Taming My
Whiskey

The Whiskeys

MELISSA FOSTER

ISBN-13: 978-1948868389

TAMING MY WHISKEY

Cover Design: Elizabeth Mackey Designs
Cover Photography: Wander Pedro Aguiar

WORLD LITERARY PRESS
PRINTED IN THE UNITED STATES OF AMERICA

A Note to Readers

If this is your first introduction to the Whiskey family, each book is written to stand alone, so dive right in and fall in love with the Whiskeys.

I have been excited to write Dixie Whiskey's story since the very first time she appeared on the page. I knew it would take a hell of a strong, confident man to earn her love and her trust, and it is clear that Dixie has found her soul mate in Jace Stone. Jace is rugged, powerful, and mysterious. And as both he and Dixie will learn, he has his own brand of romance. But at almost forty years old, Jace has never been tied down, and Dixie knows better than to sell herself short. I hope you enjoy their wild, sexy ride as Dixie and Jace try to disprove the old adage that old dogs can't learn new tricks.

In this story you will meet the Wickeds, cousins of the Whiskeys, each of whom will also be getting their own stories! You can download the Whiskey/Wicked family tree here: www.melissafoster.com/Wicked-Whiskey-Family-Tree

Each of Dixie's family members already have their own books, and her close-knit friends will also be getting their own happily ever afters. You can find the Whiskey books here: www.melissafoster.com/TheWhiskeys

Remember to sign up for my newsletter to make sure you don't miss out on future Whiskey releases:

www.MelissaFoster.com/News

For more information about my fun and emotional sexy romances, all of which can be read as stand-alone novels or as part of the larger series, visit my website:
www.MelissaFoster.com

If you prefer sweet romance with no explicit scenes or graphic language, please try the Sweet with Heat series written under my pen name, Addison Cole. You'll find the same great love stories with toned-down heat levels.

Happy reading!
~ Melissa

Chapter One

JACE STONE CLIMBED off his motorcycle early Wednesday evening, pulled off his helmet, and raked a hand through his thick dark hair. He glanced up at the sign above the door to Jillian Braden's dress shop, and a slow grin crept across his face. After years of perfecting their newest motorcycle designs, Jace and his business partner, Maddox Silver, were preparing to roll out their new Legacy line of motorcycles. Silver-Stone motorcycles were already among the most sought after in the world. The Legacy line would be the first to offer separate motorcycle designs for men and women and would secure their elite status in the industry. Jace had partnered with high-end fashion designer Jillian Braden in designing a clothing line called Leather and Lace to coincide with the launch of their new motorcycles. Today he was picking up the Leather and Lace designs, which would be featured in the Legacy calendar they were shooting next week in New York City.

The bell above the door chimed as he walked into the shop.

"Welcome to Jillian's," a cute blonde said from behind the register.

"There's the hottest biker in all of Pleasant Hill," Jillian called from the middle of the store, where she was fixing a dress on a mannequin.

The petite, burgundy-haired firecracker cruised toward him in a pair of spike heels and one of her slightly outlandish, though elegant creations. The slate-gray sleeveless minidress was ultra-short, with black trim along the hem, a crisscross skirt, and angular cutouts on the sides. The outfit left very little to the imagination, skirting a line Jace would never let any of his three younger sisters cross.

"I was sure you'd show up late given how much you drank last night," she said teasingly. They had gone out to celebrate their success with Nick and Jax, two of Jillian's brothers who were also Jace's close friends. Nick was a freestyle horse trainer, and Jax was Jillian's twin and a famous wedding dress designer.

Jace scoffed. "I've been drinking whiskey since before you were born." At six five, with a body built for a fight, it would take a hell of a lot more than a few drinks to slow him down.

"Maybe if you had the right woman in your life you wouldn't have to drink so often." She nodded toward the front of the store and said, "Annabelle is single."

"She's also about twenty-two. Sorry, babe, but I'm not into cradle robbing or commitments." Jace was in his late thirties and had spent the better part of his life creating his empire. He was used to women eyeing him like the little lady behind the register was right now, as if he were a piece of meat. Everyone wanted the big, tatted-up badass, and once they found out what he was worth, they wanted that, too. But if they knew his true penchant for leather and lace, for closing himself off emotionally, they'd probably run the other way. Most women were too meek for him anyway. They might be perfect for a night of meaningless sex, but nothing compared to soft, sexy curves and long, lean legs driven by a strong, confident woman who wasn't afraid to give him hell when he deserved it—and play a little rough in the bedroom. A woman like that was one in a million, which was just fine with Jace. He was used to living life on his terms, and he wasn't about to get strapped down by some needy chick.

"Guess that knocks me out of the running." Jillian fluttered her lashes with the tease.

When Jillian was younger, she'd hit on him relentlessly. She was gorgeous, smart, and definitely strong-willed, but Jace wasn't sexually attracted to her. In addition to their age difference, he'd known her for so long she was practically family, and despite her snarky innuendos and sexy dancing, she was a bit too refined and pure for his taste.

"You're a smart, hot chick, Jilly. You'll find the right man. You just might have to leave this town to do it." He chuckled, thinking of her five brawny brothers hulking over any man who came near her.

"You've got that right." She pushed through a door in the back of the shop and he followed her upstairs. "You saw how Nick acted last night. He was ready to tear apart the guys I danced with."

"If those guys had gotten out of hand, I'd have done more than that," Jace said with a serious glare.

"No wonder y'all are still single. I'll tell Jayla she's fighting an uphill battle," Jillian said.

His youngest sister, Jayla, had been on a matchmaking mission ever since giving birth to her son, Thane, four months ago. She and her husband, Rush, were gaga over their precious little boy. Jace couldn't deny that his adorable nephew made his insides turn to mush and his mind go down a path of wanting a kid of his own. But the minute he climbed on his motorcycle, that desire usually fell away with the rumble and roar of the engine and the freedom of the open road.

"Yes, please tell her it's not only uphill but unwanted," he said as he followed Jillian into her studio. Evening light spilled in through the windows along the far wall.

Jillian flipped on the lights, bringing the room to life. A drawing table littered with half-finished designs sat beneath the windows, and several other tables covered in fabrics and other fashion accouterments were set up around the room. Bright white walls boasted pictures of models wearing Jillian's designs, and there were dozens of mannequins wearing outfits in various stages of completion.

"You know, it wouldn't hurt if you wore a nice suit now and again," Jillian said. "Not that you don't look smokin' in jeans, but you're a *billionaire*. You should flaunt it. Women like classy men."

That was funny coming from a woman who made seven figures and acted no different than she had when she'd first started out. "Can we skip the dating advice and get to the *clothes*?"

She waved to several racks on the right side of the room. "Voilà!"

He set his helmet on a table and headed over to check out the clothes.

"I had a fitting with Sahara two weeks ago," Jillian said. "She looks positively gorgeous in everything."

Sahara Xar was the model Jace had handpicked for the calendar shoot as the face of Silver-Stone Cycles. He wanted an authentic biker, someone who knew and lived the lifestyle, not a poser. And he wanted a fresh face, someone who wasn't already on billboards or products representing other businesses. He'd searched for nearly a year, and Sahara was about as close to the *real deal* as he could get. She was an attorney, not a model, and had been referred by one of the models they hadn't chosen. She had grown up in a biker family, although she no longer lived a biker lifestyle.

Jillian lifted a hanger from the rack and hung it on a hook on the wall, displaying the corset skater-style minidress they'd designed. A zipper ran down the middle of the bodice to the waistline of the short pleated skirt. There were triangular cutouts on both sides. The tips of the triangles started just above the ribs, and the bottom of the triangle met the top of the skirt. Strips of black lace fed through eyelets on either side of the cutouts to adjust the fit. All it would take was one tug of that zipper, and it would slip off a woman's body and puddle at her feet. He'd seen the prototype outfits during the design process, but seeing them finished brought a new level of excitement.

"That's fucking *hot*," Jace said.

"Exactly the reaction we hoped for. I'm so thrilled with this line. I never thought biker attire could be *classy*, but we nailed this, Jace. There's not an ounce of skank in any one of the outfits we designed. I'd proudly wear this line, and I couldn't have come up with the concepts on my own. With your knowledge of the biker world and my creativity, we're perfect partners."

"Damn right." He'd felt lucky when she'd agreed to partner with him, and he'd never had any regrets.

Jillian ran her fingers along the edge of a cutout and said, "Adding flex in the material along the eyelets allowed a skosh more room for in-between-sized women, and I think the slightly wider front panel will work beautifully for plus-sized customers.

I'm confident that women of all sizes can comfortably and confidently wear this outfit."

"Great, because real women have curves, and I happen to enjoy those curves, so the more women we can entice into our sexy clothes, the better."

Jillian lifted a brow. "Does Jayla know you prefer curvy women?"

"Cut the shit, Jilly," he warned.

"What? I'm just saying you have a *type*. That's not a bad thing, but it explains a lot." She narrowed her eyes again like she was calculating a complex equation.

"What does *that* mean?"

"It means every time we go out for drinks, women drool over you and you never go for it. Now I understand why. You're picky."

"Jesus," he ground out. "Why did I partner with you again?"

"Because I'm awesome." She flashed a cheesy grin. "Anyway, *curve lover*, let me show you the rest of the outfits for the calendar shoot."

They looked over leather-studded hip huggers, strappy bralettes with lace overshirts, lingerie, bustiers, off-the-shoulder tops, long dresses with slits up the sides, and more, each one classier than the last. The vented jackets and warm-weather gear were just as sexy as the lingerie.

As they were making arrangements to ship the clothing to his loft in New York City, Jace's phone rang. He pulled it from his pocket and saw Shea Steele's name on the screen. Shea was the PR rep for Silver-Stone.

"It's Shea. Excuse me for a sec."

"Tell her I said hello," Jillian said as he lifted the phone to his ear.

"Hi, Shea. I'm with Jilly. Everything's all set for the shoot."

"That's great, but we have a problem," Shea said. "Sahara is out. She fell down the courthouse steps. She broke her leg and her face is all scraped up."

"Holy shit. Is she okay?"

"She'll be fine, but she can't do your shoot. I'm looking into other models, but so far the few other women you thought weren't 'all wrong' are booked. I'll keep looking, but, Jace, it took you almost a year to find Sahara. I know you're picky, but you might have to lower your standards."

"If *one* more person tells me I'm *picky*, I'm going to lose my mind." He paced, irritation escalating his voice as his mind raced through what this meant for their marketing campaign. "This person will be the *face* of Silver-Stone. There's no such thing as *too picky*."

"I get it. I understand, but we've got six *days*, Jace. How about if we use Agatha Price? I called her booking agent and she's in Hawaii, but she can be back for the shoot." Agatha Price was one of the most sought-after female tattooed models in the industry.

"No way. I'm not going to use the same model as every other Tom, Dick, and Harry. We're the *best* there is for a reason, and you of all people know how distinction matters. Legacy's top-of-the-line power, dark style, and modern edge have just enough old-school elements to make them the machines everyone will want to own and pass down to their children, and the Leather and Lace line is unlike any other biker attire on the market. The person we choose to represent Silver-Stone has to be just as unique as our products."

"Of course. How about if we delay the shoot? You can still

roll out your—"

"Hell *no*," Jace snapped. "I've got hundreds of thousands of dollars in merchandising locked in. This shoot *has* to happen on schedule. *You* were the one who convinced me that introducing the face of the company at the same time as we kick off the Legacy line was the only way to go." He looked up at the ceiling, trying to calm the frustration mounting inside him.

"I still think it is—*if* we can pull it off. The more exposure the better," Shea said. "Let me see what I can do, but we need a backup plan."

"I don't *do* backup plans. Call every modeling agency out there and tell them we need a strikingly beautiful, confident *biker* who has never done a large-scale modeling gig."

"*No impersonators.* I know the deal, but as we talked about when we were looking for Sahara, you don't really want a model, Jace. You want a biker who happens to be gorgeous and refined enough to be a model."

"Exactly."

"I'm on it," Shea reassured him.

As Jace ended the call, he heard Jillian's heels crossing the floor in his direction. If they didn't find a replacement for Sahara, it would devastate Jillian, too. She'd worked her ass off on this project. He gritted his teeth as he pocketed the phone. *Fuck.*

"Jace?"

He turned, seeing concern written all over her pretty face. "Yeah?"

"Did something happen to Sahara?"

"She fell and broke her leg. She's going to be okay, but she can't do the photo shoot."

"That's what I gathered from the things you said to Shea. I

have a model you might want to check out. She's exactly what you want—a confident, beautiful biker. She's five nine and a little on the thin side, but she's got curves in all the right places. I just made her a gorgeous dress for an event taking place this weekend. It would be easy to nip and tuck the outfits for her if she's willing to do it. She's only modeled once, and it was for me. She was in my fashion show when I launched my Multifarious line."

"Who is she?"

Jillian handed him a picture. His heart nearly stopped as he took in the tall, tatted-up redhead he knew as a smart-mouthed, quick-witted badass—the only woman he'd ever had trouble shoving into the *untouchable zone*. The one and only Dixie Whiskey, and she was *stunning*. He literally had to keep his distance from her, because she was *that* intriguing. She was not a one-night-stand type of woman. She was the woman you put on the back of your bike and never let go. He'd never seen her made up like she was in the picture, with smoky eyes and perfectly styled hair. And wearing Jillian's fancy clothes? *Holy hell.* She was pure perfection—*and* she was the younger sister of the fiercest bikers in all of Peaceful Harbor, Maryland, and the daughter of the president of the Dark Knights motorcycle club.

"Holy shit," he said in awe.

"Dixie Whiskey," Jillian said. "She's incredible, but I'm not sure if she'd do it. I just remembered that after she did my fashion show, I fielded calls from industry professionals offering her insane amounts of money to model, and she had zero interest in any of them. You know the Whiskeys. Dixie's not a model; she's *real*, Jace."

"But she modeled for you," he pointed out. Dixie was the image he'd carried in his mind when he'd been looking for the face of Silver-Stone. If he'd known she modeled, he could have saved himself months of trouble.

"Because she owed me," Jillian said.

"Why?"

Jillian's brows knitted.

"Jillian, come on," he demanded. "We need her. You know that. Why did she owe you?"

"God, you're a pain. If you tell her brothers, I'll slaughter you in your sleep."

He stared at her and crossed his arms.

"Fine!" She huffed out a breath. "I hooked her up with a guy I know here in Pleasant Hill, and I'm pretty sure you're not going to do that, so why does it matter?"

Damn right he wouldn't do that.

"I probably shouldn't have suggested it," she said. "I'm sorry. It was a dumb idea. Now that I'm thinking it through, there's no way you'll get her."

He shoved the picture in his shirt pocket, grabbed his helmet, and said, "Watch me."

"COME ON, BABY, let's make a little wager." Lance "Crow" Burke, a member of the Dark Knights who had been chasing after Dixie forever, tried to lure her into a date for the millionth time that week.

They were at Whiskey Bro's, the bar Dixie's family owned. Dixie was waitressing and Crow was playing darts with two other Dark Knights, both of whom looked amused. They knew Dixie well enough to know where this was headed. Dixie was part owner of both of her family's businesses. In addition to running the offices of Whiskey Automotive and doing the books for the bar, she had been waitressing part-time at the bar for so long, guys like Crow had become like background music—entertaining distractions.

"What'd you have in mind?" Dixie asked, fucking with him. He was good-looking enough, with pitch-black hair and angular features that made him a little too pretty for Dixie's taste, but "model hot" according to two of her closest friends, Isabel "Izzy" Ryder, and Tracey Klein, who also worked at the bar. Dixie had her bar for men set high, and it had nothing to do with looks, money, or charming pickup lines.

Dixie's great-grandfather had founded the Dark Knights. Being a biker was in her blood. She had loving, demanding parents who didn't put up with bullshit and three fiercely protective older brothers, Bones, Bullet, and Bear. Thanks to them, she'd learned to speak her mind and fight to win. The problem was, growing up with men like that had given her high expectations in a partner, just as she had high expectations for herself to never rely on a man for a damn thing besides unconditional love. She didn't want a guy who acted tough, because toughness wasn't an act. A man was either able to fearlessly stand up to any opponent or he wasn't. There was no middle ground. She also had no interest in men who rode through life on their looks, because at the end of the day, everyone would get older, saggier, grayer, or balder. And she couldn't care less about men who earned millions and tossed it around like confetti. Money couldn't buy true love. After watching her brothers open their hearts and fall in love with wonderful women, she'd seen proof of what she always knew was true. A man could wear his do-or-die spirit like armor and still have a heart of gold.

Dixie had the armor and the heart. If only her fearless knight would show up.

With a twinkle of a dare in his eyes, Crow said, "If I make a bull's-eye, you agree to go out with me Saturday night."

"You're being auctioned off Friday night, remember? Hopefully you'll get lucky and some chick will bid on you. Then you'll be *busy* Saturday night." Dixie had taken the reins to run the annual charity bachelor auction to benefit a local women's shelter. Each year a local company hosted the event. Mr. B's microbrewery, owned by their friends the Bradens, had hosted the last two years. Dixie was excited to tie the event in with the Dark Knights, and she'd made it her mission to raise more money than any of the previous auctions had. She was good at many things, but business strategizing and corralling people to work together topped the list. She'd not only signed up almost every one of the Dark Knights who were single, but she'd also already secured more than fifty thousand dollars in donations for the shelter. She'd made her goal, and the auction wasn't for another two days.

Crow winked at the other guys and said, "That's code for *she's* bidding on me."

Dixie rolled her eyes and walked away to check on other customers.

She was looking forward to the auction, but she was also nervous about it. Since all her brothers were now spoken for, she'd let her girlfriends talk her into secretly getting up onstage to be auctioned off. If her brothers got wind of their plans, they'd lock her away to ensure it didn't happen. Hell, they were so protective, their reputations preceded them. All it took was one threatening glare from Bullet, Bones, or Bear and any guy who *might* have been interested in her cowered away. If she had any hope of ever falling in love, she needed to get the hell out of Peaceful Harbor. Maybe she'd get lucky when she went to her cousin Justin Wicked's art show in Cape Cod in two weeks and would fall in love on the sandy shores of Cape Cod Bay.

Pushing that too-good-to-be-true hope aside, she went to check on her favorite sixteen-year-old, Marco Garcia. She stopped at the table where he was hunkered down over a notebook doing math homework, waiting for his older brother, Ricardo, to finish his shift as the dishwasher. "Hey, handsome. How'd you do on that science test last week?"

His big dark eyes flicked up, and a sweet smile appeared on his adorable face. A few months ago, Ricardo had tried to dine and dash without paying, and Jed, a bartender and prospect for the Dark Knights, had caught him. When Jed learned he was skipping school and stealing food for his brother, he had taken the boy under his wing and offered him a job rather than having him arrested. Now Ricardo was attending school regularly and working instead of getting into trouble. Their situation had led Jed to start the Young Knights program, in which shop owners like the Whiskeys ran mentoring programs for troubled youths. Dixie was proud of all that the Dark Knights did to help the community, and as much as she wanted to fall in love and knew it might have to happen outside of Peaceful Harbor, she had no interest in moving away from her family.

"I got an eighty-nine," Marco said proudly.

"That's my boy." She ruffled his thick, wavy hair. "Let me get you a refill."

"Thanks, Dixie."

"You bet." She picked up his empty glass and headed for the bar. She was still getting accustomed to her brother's new schedule. Bullet used to spend fifty-plus hours a week at the bar, but he'd recently gotten married and cut back. Izzy and Desmond "Diesel" Black were bartending tonight. Diesel was a mountain of muscle, with cold black eyes and no people skills, which made him the perfect replacement to watch over the bar.

Izzy was busy serving two guys at the other end of the bar, so Dixie set the glass near Diesel and said, "Pepsi for Marco, please."

Diesel lifted his square jaw in acknowledgment, and one massive hand engulfed the glass. A few milk-chocolate sprigs of hair poked out from beneath the ever-present baseball cap he wore backward. Diesel wasn't known for his personality, and he hated to be touched. But with bulbous muscles, a chest the size of Canada, and the ability to make a man scurry away with his tail between his legs with nothing more than a single terrifying glare, he was definitely all *man*. He was also a nomad, which meant he was a Dark Knight, but he moved around a lot and claimed no chapter as his own. No one had any idea how long he'd stick around this time, and nobody was brave enough to ask what he did with his time when he wasn't there, but they were glad he had stepped in to replace Bullet.

Diesel slid the drink across the bar and said, "Crow giving you trouble?"

"Nothing I can't handle."

Izzy winked at Dixie and moved in real close to Diesel. She ran her hand down the hard ridges of his muscular arm all the way to his wrist. "Do you call this *trouble?*" she asked seductively.

Diesel rose up to his full, imposing height of about six foot six, with an uncomfortable expression on his face. "Yeah, trouble for *you*," he said gruffly.

"It's called *flirting*." Izzy sighed and patted his chest. "You really need to stop calling flirting *trouble*, or you'll never get that sweet little lady to give you the time of day."

His eyes shot to Tracey, the petite brunette waitress with a cute pixie cut, who had been working there for the past few months. She'd come a long way since escaping an abusive relationship. She'd moved out of the women's shelter and was renting a room from Izzy. She was no longer painfully shy around customers, but she was deathly afraid of Diesel.

Diesel made a grunting noise and went to help a customer.

Izzy watched him walk away and said, "I kind of feel bad for him. The man will be single *forever*."

"Not if you keep schooling him on the ways of the world." Dixie picked up the drink and headed for Marco. She set the glass on the table and said, "Here you go, sweetie."

"Thanks."

The door to the bar opened, and Jace Stone strode in. Dixie dragged air into her lungs and stepped away from Marco's table, taking in Jace's sun-kissed skin, thick dark hair that brushed the collar of his T-shirt, and colorful ink snaking around his arms and peeking out from beneath his collar. *Talk about "all man…"*

His deep-set eyes surfed the room, landing on her, making her pulse quicken. His thick brows drew together, his powerful legs eating up the distance between them.

"How's my favorite Whiskey?"

His rough baritone voice was as enticing as the seductive look in his eyes, but Dixie wasn't fooling herself. Sure, Jace would slum it like the rest of them and down Jameson or Jack Daniel's in a pinch, but everyone knew his favorite whiskey came in a pricey bottle. Dixie had a feeling he had the same taste in women. She arched a brow, calling him on the bullshit line and wondering what he really wanted.

He stepped closer, his woodsy, rugged scent accentuating his potency. "What? We both know your brothers can't hold a candle to you."

She might have had a crush on him since the very second she'd first seen him, at a rally she'd gone to with her brother Bear when she was just eighteen years old, but she wasn't stupid. Jace Stone was as mysterious and unable to put down roots as Diesel. Even back then, at twenty-seven, he'd possessed the raw confidence and authoritative presence of a worldly man who took what he wanted and demanded attention. It had been more than a decade, and like good liquor, Jace Stone had gotten better with age. There was nothing *pretty* about him. His skin was tough as leather, his hands calloused, and he always looked like he needed a haircut. But while other women might find those things unkempt, to Dixie they were catnip. She even found the leather bands he wore around his wrist a turn-on.

Before she could make a fool out of herself as she had at eighteen—ogling him so openly Bear had physically *dragged* her away—she squared her shoulders, trying to ignore the butterflies partying in her stomach, and said, "What do you want, Jace?"

"I *need* you, Dixie."

She'd fantasized about hearing him say those words to her for so many years, the naive girl in her was bouncing on her toes. But she eyed him curiously, wondering what the man who could have any woman could possibly want with her. Whatever it was, she knew it wouldn't be what *she* wanted from *him*, so she said, "Get in line. So does every other guy in here."

A low laugh rumbled out, but even his cocky grin couldn't soften his edge. "Seriously, Dix. I need you to come with me to New York City this weekend to help me out with a job."

Now her interest was piqued, but she already had a *job*.

"That's the most interesting proposition I've had in a long time, but no can do. I'm slammed. I've got the bachelor auction this weekend. You remember the charity auction. The one I asked you to sign up for? I believe you said it'd be a cold day in hell before you sold your body. Yeah, *that* one," she said sharply. "Whatever *job* you need me to do can't be nearly as important as raising money for the Parkvale Women's Shelter, where women and children who have endured horrible things are trying desperately to start over." She glanced at Tracey, picking up a drink from the bar, and said, "Tracey stayed at the shelter, as did Bones's fiancée, Sarah, with two of her children, before she met Bones. Jed's fiancée, Josie, and their son, Hail, also stayed there. But I get it, Jace. You're too special to offer yourself up for a date for a good cause."

Needing to move before she said something she'd regret, she walked over to a table where three guys had just finished their beers and grabbed their empty bottles. "Refills?"

"Yeah, thanks," one of the guys said.

She walked away with the human inferno that was Jace Stone on her heels.

"Dixie, how can you be upset with me? I gave you a twenty-thousand-dollar donation for the auction."

She set the bottles on the bar and said, "Which I truly appreciate, but giving of yourself and giving money are two different things. One is easy and mindless. The other tells me who you are. It was a real eye-opener." She crossed her arms and said, "What did you need help with anyway?"

Diesel grabbed the empty bottles, and Dixie said, "Another round, please."

"I'm rolling out the Legacy line in the fall."

"So I've heard. Bear's pretty excited." In addition to working at Whiskey Automotive, Bear worked part-time designing and building custom motorcycles for Jace's company. He hadn't worked on the Legacy line, but he raved about it.

"We all are. This line is my baby. I've put blood, sweat, and tears into it. It's the first motorcycle line that will have bikes designed specifically for women. Nobody's doing that, Dix. This is a huge deal."

Bear had told her all about Jace's innovative, sleek designs for women. It was a genius idea, and it didn't surprise her that Jace had come up with it. But she couldn't help thinking about Jace *researching* the contours of women's bodies…

Diesel put three bottles on the bar, eyes locked on Jace. "*Stone*," he said evenly.

"Diesel." Jace lifted his chin in the manly greeting Dixie was accustomed to.

"Thanks, Diesel," Dixie said, and as she headed to the table with Jace beside her, she said, "Congratulations on the line, but what does it have to do with needing me?" She set the bottles down, flashed a smile at the customers, and said, "Can I get you boys anything else?"

One of them looked her up and down lasciviously. Jace stepped closer, and the guy shifted his eyes away and said, "No. We're good."

Dixie spun on her heels, grabbed Jace's arm, and dragged him to the side of the room. She felt Diesel's antennae springing and glanced at the bar, mouthing, *I'm fine!* Turning her attention to Jace, she spoke in a harsh whisper. "You just fucked up my tip, and I don't appreciate it. So whatever you have to say, say it and be gone, okay? I've got work to do."

"That guy was looking at you like you were a piece of

meat."

"No shit. They all do." Except now that she was thinking about it, Jace never had. Not once. In fact, in all the years she'd known him, this was the longest he'd ever looked at her. He didn't live in Peaceful Harbor, but he traveled there often to see his brother Jared, who *had* signed up for the auction. Jared owned a restaurant in Pleasant Hill and lived there for several months out of the year. "I have a lot to do, Jace, so if you have more to say, please get on with it."

"I'm launching a women's clothing line called Leather and Lace when we launch the Legacy line. We're making a calendar to promote the clothing and the new bikes. The photo shoot is next week, and the woman I hired to model got hurt and can't make it. I want *you* to replace her."

She blinked several times, unable to believe what she was hearing. An incredulous laugh tumbled out. "Do you even fucking *know* me, Stone? I am *not* a pinup girl!" She took a step away and he grabbed her arm, tugging her back to him and keeping her so close, she could see flecks of gold in his sexy hazel eyes.

"This is important to me, Dixie. I don't want someone who fakes being a biker. I want an authentic woman. I want *you*."

"Do I need to point out that I was your *second* choice, or maybe your *tenth*. I don't know or care, because any way you cut it, the answer is *no*. I told you, I'm not a pinup girl." She held his steady gaze with an ice-cold one of her own and said, "For the record, Whiskeys don't play second fiddle to anyone. Sorry, Stone, but you're out of luck."

"Come on, Dixie," he pleaded gruffly. "I'll let you auction me off."

"Too little, too late. The ballot is *full*." The lie felt victorious. She yanked her arm free and said, "I have customers to help. Good luck with the line. I'm sure, like everything you touch, it will turn to gold."

"With you on board, it'll be *legendary*."

"No."

He leaned closer and lowered his voice to say, "This *isn't* over, kitten."

"What the hell did you just say?" Anger simmered inside her. She poked him in his rock-hard chest and said, "I'm nobody's *kitten*, and you're *this close* to earning a knee to your groin."

"You definitely know how to use those claws, and you're so sweet I bet you *purr*," he said arrogantly. "You know you want to do it, Dix."

His eyes drilled into her, causing heat to sear through her veins and her traitorous nipples to pebble into aching peaks. Damn, he played dirty.

"Careful, Stone. This kitten *bites*."

She stormed off, as annoyed with herself for getting turned on as she was at him. *A pinup girl!* She eyed the calendars of biker chicks hanging on the walls of the bar, and her stomach plummeted. Her brothers had lusted over those types of calendars in their bedrooms when they were growing up. Jace's lack of attention over the years had left her wary but hopeful that one day he might see her as more than Bear's little sister. Now he'd quashed those hopes. No self-respecting biker would want a woman he had any interest in on a calendar for guys to jerk off to.

Jace lowered his big body into a seat at a table, and Tracey went to take his order. He nodded in Dixie's direction. Tracey headed her way with a perplexed expression. Dixie put a hand on her hip as she approached.

"What's up with Jace tonight?" Tracey asked. "He says he wants you to wait on him."

"Nothing. I'll take care of it." She stalked over to Jace's table and said, "What are you doing?"

"Ordering a beer. I'd like a Sam Adams, please." He stood up, so close she felt the heat of his body burning through her clothing. "Maybe I didn't explain how important this calendar is and what it means to me."

"*No*," she said adamantly. "I'll get you a beer, but if you're staying just to talk me into doing it, you're wasting your time."

"Then it's a good thing I have nothing *but* time on my hands until you say yes." He sat down, clasped his hands behind his head, and crossed his ankle over his knee.

Why did he have to look so annoyingly delicious?

She stalked up to the bar and joined Tracey and Izzy, who were deep in conversation.

"What was that all about?" Izzy asked.

Dixie motioned for them to huddle closer and said, "Jace wants me to model for a Silver-Stone calendar to launch his new motorcycle and clothing lines. What the hell, right? Like I'm some ditzy bimbo?"

Tracey and Izzy exchanged a wide-eyed glance.

"More like you're freaking hot and he knows it," Izzy said. "I wish he'd ask me. That would be so much fun."

"I could never do something like that." Tracey's shoulders rounded forward and she said, "But if I looked like either of you two and had your confidence, I might consider it."

"Have you two lost your minds?" Dixie pointed to a calendar on the wall. "*That* would be *me*. No way. And he called me *kitten*. What the fuck?"

Izzy burst into hysterics.

"He's got big ones to call *you* kitten," Tracey said.

"Oh, she knows just how big they are," Izzy said. "She's been dreaming about them for years."

"Do you mind, Iz?" Dixie snapped. "He wants a Sam Adams, too. I might dump it on him."

Izzy filled his order and an order for Tracey and set the glasses on the bar. "In all seriousness, you should do it. You're always in the background. Maybe this is your time to shine."

"First of all, I'd have to go to New York City—"

Tracey gasped. "I've never been there. That might be worth doing just for the trip!"

"I'm in," Izzy said. "Seriously. I'll go. Tell him I'll do it. I *love* New York."

Dixie rolled her eyes and picked up the beer. "I'll offer you up." She'd driven through New York on road trips, but she'd never spent any time there. But no matter how fun that part sounded, she wasn't going to flaunt her body in a calendar.

"Thanks, Izzy." Tracey picked up her order and walked away.

Dixie stood by the bar looking at Jace, who was watching her like a hawk, and her stomach knotted up. Even though she knew he'd been goading her by calling her *kitten*, the way his expression had changed from pleading to predatory had gotten under her skin. That was the first time he'd ever looked at her like she was an attractive, single woman, and not a friend or Bear's sister. Was it a momentary slip, or was it all part of his game to get her to agree to do the calendar shoot?

Izzy leaned across the bar and said, "I don't know how you can look at that man and say no to anything."

"It wasn't that hard." She'd been harboring hope for something more with Jace since she was eighteen. She knew it was silly, given how much time had passed, but still, she'd wished for more. If it was possible years later to break the heart of the person she'd been at eighteen, he'd managed to do it. She brought Jace his beer, and as she set it on the table, she said, "Izzy will model for you."

His brows slanted, giving him an even edgier look. "I want an authentic biker, Dixie. If I'd known you modeled, you would have been my first choice."

"I don't know where you got the crazy idea that I *model.*"

He pulled a picture from his shirt pocket and held it up. It was from the fashion show she'd done for her friend Jillian. She reached for it, and he pulled his hand back, slipping the picture into his shirt pocket.

"I want *you*, Dixie, not Izzy or anyone else."

Her heart skipped, because it was *that easy* to disregard the idea of a calendar shoot and pretend he truly *wanted* her for himself.

"You're classy and unique," he said, adding fuel to her simmering fantasy. "Just like my bikes."

Nothing like a dose of frosty reality to douse the flames.

She rolled her eyes and said, "Just what every woman wants, to be compared to a bike. Just drink your beer and be on your way."

"I'll pay you three times what you earn here."

"No."

His lips curved up and he said, "*Five* times."

"Not a chance. I told you, Whiskeys don't play second fiddle. You can pay at the bar."

He drained his glass and set it on the table. "I'd like another. As I said, I've got all night."

He wasn't kidding. Hours later, he was still seated at one of her tables, trying to convince her to take the job. He was determined, and she had to admit, he was ridiculously charming, vacillating between demanding, suggesting, flirting, and just *being* Jace. That was the most potent and charming of all, and it was what had sent her into her office to escape her attraction to him.

She'd spent the last half hour or more trying to focus on the schedules for the bar, and when that didn't work, she turned to the brochures she'd had printed for the auction. But her mind kept traveling back to Jace. It was like the universe was playing a cruel joke on her, offering up a trip to New York City with the man of her dreams and then turning him into every other man, wanting something she wasn't willing to give.

Of course, what he wanted was nothing like what most men wanted.

And that was the shame of it.

Izzy poked her head into the office. "Hey, you okay?"

"Yeah, just going over things for the auction."

"Oh, that's a good idea." Izzy sat on the edge of the desk in her red minidress, crossed her legs, and leaned back on one hand. She could be a model with her sleek black hair and hourglass figure. Jace should really take her up on the offer. "A much better idea than sitting in here mooning over the man who refused to leave."

"Is he gone?" She glanced at the clock. She hadn't realized it was so late. The bar closed ten minutes ago.

"Yes, although Diesel practically had to throw him out when we closed. He said to give you this." She reached into the cleavage of her dress and whipped out a receipt, handing it to Dixie.

24

On the back of the receipt, Jace had written, *I'd never have chosen a second fiddle in the first place if I had known #1 was available. One way or another, I'll prove that to you. JS*

Chapter Two

THEY CLOSED THE bar Friday to prepare for the bachelor auction, and with the exception of Dixie's parents, the entire Whiskey clan and most of their closest friends had shown up to help transform the understated biker bar into a festive fundraiser. Her parents were driving around town putting up signs for the event.

"I'm just saying, it's about time you make things official," Bullet said to Bones. He'd been bugging Bones about setting a wedding date ever since Sarah had given birth to their new baby, Maggie Rose, three months ago. Bullet was the most intimidating of Dixie's brothers, with a thick, unkempt beard and tattoos covering nearly every inch of his body. "Just go to the courthouse already."

"I am *not* marrying Sarah in a courthouse," Bones said evenly. He was an oncologist, the most clean-cut and even keeled of them all. But they knew what he was capable of. He was a quiet storm, and if unleashed, he would take down everything within his path. "She deserves the best of everything, and that includes a beautiful white wedding where she's the spotlight of everyone's attention."

Bones and Bullet were hanging strings of lights vertically in front of the black and white drapes they'd hung along the wall behind the stage. In between Bullet harassing Bones, they joked around with Jed and Truman, who were rearranging tables and setting up extra chairs. Both Jed and Truman worked at Whiskey Automotive. Truman and his younger brother Quincy had been honorary members of the Whiskey family since Bear befriended them when Truman was a teenager. Although Quincy couldn't get off work to help this afternoon, he'd signed up to be one of the bachelors auctioned off tonight.

"Move your skinny ass, Dix, or we'll run it over," Bear said, and then he bumped into her back. "We don't have all day."

She spun around, and he grinned. He was holding one end of a wooden table. Diesel held the other, stone-faced, as usual. They were setting up tables along the back wall for the buffet the girls were preparing in the kitchen. Their staff was too small to handle food orders for a crowd the size they anticipated, so they had decided to set up buffets of appetizer and finger foods and put donation jars on the tables.

"Really, Bear?" She stood beside a ladder she was using to hang glittery hearts the children were making from the rafters, but the area to her other side was open, and Bear could have easily gone around her. Between picking up decorations, flyers, and coordinating the efforts of the Dark Knights' wives who were going to help out at the auction, she'd been running from one thing to the next all day, and she wasn't in the mood for Bear's jokes.

Bear chuckled. "If I don't give you a hard time, who will?"

Of all her siblings, Bear was the one she'd always been closest to. He was the most playful of her brothers, although he also had a serious side. Their father had suffered a stroke when Dixie was fifteen and Bear had just graduated high school. Bullet had been overseas with the military, and Bones was studying to become a physician. Bear had stepped in, taking over for their father at the bar, and a few years later, when they lost their uncle, Bear took over managing the auto shop as well. He'd put his hopes and dreams—his *life*—on hold, giving years to their family businesses without complaint. Dixie had been thrilled when he'd taken a step back, working fewer hours at the auto shop, so he could follow his passion with Silver-Stone Cycles. She wondered if he knew about Jace's offer, but she assumed he didn't, and she wasn't about to ask and rock a boat in which she had no interest in sailing.

"Uncle Bea*h*! Look!" Kennedy, Truman and Gemma's four-year-old daughter, thrust a red paper heart up at Bear. In the middle of the heart it read BEAR LOVES CRYSTAL in thick, uneven black crayon.

"That's the best heart I've ever seen in my entire life! I do love my wife, just like I love you, munchkin." Bear set the table down and lifted Kennedy above his head.

Kennedy giggled and kicked her feet, squealing, "Uncle Bea*h*!" She looked adorable in a purple dress with her long dark hair pulled back in two pigtails secured with white bows. As Bear set her down, she said, "I made it with Auntie Cwystal, and look!"

She turned the heart around, showing him the other side, which read BEAR + CRYSTAL LOVE CUBBIE in bright blue letters. Bear looked lovingly at his wife, who was sitting with Sarah and the children while the kids played and made decorations. Crystal rubbed her baby bump and blew him a kiss. Crystal was due in less than two months, and since they didn't want to know the sex of the baby before it was born, everyone had begun referring to it as "the cub" or "Cubbie."

Kennedy blinked big brown eyes up at Bear and said, "Can you walk around Auntie Dixie so she can hang the heart up there?" She pointed to a rafter. "*Please?*"

Kennedy had had all of them wrapped around her little finger ever since Truman found her and their baby brother, Lincoln, who was now two, in a crack house with Truman's mother, who had overdosed, and his brother, Quincy, who had been strung out. Although Kennedy and Lincoln were Truman's siblings, Truman and his wife, Gemma, were raising them as their own children to give them as normal a childhood as possible. Kennedy had gone from a terrified toddler to an outgoing, loving little lady with as much sass as she had empathy for others. Lincoln had come into his own as a sweet-natured, curious little boy, and Quincy had gone through rehab and was now working at a bookstore and running Narcotics Anonymous meetings. Dixie could hardly believe how much they'd all changed in the past year and a half.

"Of course, sweetheart," Bear said.

"Thank you!" Kennedy thrust the heart into Dixie's hands and ran to Diesel, hugging his legs. "I'm gonna make you a heart, too, Uncle Diesel!"

Though she wasn't blood related, Kennedy was a true *Whiskey*. Dixie's family extended well beyond bloodlines to the families of the Dark Knights, like Diesel, and special friends, like Tracey, Jed, Josie, and others.

Diesel looked down at Kennedy, treating them all to a rare and heartwarming smile. "I'd sure like that, darlin'."

Kennedy darted toward Gemma, who was coming out of the ladies' room, and said, "Mama! Can you write *Diesel loves Kennedy* on a heart for me?"

Gemma's eyes shot to Diesel, who barked out a laugh, which was such a foreign sound, they all started laughing.

"Hey, Dix," Bear said as he lifted the table, "make sure that heart gets special attention." He winked and walked around her.

"You're a pest," Dixie said as she climbed the ladder.

As Diesel carried the table past Dixie, he said, "I'd have used a stronger word."

Dixie hung up the hearts, and then she went to check on the food preparation. She pushed through the kitchen doors, greeted by the sounds of laughter and "Treat Myself" by Meghan Trainor. The savory scents of spiced meats, gingerbread, cupcakes, and other delicious foods tempted her. The counters were covered with platters of foods and treats in various stages of completion. Finlay and Izzy were shaking their booties to the beat of the music by the ovens, while Josie and Tracey shimmied as they frosted gingerbread cookies in the shapes of muscular men posing in various athletic positions. They were using colored frosting to create black bow ties, open dress shirts, and jeans. They'd even added six-pack abs with flesh-colored frosting.

Bullet's wife, Finlay, waved Dixie over, her blond hair whipping around her face as she danced. "Dance with us!"

Dixie twirled across the room in her sky-high leather boots and miniskirt. "You guys listen to the weirdest music!" She was a lover of country and rock, though she'd dance to anything.

"Oh, shush up and dance!" Finlay said, swiveling her hips seductively in her cute pink apron. She owned a catering company and worked part-time cooking for Whiskey Bro's. She was petite and feminine, and she truly adored Bullet and all his gruffness. She'd loved him through his PTSD and brought out a tender side of him that no one had ever seen before they met.

"Penny texted a few minutes ago," Josie said as she wiggled to the music. Penny was Finlay's younger sister. She owned Luscious Licks, the ice cream shop where Josie worked part-time. "She's so excited about the auction. She's trying to earn extra tips so she has lots of cash for tonight!"

"I bet you a hundred dollars she bids on Quincy," Tracey chimed in.

Quincy and Penny had been skirting around the chemistry between them for so long, Dixie wished they would get their shit together and either take their friendship to the next level or move on so they could both find someone else who would give them all the love they deserved.

"With all the hotties I have lined up for tonight, she might have a hard time choosing," Dixie said.

"I'm bidding on Jared, that's all I know. So bitches better back off," Izzy said with a whip of her hips.

Dixie laughed. "Prepare yourself for *lots* of competition, Iz." Jace's younger brother was fun loving, like Bear, and a dead ringer for Adam Levine.

When the song ended and another began, Josie said, "Dixie, I made you special cookies, but you'd better eat them before one of the guys see them." She hurried over to a cabinet and took out a plate covered with a napkin, grinning up at Dixie. She was beautiful, with honey- and strawberry-blond hair pulled back in a ponytail and a sprinkle of elfin magic in her slightly upturned nose and high cheekbones. "I hope you like them."

Josie and Jed had recently bought Dixie's late uncle Axel's house and transformed the garage into a specialty gingerbread shop. The house had been empty for years, and Dixie was glad to see it being used again. The grand opening of Josie's shop, Ginger All the Days, was taking place the week after next, and they were all excited. Josie was Sarah's younger sister. Sarah, Josie, and their older brother, Scott, had each separately escaped their abusive parents years ago and had lost touch. Until recently, they hadn't known if the others were living or dead. Thanks to a serendipitous and emotional reunion, they'd become a family again. Scott would have been there today to help, but he had to work at the marina. They would see him tonight, though, as he was being auctioned off as one of Peaceful Harbor's most eligible bachelors.

Dixie lifted the napkin and exclaimed, "Oh my gosh! Josie! These are too cute to eat!" The gingerbread cookies were shaped like curvaceous women. White frosting outlined bodacious breasts, and black frosting formed miniskirts and half shirts. Josie had even given them green eyes, pink smirking lips, and long red, ropy hair.

"You have to eat them," Josie said. "That's what they're for!"

"We made two trays for after you're actioned off and the cat's out of the bag," Tracey explained. "Don't worry; we hid those, too."

"If you don't want them, I'll take them." Izzy held out her hand.

Finlay pushed Izzy's hand down. "You've had about a dozen cookies. Let Dixie eat them."

"I can't believe you did this for me. I love them. Thank you." Dixie hugged Josie.

Bullet barreled through the kitchen doors and said, "What's going on, Lollipop?"

Shit! All the girls crowded around Dixie as she shoved the cookies in her mouth.

"Nothing!" Izzy said.

"Cooking!" Finlay added.

"Have a cookie!" Tracey shoved a male gingerbread cookie toward Bullet, waving it so close to his face Dixie was afraid he'd swat it away.

Dixie tried to swallow, but the cookie got stuck in her throat and she started to choke. Bullet pushed one huge hand through her gaggle of conspirators, hauling her forward by the front of her shirt. He began swatting her on the back, *hard*, while holding her still with one hand around her upper arm.

"Water!" Finlay dove for a cup.

"What the hell did she swallow?" Bullet demanded, his giant arms circling her like he was going to do the Heimlich maneuver.

"Cookie!" the girls said in unison.

Dixie shook her head, trying to tell Bullet she could breathe, but all that came out was a squeak. He crushed her back against him so fast and hard, the cookie shot across the kitchen, causing all the girls to gasp.

Dixie sucked air into her lungs as they all talked at once, making sure she was okay.

"Holy crap, Bullet." Dixie rubbed her sternum. "Thank you, but I think you broke my ribs."

"Would you rather I let you choke? Shit, Dix, learn to chew." He grumbled something indiscernible. "I know you women love your cookies, but seriously..." He strode toward the door, shaking his head.

"Bullet," Finlay said sweetly. "What did you come in for?"

He cocked a grin, his features softening with adoration as he swept his arm around Finlay's waist, hauling her in for a passionate kiss. When their lips parted, he grinned lasciviously at his wife and said, "I needed a little sugar rush."

"God, she's lucky," Tracey said softly.

Finlay reached up, stroking his bearded cheeks, melting a little right before their eyes as she said, "Then give me a little more, please."

Dixie melted, too, as Bullet kissed Finlay again, more tenderly this time. She loved when their family came together for the good of others, but it was moments like these, when the love in the room was so thick it was palpable, that made her long for her own man to love. Her mind traveled to Jace. She tried to fight it, but when she thought of herself with a man, it had been his image she'd conjured for so long, their connection felt real. It wasn't, of course, especially after yesterday, when Jace had shown up at Whiskey Automotive while she was working. He'd spent the better part of an hour trying *again* to convince her to do the calendar shoot. She'd shut him down so firmly, she was sure he'd never want to see her again. She knew it was time to let her fantasies about them go, but she wasn't ready to just yet. She didn't even know how to begin to erase the beautiful badass man from her mind, much less to replace him with anyone else. Maybe tonight she'd get lucky and there would be a new man in town, someone she was destined to meet. A virile, interesting man her brothers hadn't had a chance to scare away, someone who would win her at the auction and sweep her off her feet.

A girl could dream…

And for now dreams were all Dixie had.

JACE SAT WITH the heels of his black leather boots planted in the sand, forearms resting on his knees, holding the phone between his hands as he FaceTimed with Jayla. He'd hung out with Jared earlier but hadn't been able to stop thinking about Dixie. She'd turned him down again yesterday, and he'd come to the harbor to try to clear his mind.

"Did I tell you we're going to spend a week with Kurt and Leanna at the Cape later this summer? I can't believe their little boy, Sloane, is a *toddler* already." Kurt Remington was one of Rush's younger brothers. "I know Thane will be too young to remember the visit, but I think it's important for cousins to grow up spending time together. It's never too early to start traditions like that…"

Jayla had always been a chatterbox. She went on to catch Jace up on each of Rush's siblings' lives. She and Rush were both Olympic skiers, but after hurting her shoulder a few years back, Jayla had cut back on competitions, though he had a feeling it would take an act of God to keep his determined sister off the slopes for long. She had always been strong and determined. She'd been the face of Dove for the past three years and had several other sponsorships. But for now she'd put her other obligations aside to focus on Thane, her adorable son, who was currently fast asleep in his mama's arms.

It was strange seeing his baby sister with a baby of her own, but she was an amazing mother and Jace was proud of her. She was the first of their siblings to get married, and it had been strange for Jace to step back and allow Rush to be the one to watch over her, even though Rush had been her best friend since they were kids and Jace trusted him.

Jayla was still talking a mile a minute. "Let me tell you about Rush's new training program! He's kicking ass, *of course…*"

As she talked, Jace's mind returned to Dixie. His thoughts

hadn't veered far from her since Jillian had handed him that picture, which was now safely tucked away in his wallet. He'd stared at the damn thing for hours the past two nights, seeing Dixie through much different eyes than he ever had. He was trying like hell to convince himself that seeing her differently had everything to do with how badly he wanted her to be the face of Silver-Stone, but Jace had never been good at fooling himself. He'd known the gorgeous firecracker was the woman he'd wanted to represent his company for years, but he'd been pushing away thoughts of her as anything more than Bear's younger sister for so long, he'd pulled the wool over his own eyes. Now, after going head-to-head with her, he couldn't help but see the green-eyed vixen for what she was—a fiercely determined, truly brilliant, and unfailingly strong *woman*.

"Are you even listening to me? Jace? *Jace!*"

His sister's raised voice snapped him from his thoughts. "Shit, sorry, Jay-Jay. I, uh, yeah. I'm here."

"You never zone out. What are you doing? Designing a new bike in your head? Debating opening a shop in Peaceful Harbor again? I know how much you like it there."

Although Silver-Stone had locations all over the world, they had only one headquarters, and it was in LA, where their largest manufacturing plant and most of their designers were located. When Jace wasn't traveling, he worked out of that office. Last year at this time he and Maddox had considered opening a second headquarters and manufacturing plant on the East Coast. They'd looked at Peaceful Harbor but had tabled that venture when another deal had come up for space they'd previously tried to secure for offices and retail space in Colorado, and they'd jumped on it. Now they were once again looking for an East Coast location for their second headquarters and manufacturing plant.

"No. We found a place in Boston. I'm meeting Maddox there next week for a final review of the properties." Although Peaceful Harbor would be less expensive, the property owners in Boston were offering a sweet deal that would include another prime retail location for a second Boston store in addition to the manufacturing plant and offices. If they went through with the deal, Boston would become Jace's home base. He liked his nomadic lifestyle, but spending a few months closer to his family wouldn't be a bad thing, especially now that he had a nephew.

"Sorry for zoning out earlier," he said. "I was just thinking about the photo shoot." He'd already filled her in on what had gone down with Sahara and how he was pursuing Dixie to take her place.

"If you can't get Dixie, Mia would probably model for you." All of the Stones had inherited their parents' olive skin and attractive features. Mia was five years younger than Jace and for the past several years she had worked for Jillian's cousin Josh Braden and his wife, Riley, who were famous fashion designers. Mia knew the ins and outs of modeling, and she'd do anything for him.

Unlike Dixie.

"Mia's beautiful, but she's not what I have in mind for the face of Silver-Stone."

"God, you have such ridiculously high standards. Mia is *stunning*. In my opinion, she's much prettier than that Sahara woman you were going to use."

Shea had given him the same lecture about his standards an hour ago, after he'd snubbed his nose at every model she'd presented. They were either too hard, too soft, or too...*not*

Dixie. The only person who seemed to understand his need for excellence was Maddox, who had supported his decision to go after Dixie *relentlessly.* It was no wonder they made great business partners.

"Mia is beautiful, and for that matter, so are you and Jennifer, but she's not right for my company. And you're damn right I have high standards, but so do *you.* It's who we are, Jay. Mom and Dad didn't raise pussies." His parents had unknowingly done them a favor by making them fend for themselves for the things they wanted or aspired to be. Working for everything he wanted, from his leather jacket to his college degree, forced Jace to figure out what was important to him, to strategize the best paths to success, and pushed him to excel. "Besides, when has anyone gotten *anywhere* settling for a damn thing?"

"Well…Jen doesn't have such high standards, at least not in the male-companion department."

"Don't get me started on Jenny." Their sister Jennifer had an affinity for playing around with men, and she wasn't the least bit shy about owning it. It had long been a bone of contention between her and Jace.

"I know, I know. Do you think you'll be able to get the woman you want? Dixie? I love her name, by the way. Is that her biker name or her real name?"

"When have you ever known me not to get what I go after? And I have no idea if Dixie is her real name." But now that she'd brought that up, he wanted to know the answer.

Jayla brushed a kiss over Thane's forehead. "From what you said about her, it sounds like she's as stubborn as you are. You might have met your match. Then what?"

"I don't do what-ifs. You know that. I'll convince her to do it." His jaw clenched tight at the thought of Dixie continuing to turn him down. There was no way he'd let that happen. She wasn't second fucking fiddle to anyone, and he'd sure as hell prove it to her.

The alarm on his phone went off, and he quickly silenced it. He'd set it so he didn't miss the auction. He hadn't planned on going. He hated shit like that, buying dates with people based on looks, even if for charity. But the event was important to Dixie, and that kicked it to the top of his priority list in a way that hadn't registered before. Attending the auction was not about getting her to accept his offer. He had plenty of time to focus on that *tomorrow*. Dixie's comment about his donation telling her *who he was* had been eating away at him. She'd pointed out a flaw in him that he hadn't realized existed, and he didn't like it. When Jace didn't like things, he fixed them. Tonight was about showing Dixie that he wasn't a self-absorbed prick.

"I can think of one way to get Dixie to agree," Jayla said, drawing his attention away from his thoughts. "Have you tried flirting with her?"

"She's not that kind of woman."

Jayla laughed. "Are you kidding? *All* single women like to be flirted with by hot, rich guys."

"She doesn't give two shits about money. I've got to get going, Jay," he said as he pushed to his feet and brushed the sand from his jeans. Dixie's voice slammed into him, her words grating on his nerves. *Whiskeys don't play second fiddle to anyone.* He had no idea *when* proving she had always been his first choice for the face of his company had turned into proving he was better than she thought he was. But it *had*, and the more he thought about her comment, the more it bothered him. He wasn't some privileged kid who had ridden Daddy's tailcoats to success. His parents hadn't had two nickels to rub together. He'd worked his ass off to get where he was, and he was still working his ass off, growing the company, building better bikes. He'd always been proud that he gave a large percentage of everything he earned to charities, and he didn't like the way her comment made that feel dirty.

There was no way in hell he was going to let Dixie believe he thought he was too good to give of his time.

"Date?" Jayla asked hopefully.

"Auction." He headed for the parking lot.

Her eyes lit up. "I thought you weren't going?"

"I wasn't. Now I am."

"Good! Then you can video Jared when he's auctioned off. *Pleeease!* We can watch it when you come for dinner Sunday night with Mia and Jennifer. They'll be so excited to see it. Please, Jace? Please, please, *please?*"

He gave her a knock-it off look, knowing she wouldn't. He was looking forward to seeing his sisters, who all lived in New York City.

"Come on!" Jayla pleaded, her brows knitted together so tight a deep vee appeared between her eyes. "I'll stop bugging you about finding your soul mate!"

It didn't matter that Jayla was thirty years old; she'd always be his baby sister, and there wasn't much he wouldn't do for her. Some things just took more negotiating than others.

"*Done.*" He chuckled.

She did a silent happy dance, being careful not to wake Thane, grinning from ear to ear. "I love you so much right now!"

"I love you, too. Kiss my little buddy for me."

"He misses you."

"I miss him, too." He knew she was just buying time to keep him on the phone. Jace traveled so often, they sometimes went for long stretches without seeing each other or even talking on the phone, catching up with texts as he was able.

"Fingers and toes crossed for Jared to get won by a great woman who loves to eat and for Dixie to fall prey to your charms and agree to do the shoot!"

God, he loved her enthusiasm. He stood by his bike, surrounded by the scents of the sea and sand, missing his family, and said, "I'll let you know when she says yes, because she will, Jay. Now I really have to go."

"Okay," she said quietly, wiggling her fingers in her usual wave. "Good luck, Jacey."

She didn't use the nickname she'd called him since she was too young to walk very often, but she always did when they said goodbye. And it did him in every single time.

He said goodbye, missing her even more as he pocketed his phone. He pulled on his helmet and straddled his bike. He had a fleet of bikes, but this one was his favorite. It wasn't his fastest or his sleekest motorcycle, but it was the most important model he'd ever built. It was a slightly upgraded version of the very first motorcycle line he'd ever developed, the Stroke, which had catapulted his company into an elite level of an industry that had once seemed untouchable.

His bike roared to life. Even though it was more than a decade old, it still purred like a tiger, underscoring how much quality mattered.

And there was no higher quality than the frustratingly stubborn green-eyed woman he was going to see.

Chapter Three

THERE WAS STANDING room only at Whiskey Bro's. It was amazing what the promise of hot single men and a good cause could do to a place. Beyond the usual bearded, tattooed bikers and black leather vests boasting Dark Knights patches, there was a sea of conservative men and women, yuppies sporting perfectly coiffed hair, and hipsters who worked too hard at looking cool. Most of the women carried bidding paddles with numbers on them. The Rebels, a band made up of members of the Dark Knights, played in the back of the bar. The main stage was lit up like it was an award ceremony, with black and white curtains and hundreds of lights. Jace picked up a brochure from a table by the door and shoved it in his back pocket, scanning the dancing and mingling crowd for Dixie.

His gaze skirted over women in short dresses and tight jeans who were ogling him as they sucked down drinks. He saw a group of Dixie's girlfriends and sisters-in-law huddled by the stage talking animatedly, but Dixie wasn't with them. He spotted Biggs, Dixie's father, standing by the bar talking with Diesel and Bullet. Biggs was a rough and gruff biker to the core, rivaling Bullet's size and attitude. Though a stroke had stolen

Biggs's ability to ride his motorcycle and left him with a slight droop on one side of his face, the need for a cane, and slow speech, Jace knew Biggs would step into a brawl without an ounce of fear to keep his town safe.

Jace's face broke into a wide smile when Dixie's mother pushed through the crowd in front of him. Red was a dead ringer for Sharon Osbourne, and as usual, she was dressed in black from her blouse and jeans all the way down to her biker boots. She was the coolest mother on the planet, and Jace was honored to be treated like one of her own. Then again, she treated just about everyone that way. Jace's mother was kind and generous, but she was also conservative. Although she was proud of Jace, she didn't like tattoos or leather, and she didn't understand why he had loved motorcycles for as long as he could remember. He didn't understand it, either, but even as a little kid he'd been captivated by the roar of their engines and the sleek images in magazines.

Red's green eyes brightened. "I knew you'd come. Get in here and give me a hug, you big, handsome devil."

"How's it going, Red?"

"The community has come together, I have all of my babies under one roof, and our family continues to grow. Life is *good*, Jace." She slipped her hand around his arm as if he were going to lead her onto a dance floor and said, "And now *you're* here. You let a lot of women down by not signing up to be auctioned off."

"Sorry, Red. It's not my style."

"Yes, I know. You're like a mix of all my boys: tough, smart, funny, with no patience for bullshit. I get it. And I know how much Dixie appreciated your donation. She raved about how generous you were."

He scoffed. "You don't have to say that, Red. I know she was pissed that I wouldn't agree to get up on that stage."

"Well, yes, but that's because she's competitive with herself, and she was determined to get the best men around in on this. Dixie doesn't like to lose." She waved to the crowd. "Can you believe she pulled this off? When she gets something in her head, she's like a dog with a bone. Between you and me, while my boys are all impressive in their own rights, my girl's the brains behind most good things that happen to this family. Anyway, I assume you're here to support Jared? He's over there by the bachelor table."

She pointed through a gap in the crowd. Jared was talking with Nick and Jax Braden, and too-cocky-for-his-own-good Dr. Jon Butterscotch. Quincy Gritt was sitting at a table with a number of Dark Knights and a few guys Jace didn't recognize, but he assumed they were also being auctioned off.

"Actually, I'd like to find Dixie before things get underway. Have you seen her?"

"She's in demand tonight. I saw her by the buffet table on the other side of the crowd a little while ago." She looked into the crowd, bobbing to peer around people. "There she is, with Dr. Rhys. Now, *there's* an eligible bachelor for you, and he's got eyes for my girl."

Jace followed her gaze, and Dixie's flame-red hair came into view. She clutched a clipboard to her chest, her tempting mouth curved up in a radiant smile, her gorgeous eyes trained on...a fucking *movie star*. The dark-haired, clean-cut dude was *pretty*. *Christ*, was that the kind of guy she was into? A sharp, *annoying* streak of jealousy sliced through Jace's chest.

Dixie lowered the clipboard, and *fucking hell*...Heat scorched through him as he drank in the draped neckline of her too damn short sparkly black dress, which clung to her curves. The neckline draped elegantly between her breasts, almost all the way to her belly button. The shimmery black dress was held up by a thin silver chain hooked to a tiny strip of material above each breast. The chain wrapped around her neck several times, tight as a choker, and also looser, lying in seductive layers against her creamy skin. Jace's cock twitched greedily, and his eyes shifted to the dude again. His hands curled into fists. Jace didn't *do* jealousy, and the unfamiliar sensation burning up his spine pissed him off, but he couldn't shake it any more than he could tear his eyes away from Dixie.

Red patted his arm and said, "Stick around. My baby girl is going to surprise everyone tonight, and you're *not* going to want to miss it." She winked and disappeared into the crowd.

Jace was laser focused on Dixie as he strode forward, parting the crowd with his sheer size. He reminded himself he wasn't there to stake claim to Dixie, but the closer he got to her, the more possessive his thoughts became. How had this happened? What kind of vortex had opened that he could no longer shove those thoughts away?

Someone grabbed his arm, and he whipped his head to the side. "What the hell—"

"You came!" Jillian bounced on the toes of her sky-high heels, her eyes dancing with excitement. "Sit with us!" She waved to the table, around which were a number of her cousins from Peaceful Harbor.

"How's it going, Stone?" Sam Braden, an old friend who owned an adventure company, stood to shake his hand. He and his wife, Faith, had recently welcomed their first child, a baby girl named Raeanne. "It's been too long, man. Good to see you."

"It sure has." Jace nodded a hello to Faith, and then looked at Dixie again. His gut clenched as she leaned closer to the pretty boy.

"Why aren't you on the auction block tonight?" Sam asked as he sat down beside Faith. "Afraid you can't measure up to the Bradens?"

"Hardly," Jace said absently, his attention going right back to Dixie.

Jillian was still holding his arm, chatting up a storm. "We're all here to support Nick and Jax! And Jared is looking *hot*. I can't wait to see…"

Her voice turned to white noise as Dixie glanced in his direction, and their eyes caught. The look of shock on her face was unsettling.

Jillian smacked him in the chest. "Jace!"

"Jesus, Jilly," he said, meeting her annoyed expression.

"You weren't even listening to me!"

"I was," he lied. He heard Sam and his brothers chuckle and knew he'd been caught.

"Oh really?" Jillian said with a hand on her hip. "I said I was going to win *Jared*, take him to a hotel, and tie him to a bed to do dirty things to him."

Jace gritted his teeth. "The *fuck* you are."

She smirked, her slim brows lifting. "See? You didn't hear a word I said. But I get it. Go get Dixie before Dr. Rhys, the hottest obstetrician around, plants his own baby in her pretty little belly."

Her words sent fire through his veins. He took Jillian by the shoulder and guided her into her seat. He set a serious stare on Sam and said, "Do *not* let her bid on Jared. My brother would eat her alive."

"Good to know," Jillian said with a happy little shoulder wiggle.

Sam and his other brothers glowered at her. With Jillian's virtue taken care of, Jace went to protect Dixie's. As he approached, her eyes flicked nervously toward him, turning dark and heated. She must have realized how much she was giving away, because those telling eyes moved to the dreamy doctor, where they remained.

"Thanks again, Dix," Dr. Rhys said. "I need to catch up with Wayne before you feed us to the animals." A boyish smile appeared on his too-pretty face, exposing straight, winter-white teeth, and then he headed for Bones.

Bones was Wayne Whiskey's biker name, just as Bullet and Bear were Dixie's other brothers' biker names. Jace found himself wondering again if Dixie was her real name or her biker name. He had a feeling it was her real name. He simply couldn't imagine her going by any other name. *Except maybe Kitten.*

Jon Butterscotch appeared out of nowhere, crowding in on Dixie. Dixie took a step back as he said, "You got enough cash to win me tonight, gorgeous?"

Jace gritted his teeth. At this rate he was going to break them before the night was over. Jon's short-sleeved white button-down made his year-round tan seem even darker. Chicks thought he had it *all* going on. A well-respected doctor and adrenaline junkie who ran, biked, and swam in races whenever he got the chance *and* drove a motorcycle. But Jace had seen him in action and knew he was also a player. He wasn't about to let Jon get his paws on Dixie.

Dixie rolled her eyes. "Why would I pay for what any woman in Peaceful Harbor can get for free?"

Jace put a hand on Dixie's lower back, glad she knew the

truth. He lowered his chin, holding Jon's gaze, and said, "*Beat it*, Butterscotch."

Confusion rose in Jon's eyes as they darted between Dixie and Jace, but he was a smart man. He put his hands up in surrender and backed away, heading over to his business partner, Sam's brother Cole.

"*Hand*, Stone. Move it," Dixie said sternly.

Why did her fierceness turn him on?

He knew damn well why. Because now that he'd actually allowed himself to deal with her on a one-on-one level, as capable adults, she was no longer the Dixie Whiskey who was locked firmly in the off-limits little-sister department. She was Dixie Whiskey, a challenging woman who could handle herself like a strong woman should.

And that was dangerous.

He followed the path of skin down the center of her body and caught a quick glimpse of her stiletto heels, black with silver spikes all over them, sexy red toenails peeking out from the open front. He wasn't a guy who needed to jump off a building to see if he could fly. That kind of danger didn't appeal to him. But danger of the Dixie Whiskey kind? A woman who would test his patience, his boundaries, and match him point for point? Hell yes, baby. He fucking loved that.

"Jace, I already gave you my answer, and I don't have time to argue with you. In case you haven't noticed, I've got an event to manage."

He wasn't the man Dixie needed, but as guys gawked at her long, lean legs and deep, delicious cleavage, his protective urges surged. Like a king lion protecting the queen of the pride, he stepped closer so she had no choice but to look into his eyes and said, "I'm not here to get you to change your mind."

She set her jaw, her eyes narrowing as she cocked a brow.

"I'm here because you were *right*. There is a difference between donating money and giving my time. I somehow missed that error in my ways, and I appreciate the kick in the ass. I'm better than just a money guy—you'll see."

Her gaze softened a little and her lips parted, but she didn't say a word.

"But I can't say I'm sorry for not agreeing to get on that stage," he said gruffly.

Annoyance clamped her jaw tight again.

He put a hand on her hip, loving the way her softness filled his palm. The air around them sizzled despite her annoyance as he said, "There's only one woman in Peaceful Harbor worthy of my time, and she's busy wrangling men for a good cause."

She inhaled sharply, her feminine scent drawing him even closer.

He lowered his voice for her ears only and said, "You look gorgeous tonight, kitten."

THE AIR RUSHED from Dixie's lungs as Jace strode casually up to the bar, accepting a manly embrace from her father and a handshake from Bullet as if he hadn't just set her entire body aflame and left her wondering what the hell was happening. She needed to *move*, to stop staring at him, but for the first time in her life, Dixie felt completely discombobulated. Her legs were as wobbly as a newborn foal's, and her heart was racing.

Her mother came to her side and followed her gaze up to the bar. "Look at your daddy, so handsome in his leather vest, doing what he does best. Taking care of family. Even after all these years, that man still takes my breath away."

"Uh-huh," Dixie said, trying to breathe deep enough to fill her lungs.

"Seems like a certain someone has the same effect on you, sweetheart."

"What?" Dixie snapped, tearing her eyes from Jace and meeting her mother's amused expression. "No he does *not*. He's infuriating and arrogant."

Dixie's eyes moved traitorously back to Jace as he climbed onto a barstool with his back to the bar. He locked those piercing eyes on her, knocking her legs out from under her again. She groaned and spun on her heels, slamming right into Quincy with an *oomph*.

"Whoa, sorry, Dix," Quincy said, his clear blue eyes wide and alert, so different from the strung-out kid he'd been when he'd first reconnected with Truman. His light brown hair had gotten blonder from the sun, and he'd brushed it away from his face. "Hey, you okay? You look a little frazzled…or *drunk*."

"I'm *fine*," she snapped, feeling so far from *fine* she couldn't even remember how to spell the word.

Her mother chuckled and said, "We're starting in ten minutes, sweetheart. If you need to do a shot to calm those nerves, get it quick."

"I'm not going anywhere near that bar," Dixie grumbled.

"Suit yourself." Her mother walked away.

"What's going on with you?" Quincy asked. He looked at the bar, scanning the people around it, and said, "Is someone bugging you? Need me to take care of it?"

It was all Dixie could do to laugh incredulously. "Unless you have one of those mind wipers from *Men in Black*, then no, you can't take care of it."

"Hey, I've got connections." He waggled his brows. "Stress getting to you? You nailed the event. I heard people saying they were ready to bid a *thousand* bucks."

"I hope Penny made lots of tips today," Dixie said, chancing a look around the room while avoiding the bar area completely. It didn't help. Energy radiated off Jace like flames, taking up residence in the very air she breathed.

"I see *lots* of familiar ladies who frequent the bookstore. I'd say she'd better have had a good *month*."

Quincy crossed his arms over his chest, his gaze skating around the room. When he was only thirteen years old, he'd killed a man for raping his mother. Truman, who was nine years older than Quincy and had always taken care of him since their drugged-out mother never could, had confessed to the crime he hadn't committed and served six years in prison. To say Quincy had demons was an understatement. Like so many of the men there tonight, he wore the ghosts of his past in the ink decorating his arms. But Quincy was a good man and a brilliant mathematician. He'd filled in for Dixie last fall when she'd taken a road trip, and he'd done a phenomenal job handling the administrative duties and payroll for the shop and the bar.

"Just promise me one thing," Dixie said. "If you're won by Miss America tonight and you two get all hot and heavy, you'll still fill in for me while I'm at the Cape the week after next?"

"I have it on my calendar. Wednesday through Sunday. I'd never let you down, Dix. Not even for a great piece of ass." He nodded toward Finlay, Izzy, and the rest of the girls making their way toward them. "Looks like the cavalry is coming. I think I'll go give the bookstore ladies a peek at the stallion before the ponies take the stage. I wouldn't want them to waste their money."

He strutted off, and a moment later Izzy looped her hand through one of Dixie's arms. Crystal did the same on her other side. The rest of the girls crowded around her as they dragged her toward the ladies' room.

"Let's go, Dixie Lee. It's time to get you ready for your big debut," Crystal said excitedly.

She'd been so sidetracked by Jace, she had completely forgotten she was being auctioned off. Quincy might not have those mind-wiping powers she needed, but Jace sure did. Unfortunately, he was erasing all the *wrong* thoughts.

"We've got to make sure you earn more than all the guys combined," Izzy said. "Go big or go home, right, girls?"

"Yes!" they cheered in unison.

"I cannot wait to see everyone's faces." Gemma winced and said, "You guys, I almost made a mistake and said something to Tru about it last night."

Josie gasped. "I almost spilled the beans to Jed, too!"

Dixie was getting more nervous by the second. Her nerves flamed as her mother fell into step with them.

"Are we ready?" Red said in a hushed tone.

"I'm not," Sarah said as they crowded into the ladies' room. "I'm a nervous wreck. I hate keeping secrets, especially from Bones. I had a dream last night that when he found out I knew about Dixie being auctioned off, he canceled our engagement!"

"What?" Finlay said loudly. "He'd never do that."

"Bones adores you," Gemma said.

"The man proudly drives the *Bones Mobile* around town with the kids. He's yours for life," Crystal pointed out. Bear had built a special vehicle so Bones could drive his kids around in something that resembled a motorcycle. The Bones Mobile had the front end of a motorcycle and the back end of a sports car, with sides and a roof protecting three back seats with five-point harnesses.

Red took Sarah's hand, smiling warmly. "Honey, my son waited his whole life to find you and the kids. He's not going to let you go for anything, especially not for helping Dixie break free of the chains that bind her. Don't you *ever* worry about that. He'll understand."

The worry cleared from Sarah's eyes. "You're right. I'm just overtired and worrying over every little thing. Maggie Rose hasn't been sleeping very well lately. I think she's starting to teethe."

"Or maybe you and your hot-doc hubby-to-be are keeping her up at night." Crystal nudged Finlay and said, "Bet you and Bullet will need to keep your kids in the garage so you don't wake them up at night with your wild mattress wrestling."

Finlay blushed and covered her face.

"They're my *brothers*," Dixie reminded Crystal.

Everyone else cracked up.

"Okay, ladies, let's focus before the guys come in here to get us," Red said, moving closer to Dixie. She looked her daughter up and down, ran her fingers through the ends of Dixie's long hair, and sighed. "You're perfect just as you are."

"Jace sure thinks so," Tracey said from behind Red, and all eyes turned toward her. "What? He's been staring at her since he came in."

"Along with most of the other guys in this place," Izzy said, giving Dixie an I've-got-your-back look. "Can you blame them? Dixie's got it *all* going on."

"Damn right I do." Dixie turned toward the mirror, and the girls crowded around, primping her hair, smoothing her dress, and fixing the slinky silver chains around her neck. "*God*, I love this dress. Jilly is amazing, isn't she?"

"It's stunning," Gemma said, "But you make everything look amazing. I'd give anything to have your legs."

"I want her boobs," Tracey said, grabbing her own tiny breasts.

Josie nodded emphatically. "Me too!"

Sarah said, "I'll take her cute butt."

Dixie laughed. "You guys are all *gorgeous*. I'm tall and gangly! I'd love to have any of your figures."

"Even mine?" Crystal rubbed her baby bump, fluttering her lashes.

"Definitely *not*," Dixie said. "But when Cubbie is born, I'll gladly love him or her up as often as you and Bear will let me."

Red hiked a thumb over her shoulder and said, "Get in the back of the line, Dix. That baby's *mine*."

A loud *rap, rap, rap* on the bathroom door startled them, and they squealed, huddling together.

"Hen party's over!" Bullet's gruff voice came through the closed door.

"Coming!" Red called out. She turned to the girls with a mischievous look in her eyes and said, "Ready to pull off the greatest Whiskey feat yet?"

Everyone cheered, "Yes!" Even Dixie, although she wasn't nearly ready.

She was suddenly scared shitless. She hadn't thought this through. What if her brothers caused a huge scene? What if nobody bid on her and she made a fool of herself? She gripped the clipboard so tight her fingers shook as they pushed through the door in a whispering huddle. Dixie felt Jace's eyes on her, but she refused to look anywhere but at her friends as the girls hurriedly took their seats with their significant others, and Tracey and Izzy joined them at their table. Diesel strode over and stood guard beside Tracey. Tracey's shoulders rounded forward, and she whispered something to Crystal, her discomfort palpable. As the scene unfolded, Dixie realized her own discomfort was probably just as evident. Jace had messed with her head so badly, he'd knocked her off her game.

Nobody knocks me off my game.

She straightened her spine, searching the room for Jace. He stood by the bar, watching her intently with a coy expression.

Fuck coy.

You want to mess with me, you'd better bring the biggest ones you've got, buddy.

Dixie tipped her chin up, thrust out her chest, and turned the heat up a million degrees as she sauntered toward the stage with an extra sway to her hips. She hadn't been oblivious to the men checking her out all evening, though she'd paid them no mind. Now she made eye contact, doling out seductive winks and smiles like never before. She felt Jace's stare burning through her skin, and it only drove her confidence higher.

The bachelors were seated at the table by the stage, grinning like fools. Jon Butterscotch was waving to women, and Quincy had fierce eye contact going on with a table of chicks. Just beyond the other side of the stage, Chicki Redmond, Red's best friend and the wife of a Dark Knight, sat ready to register the winning bids and take donations.

Dixie put a hand on Jared's shoulder and bent at the waist between him and Scott, Sarah and Josie's brother, purposely giving Jace a view of her ass. Yeah, she had a great ass. She walked a boatload of miles every week running the businesses and waitressing at the bar. Other parts of her weren't so bad either. She'd long ago embraced her tall, slim, though slightly curvy figure for what it was. She'd never have the hourglass shape of a Kardashian, but she'd never have their baggage, either, and for that she was grateful.

"You boys doing okay?" she asked. "You're first up, Jared. Are you nervous?"

"I haven't been nervous about a *performance* since my first time with a girl." Jared and Scott bumped fists, chuckling. "I just feel sorry for all the women who *won't* win me. You sure you don't want to auction off a week's worth of dates for us?"

"Not tonight, but I'm sure you'd be booked solid." She patted his shoulder. "How about you, Scott? Are you ready?"

"Hell yes. But get ready for a cat fight. The ladies are hot for me tonight."

"I'm ready." Dixie chuckled and straightened up. She couldn't help but steal a glance at Jace as she stepped back. Jace lifted his chin, no longer looking quite so coy. In fact, he looked downright irritated.

Good.

She turned toward the stage, consulting the clipboard, even though she had the lineup memorized. She needed something to focus on other than Jace's reaction.

"Thank you all for coming tonight," her father said into the mic, and the crowd exploded with applause and cheers. He stood in the middle of the stage gripping his cane, wearing a T-shirt, a black leather vest, and the same scuffed boots he'd worn for decades. He didn't dress up, and he didn't give a damn what anyone else thought of his appearance, as underscored by his unkempt gray beard and thoroughly inked flesh. His leathery skin was mapped with deep grooves earned from a lifetime of riding under the harsh sun, and the left side of his face drooped from his stroke. Still, he was the epitome of strength and confidence.

As Dixie listened to her father explain that the proceeds of the auction would benefit the Parkvale Women's Shelter, she filled with pride. Her father was a warrior, a protector, and a heck of a good man. He was a tough parent, with strict beliefs about how to treat others and what roles women and men should play in each other's lives. She may not agree with some of his protective barriers, but she respected them and she respected him *immensely*.

Her father looked directly at her and said, "Now, let's hear it for my beautiful daughter, Dixie, who spent weeks planning and coordinating every aspect of this event, from the food and the signage to soliciting donations and convincing each of these badass men to step onto the auction block."

More applause and cheers rang out. Her brothers and friends hollered things like "Dixie rocks!" and "Way to go, Dix!"

She waved, her stomach twisting into knots as she murmured, "Thank you."

She *really* hadn't thought this through. She'd been worried about her brothers getting upset, but she hadn't thought too hard about her father. Her brothers were always in her face, trying to keep her safe—or in line. But her father was the quiet force behind them, the Dalai Lama of the Dark Knights. Her brothers were protective of her and of each other because their father demanded it, and he demanded it because he loved them—all of them. His blood-born children as well as the people who had become family, like the families of the Dark Knights, Quincy, Tracey, Scott, Tru and Gemma, Josie and Jed, and all their children.

Would taking this stand, getting up on that stage and being

auctioned off, be a slap in the face to her father? An act of public disrespect?

Would he ever forgive her?

"I assume you all know how this works," her father said. "But for those who have never been to a bachelor auction, there are rules. The first rule is to bid *high*."

The crowd laughed.

"I'm not kidding," he said. Then his expression turned serious, and the crowd silenced. "I haven't seen some of you in our bar before, so the second rule is for you. If you start a fight or cause any bullshit, you'll have my boys to deal with."

Every Dark Knight in the place rose to their feet, proudly showing off their leathers and patches. Even the clean-cut members looked like forces to be reckoned with. A low murmur rumbled through the crowd.

Her father nodded, and the men sat down. "Rule number three is for the winners of the auction. If you win a date, you will adhere to the rules for those dates, which will be handed to you upon payment by the lovely Chicki Redmond." He lifted his cane, pointing it at Chicki, who waggled her finger toward the crowd, eliciting another low murmur. "Now, let's get this show on the road with bachelor number one, Jared Stone."

Chapter Four

THE BAND PLAYED "Moves Like Jagger" as Jared strutted up to the stage in his jeans and T-shirt, his tattooed arms on display, and the crowd went wild. Women screamed, guys whistled, and Jared ate it all up, turning as he danced his way over to Biggs and the music died down. He handed Biggs the card Dixie had prepared for her father to read, as she'd done for each of the bachelors. She'd had fun preparing them and picking out songs for each of the contestants. Her friends had written her card and chosen her song, but they'd given it to her mother and refused to tell her what they'd written or what song they'd chosen.

"Settle down, ladies, and let me read you the goods on this fine gentleman," Biggs said in a slow drawl, and the din of the crowd eventually died down. He leaned his cane against his leg and read from the card as Jared waved and winked at the audience. "Jared Stone is a chef by trade, and you know what that means. He's got magic hands."

Jared held up his hands and said, "Yeah, baby! Magic!"

Women cheered. Biggs glowered at Dixie, but she couldn't stop smiling. It was just the reaction from the crowd she'd hoped for.

"Jared's got tons of energy," Biggs continued. "If his jaw isn't jumping, his legs are, so if you win this hot bachelor, get ready to pull an all-nighter." He lifted his gaze to the cheering audience and chuckled as Jared began hip thrusting. "This scorching-hot Adam Levine lookalike owns several restaurants and clothing stores. He's sure to keep your body happy, your mouth full, and don't worry about your tattered clothes. He'll replace anything he tears off your body." His eyes shot angrily to Dixie as more *whoops* rang out. "I think we're in for a long night."

The band started playing "Moves Like Jagger" again, and Jared broke into a sexy dance, earning more applause and whistles. Dixie felt the heat of Jace's stare boring into her and told herself she was imagining it. She moved to the beat, swaying her hips and shoulders to try to work off her nervous energy as Biggs started the auction process, but she couldn't shake the feeling that Jace was watching her every move. That should probably annoy her, but it revved her up, despite his earlier use of the endearment *kitten*. She didn't like pet names, especially terms that seemed soft and submissive. But when he'd said it, it had sounded smoldering and sexy, as much of an annoyance as it was a turn-on. The urge to see if her mind was playing tricks on her was too strong. She tried to act casual as her gaze rolled over the cheering crowd, coming to a heart-thundering *halt* at the predatory look on Jace's face.

"Sold to Jillian Braden, number two sixty-nine," Biggs called out.

Jace shot an angry glare in Jillian's direction. Jillian was jumping up and down, clapping and screaming.

"Braden!" Jace's deep voice boomed across the room at the

same time Nick and Jax shot to their feet at the bachelor table and seethed, "Sam!"

The crowd silenced as Sam Braden pushed to his feet, the three protective men glaring at him. He held his palms up toward the ceiling and said, "I tried, but it's *Jilly!*"

Laughter erupted as Jillian strutted proudly toward Chicki, ignoring the ruckus the men had made.

Red strode onto the stage and took the mic from Biggs, who chuckled and stroked his beard, stepping back to give Red the floor. "Listen up, gentlemen. This is for *charity*. Nobody's going to be taking advantage of your sisters, cousins, friends, or acquaintances. We'll see to that." She looked pointedly at Jace, then at Nick, and finally, at Jax and said, "Calm your jets or I'll haul all y'all out of here by your ears. *Got it?*"

When there was no response past a grumble, Red said, "What was that?"

"Got it," the three grumbling men said louder.

"Okay, then let the night roll on." She handed Biggs the microphone, kissed him smack on the lips, and strutted off the stage as more applause rang out, setting the tone for the rest of the night.

Hours later, when they finally got down to the last two bachelors, Dixie was nearing her wit's end. As if she wasn't nervous enough as her turn to get auctioned off neared, Jace had set his sights on Dixie again. And like an addict craving her favorite drug, she couldn't resist getting her next hit, looking at him over and over again. Every heated glance amped up the electricity between them, until she was sure they'd catch fire.

Biggs called Jon Butterscotch up to the stage, and the crowd went wild.

The band played "SexyBack" as Jon strode onto the stage.

He took the mic from Biggs and said, "Fifty shades of sweetness at your service, ladies. Who's going to get the first lick?"

The ladies shot to their feet, clapping and screaming.

Biggs ripped the mic from Jon's hands and said, "I can see Dr. Butterscotch needs no further introduction." He stepped back, allowing Jon to take over.

Jon swaggered to the front of the stage, splayed his arms, and made a dramatic show of gyrating his hips. He grabbed the front of his shirt with both hands and tore it open. Buttons flew through the air, inciting more excited squeals. He shrugged his shirt off and whipped it around over his head, then tossed it into the crowd.

One of Crow's sisters won a date with Jon, which caused several of the Dark Knights to send threatening glares in his direction. Dixie knew what it felt like to be the cause of that type of scrutiny. Her stomach knotted tighter. She glanced at her family sitting at a table near the stage, cheering as Biggs called Quincy up to the tune of "You Sexy Thing." All of her burly brothers and their beautiful wives cheered him on as he strode coolly and confidently to the middle of the stage, flashing his famous smirk. Quincy opened his arms, giving the screaming ladies a good long look at his gorgeous self before turning around and shaking his ass, earning more whoops and cheers.

"Three hundred dollars!" a woman yelled from a table of twentysomethings. They all shot to their feet, except a cute brunette wearing black-framed glasses who looked like she wished she was invisible.

"Looks like my boy Quincy needs no introduction either. I need the number from your bidding paddle, sweetheart," Biggs said.

The women looked anxiously at each other. One of the girls

grabbed the paddle from the cute brunette and waved it, yelling, "Three hundred!"

Dixie looked at Penny, who was sitting next to Josie. They were whispering behind their hands. Penny hadn't bid on anyone, but she looked like she was having a great time.

"Do I hear three hundred and ten?" Biggs's voice boomed through the room.

Quincy started gyrating in a sexy dance as he pointed out at the crowd. He wiggled his fingers in a come-hither gesture, and more bids rang out, driving the winning bid all the way up to one thousand dollars!

"Sold, to—"

"Veronica Wescott!" the winning group of girls screamed. Two of them hauled the embarrassed bespectacled brunette to her feet and hollered, "Roni Wescott! Roni Wescott is the winner!"

Dixie felt as nervous as Roni Wescott looked. She was *next*. Her palms sweated as her friends turned to look at her with supportive smiles, giving her the thumbs-up. She stole a glance at Jace. He was watching her, clapping along with everyone else as Biggs announced the winner.

Jace mouthed, *Nice job*, and winked.

Oh God, was she really going to get up on that stage and be auctioned off? Would Jace bid? What if he didn't? She turned away, feeling queasy, and watched her mother cross the stage to join her father.

Biggs kissed Red, and then he said, "That was a hell of an auction!" Applause rang out anew, and Biggs made a settle-down motion with his hand, quieting the chaos. "Before we wrap up and celebrate, my beautiful queen would like to say a few words." He handed the microphone to Red, eliciting more cheers.

"I can't imagine a more successful auction. We greatly appreciate the community coming together and supporting the needs of women and families who are going through hard times." Red looked warmly at Sarah, and Bones kissed Sarah's temple. She shifted her gaze to Josie, tucked beneath Jed's arm, and then her motherly gaze landed on Tracey, who blushed. "As you may know, the Dark Knights started the Parkvale Women's Center, and our very own Eva and Sunny Yeun, the best mother-daughter team around, run the program." Red motioned toward the Yeuns, earning another round of applause. "They're changing and saving lives on a daily basis, and events like this make it possible for them to continue their good work. And tonight wouldn't have been so successful without our bright and talented daughter, Dixie. Let's welcome Dixie to the stage."

"Way to go, Dixie!" a number of men called out between hoots and whistles.

Dixie tried to ignore the swarm of bees in her stomach as she joined her parents. Thank God she was used to walking in spike heels, or she would probably have stumbled in her nervousness. The secretive look in her mother's eyes made her even more anxious.

I can do this. I can do this. I can do this.

Her father reached for her hand, and his beard tickled as he kissed her cheek. "I'm proud of you, princess."

He used that endearment so sparingly, it shot straight to Dixie's heart. *Oh God! Can I do this? Please don't hate me, Dad!*

She stood between her parents, looking at Jace over the crowd, and her pulse spiked at the grin on his face.

"Dixie not only took the reins for this event with both

hands," Red said proudly, "but she put her heart and soul into it, reaching out to individuals and companies, all while managing our family businesses."

Dixie kept forcing herself to redirect her gaze, but like metal to magnet, it zipped back to Jace time and time again.

"We have a big surprise for you tonight," Red said.

"We do?" Biggs asked.

"We do!" Red exclaimed.

Dixie gulped a breath.

Her mother took her hand, squeezing it supportively as she led her to the front of the stage. "Anyone who has attended these auctions over the years knows that one of the rules is that the hosting family must have one family member on the auction block, and since all of our handsome boys are taken..." She stepped back, motioning toward Dixie, and said, "I present to you our lovely princess."

The room went dead silent.

The band started playing "Dear Future Husband" by Meghan Trainor. Dixie shot an are-you-kidding-me glare at her friends and sisters-in-law, who all cracked up.

Bullet busted out a laugh and said, "Good one, Red!"

Laughter rumbled through the crowd, sending anger rushing through Dixie's veins.

"Hey!" Dixie hollered. "What the *hell*, people? Did you not hear Red? I'm up for auction. Let's get the bidding started!"

Bullet's face turned stone-cold. "Over my dead body." He pushed to his feet, glowering at Bear and Bones, which was enough to bring every other Dark Knight to their feet, arms crossed, their menacing stares roaming over the murmuring and gasping crowd.

Bear and Bones exchanged an uncomfortable glance, though

they did not stand.

Dixie saw fear on women's faces and confusion on some of the men's, making her even angrier *and* embarrassed. She crossed and uncrossed her arms. The Dark Knights were scattered through the room like unwanted sentinels, scaring off anyone who may have wanted to bid. She gritted her teeth, hoping nobody could hear her hammering heart, which pounded in her ears like a bass drum on steroids. Every passing second felt interminable. The pit of her stomach burned as Bones leaned back in his chair, making no move to stand. Crystal said something to Bear. He cocked a grin, put his arm around her, and remained seated, nodding supportively at Dixie.

Dixie felt a modicum of relief, but it was short-lived as Bullet moved forward, his eyes so angry they looked pitch-black. His shoulders were high and tight, his biceps twitched, and his fingers curled into fists, ready to take down anyone in his path.

"*Off* the stage, Dixie," Bullet commanded, planting himself in front of the stage, a formidable barrier between her and potential bidders.

"*No.*" Dixie squared her shoulders, refusing to be shut down any longer.

"My son seems to have forgotten his manners," Red said lightly as she stepped off the stage and went to stand beside Bullet. "Let's get the bidding started, shall we?"

Dixie heard the masked tension in her mother's voice. The room was unnervingly silent, save for the tension crackling in the air.

Bullet crossed his arms over his broad chest, turning to face the crowd, his voice low and threatening as he said, "Anyone who bids will deal with me."

"Come on, Bullet. Don't ruin the night." Jon stood up and said, "I'll bid five hundred dollars!"

"Sit *down*, Butterscotch," Bullet seethed.

Jon sat obediently. Dixie rolled her eyes. Were there no more real men in the world?

A tough-looking blond guy on the other side of the room stepped forward, and Dixie's hopes lifted.

Bullet snapped his head in the guy's direction and barked, "Back off or I'll take you down."

Anger and embarrassment consumed Dixie. "Is this how it's going to be? Nobody's got big enough balls to stand up to my brother? Well, if that's how it is, then y'all aren't man enough for—"

"Thirty thousand dollars." Jace's deep voice thundered through the room.

There was a collective gasp and a rumble of shocked murmurs.

Dixie's heart sped up even faster as the crowd parted, and Jace strode confidently to the front of the room, stopping inches from Bullet.

"You're playing with fire, Stone," Bullet growled.

"*Thirty-five* thousand," Jace said authoritatively, holding Bullet's stare.

His complete disregard for Bullet's warning had Bullet stepping closer. "Don't fuck with me, Stone."

Jace's eyes flicked up to Dixie, and a slow grin spread across his handsome face as he said, "Make it forty thousand, and I'll volunteer at the shelter the next time I'm in town."

Gasps and sounds of shock rose from the crowd.

Dixie was breathing so hard, she thought she might faint. She'd never seen anyone stand up to, or *ignore*, Bullet like that.

Plus, Jace was offering up his *time*. Her hopes soared. Maybe she hadn't been misguidedly crushing on Jace for all these years after all. *Maybe...*

And then it hit her.

And her hopes came crashing down.

Jace wasn't bidding on a date. He was buying her so she'd be in the calendar.

Anger sent Dixie stomping down the steps to the two angry giants. She pointed at Bullet and said, "Back off. *Now.*" She turned furiously to Jace and said, "If you think you can buy me to do that calendar shoot, you're *wrong.*"

"Hey, I'm just trying to win a date, Dix," Jace said. "Any woman strong enough to get up on that stage is worth a hell of a lot more than forty grand."

He said it with such vehemence, her heart leapt.

"What *calendar?*" Bullet eyed Jace.

Jace was still looking at her, and for the first time, she thought he was *really* seeing her.

"He wants me to model for the Silver-Stone motorcycle calendar," she said a little absently.

"Fuck no! You are not going to be the chick on a spank-bank calendar." Bullet bared his teeth and seethed, "I should tear you apart, Stone."

"Go for it." Jace winked at Dixie, completely unflappable, which was so damn sexy she nearly lost her breath.

"*Boys...*" Biggs said with an air of warning.

Bear and Bones rushed over.

"Sorry, Jace, but she's my little sister. I really don't want her in one of those calendars," Bear said.

"Sorry, Dix," Bones said. "But I'm with them. You're not doing the calendar."

Dixie was sick of being told what to do, and if she was ever going to break out of this little-sister mold, it had to be now. She threw her arms up, looking incredulously at her brothers, and said, "You know what?" She turned toward Jace and said, "I'm *in*. I'm doing the calendar."

BIGGS WAS LIMPING toward them with a stern expression, and Dixie's brothers were hollering angrily. But Jace couldn't take his eyes off Dixie as he said, "And my date?"

For the first time in as long as he could remember, he actually *wanted* to go on a date. *A fucking date.* Not a hookup, but an honest-to-goodness date. The desire shocked the hell out of him. The crowd silenced, as if everyone in the bar was holding their breath, except Bullet, who was breathing fire, muttering threats.

Red made an excited little sound.

Dixie's lips curved up, and she said, "Sold, for one date!"

The room erupted in *whoops* and cheers.

Like a damn teenager, Jace pumped his fist. "Yes!"

"Biggs," Bullet growled as his father came to his side. "You got something to say about this?"

Biggs stroked his beard, eyeing all of them. "Hell yes, I have something to say." He looked out at the crowd, eyeing the Knights that had circled them, standing guard, and gave a single curt nod.

It felt like the whole room exhaled as the men who would give their lives for the brotherhood eased their protective stances and backed away.

"We're real sorry for the interruption," Biggs said loudly to the crowd. "Y'all can go celebrate. This is a family matter now. There's nothing else to see here." He waited as people made their way toward the buffet tables. Then he turned to Bullet and said, "Thank you for doing exactly as I taught you." His eyes moved between his three sons. "You boys make me proud every single day, and you always have."

Bullet's chest puffed up with the *take-that* look he gave Jace.

Biggs's keen eyes found Dixie, and Jace stepped closer to her, shocking himself, and apparently her family, as they all looked curiously at him. He didn't step back. Biggs held his gaze for another beat before turning his attention to his daughter. Dixie shifted on her high heels, her beautiful green eyes moving nervously to Red's. Red's supportive nod was almost imperceptible. If Jace hadn't been looking for it, he would have missed it. A little smirk of confidence lifted Dixie's lips, and she met her father's steady gaze.

"Princess, I raised you to be tough, to speak your mind, and to be as ballsy as your brothers," Biggs said in a serious tone. "I expected you'd rebel one day. Or *maybe stake claim to your life* is a better way to say it. Though, I have to admit, I never expected your mama to be in on it." He looked at Red and said, "You and I are going to have a little talk later."

"I look forward to it," Red said sassily.

Biggs glanced over Bullet's shoulder at Dixie's sisters-in-law and friends, huddled together and watching them intently. The girls stilled like deer caught in headlights. The second Biggs looked at Red and Dixie, the girls huddled together again, whispering behind their hands.

"It looks like you ladies have formed a club of your own," Biggs said. "Every club needs a powerful leader and a strong second. Well played, ladies. Well played."

Relief swept over Dixie's face, and she threw her arms around Biggs. "Thank you, Dad. I didn't mean to disrespect you. I just...It started as a joke, but then it wasn't..."

"Are you fucking kidding me?" Bullet grumbled, scowling at Jace.

"What do you think I'm going to do, Whiskey? Spit it out," Jace challenged.

"*Boys*," Red said. "Can't we play nice?"

"I mean no disrespect, Red, but I'd like to hear Bullet's answer."

Bullet ground his teeth together, his hands fisting as his wife, Finlay, a pretty little blonde, came to his side. She unfurled his fingers and slid her hand into his with a sweet smile. The tension in Bullet's jaw eased as she said, "Are you guys almost ready for some food?"

"Soon, sweetheart." Bullet lifted colder eyes to Jace and said, "You're putting my sister in a calendar that she has no business being in."

"That's *my* decision to make," Dixie snapped.

Bullet opened his mouth to speak, but Finlay patted his stomach and said, "She's right."

"Bullet, you're an admirable man and a fine brother," Red said. "But you boys have each had your time to shine. Now it's Dixie's turn. You've taught her to be the fierce lioness she is. I know letting go is hard—I've had to do it several times already—but you need to loosen those reins or you're going to push her away." She handed Jace a card and said, "Congratulations on your date."

"Thank you." Jace shoved the card in his pocket. "Bullet, how about you and I sit down, and I'll show you what I have in mind for the calendar? I've got three sisters. I know what lines not to cross. And Dixie is not going to just be a model. She's going to be the *face* of Silver-Stone, which in the business world is the equivalent to Red being Biggs's *queen*."

"Red isn't on a calendar," Bullet said sharply.

"You're right. But you do realize Dixie's gorgeous and guys are looking at her all the time. Now she'll have a company behind her, a legal team, a public relations group. She'll have *me* demanding respect for her."

"What else will you *demand*, Stone?" Bullet challenged.

He sensed Dixie holding her breath and said, "Not a thing. *Ever*."

Bullet narrowed his eyes and said, "With a forty-thousand-dollar investment, I'm not sure I believe that."

"It's a donation to charity, Bullet, not a brothel payment."

Bear chuckled. "I'm not thrilled about this calendar, but you two can fight this out. I want to go spend time with my wife." He offered his hand to Jace, and when Jace shook it, he said, "Thanks for the donation. The shelter needs it."

"I trust you boys to be civil," Biggs said, reaching for Red's hand. "If you'll excuse me, my woman and I are going to have a little talk."

Red patted Bullet's cheek and said, "Remember what I said, honey."

"He will," Finlay promised.

Red winked at Jace, blew a kiss to Dixie, and said, "Bones, maybe you want to spend time with Sarah, too?"

Bones glanced at Bullet and said, "You cool? Most of the people here were ready to piss their pants when you lost it."

Bullet nodded.

"Good," Bones said. "Jace, I'd like to see what you have

planned for the calendar when you have time. When and where is the shoot taking place?"

"Monday and Tuesday in New York City. We'll leave Sunday and be back Wednesday. I'll grab you after I settle up my donation with Chicki."

"Oh, shoot." Dixie looked around the room. "If I'm going away, I need to talk to Tracey about taking my waitressing shift and to Quincy about handling the auto shop while I'm gone."

"Congratulations on winning a date with Dixie," Finlay said. She went up on her toes, pulling Bullet down so she could say something into his ear.

Bullet made an appreciative sound and said, "Stone, grab me when you talk to Bones."

"Will do."

When they walked away, Dixie let out a loud, exasperated breath and said, "Oh my God. What a nightmare."

Jace stepped closer and said, "I'm glad you changed your mind."

"You have my brothers to thank for that."

She said it so sharply, it rubbed Jace the wrong way. "It wasn't my intent to even talk about the calendar photo shoot tonight. I came to support your efforts with the auction, which you pulled off beautifully, by the way."

"Thank you, but it's okay. I know your time is running out to find a model."

"I'm being serious, Dixie. I didn't come here to pressure you. I came here to make a change. To give of my time, not my money. I had no idea you were going to be auctioned off, and I'm glad I won the date, but I don't want you to do the shoot because you felt pushed into a corner or just to stick it to your brothers."

A snarky smile lifted her lips and she said, "You had no problem pushing me into a corner for the last two days."

"You're right, and I realize that it doesn't matter how much I want you to be the face of my company. Doing something like this calendar will bring you international exposure, and that's a lot of pressure. It could upend your life in a way I hadn't considered. A photo shoot like this will probably lead to ads on television, in magazines, billboards…"

"*What?* I thought this was a *one*-time thing."

He scrubbed a hand over his beard, wincing at his own impulsiveness. Shea thought he'd been a pain in the ass trying to find someone who lived up to Dixie. Once Dixie was in the calendar, once she truly became the face of Silver-Stone, no one else would ever be right enough to fill her shoes. That wasn't a fair position to put Dixie in without her knowledge, so he said, "I know. That's my fault. I've had you in my mind as the face of Silver-Stone for so long, I got excited at the possibility of you actually agreeing to do the calendar and I didn't think beyond it. Seriously, I want you to think about it. I don't want you to feel pressured."

She studied his face with a curious expression and said, "Why did you bid on me if it wasn't to try to buy my agreement to do the calendar?"

"I'm not entirely sure. I saw you up there, and it just happened. I didn't like how it was playing out. I hated the anger and embarrassment I saw in your eyes." *And I hate the thought of another man's hands on you.* He kept that to himself, because he didn't understand why he felt it so viscerally.

She crossed her arms and said, "So you were *rescuing* me?"

He closed the distance between them and said, "No. You aren't someone who needs rescuing. I was selfishly taking advantage of an opportunity, and if that makes me a dick, then it does. I think we both realize it's about time we get to know each other better."

Her breathing hitched, and hell if he didn't love that little tell. He put a hand on her hip as he felt her sway forward. "Tell you what. How about we take advantage of the night and share a dance? We'll put your answer off until tomorrow, okay?"

"About the date?" she challenged.

"No, kitten. You're mine for one night. That deal is sealed," he said as he led her into the dancing crowd. "I was talking about the calendar."

As he drew her into his arms, she said, "If you call me kitten again, my claws are going to come out."

"Now you're taunting me with dirty promises?"

"Jace! Dixie!" Jillian hurried over to them like she was on a mission. She plastered herself to the two of them, one arm around Dixie, one arm around Jace, and said, "I'm cutting in before you two start going at it on the dance floor."

Bloody hell.

"We are *not* going at it," Dixie said with enough of a bite to sting.

Jillian wobbled her head from side to side with a sarcastic, "*Uh-huh.* Dixie, you were the *bomb* up there! You were like the Rosa Parks of the Whiskeys, breaking free, everyone else be damned! You're an inspiration to single girls with overbearing brothers everywhere." She patted Jace's side and said, "And, Jace! I wondered what that bid was about, but"—she whistled— "now I can see. Sparks are flying all around you two. Poor Finlay is doing everything she can to distract Bullet. He's over there chewing on nails by the bar."

"Okay, Jilly. *Enough.*" Jace couldn't keep the sharpness from his tone. "I thought I told you not to bid on Jared."

Jillian rolled her eyes. "And what gave you the idea I'd listen? Once Izzy started bidding, I got carried away with winning. Speaking of Jared, he's with Nick and Jax, who I'm sure are laying down ground rules right now." She lowered her voice and said, "Every one of which I intend to break."

"*Jilly*," Jace warned.

"You're not even my brother, so back off. One day all the men in the world will realize we women can think for ourselves, and then what will you have to worry about?" Jillian smiled and said, "I'll let you get back to your hot-and-heavy dancing. I just wanted to say congratulations, and, Dixie, Jace was so enthralled with you as the face of Silver-Stone, he stole my picture! I already altered the clothes for the shoot to fit you. It's a good thing I made that dress for you, Dixie, or I wouldn't have known your measurements. Jace, you can pick them up tomorrow. Good luck at the shoot."

She flitted away with a bounce in her step, and Dixie's eyes went cold. "What did she mean that she altered the clothes to fit me?"

"I figured you might come around and I was worried she wouldn't have time to do the alterations if I didn't get her started."

Dixie stepped back, anger and hurt warring in her eyes. "So what was all that crap about not even wanting to bring up the calendar shoot tonight?"

"I wasn't going to talk about it. *You're* the one who brought it up. I was just covering my ass, Dix. I had planned on talking with you tomorrow, and hoped I'd be able to convince you to do the calendar."

"It was a dick move." She whirled around to storm off.

Jace grabbed her hand, hauling her back into his arms, and held her tight despite the fumes coming out her ears. "There's the tempting claws I keep hearing about."

"Cut the shit, Jace. This whole thing was a lie," she seethed.

"I don't lie, Dixie."

Her jaw clenched tight again.

"I respect the hell out of you, and lying would undermine that. I wouldn't be here right now if I didn't."

She glared at him, eyes narrow, lips pursed. "Then maybe you're just covering your ass right *now* because you're afraid of what Bullet might do if he found out you played me."

He scoffed. "Bullet would put up a hell of a fight, and he'd probably fight to the death to preserve your honor." He lowered his mouth beside her ear and said, "But so would I, and I don't lose. *Ever.*" Drawing back, he saw surprise and something *darker* simmering in her eyes, and man, he liked it. "I told you the truth. I was covering my ass with Jilly, and yeah, I thought you'd eventually come around. That doesn't make me a dick. It makes me a *confident*, smart businessman."

"It also makes you an ass."

"I've been called worse. The bottom line is, I told you not to answer tonight. The ball is in your court. Do you want to turn me down? For the *calendar*?" he clarified. "Either way, you're still mine for one date."

Holding his gaze with fire in her eyes, she said, "*No.* It makes me want to do it even more." She put her arms around his neck and said, "Dance with me before I change my mind."

Thank God. "Not a hardship, Dix."

"What if I say no tomorrow?" she challenged.

"Then I'll be fucked. Not only would I be out of time, but also coming this close to having my number-one choice as the face of my company has solidified in my mind how right it is. Nobody else will do."

They danced wordlessly, and a few minutes later he felt the tension ease from Dixie's body. He slid his hand up her back, threading his fingers through the ends of her hair. He'd been dying to touch her glorious mane for years. She inhaled sharply, sending a rush of pure satisfaction through him, and he couldn't resist fisting his fingers in the silky strands.

"I have a feeling you're trouble, Stone," she said breathily.

"Of the very best kind."

Chapter Five

DIXIE ARRIVED AT Whiskey Automotive an hour early Saturday morning and was surprised to see all three of her brothers' vehicles parked out front. It wasn't unusual for her brothers to get together without her. They'd been having what she referred to as *penis parties*—discussions among the men—for as long as she could remember. When they were younger, they'd discuss girls or bikes, but these days they usually discussed club business. In true motorcycle club fashion, women weren't allowed to be members of the Dark Knights. That bothered her to no end, but there were certain battles she couldn't win, and club regulations were at the top of the list.

Her office was in the rear of the auto shop, and she hoped they weren't using it. She wanted to get things in order before meeting with Quincy about taking over for her while she was gone.

She slid her black leather backpack off one shoulder, grabbed her helmet, and headed inside. Bullet stood with his back against the counter. He lifted his chin in greeting. He'd been giving her the cold shoulder since she'd said she'd do the calendar shoot.

"Hey, Dix," Bones said from his perch on the couch. He looked sharp in dark slacks, a crisp white dress shirt, and a striped tie.

"Hi." She closed the door behind her.

Bear came through the door from the shop and said, "I had a feeling you'd be early today."

"Don't worry," she said, walking past him. "I'm not going to be in your way. I've got stuff to do."

"Hold on. We're here to talk to you," Bear said.

Dixie took a moment before turning to face them. She'd seen them talking with Jace for more than an hour last night, and she was not in the mood to be given grief about the calendar shoot. She was nervous enough about doing it—and about all the sparks flying between her and Jace. She'd been up half the night trying to figure out if she was making a mistake. Modeling for a calendar went against everything she believed women should be, but everything about *Jace* spoke to the deepest parts of her. No man had ever made her feel the way he did, and she knew how important the calendar was to him. More importantly, she knew his company was an *extension* of him. Bear was always raving about Jace and Maddox and how committed to excellence they were in every aspect of the business. She respected Jace's high standards because they were on par with hers, and that was hard to find. She'd made light of Jace comparing her to his motorcycles, but the truth was, she knew what it meant to be associated with a brand Jace had dedicated his life to building. And she knew his comparison had been the highest of praise, even if it wasn't meant romantically.

It would be an honor to be the face of Silver-Stone, and she also understood where her brothers were coming from, because she still wasn't sure she wanted to be the person men drooled over. But that was *her* decision to make, not theirs.

"If you're going to give me shit about the calendar, you can keep it to yourselves," she said, turning to face them.

"We're not," Bear said.

Bones pushed to his feet, and Bullet shifted his eyes away, telling her exactly who was and wasn't on board. Outside of dating, she could count on one hand how many times in her adult life her brothers *hadn't* supported her decisions. To have Bullet on the opposite side made her decision even more difficult. But nobody ever said breaking out from beneath her brothers' overprotective wings would be easy. She was ready to face whatever they doled out.

"I'm going to let everyone speak for themselves," Bear said, "but I wanted to say that I'm sorry for jumping all over you and Jace last night about the calendar. You've always had my back, Dix, and I should have had yours. I was okay with you being auctioned off—"

Bullet cleared his throat and pushed from the counter, crossing his arms.

Bear gave him a disapproving look and said, "But the calendar took me by surprise. I know the quality and class of Silver-Stone, and I support your decision to be in the calendar."

"Thank you. I appreciate that." She breathed a sigh of relief.

Bear was always the first to stand up for her. When their grandfather passed down the bar, although he gave each of them an equal share in the business, he made it clear that only the *men* were to run it. Dixie had never wanted anything *but* to run and grow their family businesses. On paper, she was an equal partner, but when it came down to having the authority to make final developmental business decisions, she was stymied because she wasn't in the penis club. Last year, when Bear decided to follow his heart and take the job with Silver-Stone, he went to bat for Dixie, offering to sell her his shares of the business, which would have given her a majority vote. Bones and Bullet had followed suit. It was only then that they learned that their father had wanted more for Dixie than to work at a bar and an auto shop. He'd held on to the notion of following their grandfather's wishes, hoping it would push Dixie to do bigger, better things with her life. Once her brothers had united in their support, her father had relented, accepting that running the businesses that had been in their family for generations was where her heart lay. She was now included in making all major decisions for both of the businesses.

She glanced at Bullet, wondering what life would be like without that united front, but she couldn't read his serious expression.

Bones stepped forward as if he were taking the floor and said, "We talked to Jace for a long time last night. He told us his vision for the calendar and described the clothing line he and Jilly designed. It all sounds very classy. It's no wonder he wanted you to represent Silver-Stone. But after I went home last night I spent a long time talking to Sarah about this whole situation. She asked what I would do if Lila or Maggie Rose wanted to pose for a calendar like this when they were older." His lips quirked up in a perplexed smile. Lila was only a year and a half old, and Maggie Rose was just three months. "My first reaction was the same as Bullet's was last night. *Over my dead body.* But then Sarah asked what I would do if Bradley grew up and wanted to model for a calendar. I caught myself saying exactly what you think I'd say, and I didn't like it."

"No surprise there," she said. "But I get it. I'm not sure I'd want your girls on a calendar either." She wasn't even sure she wanted herself on one.

"Sarah told me that if I stood in the way of our girls when they're your age, I'd lose them, and I think she's right. I don't want to lose you, Dix. So there's that. But there's also something much bigger at play here, something else I was missing. Everyone talks about how much of Bear's life he dedicated to our companies, and it's true. If it hadn't been for him, we might not have been able to hold on to the bar when Dad had his stroke, or the auto shop after Axel died. But there's another truth that's equally important. You gave your all to our family businesses long before last year, when Dad finally agreed to give you an equal voice in the companies, which you should have had all along. Bear might have been the face of this place and the bar when you were a teenager, but you stood behind him, helping when you could as you went through school. And when you graduated from college, you could have done anything, Dix. We all know that. You're the smartest of all of us."

Her throat thickened with emotion. That meant a lot coming from the man *she* believed was the smartest of them all.

"You chose to stick around and helped take our companies to new heights. You *deserve* to do whatever makes you happy, and truth be told, whether we like it or not doesn't matter." Bones stepped forward and embraced her. "I have to get to the office, but congratulations. Mom's right. It's your turn to shine."

She inhaled deeply, overwhelmed with emotion. "Thanks. I'll have to remember to call Sarah and thank her, too."

Bones headed for the door and said, "Don't worry. I thanked her *quite thoroughly.*"

"*Ew!* That's not something I want to picture," she hollered after him as he walked out.

Bear chuckled and said, "I'm going to work. Bullet, are you going to be civil?"

"Beat it, bro," Bullet growled. He waited for Bear to walk out, then said, "You know they hate the idea of seeing you in a calendar as much as I do."

"That's okay. They still support me, and that's what matters."

"I don't like this shit, Dix, and I don't like Jace buying a date with you, either."

"Why not?" She crossed her arms, needing the armor. "You've always trusted him. You're *friends* with him. You've hung out, ridden together, and always had each other's backs."

"Yeah, when he wasn't going after you."

Dixie had only lied to her brothers about one thing—going on dates. She didn't like to lie, but it was easier than facing this type of scrutiny, which was why she was going to lie now. "He's not going after me, Bullet. I'm pretty sure that despite what he said, he only bid on me because it was a chance to get me to do the calendar."

Bullet scoffed. "If you believe that, then I haven't taught you shit."

He mirrored her stance, puffing out his chest and crossing his arms, making her feel their size difference. Before joining the military, Bullet had been the one to show her just how strong she was. He'd taught her to be tough and had shown her everything from how to stand so she looked fearless even when she was scared to how to fight. Those lessons had served her well, and she called upon them now as she didn't back down.

"Can you stop being my overprotective brother for just a second, please? I'm thirty-one years old, Bullet. A grown woman. I've always respected you and supported your choices.

It would be great if you could do the same for me."

"And what if some asshole sees that calendar and sets his sights on you? What if you end up with a crazy stalker?" Anger billowed off him.

"If I do this calendar, thousands of jerks will see me," she snapped. "But you taught me to handle myself, remember?"

He scoffed. "You're tough, Dixie, but you're no match for a man Bear's size, much less mine. What if you're on one of your trips to the Cape, or busy with that fucking book club of yours and off God knows where for a meeting, and a guy comes after you?"

It dawned on her that Bullet *wasn't* trying to control what she did. He was afraid *he* couldn't protect her. She was momentarily stunned as she tried to reconcile Bullet being afraid of *anything*. He'd spent years in the Special Forces, and he'd nearly died. But he hadn't told any of them except Bones, whom he'd sworn to secrecy, when he was lying in the hospital holding on to his life by a thread because he'd been protecting them even then. Why hadn't she realized this before?

"Then I'll figure something out," she said. "I want to live my life, Bullet, and whether that means I want to pose for a calendar, go out with Jace Stone, or go out with any other man, those are *my* decisions to make. Not yours. You can hate my decisions and still support me."

Bullet's face contorted with confusion. "No I can't."

"Sure you can. Do you think I liked it when you joined the military, knowing you could die? Not seeing you for months at a time?"

"That was different."

"Was it? Because from where I'm standing, it looks pretty similar. I cried when you left. Did you know that?"

"You did not, Dix. You told me to go kick some ass and said you were going to rifle through my things."

She smiled with the memory. "I did both those things. I still have the sweatshirts and T-shirt I stole from your drawers." She lowered her arms and said, "Do you know why I took them? Because I missed you, Bullet. You made a decision for yourself, and I had no control, but I didn't try to stand in your way or make you feel guilty."

"I get what you're saying, Dix, and I'm sorry, but it doesn't matter what you say. I'm not going to be okay with you on a biker calendar, regardless of how classy it is. To Jace's credit, he did make it sound like it was going to be a nice one."

"I'm fine with you not being okay with it," she said, even though it stung. "But can't you find it in your heart to be upset over it without treating me like the enemy?"

"You're never the enemy. I just don't like it."

"Well, you looked like you wanted to kill me when you realized I was going to be auctioned off, and you were definitely ready to tear Jace apart when he bid on me. He didn't deserve that."

Arms still crossed, Bullet said, "I'd never hurt you, but Stone's a different story. He had no business asking you to do that calendar in the first place."

"I could argue that six ways to heaven and back, but I won't." She reached up and tugged his beard. "I love you, Bullet, and I'm glad you worry about me. I can see that's not going to change. We're both going to have to find a way to be okay moving forward, because I'm done dating in other towns to avoid the look you're giving me right now."

"Thank God. I'm sick of sending guys to check up on the losers Jilly sets you up with."

Her jaw dropped. "You knew…?"

"You're my sister. Someone's got to watch out for you."

"You're unbelievable." Although she should have realized he'd pull a stunt like that. He always seemed to know what every one of them was doing. "It's a good thing I love you, because I kind of hate you right now."

He hooked an arm around her neck and tugged her into a hug. "You can hate me and still support my decisions."

"Asshole," she said against his chest.

"Yeah, I am," Bullet said as Quincy came through the shop door. "I love you, Dix, but I'm not buying one of those damn calendars."

"Well, I sure as hell am!" Quincy put his hands on his hips, his blue eyes glittering devilishly. "Everyone was talking about you last night, Dix, saying how brave you were to stand up to your brothers and get auctioned off and how proud they were of you for doing the calendar. Congrats, by the way. Super-cool gig. Of course, the showdown between Bullet and Jace was also a hot topic."

Anger rose anew in Bullet's eyes.

"Go for a ride before work so you don't kill someone." Dixie kissed Bullet's cheek and said, "We're on the same team, remember?"

"Right." He nodded at Quincy and said, "You sure you're cool taking over here while she's in New York, and again when she goes to the Cape?"

"Definitely. I've already cleared my schedule at the bookstore." He cocked a grin and said, "It'll give me more time to get my homework done, too, without all those hot women distracting me."

Bullet chuckled. He and Quincy talked for a few minutes

before Bullet left, and then Quincy and Dixie headed into her office. Truman and Bear were talking beside a car with the hood up.

"Hey, Tru," Dixie said as they walked past. "I ordered the part for the Finnegans' truck. It should be here Monday."

"Cool," Truman said. "Hi, Quincy."

"Morning, bro," Quincy said, and then he followed Dixie into her office. "So, Dix, what are you going to do with all your extra time without the auction to plan?"

As they settled into their chairs, Dixie said, "I'm never at a loss for work." She was dying to ask him about Penny not bidding on him, but as much as she wanted to pry, she worried that maybe it was a sore spot. Instead, she said, "The girl who won you last night sure was cute."

"Roni? Yeah, she's gorgeous and super sweet, but *really* shy, or cautious or *something*. She said her friends dragged her to the auction and paid for everything. She didn't even want to go."

"Does that mean you're not going on a date with her?" Dixie pulled a notebook from her backpack and set it on the desk.

"Are you kidding? It made her even *more* intriguing. Have you not figured out that I enjoy the chase? Roni said she's busy for the next several weeks, but her friends pulled me aside and said she hadn't dated in a long time and she was just nervous." He sat back and said, "I'm a whole lotta man for any woman. She'll get over it."

Dixie chuckled as she booted up her computer and decided to step into muddy waters. "What about you and Penny?"

"I think we've both known for a while that we sailed right past our chance for romance into a friendship that neither one of us wants to jeopardize. It's not like we were in love or anything. You've got to remember that until I got clean, I never had real friends. I don't take friendships lightly. I know what it's like not to have anyone to turn to, and I hope to be friends with you and your family, Penny, Jed, Scott, Izzy, and everyone else we hang out with forever."

"I guess that's why she didn't bid on you last night."

"I asked her about that. She said when she saw all those other women bidding, she was *happy* for me, not jealous. We're cool. No worries there. But you know me. I'll always tease her about missing out..."

"I'm sure you will." Thinking about how long she'd been crushing on Jace, she said, "You never know what the future will hold."

"You've got that right. What about you and Jace? If he steals you away from the Harbor, you'll leave a string of broken hearts behind."

Dixie rolled her eyes, but her insides were thrumming just thinking about the things Jace had insinuated last night, and the way it felt to be in his arms, dancing so close she could feel his heart beating.

"Not you, too. There's nothing going on with me and Jace." She opened the notebook and said, "Moving on to"—*safer*— "more important subjects, I assume you remember how to do the payroll for both the shop and the bar, and the bank deposits, but what about special orders? If not, Jed can help you with that."

Quincy smirked. "Does Jace know you're a master at changing subjects?"

"*Quincy*," she warned.

"Hey, just asking..." He leaned forward, scanning the list she'd written in the notebook. His eyes shifted to the back of the previous page, on which was the list of clothes she wanted to bring to New York.

She slapped her hand over the list.

His amused eyes shot up as he said, "Black lace top? Strapless bra? Thigh-high stockings?"

"I'm *modeling*! I need to be prepared." She slapped the notebook closed.

"For *anything*, apparently."

JACE STOOD ON Jared's back deck late Saturday afternoon talking on the phone with Maddox. Jared lived on a few wooded acres overlooking the harbor. Like Jace, Jared owned several properties near his various business locations, but this was by far Jace's favorite. There was something charming about small towns like Pleasant Hill and Peaceful Harbor, where bikers took part in community events and looked out for residents and business owners. The idea of the auction had been unappealing to Jace, but last night had changed that. Seeing people who probably went to great lengths to avoid a tough biker bar like Whiskey Bro's putting aside their assumptions and fears and coming together for a good cause was incredible. He spent so much time in big cities, he didn't have a community to call his own. It made him want to be more involved, and he had Dixie to thank for opening his eyes.

"I still can't believe you got Dixie to agree to do the shoot." Maddox's voice was tough as leather and as powerful as the bikes they designed. "I know you handpicked Sahara, but we both know you were never sold on her. If I didn't know better,

I'd think you rigged her fall."

Jace chuckled. "Sahara was the best of all the women I saw, but you know the score. Does a Harley compare to a Silver-Stone?"

"You've got a point. Good job, Jace. I know Dixie has the look and the attitude. I just hope she can pull off modeling."

"Jilly said she's great." After seeing how she'd handled the event last night and how beautiful she'd looked standing on the stage in that knockout dress before all the bullshit went down, Jace had no doubt she could pull it off. She was mouth-wateringly gorgeous and elegant, with a hint of attitude that gave her the unique edge he had always admired.

"Have you talked with her about the contracts and waivers?" Maddox asked.

"Yes. They were sent to Court Sharpe, Dixie's attorney, earlier today. She's already signed them, and Court returned them to the legal department. We're all set," Jace said.

He'd half expected Dixie to regret her decision this morning, once she'd had time to calm down after Bullet's showdown. He'd also expected her to try to negotiate her way out of the various in-person marketing obligations included in the contract, but she hadn't balked at the six events she'd attend as the face of Silver-Stone during the twelve-week period after the launch, or the ongoing marketing efforts that called for six annual appearances over the next three years. He was elated, and he'd sent her two dozen roses as a thank-you. Outside of his sisters and mother, he'd never sent a woman roses before, but this morning he'd been overwhelmed, both personally and professionally.

Spending more time with Dixie had opened a portal to desires he'd been locking down for years. The *man* in him wanted to send her flowers, but if he'd sent them as a solely personal gesture, he worried it would send the message of a promise he wasn't ready to make. Making the flowers a thank-you gift was the perfect solution. After all, the only woman he thought worthy of being the face of Silver-Stone had agreed to step in, and for that he was grateful.

He was also pleased when she'd texted, *There aren't many firsts in life, and you've given me two of them.* Thank you. He'd responded with, *Now you've got me curious…*

His phone had vibrated seconds later with, *Get your mind out of the gutter. Roses and being in a calendar.* He'd immediately thought of several dark, erotic firsts he'd like to introduce her to, each one ramping up his desires.

"Great. I'll make sure the jewelry is delivered for the shoot." Maddox said, bringing his mind back to the conversation. Maddox's brother Sterling was a jeweler, and he was providing accessories for the shoot. "I'll see you in Boston Thursday. I'm catching a flight to LA afterward to meet with our engineers. When do you head out? Are we still on for dinner next Sunday?"

"Yeah. I arrive Sunday afternoon, and barring any unfore-seen circumstances, I'll be in LA until the launch." If all went well Thursday, they'd be signing off on the Boston space the following week. Between dealing with the Boston buildouts and logistics and preparing for the launch of the Legacy and Leather and Lace lines, the next few weeks would be a bear.

"With the exception of the meetings in Oregon and Mexico in July and the locations you're scouting in Ohio and Pennsyl-vania in August," Maddox reminded him.

"Right, of course." Flying out to different locations for a few days here and there had become so much a part of his life, he no longer considered them needing mention.

He and Maddox talked business for a while longer, and as he ended the call, Jared stepped onto the porch. Jared was the youngest of the Stone siblings. Ever since he was a kid, he'd been unable to sit still. If he wasn't physically on the move, his jaw was jumping or his leg was bouncing. He was sharp and witty, gave off an edgy, eclectic vibe, had a passion for cooking and high-risk business and a hatred of all things trendy. He was the polar opposite of his business partner, Seth Braden, who had been named as one of *Forbes*'s most eligible bachelors and was about as laid-back and low-key as a guy could get. But somehow they made an incredibly successful team. Jared and Jace weren't very similar either, except when it came to remaining grounded and remembering where they'd come from. While Jace created scholarships and mentoring programs for up-and-coming designers and engineers, Jared made it a point to put in time at each of his restaurants and retail operations and spend a few weeks every year working alongside their chefs and directors.

Jace pocketed his phone and said, "You heading to the restaurant?"

"Yeah, soon," he said, pacing the deck.

"I wish you could make it to the city tomorrow. The girls miss seeing you." Jace had spoken to Jennifer and Mia earlier, and both had asked him to drag Jared with him to the city. But Jace had long ago stopped trying to drag his siblings anywhere. He'd also spoken to Jayla, who was not pleased that Jace had totally forgotten to video Jared when he was on the stage. She didn't need to know it was because he'd been too damn taken with Dixie to think of anything else.

"I'll get there soon." *Soon* was Jared's go-to response for everything.

Jared came by his unwillingness to be nailed down for social visits honestly. He'd picked it up from Jace. Although now that Jayla had a baby, Jace realized how fast the years were flying by, and he was trying to get better about keeping in touch and seeing family.

"You catch any more hell from Bullet today?" Jared asked.

"Nah. He's just watching out for Dixie. He said his piece. Now he'll wait to see if the calendar blows up in her face so he can come after me if it does. Where'd you disappear to last night?" Jared had left the auction before Jace, and he hadn't gotten home until after two in the morning.

Jared leaned against the deck with a cocky expression, then pushed off, pacing again as he said, "Had to soothe a friend's broken heart for losing out when she bid on me."

"Christ, Jared. Promise me you won't be a dick to Jilly."

"I'm never a dick. I mean, I'll *share* my dick, but I treat all my ladies well."

Jace stepped in his path and said, "Do *not* cross that line with Jilly. I don't care how much she messes with your libido, in her heart, she's a white-picket-fence girl. Got it?"

Jared cringed. "If she were a white-picket-fence girl, she shouldn't have bid on me."

"No shit. Keep that in mind. She's got a hint of Dixie in her, only Dixie can handle any flack she catches from her rebellions. Jilly doesn't have the benefit of being brought up in a rough environment. She's a lady through and through. To her, it's all fun and games. You have to remember who she is. She's used to guys who wear ties, not guys who use them for sex games. Unless you want Nick Braden breathing fire down your back, watch yourself."

"I can handle Nick Braden."

Jace spoke through gritted teeth as he said, "I don't know about that, but you sure as hell can't handle me."

Jared scoffed. "Fine, dude. Geez. Didn't you get enough of that big-brother shit when our sisters were younger?"

"Just watching out for a friend." He stepped back, and Jared began pacing again. "You still cool with me leaving my bike in your garage? It'll be a few weeks before I can head back to the Harbor. I've got a car taking us to the airport."

"Sure, whatever." Jared stretched and looked up at the sky. "What're you doing tonight? You should stop by for a drink at the restaurant."

Jace had planned on giving Dixie—*and himself*—space tonight and diving into work to keep his mind off her. He'd been *this close* to kissing her last night, and that would be a bad idea, no matter how much he wanted her. She was as rooted to Peaceful Harbor as Jace was to the open road. But a drink with Dixie sounded a whole lot better than trying not to think about her.

Jared stepped into the house and turned around. Holding either side of the doorframe, he leaned outside and said, "Don't think too hard. I'm pretty sure I see smoke coming out of your ears."

"Fuck off." He followed Jared in and said, "Maybe I'll see you later."

"Only if you're lucky," Jared said on his way out the front door.

Chapter Six

"YOU'LL COME BY and get the roses?" Dixie asked Izzy over the phone Saturday evening, eyeing the enormous bouquet of roses Jace had sent to her at the auto shop to thank her for agreeing to do the shoot. They were gorgeous and unexpected, and it was the first time she'd ever been sent flowers. She'd been staring at them all day. She couldn't carry them home on her motorcycle, and she and Jace were leaving tomorrow, so she wasn't going to be there to enjoy them. That was why she'd offered them to Izzy.

"Of course. When do you leave?" Izzy asked.

Izzy had already tried to convince her that flowers meant something more than *thank you*. Although Dixie had shut her down, it was all she could think about, adding to a long list of other Jace-related thoughts.

"Tomorrow afternoon, and I'll be back Wednesday." She gathered her belongings and shoved them into her backpack. Jace had made their travel arrangements, and he was picking her up tomorrow afternoon for a three o'clock flight. Signing the legal paperwork made the whole venture even more real. She still couldn't believe she was really going to New York with Jace and doing a photo shoot. "Iz, I've been second-guessing myself all day. This is so important to Jace. What if I screw up?"

"Stop worrying. You're going to nail the shoot. When you did Jilly's show, you walked the runway like a pro."

"I'm not too worried about that. As much as I hate the idea of being in the calendar, it was the perfect way to finally put my foot down with my family, and I think the shoot will be fun. I'm more worried about being around *Jace*. In all the years I've known him, he's *never* flirted with me, and last night he was definitely flirting. Not like Crow or Jon, who outright proposition me all the time. It was like he was taunting me with ideas that *could* lead to more but he wasn't committing to it."

"Which is really surprising, because I've always thought Jace was the type of guy to stake his claim, you know? Like Bullet asking Finlay to take a *ride on the Bullet train.* Although forty grand stakes a claim in a pretty major way, don't you think?"

"That was for charity." At least that was what she'd told herself all day. "I've never thought of Jace being like Bullet with women. I've never heard him be crass. I mean, he talks shit with the guys, but he's more mysterious to me on the male-female interaction front. Come to think of it, I've never actually *seen* him with a woman, have you?" She guessed that wasn't so strange, considering he didn't live there. She wasn't even sure where he lived. He usually came into town for a day or two, then took off.

"I've seen him dirty dancing with Jilly a few times when they were out at clubs with Nick and some of her other brothers. You should see Nick when they dance." She barked out a laugh. "If looks could kill…"

"Do you think Jace and Jilly have hooked up?" A streak of jealousy shot through her. She couldn't *stop* thinking about what he'd said when she'd asked him why he'd bid on her. *I was selfishly taking advantage of an opportunity, and if that makes me a dick, then it does. I think we both realize it's about time we get to know each other better.* Had he ever said that to Jillian?

"No," Izzy said emphatically. "I didn't mean that. Nick is like Bullet. He goes all caveman on anyone who comes near Jilly. I think the reason he lets Jace dance with her is to keep other guys away, but he clearly doesn't like it. Didn't you see Nick threaten Jared last night?"

"No, but I was a little sidetracked." She slung her backpack over her shoulder, taking one last long look at the flowers. She'd taken a dozen pictures of them. Jace had made her whole day with those roses. Maybe Izzy was right and they did mean more...

Trying to push those thoughts away, she grabbed her helmet and left her office. Truman and Bear had already gone for the day. As she turned off the lights in the shop, she heard the roar of a motorcycle. "Someone just pulled up. I hope it's not a customer. I was really looking forward to getting home, packing, and then getting lost in our book club novel. Have you started it?" She and Izzy were in an online book club that she'd learned about through a friend of her cousin Justin when she was in Cape Cod last September. Dixie hoped reading might distract her from thinking about Jace, and she was definitely packing the novel to keep her mind occupied at night in New York.

"Oh my God, *yessss*," Izzy said dramatically. "It's so freaking hot. You might want to read it in an ice bath."

"Good. I need some sex in my life, even if fictional." She went into the lobby and peered out the window. Her pulse quickened at the sight of Jace pulling off his helmet and setting it on the seat of his motorcycle. "Shit. Jace is *here.*"

"Damn, girl. He must want you something *bad.*"

"You're not helping." Though the idea made her all sorts of happy—and confused—because Jace's life was who-knew-where.

Izzy laughed and said, "Yes I am! I want you to get a piece of that fine-looking man. From what you've told me, you've been crushing on him forever. *Go!* Call me later, or tomorrow. Oh, what if you spend the night with him?"

"Izzy!"

"You can't tell me you're not all kinds of excited that he's there, especially after the *flowers.* I want all the details!"

That was the problem. She was *too* excited.

Dixie ended the call, cut the lights in the lobby, and inhaled a calming breath. It didn't help. She headed outside, getting more nervous by the second as the scorching-hot biker came into view. That slow smile that had crept across his lips and set off an inferno inside her last night slid into place as he approached. She tried to focus on locking the door, but his rugged, woodsy cologne carried in the breeze, and when she turned, he was *right there*, causing her temperature to spike.

"Hi." She headed for her bike to keep from getting lost in him again. "If you're looking for Bear, he's long gone."

"I'm looking for *you*, Dix. I thought we could head over to Nova Lounge to grab a drink and talk about the shoot."

She'd fantasized about being swept off her feet by Jace Stone hundreds of times, and not once did they include the words *talk about the shoot.* Maybe last night's comment meant they should get to know each other better *because of the shoot.* Could she have misread him that badly?

She looked down at her Whiskey Automotive shirt, skinny

jeans, and boots, and said, "I'm not dressed for Nova. We could go to Whiskey Bro's, but I thought we covered everything about the shoot last night."

He leisurely dragged his eyes up and down her body and stepped closer. *Sweet baby Jesus.* He sent her lady parts into a frenzy. *Big trouble* didn't even begin to describe this man.

"You look incredible, but if you're uncomfortable going to Nova, I'll take you for a burger and we'll go someplace else where we can talk. But I'm *not* taking you to the bar where you work. Do you want to leave your backpack here or bring it?"

"Fine. I guess you can claim the date you won last night." She shrugged off her backpack and locked it in the compartment on her bike. She pulled out her keys and said, "Where to? I'll follow you."

He took the keys from her hand and said, "My bike, and this is *not* the date I won."

The urge to pick apart that claim was so strong, she nearly challenged him. But she was even more sidetracked by what he'd asked her to do. She eyed his bike, her heart pounding frantically. "Around here, putting a woman on the back of your bike means something." It meant more than something; it meant *everything.* It was the most widely recognized way a biker could claim a woman.

He flashed an arrogant grin and climbed on his bike as he said, "For once in your life, stop giving a man shit and climb on."

She told herself she was being stupid, that he was playing some sort of game, toying with her emotions, though she couldn't figure out why he'd do that. Even if he was toying with her, she *wanted* to climb on his bike more than she wanted her next breath.

He put on his helmet as she straddled his bike, and *years* of greedy fantasies coalesced. Despite her best efforts not to get carried away, heat and hope whirled inside her. She pulled on her helmet and wrapped her arms around him. He covered her hands with his, pulling them tighter, crushing her chest against his back. She imagined him smirking as the engine roared to life. Most women would think it was the vibration of the engine making their body tingle and hum. But Dixie had been riding motorcycles so long, she knew the difference between an engine working its magic and Jace Stone making every ion in her body sizzle and spark.

As he cruised out of the parking lot and headed for the main drag, she relied on lies to try to regain control of her runaway hormones. She told herself the heat creeping up her thighs was caused by the warm leather seat and that she was done letting him toy with her emotions. She'd nix that shit as soon as they got wherever they were going.

After picking up burgers and bottled drinks, and *not* putting the kibosh on *anything*, Jace drove across the main drag and followed the winding roads that led into the mountains. Dixie knew these roads by heart, and she never tired of the umbrella of trees and woodsy scents. She loved them just as much as she enjoyed the open skies and salty air of the harbor. Sitting in the woods on her favorite overlook and burying her toes in the sand gazing out over the endless sea brought the same sense of freedom as riding her bike. But neither was as incredible as sitting on the back of Jace Stone's bike, wrapped around his strong body. She could get addicted to the feel of his muscles flexing against her inner thighs, chest, and arms.

Who was she kidding?

She already was addicted…

Jace pulled off the mountain road, following the narrow trail Dixie had frequented when she was younger and had recently started visiting again. Even her brothers didn't know she went there when she needed to be alone. Jace drove swiftly up the winding mountain trail like he knew it well, too, which was surprising. Dixie's tire tracks from last week were still visible in the crushed leaves and dirt.

The trail ended abruptly at the thicker forest. Dixie climbed off the bike, whipped off her helmet, and shook out her hair. "What are we doing here?"

"There's an overlook up ahead."

"How do you know about this place?"

He set his helmet on the bike and grabbed the bag of food and drinks from the storage compartment. "I found it last year when we were considering opening a shop here." As they walked through the woods, he said, "When I first found it, the trail looked like it hadn't been used in years. I must have walked it twenty times while I was here. And the next time I was in town, I thought, *fuck it*, and rode my bike down it."

He pushed through the last of the tall pines separating the woods from the overlook and held the branches back for Dixie to walk by. They crossed the bumpy, brush-covered ground to a large outcropping of boulders. The side of the mountain spilled out before them, as glorious and lush as it was the first time Dixie had gone there.

"It's bizarre to think that the first people to discover Peaceful Harbor camped in these woods," Jace said as they sat down on a boulder.

"How do you know that?"

He shrugged. "I like history."

That was an interesting fact she hadn't expected. She hadn't pegged him as the kind of guy who would seek out a place's history. "How on earth did you go from suggesting Nova Lounge to bringing me here? What's up your sleeve, Stone? If you're afraid I'm going to back out of the shoot, I'm not. You don't have to play games with me."

He set the food and drinks between them and said, "You know me well enough to realize I don't play games."

"Do I?" she challenged, wanting to get into his head.

"You will. Is it a fucking crime to want to spend time getting to know you better?"

"You've known me since I was a teenager, and suddenly you want to know me better? Buy me dinner? Bring me to *my* secret spot? That part's a little unnerving. How did you know I come here?"

"Jesus, Dixie. You've got a lot of mistrust bottled up inside you. I had no idea this was *your* spot. I told you I happened upon it last year and liked the view."

"You didn't know?" she said sarcastically. She grabbed a burger and unwrapped it. She wanted to believe him, but at the same time, she was afraid to. He was showing her a completely unexpected side of himself, and she had no idea what that meant, if anything.

"I'm not a stalker, for fuck's sake. You sure don't need Bullet to scare me off. You're doing a pretty good job of it yourself."

She eyed him and took a bite of her burger, buying time to mull over the situation, and feeling like an ass for pushing him into a corner. "Sorry. You keep taking me off guard."

"I'm good at that. Just take me at face value, Dix. What you see is what you get. No games, no bullshit, which seems to be how you operate, too."

"Yeah, you could say that. Did you *really* just find this place?"

"*Yes.* Stop asking. What about you? How'd you find it? How often do you come here?"

In her experience, guys who had something to hide had shifty eyes. She watched him take a bite of his burger, his eyes never wavering from her face. Okay, she decided. She'd take him at face value and not worry about the *why*s this evening.

"I found it when I was a teenager, the year my dad had his stroke," she said, realizing she'd never before exposed her hidden oasis, or her reasons for finding it, to anyone. "Bear was taking care of the bar, my mom was nursing my dad back to health, and Bullet and Bones were away. When things got to be too much, I'd come here."

JACE SAW A hint of sadness in Dixie's eyes, and it tugged at something deep inside him. "It must have been hard watching your father go through that."

"My father, Bear, my mom. It affected everyone. Bullet and Bones weren't around, but I think that made it even harder for them. It was a little terrifying, to be honest. You think you know your family, and then something like that happens and it changes everything. I always knew we were strong, but that made us even stronger as a group *and* individually."

"How old were you?"

"Almost sixteen."

So young...

He'd met Dixie when she was eighteen, and she was already

a tough, take-no-bullshit spitfire. He wondered if she had been that way before her father's stroke. At sixteen a girl's biggest concern should be the cute boy she liked or seeing a concert with her friends, not wondering if her father was going to live or die.

"How'd you get here without a driver's license?"

The corner of her mouth lifted, and her gorgeous eyes glimmered with rebellion. "Do you think I'd let something like that keep me trapped?"

He laughed. He liked knowing she'd always had a fiery spirit. It made him want to know more about her and the things she'd been through. "Not even for a minute. Sounds like you were a rebellious little thing."

She held up her finger and thumb and mouthed, *A little bit.* "I took my mom's motorcycle. I've been riding since I was fourteen."

"And you came out here to escape the stress and sadness? To wrap your head around things?"

"You could say that. The first year I mostly tossed prayers up to the powers that be, cried, you know, that sort of thing. Later I'd come and debate whether I should go away to school or stick around after graduation. But sticking around wasn't an option. My family practically pushed me out the door once I graduated high school. They were dead set on me attending college."

"I'm sure they were just looking out for you and didn't want you to give up your future."

"When is my family *not* looking out for me?" she said sarcastically. "I kind of hated that they made me go away. But to be honest, that's one instance where I'm glad they told me what to do. I've done more for the family with what I learned while I was at school than I could have if I'd stuck around and never gotten any further education."

"Bear raves about you and what you've done for your family's businesses."

She smiled like hearing it meant a lot to her, but she said, "We all do what we can." She took a bite of her burger, and they finished eating in comfortable silence.

Jace put their trash in the bag and said, "After seeing what you pulled off last night and the way you stood up to your family, I have a feeling you do more than just what you *can*."

"There's no sense in doing anything half-assed."

"I've got to agree with you there. Do you feel better now that you've taken a stand with them? Where do you go from here?"

Her finely manicured brows knitted. "*Go?*"

"You took quite a stance, getting up on that stage to be auctioned off and agreeing to be in a calendar after turning me down flat. You must have stood up to them for a reason. Do you want to get out of your family's businesses or something?"

"No, not at all. I *love* running the companies, working with the community, and with my family, even though they drive me crazy sometimes. I just needed breathing room. It's suffocating always being watched and told what I can and can't do. You wouldn't know anything about that, but I bet your sisters do."

"I'm not Bullet."

She rolled her eyes. "Jilly told me about what you did when you heard she was going to bid on Jared."

"Because Jilly's a lady and while my brother's a great guy, he's not very good with self-control. He acts now, regrets later. I know Jilly. Dating what she calls a *bad boy* is a game to her. Jared's not the guy to play that game with."

"But you are?" she asked casually.

"I don't want to date Jilly."

She laughed. "I didn't mean that."

"Trust me, I *know* how to hold back. I'm a fucking expert at it."

"How do I know I can believe that?"

He debated giving her a pat answer, but Dixie was just pushy enough to browbeat him until he came clean, so he held her gaze and said, "Because I've thought you were gorgeous since you were a smart-ass eighteen-year-old looking at me like I was made of your favorite chocolate cake, and I've never done a damn thing about it."

She snapped her mouth closed and visually *gulped*, but her eyes never left his.

A battle raged inside him. He could lean forward, push his hand to the nape of her beautiful neck, and draw her luscious mouth to his, taking the taste he so desperately wanted. Or he could behave, be smart, and take things slow.

A flock of birds flew across the sky behind Dixie, and the movement snapped him from his trance. He blinked several times, mentally circling back to her earlier comment to redirect his thoughts.

"I never breathed down my sisters' backs the way your brothers do with you. I've always protected them, but I believe in giving them space and stepping in when they need me. We're having dinner with them tomorrow night. You can ask them for yourself."

Her eyes widened. "We're having dinner with your sisters? I don't need to take up your time with your family, Jace. I'll just hang out in the hotel."

"Hotel? No way, Dix. You're staying with me at my loft,

MELISSA FOSTER

and my sisters would have my ass if I don't bring you along. Jayla just had a baby and she loves showing him off." It hadn't dawned on him until this very second how tempting her staying at his loft would be, but he wasn't about to change his mind.

"Was that the plan with the model you first booked? To stay at your loft?"

"Hell no."

"Then why are you asking me to stay there?"

"Because I know you, Dix. You're a friend. Besides, your brothers would get in my face if I let you loose in New York City. I've got to keep my eyes on you."

She lifted her chin in a challenge, but her eyes turned hungry and dark as she said, "Are those the *only* reasons?"

"What do you think?" They were playing with fire, and he wasn't nearly ready to stop.

"I think you want to get more than your eyes on me."

Without thinking, he leaned in so close he could feel her breath on his lips and said, "I'd like to get every inch of my body on you and burrow so deep inside you that you still feel me the next *week.*" *Fuck. Where did that come from?* He had more of Jared's impulsiveness in him than he knew—at least where Dixie was concerned. He had no business being there with her, much less taunting them both with his lascivious thoughts.

Her breathing hitched, but she didn't look away. She swayed *closer.*

Hot. As. Fuck.

He ground his teeth together, struggling to get himself back in check. He forced himself to sit up, putting space between them. He needed to shut down the electricity arcing between them so he could think straight, so he said, "But settling down isn't on my radar, and you, sweet Dixie, have roots so deep they're buried well below the sea."

She pressed her lips together, hurt and anger swimming in her eyes. Man, he hated that, but it needed to be said. Otherwise she'd just think he was a pussy for not taking the kiss he was sure they both wanted.

She sat up and reached for a bottle of water.

He snagged it, removed the cap, and handed it to her. When her brows slanted, he said, "I know you can do it yourself, but my old man brought me up right."

"Your father tells women the dirty things he wants to do to them, then gives them whiplash by saying he can't?" She took a drink. "Nice family you have there."

He chuckled and reached for the bottle.

"Maybe you should drink from the other bottle so you don't sprout *roots*," she said sharply. "They could be contagious."

"Your mouth hasn't been on that one." He took the bottle from her hand, enjoying the blush on her cheeks. "Never thought I'd see the day Dixie Whiskey blushed. You'd think my earlier comment would have earned a blush first." He sucked down a drink and said, "It's definitely sweeter after you."

He offered her the bottle and she shook her head. She leaned back on her hands and gazed out at the setting sun. She was gorgeous, with all that thick red hair tumbling over her shoulders. She might be tough, but there was nothing tough about her delicate features. High cheekbones, a slender nose, and temptingly plump lips with a sweet bow in the middle. How could this sexy, challenging woman still be single? How could she never have been sent roses before? If she were *his*, he would shower her in all the pretty things she deserved. The unfamiliar thought hit him right in the center of his chest. The urge to kiss her was so strong, he felt himself leaning closer.

He cleared his throat to try to clear his head, and she glanced over, catching him staring. Instead of getting shy like other women might, she dragged her eyes down his chest. Man, that was *hot*. She knew how to push all his buttons.

"You're a hard man to read," she said. "It's confusing."

"Something tells me you eat easy-to-read men for dinner," he said, though the idea of Dixie *eating* any other man made his blood boil.

"You think you know me?"

He set the water down and leaned back on one hand, angling his body toward her. "No. I think I know some things about you, the things you want men to see. But I want to get to know more about you, Dixie. The real you."

Her eyes widened, and just as quickly they narrowed, as if she realized she was giving away how much she liked the sound of what he'd said. "Why?"

"You're a ballbuster."

"As I said, *why?*" she asked with unfaltering confidence. "You just told me nothing can happen between us."

He moved the trash and the bottles from between them and shifted closer, enjoying the sparks flying around them. "Because until the other day, I'd only allowed myself to see you as a little sister to your brothers. But I can't do that anymore. You're so much more than anyone's little sister. You've gotten under my skin, like a fever I can't shake."

"Whiskey fever," she said breathily.

"That's pretty accurate."

"No, I mean, it's a real thing. Ask my sisters-in-law. Once they felt an attraction to my brothers, there was no turning it off." Worry washed over her face.

"There must be a remedy, some way to satisfy the urge, get rid of the fever?"

They gazed into each other's eyes, the air between them pulsing to the beat of their lustful breaths. Her eyes held a challenge, and his body ached to take her up on it.

But he'd already caused enough trouble, so he said, "Then we'd better get out of here before we do something you'll regret."

She scowled, and hell if that didn't add fuel to their inferno.

He grabbed the trash and reluctantly pushed to his feet. He reached out to help her up. She stared at his hand for a long time before finally taking it and rising to her feet.

She set those challenging eyes on him and said, "I never pegged you for a tease."

Every fiber of his being wanted to grab her by the shoulders and kiss her until she was begging for more, showing her just how much he liked to tease, with his hands, his mouth, his body...

Instead, he ground out, "That makes two of us," and headed back toward the trail.

Chapter Seven

"THE VIEW FROM upstairs is incredible," Jace said as he unlocked the door to Silver-Stone's Lexington Avenue store late Sunday afternoon. He lived on the top floor of the building and there was a side entrance that led to the elevator, but he wanted to show Dixie the retail operation first.

"The view from right here is pretty great, too," she said seductively.

He glanced over his shoulder, catching her checking out his ass. She'd been flirting with him all afternoon and had cranked up her sass by about a zillion degrees. He wondered if she was taunting him as some sort of payback for the things he'd said last night or if this was who Dixie was outside of the watchful eyes of her family back in Peaceful Harbor. Whatever the reason, it was doing the trick. Between her sexy comments and her fuck-me outfit—skimpy cutoffs, knee-high black boots, and a black T-shirt that had TATTOOED BOYS ARE MY FAVORITE TOYS—he needed an ice bath for his dirty mind. She'd turned so many heads in the airport, on the plane, and now, on the busy sidewalk, he felt like a giant green-eyed monster was perched on his back. Thank God the store was closed. The last thing he needed was to get jealous over his employees.

She raised a brow and said, "They say this city never sleeps. Do you think that means the Big Apple is full of workaholics, or that everyone's up having wild sex all night?"

Damn, she was good. About ten dirty retorts sailed through his mind, but he wasn't going to touch that comment with a ten-foot pole. He pushed the door open and waved her in. "After you."

She sauntered past, and his gaze was riveted to her long legs and gorgeous ass. He carried her luggage inside and set it down along with his duffel, locking the door behind them.

"Wow, I knew Silver-Stone was big, but I've never seen anything like this." She turned in a slow circle, admiring the store.

"It's our flagship store," he said proudly.

This was the largest of their one hundred and twenty-two retail operations. While they had about half as many retail outlets as their closest competitor, Silver-Stone had outsold the competition for the past four years. The addition of several exclusive Silver-Stone dealers in Mexico and Canada had brought significant sales increases, to the tune of more than seventy-two percent annually.

He watched Dixie as she walked around, running her fingers over helmets, T-shirts, leather jackets and boots, and eyeing the trinkets they sold. She went to the motorcycles at the front of the store and traced the sleek lines of several of the bikes.

She tossed her thick mane over her shoulder and said, "Mind if I sit on this one?"

"Go for it." He went to her as she straddled an S-S Classic, gripping the handlebars and wiggling her ass on the leather seat.

"Feels *good*." She put both hands on the sides of the seat just inside her thighs and leaned forward, thrusting out her chest as she said, "Nice *girth*. I can't help but wonder if everything about *you* is just as impressive."

Strangled laughter fell from his lips. "What are you doing, Dix?"

She wiggled her shoulders, still posing on the bike like a sexy little minx, and said, "Just saying what's on my mind."

He gritted his teeth, trying his damnedest not to act on the white-hot lust that had been scorching through him for days. She threw one long leg over the bike and pushed to her feet, stalking toward him like a jaguar on the prowl. Her eyes said *fuck me*, but when she stopped inches from him and thrust out one hip, her body language was far more challenging. She didn't say a word for a long stretch of time. Her gaze traveled from his eyes to his mouth, lingering there so long heat stroked down his chest. Her tongue slid over the curves of her upper lip, then slowly traced her lower lip, and *holy hell*, he had visions of her mouth wrapped around his cock, his hands fisted in her hair.

And just like that, he was rock hard.

"Or maybe things aren't quite so impressive," she said evenly, chin dipped slightly, her voice toying with him. "Maybe that's why you think I'd regret it if we got together."

He closed the distance between them, planting one foot beside hers, so his broad chest brushed her breasts, and spoke in a low, firm voice. "If I had less self-control, I'd bend you over that bike and show you just how wrong you are."

"Why all the control, Stone? Is it because I'm doing the calendar?"

"I don't normally mix business with pleasure, but as asinine as it sounds, *no*, it doesn't have anything to do with that. Though it definitely *should*. I can't be the stick-around guy you need, Dixie, and I don't want to regret ruining you for any other man."

She made a frustrated sound and stalked away.

He caught up to her in two long strides and grabbed her by the arm, spinning her around. "What're you doing, Dixie?" he seethed. "I'm not the guy for you. Why are you pushing my buttons when you know I'll only break your heart?"

She lifted her chin and said, "What makes you think I'm looking for a man to give my heart to?"

Christ, she was putting up a brave face, but there was no disguising the vulnerability in her eyes. He was drowning in mixed emotions. He wanted to take her into his arms, into his *bed*, and worship her until she never felt that way again. But he knew what he had to do, so he said, "I never said you were, but I know you're not looking for a guy like me."

Anger flickered in her eyes. "How about you let *me* decide for myself?"

How could he have been so blind to his own actions? His chest constricted with the realization that last night when he'd told her she'd regret being with him, he'd taken away her ability to decide for herself the same way her brothers always had. *Fuck.* Now he was in a bigger quandary. In the space of a second, he weighed his options—give in to his desires and devour her until she lay boneless and sated in his arms, or do the right thing and protect Dixie by staying on the safe side of the line he'd drawn in the sand.

Before he could decide how to respond, she said, "I like my men a little more decisive than this, Stone."

The challenge in her voice shredded his control.

Fuck the line.

He swept one arm around her waist, drawing her against

him, and the air rushed from her lungs. Her gaze softened and her lips curved up as "Jace," fell hot and breathy from her lips.

A shrill, repetitive ringing sounded in his pocket, and he ground out a curse.

"One of your harem?" Dixie said snarkily.

"My *sister* Jennifer," he said as the sound blared again. "I don't do harems. I'm not good at *sharing*." Answering the phone was the last thing he wanted to do, but he and Dixie were expected for dinner soon and he didn't want his sisters to worry.

"Surprising for a guy who thinks he's as good as chocolate cake." The shrill sound sliced through the tension. She leaned closer and whispered, "Better get that."

"This isn't over." He reluctantly released her to answer the phone.

As he put the phone to his ear, Dixie said, "Once again, *my* decision, *not* yours."

DIXIE COULD BARELY breathe. Her body thrummed, her nerves were on fire, and her heart was going to beat right out of her chest. She hadn't meant to go after Jace so aggressively, but she'd spent the night being as turned on as she was angry. Why did every man in her life try to make her decisions for her?

Jace was funny and kind to his sister, his voice light and reassuring. But the second he ended the call, he turned brooding and serious again, silently leading Dixie into the elevator. They'd been seconds away from kissing before his stupid phone rang, and she *wanted* that kiss. She stole a glance at him as they rode up the elevator to his apartment. The tension was so thick she could stack it up and build a fort. His eyes were locked on the elevator doors, the muscles in his jaw twitching. He carried one of her bags in each hand, his black leather duffel slung over his shoulder. He was so big and broad, he made the elevator seem far too small.

The elevator opened directly into his apartment, and he motioned for her to go in. When he told her that he lived above the store, she'd expected a modest apartment, not an enormous two-story, industrial-type loft with an open floor plan and incredible views of the city. The walls were brick, the floors earth-tone marble and rich, dark wood. Two black leather sofas and two armchairs created a nook to their right, with a slate-gray throw rug beneath a glass-and-steel coffee table. On the wall behind the nook was a row of built-in bookcases and an archway that led into an office. Beyond the couches was a sleek black bar with four silver barstools. Expensive-looking cabinetry lined the wall behind the bar, and under-cabinet lights illuminated the counters. To their left was a stainless-steel kitchen, all clean lines and sharp corners. A gorgeous black table sat in front of the windows, and thick chains hung from the ceiling with downward-pointing lights. There were a few black-and-steel tables throughout the space with candles and open notebooks littering their surfaces. Everything in the place reminded her of Jace—sleek, sharp, and strong. But he didn't seem like the kind of guy who used candles, and she wondered if they were for the benefit of the women he entertained. That thought made her a little queasy, so she refocused on her surroundings.

While the right side of the loft had two-story ceilings, the left side didn't. Beside the kitchen, a black-metal staircase with stainless-steel posts and wires led to a second-floor balcony spanning the width of the apartment. She saw three doors and assumed they were bedrooms.

"You live in the *penthouse*?"

"Yeah," he said in a clipped tone, heading for the staircase with their bags. "The bedrooms are upstairs."

She followed him up, and he set her bags inside the first door, turning to her with an expression that looked a little angry and a bit grief-stricken.

"Listen, Dix, I didn't mean to be an ass last night. I wasn't trying to take any decisions out of your hands."

"No? Then maybe you should have said that *you* didn't want to do anything *you* might regret."

"You're absolutely right. This is all new to me. Usually, if I want a woman—"

"Stop." She held up her hand. "I don't want to hear about the women you've been with any more than you want to hear about men I've been with. This isn't about anyone but the two of us."

His jaw tightened again, and he ground out, "Right, sorry." His eyes trained on hers, and he said, "You know I want you."

Hearing him say that, and the way he was looking at her, with as much desire as restraint, made her body tingle with anticipation.

"You have invaded my every thought, and I can't just turn off wanting you. But no matter how incredible we'd be together, and trust me, we would be fucking fantastic, almost kissing you was a mistake. I respect you too much to be the guy who takes advantage of this situation. The bottom line is, a night or two of immense pleasure that can't lead to anything else isn't worth hurting you."

"I appreciate your concern for my well-being, but I'm not a pushover. I'd never let you, or any other man, take advantage of me. So if that's what's going on in that head of yours, you can hit your delete button and wipe it clean."

He cocked a grin. "If only it were that easy. You can't turn off respect."

God, he was adorable, which was a strange thing to think about a large, powerful man like Jace, but he seemed to really be struggling with this. When she'd been in his arms, she'd felt his desire from his piercing gaze to the hard heat behind his zipper, and she wanted it *all*. But he was so damn righteous, she was obviously going to need to give him another little push.

"Well, make up your mind, Stone, because it's not *my* heart you should be worrying about. Better men than you have tried to tame this Whiskey, when all I really want is a good time. Now, if you'll excuse me, I'm going to get changed before we leave to have dinner with your family." She couldn't help pushing his buttons and said, "Maybe you should take a cold shower, unless you'd like them to see you with a raging hard-on."

He ground out a curse, and she walked into her room, smiling like a peacock. But as she unpacked, she could hear Jace's shower through the wall, and she imagined him naked, water streaming down his chest and abs to the formidable *machine* between his legs, and she started to sweat. Was he taking that into his own hands? Stroking himself to relieve the pressure they'd built up?

Her pulse quickened, and she closed her eyes, biting her lip as she conjured an image of Jace, naked and wet, touching himself to visions of her in his mind. She pictured his jaw clenching, his hips thrusting, and the aggressive sounds he'd make when he came.

She exhaled a long, uneven breath and headed for her own cold shower.

Chapter Eight

DIXIE WONDERED HOW many sides of Jace she was going to be treated to seeing tonight. From the moment they'd left his apartment, the heat between them had been simmering, thankfully at a level below *boiling*, which it had been at before they'd hit the showers. They'd caught a cab to Rush and Jayla's, and on the way over, Jace gave her the rundown on his siblings and Jayla's husband, Rush. She hadn't been nervous about meeting Jace's family. She was around new people all the time, and she took it in stride. But as they climbed the steps to his sister's brownstone, Jace glanced over, sending another *zing* through her, and her nerves flared to life. She hoped his siblings wouldn't notice the sexual tension hovering over them like clouds.

The door swung open, and three beautiful brunettes peered out with bright smiles. *Wow.* There was no shortage of good-looking genes in the Stone family. It was easy to tell his sisters apart by Jace's descriptions alone.

"Jace!" Jayla squealed and leapt into Jace's arms. She had to be the new mom, and the sister with whom Jace was closest.

Jace laughed heartily as he embraced her, holding the gift

he'd brought for her baby, Thane, in one hand. "Hi, Jay Jay."

He sounded so carefree, it took Dixie by surprise and helped ease her anxiety. It was heartwarming to see big, burly Jace softening with the embrace.

As Jace set Jayla on her feet and handed her the gift he'd brought for Thane, another sister stepped forward with a warm expression. Dixie recognized Mia by her clothes alone. Jace had described her as a *bundle of energy who cruised around in skinny jeans, low-cut blouses, and sky-high heels, who worked in the fashion industry.* Tonight her skinny jeans were white, her spaghetti-strap blouse vibrant red, and her heels were taller than Dixie's spike-heeled boots. Her hair was the darkest of the three sisters', while Jayla's was the lightest shade of brown.

"Hi. I'm Mia. You must be Dixie. We've heard so much about you!"

"Yes," Dixie said. "It's nice to meet you."

Jennifer, the high school principal who Jace had said was *professional during the day and vamped it up in her off hours,* pushed past Mia, wearing a black minidress. Her hair fell to the middle of her back in natural waves. "Hi. I'm Jennifer, and the one smothering Jace is Jayla." She hugged Dixie, and then she stood back and looked Dixie up and down. She set her hands on her hips and said, "Damn, girl, Jace wasn't kidding. You're *gorgeous.* You definitely deserve to be the face of Silver-Stone. I love your tattoos."

"Thank you. I'm getting nervous about the shoot tomorrow." She had been trying not to think about it, because every time she did, she froze inside. She'd thought she could pull it off as she had with Jillian's fashion show, when she'd just walked down the catwalk strutting her stuff. But this was going to be *way* different. Earlier, Jace had reiterated that they would be taking still shots, which was making her more nervous than being a moving target. In the cab on the way over Jace had pointed to a billboard and said that she'd be up there one day representing Silver-Stone. She wasn't sure if he was kidding or not, but it was overwhelming to think about. She looked at him as he hugged Mia, and he winked, setting her nerves on fire again.

"You're going to be *phenomenal*," he said confidently. "You couldn't screw this up if you tried, Dix. That's why I chose you. You're Dixie Whiskey, biker chick extraordinaire, from the tip of your gorgeous head to the soles of your leather boots. It not only runs in your blood, but it's in your bones. You can't lose that, fake it, *or* fuck it up."

"Wow," Jayla said with a grin.

Wow is right. His vehemence made her want to believe him.

"You'll kick ass," Jennifer said. "And Jayla can give you tips if you need them. She's done tons of sponsorship photo shoots."

"Definitely," Jayla said. "Mia too. She works with models all the time."

"Absolutely," Mia agreed.

Dixie felt better just knowing she had a few friendly females to lean on. "Thank you. And thanks for letting me tag along tonight."

"We wouldn't have it any other way." Jayla went in for a hug and said, "Jace never brings women home, so we're all pretty curious."

"*Jayla*," Jace warned as they followed his sisters inside.

"Oh, please," Jennifer said. "Like you didn't know we'd be curious?"

"You used to question all the guys we went out with. Now it's *our* turn," Mia said.

Jace's jaw clenched as they went into the living room, and Dixie had to chuckle to herself. She loved watching him squirm. There was definite power in having sisters to outnumber the males in the family.

Rush and Jayla's home was warm and welcoming, with brightly colored furniture and throw blankets draped over the backs of the sofa and armchairs. Bookshelves held more family photos than books, and the walls were decorated with winter-themed landscapes and more family pictures. French doors led to a balcony with flower boxes overflowing with colorful blooms. The open floor plan revealed a dining room and a kitchen that were just as cozy.

"So, do you have brothers or sisters?" Mia asked.

"Yes, I have three brothers. Bones, Bullet, and Bear."

"And I thought our parents were weird giving us all J names just because their names are Jacob and Janice," Mia said.

"Those are my brother's biker names," Dixie said. "Their real names are Brandon, Wayne, and Robert."

"Is Dixie your biker name?" Jayla asked.

Jace cocked his head, as if he wanted to know the answer, too.

"It's my real name. Dixie Lee Whiskey." Dixie shook her head and said, "I know. I should be wearing cowgirl boots with a name like that. But I'm confused. Mia, what did you mean by *J names*? Your name starts with an *M*."

"Mia's first name is Jocelyn. Mia is her middle name. She rebelled in sixth grade, refusing to be called Jocelyn. She's been Mia ever since." Jennifer nudged Dixie and said, "Let's get back to your badass biker brothers. Are they single?"

"Christ, Jen," Jace said. "They're all taken, and the last thing you need is a biker."

Jayla's eyes widened, and she said, "Careful, Jace. You're going to ruin your chances with Dixie."

"Oh, I know just what your brother is like." Dixie met Jace's annoyed gaze, and sparks burned right through the annoyance. She quickly shifted her focus to Jayla opening the gift Jace had brought.

Jayla opened the box and held up a tiny black leather jacket. There was a collective "aw" from Dixie and his sisters.

"This is the cutest thing I've ever seen! Thank you, Jace!" Jayla set the box down on the coffee table and Mia snagged the jacket from Jayla's hand.

"Look!" Mia turned the jacket around, showing them the Silver-Stone logo on the back, and they all laughed.

While his sisters gushed over the jacket, Dixie silently swooned over the joy in Jace's eyes as he ate up his sisters' happiness.

"The little dude needs to be kept in style," Jace said casually. "Where is my little buddy?"

"Rush is upstairs changing Thane. They'll be right down. Can I get you drinks?" Jayla asked. "I made sangria."

As if on cue, a tall, handsome man with short brown hair and bright blue eyes descended the steps with a baby in his arms and said, "Sounds good to me. If you wait a sec, I'll help you, Jay."

"Good to see you, man." Jace pulled his brother-in-law into a manly one-arm embrace, careful not to squish the baby. "Rush, this is Dixie Whiskey, the new face of Silver-Stone."

It was weird to hear herself described that way. Was that how Jace saw her now? As the face of his company above all else? Maybe he *was* holding back because they were working together. That made her even more nervous about them *and* the photo shoot.

"It's nice to meet you," Rush said. "It's easy to see why Jace is so stoked about you doing the calendar."

"Thank you. I'm not a model or anything; it's still a little nerve-racking," she confessed.

"Jay and I have both done loads of advertisements and commercials for sponsors," Rush said. "Want my best advice?"

"Yes, please."

Rush cocked a grin and said, "Tell yourself you're a teenager again, showing off for your biggest crush. It's amazing what happens when you allow yourself to revert to feeling invincible in the way you did before you were forced to grow up and realize you're only human after all. Jay and I both found that if we mentally put ourselves back to that stage of our lives, we could pull off anything. Hell, I still use that tactic when I'm nervous."

"It really works," Jayla said. "Of course, Rush *was* my teen-age crush."

Rush said, "And Jay was mine."

Dixie glanced at Jace, and a wave of memories hit her. At eighteen she'd strutted around Jace, taunting him with her nubile body, believing with her whole heart that she could have him. She remembered how he'd described what she did to him back then, and a burst of invincibility hit her. *Damn, Rush is right.*

"Thanks. I'll definitely try that." Dixie looked at the precious bundle in his arms and her heart melted. "Oh my goodness, look at this little guy." She reached out to tickle the baby's foot and said, "Hi, Thane. You are just the cutest little thing."

"Relinquish the little dude," Jace said as he took the baby

from Rush's arms and cuddled Thane against his chest. He brushed his nose over the baby's forehead, and a soft smile lifted Jace's lips.

"He's such a baby hog," Jennifer teased.

"Who would have guessed?" Dixie's insides turned to mush at the sight of him loving up the baby, pushing her worries about why Jace was holding back out of her mind. Seeing him with that tiny baby brought all sorts of strange new warm and fuzzy emotions.

Jace lifted his eyes to hers, and the electricity that had been buzzing between them morphed to something softer, *deeper*. *Oh boy*. This side of him might be even more potent than the animalistic side she knew he was keeping tethered.

"Do you have kids?" Jayla asked, snapping her from her reverie.

"No, but I have lots of nieces and nephews. I *love* babies." She put out her finger, and the baby wrapped his little hand around it.

Jayla sidled up to Jace and said, "You hear that, Jace? Dixie *loves* babies."

"Good Lord, Jay, don't push her in that direction." Jennifer shook her head. "Trust me, Dixie, you don't want to go there with Jace. I've been with guys like him. It's work *first*, *second*, and *third*. He's also the hardest man to get in touch with, and when you do, he's all wrapped up in his own head. That'll never change."

"*Hey*," Jace warned.

Mia scowled at Jennifer. "I don't know what you're talking about. Jace would be a great father. He was always there for us."

"He even changes diapers," Jayla said. "He's a *great* babysitter. When he has time, I mean. Of course he's a busy guy. He runs a *huge*, successful company."

Dixie felt like she was listening to a debate about the pros and cons of Jace Stone. Not that she needed to hear it when she had her own list.

"I'm not saying he's a bad guy," Jennifer explained. "I mean, he *does* have that scholarship program for underprivileged kids, and he's a great brother."

"*He's* right here," Jace said.

"Scholarship program?" Dixie asked.

"It's *nothing*," Jace snapped.

"He's so modest. As soon as Jace was in a position where he could do it, he started a scholarship program for underprivileged kids who want to study engineering," Mia explained. "He also awards internships *and* he started a mentoring program within Silver-Stone that he takes part in." She glared at Jennifer and said, "As I said, he's a great brother, and he'd make a great father. Just ignore Jennifer's comments."

"What are you talking about?" Jennifer shot a look at Jace and said, "You have always said you were married to your business, am I right?" She didn't give Jace time to answer, and his annoyed expression gave nothing away. "I'm just warning Dixie not to get her hopes up because you're charming when you try to be. You *know* you're not going to settle down and become a baby daddy any time soon."

Holy cow. What did they think was going on between her and Jace? She was as blown away by that as she was at learning about the programs he'd set up.

"How do you know he's not? Priorities change," Mia snapped. Then, softer, she said, "Although you are getting old, Jace. If you want kids, you should probably get on the stick. You've already blown the life plan I had for you."

Jace glowered at her.

"Whoa." Dixie waved her hands. "Jace and I aren't dating. We're just doing this calendar together."

His sisters exchanged a confused look.

"Oh," Jayla said. "I'm sorry. The way you two were looking at each other just now…"

"*Enough*," Jace demanded, turning a displeased stare on his sisters. "Aren't we here for dinner?"

Rush chuckled and said, "It's times like these that make me glad I have only one sister. We should get dinner on the table before Dixie bolts or Jace loses his cool."

"I've got three older brothers who harass me all the time," Dixie said. "It's nice to experience what it's like when the tables are turned. Although I could use some of that sangria you mentioned."

"Make it *tequila*," Jace said, giving her another dark look.

"Yes!" Jayla bounced on her toes and then she grabbed Mia's arm, pulling her toward the kitchen as she lowered her voice to say, "I love her! We'll get them drunk and learn all their secrets."

"You have to excuse Jayla," Jennifer said. "Ever since birthing that adorable spawn, she's been on a mission to marry us all off. I'll go keep them in line."

"And I'll keep *her* in line." Rush followed Jennifer into the kitchen.

"I HAVE A feeling it's going to be a long night," Jace said, although he'd known it was going to be a long night when

Dixie had come downstairs from her bedroom wearing a black leather miniskirt, skintight knit tank top, and spike-heeled knee-high boots.

"I *love* your sisters. I wonder how different my life would have been if I'd had sisters." Dixie brushed her hand over Thane's forehead with a tender gaze and said, "Do you think they'd mind if I held him for a minute?"

"Of course not." Jace handed her the baby, and his heart squeezed as she nuzzled against Thane's cheek.

"I love the way babies smell," she said softly. Then she looked at Jace and said, "What did Mia mean when she said you blew her life plan?"

Jace glanced into the kitchen, catching his sisters watching them like hawks. The girls startled, turning and bumping into each other. Jace chuckled, glad they liked Dixie, though he'd known they would. "Mia's a big-time planner. She's had all of our lives planned since she was a teenager. I think Jennifer and I both blew her plans, although Jayla and Rush turned out just like she'd anticipated. They've been best friends since they were kids."

"They're lucky to have a foundation of friendship." She glanced into the kitchen.

Jace followed her gaze, seeing Rush's arms around Jayla as he lowered his lips to hers. "They're good together."

His sisters started carrying platters of food to the table.

"Why did they think we were *together*?" Dixie asked.

He lifted one shoulder in a halfhearted shrug. "Maybe because I haven't brought a woman to dinner since I was a teenager. Now I remember why."

"That's not why," Jennifer called from the dining room. "It's because we've heard about *Dixie* for *years*."

"Always off-the-cuff," Jayla added, waving them into the dining room. "As if the comments were no big deal. He'd say something like, 'You wouldn't catch Dixie putting up with that crap.'"

"My favorite was while he was looking for a model for the face of Silver-Stone." Mia lowered her voice an octave. "'That girl's got nothing on Dixie Whiskey!'" She pulled out a chair and sat down as she said, "We always had a feeling there was something more there."

"*We?*" Jace asked.

All three sisters waved at him, and then Rush raised his hand and said, "Me too, bro. Sorry."

"You all have *wild* imaginations," Jace grumbled, trying to remember if he'd ever said those things. He knew he'd thought them, but he hadn't been aware he'd ever said them to his family. "You all made that shit up."

"No we didn't," his sisters argued.

Dixie was watching him with an expression he'd never seen, like she knew his secrets. Until this very moment, he'd thought he'd kept them close to his chest.

"Sorry, not sorry," Jayla said to Jace. "Dixie, why don't I put Thane in the swing so you can eat?"

"Okay, but just one more snuggle. He's the sweetest little guy." Dixie hugged the baby, nuzzling against him with her eyes closed, before handing him to Jayla.

Jace pulled out a chair for Dixie, and then he sat beside her and said, "Sorry about all this."

"I'm not. It's all very *enlightening.*"

He wanted to kiss that sass right off her lips. Instead, as everyone filled their plates with lasagna, he focused on catching up with his siblings and said, "Jennifer, did you get your dishwasher fixed?"

"Yes, *finally*," Jennifer said with a sigh.

"Good. And did you handle that situation with those boys who were getting in trouble just so they would be sent to your office?" His sister had always had a trail of teenage boys following her like panting puppies, and she was pretty good at shutting down the ones who got too big for their britches, but he liked to keep tabs on the situation. "They need to find a better outlet for their hormones."

"Yes, I handled it," Jennifer said. "Remember when you had the hots for Ms. Malone, the French teacher? You were just as bad."

"Exactly. That's how I know you need to shut it down," he said sternly. "What about your summer vacation? Have you decided if you're going away this year?" Jennifer didn't earn much money, and because of that, she didn't always take vacations.

"Not yet. I'm pricing out different locations, trying to decide if I should go someplace all inclusive or not." Jennifer glanced around the table and said, "I guess it doesn't really matter. Give me a sandy beach and hot cabana boys and I'm good."

"Just—"

"I *know*." Jennifer rolled her eyes. "Let you know my flight plans and text you every day so you know I haven't been absconded with by some psycho."

Dixie leaned closer to him and said, "*This* is what you call giving your sisters space? You're just as bad as my brothers."

"I am not," Jace argued. "If I were your brothers, I'd handle those teenage boys myself, I'd have made arrangements for her dishwasher to be fixed the second I'd heard about it, and I wouldn't just ask for a text—I'd show up at the beach."

"Whoa, do your brothers do that?" Jennifer asked. "That would drive me crazy."

"Pretty much. They're very protective of me," Dixie said. "I'm working on getting out from under their watchful eyes."

"For what it's worth, Jace was more of a hovering force when we were younger," Mia said. "But he hasn't been like that for years. He's like the umbrella you keep in your trunk. You don't really need him for day-to-day showers, but when that monsoon hits, you're glad you've got it."

Dixie turned a warmer expression to Jace and said, "I guess I misjudged you. You really are different."

"You'll never find another man like him," Jayla said in a not-so-subtle nudge.

Dixie's leg brushed Jace's under the table, and he found himself staring at her again.

He tried to distract himself and said, "Are you girls done trying to sell me to Dixie?"

"No," Mia and Jayla said in unison.

Jace reached into his back pocket and tossed an envelope to Jennifer.

"What's this?" Jennifer opened the envelope and pulled out a brochure.

"Maddox's relatives have a place on Silver Island. I got you a room for ten days. They'll honor it until you feel like going, even if it's not this year." He put a forkful of food in his mouth as his sisters squealed. Jennifer popped to her feet and dove into him for a hug.

"My brothers definitely *don't* do that," Dixie said, looking at him like he'd just hung the moon.

"I'm googling that island." Jayla pulled out her phone as

Jennifer took her seat, and they passed the brochure around the table.

"Nice, Jace," Rush said. "Don't let my sister know you did that or she'll be tapping on my shoulder next."

"Wait a second, Jace. You've been Maddox's partner for years, and this is the first we're hearing about his family having a place on an island that just *happens* to have their name?" Mia pointed her fork at him and said, "Spill it."

"Nothing to spill. You know I don't like mixing business with pleasure."

Dixie fidgeted with her napkin, and he realized what he'd said.

"Oh no." Jennifer pointed at him. "Did you set up some old man to hover over me? Because if you did—"

"Relax," he said. "I didn't arrange any such thing. If you'd rather not go, give it to Mia or Jayla."

Jennifer pressed the brochure to her chest and said, "I want it! Thank you. It's just…it's a lot."

"It's not, and you deserve it. You work your ass off at that school. I got you guys something, too." He always tried to bring a little something if he hadn't seen his sisters for a while, but he was careful not to give them anything that would make them feel like he thought they couldn't provide for themselves.

He pulled out another envelope from his pocket and handed it to Jayla. "Mom and Dad massages. It was a package thing for new parents at that spa you like. I figured you and Rush could use some pampering. If I'm in town, I'll watch Thane for you. I know you can afford to get whatever you want, but I also know that neither of you will put yourselves before your baby."

Rush squeezed Jayla's hand, and they both thanked him.

"Mia, you have a gift coming in the mail."

"I do?" Mia asked.

"A pair of the Leather and Lace stilettos you've been bugging me about should arrive next week."

"Oh my gosh!" Mia gushed. "I've wanted those since you first showed me the designs! Thank you so much, Jace."

"You loved the heels. It's not a big deal. How's that new boutique at the Cape coming along?"

Mia's eyes lit up. "It's going to be amazing. I leave in a couple weeks to get together with the designers at the Cape. I'm excited to see it all come together."

"The Cape? As in Cape Cod?" Dixie asked.

"Yes. My boss is opening a new boutique in one of his brother's resorts—Ocean Edge, in Brewster. Do you know of it?" Mia asked.

"Not of the resort specifically, but I know the Cape. I'm going to Wellfleet next week. My cousin Justin is showing his sculptures at a gallery, and I'm going to the opening. I was there in the fall. My cousins and uncle are members of the Cape Cod chapter of the Dark Knights. Have you heard of them?"

"Dark Knights?" Jennifer asked.

"It's a motorcycle club. My great-grandfather founded the Maryland chapter, and my relatives founded and are involved in other chapters, on the Cape and in Harborside, Massachusetts, in Colorado, and a few other places," she explained.

"Like a *gang*?" Jayla asked, her eyes skirting to Jace.

"No," Jace answered.

"A club is different than a gang," Dixie explained. "It's basically a group of guys who like to ride and have similar beliefs and lifestyles. They watch over the community, stop bullying, help people in need, that sort of thing. It's like one big family."

"Wow, you're even more perfect for Jace than I thought," Jayla said, looking at Jace with a pushy expression.

"Jayla, cut it out," Jace warned.

"I'm just noting a fact," Jayla said casually.

Dixie nudged Jace's arm and said, "Relax. She's just giving you a hard time."

"Do you go to Bikes on the Beach, too?" Mia asked. "Jace goes every year."

"I've been going so long, I know most of the local bikers around the Cape, including your cousin Justin Wicked's family and most of the Dark Knights," Jace explained.

"That's not surprising. Their community is closely knit, like Peaceful Harbor," Dixie said. "My cousins go every year, but I never do. Those events are like one big drinking fest, and I get enough of that working at my family's bar. But I do hope to go to the drive-in theater while I'm there. I love drive-ins and there aren't any where I live."

"Jared told me about the drive-in. It's on my to-do list," Mia said. "I want to hear about your family's bar. How cool is it to own a bar? What's it like?"

"It's kind of a biker dive, but I love it. During the day it's family friendly, but at night it can get rowdy." Dixie's whole face brightened as she told them about the bar, and the auto shop, and what she did for each of the businesses. The pride in her voice was inescapable.

"You handle the books and administration for both of the businesses *and* waitress part-time?" Jennifer asked. "That sounds like a lot. How do you find time to date?"

"Or *read*?" Mia asked.

Jennifer rolled her eyes. "You and your fictional romance."

"Dating is a touchy subject," Dixie said. "Because of my

brothers' reputations for protecting me, *most* guys stay away."

She looked pointedly at Jace, and he knew she was thinking about how he hadn't backed down. If he was reading her expression correctly, she liked it a hell of a lot.

"I rely on fictional romance more often than I'd like, too," Dixie confessed. "But I'm part of this great online romance book club. We have members all over the world, but the girls who started it live in Wellfleet. I'll probably see some of them when I go for Justin's art show. We're reading an erotic romance right now." She looked tauntingly at Jace and said, "I *love* erotic romance."

His interest piqued.

She rubbed her leg against his under the table, and he shot her a warning look. She feigned an innocent smile as she ran her fingers along his outer thigh.

"I want in on that book club," Jennifer said.

Jace ground his teeth together. He didn't give a rat's ass about the book club, but he wanted in on *Dixie*, and hell if he was going to let her get him hot and bothered in front of his family. It was time for a little payback. He palmed her bare thigh, schooling his expression as her flesh heated. He felt her muscles tense as he slid his hand along her silky skin, beneath her skirt.

She finished her sangria in one gulp.

Pleased with her reaction, he left his hand there, feeling the heat radiating between her legs. He speared a piece of lasagna with his fork, as if he were just enjoying dinner as the girls chatted. He could practically feel Dixie's heartbeat pulsing in the air around them.

"I want to join the book club, too!" Mia exclaimed. "At least that way I'd have friends to talk about my fictional boyfriends with."

Jayla looked playfully at Rush and said, "How can we sign up?"

Jace scanned his sisters' faces, making sure they were clueless about his furtive touches. They were so busy talking about the book club, no one missed a beat—and neither did he. As Dixie talked about forums and FaceTime meetings, he brushed his fingers higher, feeling the damp heat of her panties.

She squeezed her legs together as she said, "I'll give you all the *details* after dinner." *Details* came out breathy. "The book we're reading right now is *so* good. The hero is totally alpha. He takes what he wants, but he really gets off on giving pleasure, too." She looked at Jace as she said, "There's nothing hotter than a man who knows what he wants and goes after it."

"*Yes*," Jennifer agreed.

Rush leaned in and kissed Jayla. Then he said, "My wife can attest to that."

Dixie's eyes never left Jace's face. He'd thought he'd shocked her, but she was enjoying every second of his secret touches, probably feeling like she *won*. That was hot as sin, but he'd played right into her skillful hands.

Needing to turn the tables, he withdrew his hand, earning a harsh glare from Dixie.

Oh yeah, kitten, bring those claws out.

Jace leaned leisurely back in his chair and said, "So, Rush, tell me about the new training program Jayla mentioned." The heat of Dixie's stare seared into him.

Over the next two hours, Dixie brought those kitten claws out, taunting and teasing him and getting frustrated when he wouldn't play along. It was killing him not to react to her sexy double entendres and seductive glances, but if he touched her again, he wasn't going to stop. As if that wasn't torture enough, everything *else* she did during the evening drew him deeper into her, from loving up Thane to giggling and whispering with his sisters in the kitchen, spearing pieces of chocolate cake as they whispered behind their hands. She looked feminine and joyous, like she had nothing to prove.

Dixie almost always looked like she had something to prove.

Witnessing this side of her was so captivating, Jace felt spellbound.

She got teary eyed when she told them about the night Truman found his baby siblings and again when she told them about her father suffering a stroke and her mother sticking by him night and day, nursing him back to health. She'd gone on to tell stories about each of her family members, and she even told them about what had gone down at the auction. It was easy to see how much her family meant to her, but when she told them what it was like to watch Finlay fall in love with her gruffest, most closed-off brother, Jace noticed something special about how much Bullet's happiness meant to Dixie. Her love for her family clearly outshined the hard feelings she had about living in her brothers' shadows.

As they got ready to leave, all the girls pumped up Dixie for the photo shoot, telling her how fantastic she would do and wishing her luck. They exchanged phone numbers, and apparently Dixie's book club was getting three new members. After hugs and promises from Jace to send them a few pictures from the shoot, and from Dixie to keep in touch, Jace hailed a cab.

"Your family is *amazing*," Dixie said as the cab pulled away from the curb.

Her skirt was hiked up so high, his fingers burned with the

memory of brushing against her panties. He gritted his teeth so hard he was sure they'd crack.

"I wish I had sisters. The dynamics are so different between your family and mine. And *Thane?*" Dixie sighed, pressing her hand over her heart. "He's so sweet. I don't know how you stand it. He's going to be a heartbreaker, just like his uncle…"

She went on about how much fun she'd had and how his sisters and Rush had helped calm her nerves about the shoot tomorrow. Jace tried to focus on what she was saying, but he couldn't take his eyes off her long legs. His mind was a whirlwind of Dixie laughing, taunting, and *challenging*. While she talked about tomorrow, he struggled with how he was going to make it through the night.

Family and loyalty were the two things Jace held closest to his heart, and as all the newly discovered parts of Dixie came together, he realized she was unknowingly finding her way there, too.

He thought about that as he helped her from the cab and ushered her inside the building and into the elevator. She stopped talking, and her eyes found his. He should have taken the stairs, because he felt himself getting lost in her.

"Did you hear a word I said?" she asked softly as the elevator doors closed.

He stepped in front of her, and those green eyes went dark as a forest, reeling him right in. He ignored her question, needing her mouth on his, and said, "We both know I'm not the guy you need. I don't answer to anyone, Dix, and I can't give you forever. Hell, I can't give you next week. You want to make your own decisions? You'd better make it fast, kitten, because I'm one breath away from feasting on you."

"You're the guy I need *right now.*"

She grabbed the front of his shirt and tugged. His mouth crashed over hers, and her back hit the wall *hard*. He ground against her hips, letting her feel the effect she had on him. She tasted sweet and sinful, like all his favorite things wrapped up into one delicious package. He pushed his hands into her hair, fisting them and angling her mouth beneath his as he took the kiss deeper. He was rough and greedy, and she was just as eager, rocking her hips, clawing at his arms, back, and head. Blood pounded through his veins as their tongues tangled fierce and hungry. He tugged her hair, eliciting a moan that shot through him like lightning. The elevator doors opened, but he refused to release her. They stumbled into his apartment eating at each other's mouths, and he backed her up against the wall without breaking their connection. Years of repressed desire surged inside him. He wanted to touch all of her at once, to taste her, to feel her come on his mouth, his hands, his *cock*. He groped her breast with one hand, his other hand pushing beneath her skirt as they kissed.

She moaned into his mouth, rocking her hips as he slid his fingers beneath her panties and cupped her sex, feeling her wetness against his palm. The heat of her desire branded his skin as he dragged his fingers slowly along her swollen sex, drawing out her neediness. Another long, hungry sound sailed from her lungs to his, and he quickened his pace, teasing her with his fingers as his thumb found its mark and she gasped. He drew back, needing to see her beautiful face as he claimed her. God, she was gorgeous.

"Open your eyes," he demanded. Her eyes fluttered open, and the passion welling in them burned through him like hot coals.

Biting back the words perched on the tip of his tongue—*you destroy me*—he ground out, "*Fuck*, Dixie," and yanked her top and bra up, exposing her breasts. He continued teasing her down below as he lowered his mouth and dragged his tongue over and around one taut peak. When her eyes fluttered closed, he said, "*Open*," and stilled his hand between her legs. Her eyes flew open, and he held her gaze as he simultaneously sucked the peak into his mouth and thrust his fingers into her velvety heat.

She gasped, her fingernails digging into the backs of his arms, using him for leverage as she fucked his fingers and he sucked and licked, bit and teased her gorgeous breast. He rose, grinding his cock against her hip as he reclaimed her mouth, and sped up the strokes of his fingers. She whimpered into the kiss, a needy, sexy noise that spurred him on. He kissed her rougher, thrust his fingers faster, until her muscles flexed and her orgasm claimed her. Her sex pulsed around his fingers, her hips bucked wildly, and a stream of lustful sounds poured from her lungs. The sight of her coming apart, the sounds she made, and her alluring scent, were magnificent, but they still weren't enough. He wasn't normally such a greedy bastard, but Dixie changed everything.

She came down from the peak, breathless and panting. His body was on fire. His muscles burned with restraint as he searched her eyes for, and *found*, the green light to take them further. Lust shot through him, and a rough noise rumbled out as he shoved her skirt up to her waist and tore her panties down—and *off*. Kneeling in front of her, he planted his hands on her thighs, spreading them wide, and sealed his mouth over her sex, taking his first *real* taste of her. She was sweeter than honey, more addicting than any drug. If euphoria had a taste, it would be *Dixie*.

She buried her hands in his hair as he took his fill. He lifted one of her long legs over his shoulder, angling her hips so he could delve deeper. He fucked her with his tongue, teased her with his fingers. Her body trembled and shook as she inhaled sharp little gasps, moaning and pleading for more. He took her clit between his teeth, using his fingers to stroke the secret spot inside her that sent her soaring again.

"*Jace!*"

Hearing his name sail from her lips in the throes of passion made him want to hear it again. He withdrew his fingers from her slick channel and feasted on her sweetness again.

"*Ohgodohgodohgod*," she panted out as he worked his magic, catapulting her back into oblivion.

He stayed with her, savoring every moment through her very last aftershock. He trailed a series of lighter kisses over and around her sex and along her inner thighs. Each touch caused a sharp inhalation. That sound spiked through him like a gift. Her trembling hands clutched his arms as he rose to his feet. He felt different, as if he'd experienced something life altering. He told himself it was just sex, but the pleasure and approval in her eyes tugged at something deep in his chest. He reclaimed her luscious mouth, rough and wicked, trying to chase those unnerving sensations away. But when she wound her arms around him, pressing her hands to his back, holding him like she never wanted to let go, something inside him shifted. His efforts slowed. He *wanted* to be held by her, to be wanted for more than the pleasure he'd give, to be needed by the woman who needed nobody. His tongue stroked hers sensually, *meaningfully*, different than he'd ever kissed another woman.

He kissed the edge of her mouth and bowed his head beside hers, their bodies still pressed together. Her heart pounded rapidly against his chest, her hands slid down his back, clutching his ass. His hips thrust involuntarily. The depth of their connection tripped him up, and warning bells sounded in his head. *Jesus fuck.* If he felt like this from just going down on her, what would it be like when he was buried deep inside her?

Hating what he was about to do, when what he really wanted was to carry her to his bed and claim every inch of her, he closed his eyes, savoring the moment, and said, "You've got a big day tomorrow. You should get some sleep."

"Yeah," she whispered.

He stepped back, fixed her shirt and skirt, and retrieved her panties.

Black silk.

Fuck.

He placed them in her shaky hand and wrapped his fingers around hers, bringing her eyes up to his. Another unfamiliar blow from within nearly bowled him over. His head spun. If he didn't put space between them he'd end up keeping her up all night, and she had had him in such a tizzy, Lord only knew who he'd be in the morning.

He pressed his lips to hers in a slightly angry kiss and said, "You'll do great tomorrow," and headed for the bar on the opposite side of the room.

He watched her walk upstairs as he poured himself a stiff drink, wondering just how many cold showers a man could survive.

Chapter Nine

"DAMN THOSE STONES and their magical mouths," Izzy said to Dixie on the phone early Monday morning.

Dixie stopped cold in front of her bedroom window. "What do *you* know about the *Stones'* magical mouths?"

"Um…"

Her stomach sank. "Isabel Ryder, have you and Jace…?"

"No!" Izzy snapped. "I *might* have hooked up with Jared once or twice. I knew him when I lived in Boston. I worked in restaurants, remember?"

"Holy shit. You never told me! That's why you were so pissed when Jilly won him in the auction."

"I wasn't pissed, and you didn't call to talk about *me* this morning. We need to get *your* head back in the game."

She was right. Jace had blown Dixie's mind last night. She'd loved every single second of being close to him—every scintillating kiss, every rough touch, the way his beard scratched her mouth, cheeks, and *thighs. Delicious!* She'd walked upstairs feeling like she was floating on a cloud, her body humming and her hopeful heart craving more. She'd slept better than she had in years, and she'd woken up in the best mood, full of energy and ready to conquer the photo shoot. But as she'd showered and dressed, she'd relived their night over and over again, and no matter how many ways she tried to rewrite it, the last time Jace had kissed her had been markedly different from all the rest. It had felt mad or spiteful, *something* far from pleasure filled, the way all the others had felt. That reality had brought her confidence crashing down. She'd gotten herself all worked up, wondering if he could have regretted getting together that quickly and had finally given in and called Izzy so her friend could talk her off the ledge.

"Yes, let's focus. I've got to leave in twenty minutes for the shoot, and I can't bring myself to face Jace. Everything was so incredible all the way up to that last kiss. But that kiss…" A pain sliced through her.

"You're the toughest woman I know, Dix. You're going to ice down your heart, pull up your big-girl panties, and pretend last night didn't matter one way or another. You were in it for a good time, just like you told him."

"Tell that to the nest of bees in my stomach," Dixie mumbled.

"Fuck the bees. In fact, embrace the discomfort and use it to fuel your confidence. There's no way he regrets being with you. You're awesome and he knows it. The man laid down forty grand for a date with you."

"Charity donation," Dixie reminded her, although he'd stood up to Bullet and he'd revealed how long he'd wanted to be with her, so maybe she *was* overanalyzing that last kiss.

But what if she wasn't?

"That's still a lot of money, Dix. You know men would line up to be with you if your brothers would let them."

"You're right." Dixie strode over to the mirror, giving herself a once-over. She looked damn good in her jeans and tank top. She stood up taller, tossed her hair over her shoulders, and forced her confidence to the forefront. "Nobody fucks with Dixie Whiskey."

"There's the girl I know and love! You're going to march downstairs, look that big stud in the eyes, and act like last night was just one in a string of good times in which men have pleasured you."

"Right. He'll think I'm a slut."

Izzy laughed. "But *we* know the truth, and that's all that matters. Listen, this morning is about saving your pride and protecting your heart. On the off chance that he's an asshole, or that his conscience got the better of him because he's a loner and feels guilty about hooking up with you, you can't let him know it bothers you."

"I know you're right. And he's *not* an asshole. He gave me plenty of chances to say no. I baited him until he couldn't resist me."

"Because you're awesome like that."

Dixie could hear her friend's smile, and it helped ease her nerves. "Yeah, I am. You know, he's the *only* man I've ever pushed like that."

"Crushing on a guy for more than a decade will do that to you. You've got this, Dix. I wish I were there. Do you want me to call my cousin's wife to come see you? She's a model and lives in New York. She could walk you through the shoot if you freeze up. *Oh!* I have a great idea. Maybe her husband could bring a few of his hot friends to make Jace a little jealous or at least uncomfortable. Paybacks are so fun."

"No thank you," Dixie said. "After the way he stood up to my brothers, I'm pretty sure *nothing* makes Jace uncomfortable.

Besides, I don't need rescuing. I just needed a pep talk. I'm okay now. Thanks, Iz."

"Hey, even though it feels weird right now, I'm so happy you got to finally make out with him. At least you aren't left wondering what kissing him would be like."

"That's true, but try telling that to my body. Last night left me even more curious about other things." Like what it would feel like to pleasure *him* with her hands and mouth, to be lying beneath his powerful body as their bodies came together…

A shiver of heat traveled down her spine.

"Well, don't let him know that," Izzy said sharply. "Or he'll tell you he doesn't regret it just so you'll blow him."

"You need to stop talking because that makes me want to tell him."

Izzy laughed. "Are you sure you're okay?"

"Yes. I've got this. Thanks for talking me off the ledge."

"Anytime. I forgot to tell you that I saw your parents at the grocery store. Your mom is raving to *everyone* about you doing the calendar. They're so proud of you, Dix. We all are. You're going to be amazing today. Have fun with it. Think of this as your coming-out party. You've broken free from your little-sister reins. The world is your playground."

There was only one playground she was interested in, and right now trying to navigate it was like trying to jump over a jungle gym.

Good thing she had long legs.

After they ended the call, Dixie inhaled a few deep breaths, grabbed her bag, and headed downstairs to face the man with the magical mouth.

Jace was reading something on his phone, leaning over the counter as she descended the stairs. His jeans hugged his fine ass. Damn he looked good. She remembered how delicious his hard body had felt against hers, and her pulse quickened. He was so *big* and broad, when she was in his arms she felt more feminine than she ever had.

He turned and their gazes collided, setting off a ricochet of electricity inside her.

"Good morning," she said casually, dropping her bag on the table.

He filled a cup with coffee and handed it to her, studying her face. "You okay this morning?"

"Sure. Just a little nervous about the shoot. No big deal. I'll get over it." She poured creamer into her coffee and leaned her butt against the counter, feeling the weight of his scrutinizing gaze as he leisurely sipped his coffee.

"I meant about last night. Are we cool?"

"Totally," she lied, trying to sound tough, which was weird, because she'd never had to *try* to sound tough before. "Sorry I didn't get a chance to reciprocate."

His lips quirked up, and she immediately regretted what she'd said. Izzy was right. What man would turn down a blow job?

He stepped closer, planting himself in front of her, and set his coffee cup on the counter. Then he took hers and placed it next to his. Without a word, he put his hands on the edge of the counter beside her hips, boxing her in and making her heart race.

"Can I help you?" she said teasingly.

"Your eyes are glowing."

A nervous laugh bubbled out. "What?"

"Your eyes are usually not quite dark enough to be forest green, more of a jade. But when you lied about the ballot for the auction being full, they glowed lighter, like they are now, more of an emerald color."

Holy cow. The only other person who had ever noticed the way her eyes changed colors was her mother. Her mother had once told her that she'd had to find some telling sign, because Dixie was so good at pulling the wool over everyone's eyes.

Except, apparently, Jace Stone's.

"So, I'll ask again," he said evenly. "Are you okay? Are we cool?"

She lifted her chin, refusing to show him the effect he had on her, and said, "Yes. We were just having fun. I know there's nothing more between us. We're on the same page."

He squinted, staring directly into her eyes for a long, silent moment, before saying, "If that's your story, I guess you're sticking with it." He leaned closer, brushing his beard over her cheek, sending shivers of heat to her core. He spoke just above a whisper as he said, "You, Dixie Whiskey, are my new favorite dessert. I don't need you to reciprocate, but I'd love to have seconds. Ball's in your court..." He pushed from the counter and said, "We'd better get a move on. The car will be here in ten minutes to take us to the shoot."

She tried to pick her jaw up off the floor and respond, but it was a lost cause.

A few minutes later he said, "Coming, Dix?"

"*Not yet*," she said under her breath as she grabbed her bag, wondering how she was going to make it through the shoot with *that offer* hanging over her head.

SHEA HAD WORKED with their marketing department to handle all of the logistics for the shoot, from the set to the photographer, makeup and hairstylist, and a general stylist to help Dixie with outfits and accessories. Jace had seen pictures of the warehouse where they were shooting and had thought it was the perfect location, but it was even better in person. The combination of brick and stone was gritty and edgy and would be the perfect backdrop for their sleek motorcycles. Two guys from their local store were there to handle the six Legacy bikes Jace had brought in for the shoot. Though the bikes were gorgeous machines on their own, he knew Dixie would make them look even more desirable.

He hadn't been able to stop thinking about her since last night. He'd had a hell of a time staying in his own bed, knowing she was only a few feet away, sated and flushed. Maybe it was because they'd gotten closer, or because he'd finally gotten a taste of the woman he'd wanted for so long, but when she'd come downstairs this morning looking badass and beautiful as usual, with an underlying hint of vulnerability, she'd taken his breath away. But her cool answers had bothered him. He'd *had* to try to find out where her head was. He hadn't planned on making her even more nervous with his comment, but her reaction to it had told him everything he needed to know. She'd snagged a bottle of whiskey before leaving the apartment *to get through the shoot.* She'd been quiet on the drive over, nervous about the shoot and texting with his sisters, who had wished her luck. The second they arrived, she was swept away to get ready for the shoot.

He was glad they'd have a distraction today, because one night with Dixie definitely wasn't enough.

As if the universe knew he needed to get his head out of the clouds, the photographer, Hawk Pennington, arrived while Dixie was getting her hair and makeup done.

"Hawk, thanks for coming out." Jace shook his hand.

Hawk had been referred by Lenore "Leni" Steele, one of Shea's top marketing representatives and a valued member of Silver-Stone's marketing team. Hawk's reputation spoke for itself. He'd published several photo spreads of A-list celebrities, sports figures, and some of the wealthiest families in the world. But equally important to Jace was his knowledge of the biker world. In an effort to keep the calendar as authentic as possible, Jace had wanted a photographer who was also a biker, and Hawk was a Dark Knight. Although dressed in maroon pants, leather suspenders, and a gray button-down, he looked more like a hipster than a biker. His eyeglasses were multicolored, his hair was swept back in a trendy cut, longer on top, neatly shaved on the sides, and his beard was thick but neat.

"Nice to see you again," Hawk said as his assistants went to work setting up their equipment. "This is a great location. I went over the shoot with Shea last week. I understand we'll be shooting inside and out, twelve final calendar images, plus a cover shot, a number of merchandising shots for advertisements and cutouts, with one model, several bikes. You're going for 'classy with an edge,' primarily a male audience for the calendar, but the clothing needs to be as prominent as the bike. Has anything changed?"

"No. That's all correct."

"I assume you're going to be handling the motorcycles?"

"Yes. We have men who will do whatever is necessary."

"Great, then I'll check out the space and get my guys set up while your model gets ready."

Hawk headed for the warehouse, and Jace went to check on

Dixie. They'd set up a dressing room in one of the office spaces. As he walked through the door, he nearly crashed into her.

Dixie put her hands on her hips, scowling at him. Her hair was tousled and wild, her eyes were made up too dark, her cheeks too pink, and her lips too red. "This is what you call *classy*? I look like a high-end hooker."

What the hell is that makeup artist doing? "Wash that shit off your face and brush your hair. I'll take care of this."

"Damn right you will, or I'll be on the next plane out of here." She stormed off toward the ladies' room.

Jace strode into the dressing room, where Indi Oliver, the hair and makeup artist, a twentysomething with long blond hair and big blue eyes, was organizing brushes and makeup on a table.

"Hello, Mr. Stone," she said when he walked in.

"Hi." Jace tried to tamp down his frustration. "I'm not sure what look you were going for, but I want *Dixie*, not some tramped-up version of her."

"Oh, goodness. I was told you wanted sexy and *edgy*," she said with furrowed brows.

"Then we're using the wrong word. *Classy*, not *clownlike*. Dixie is a stunning woman. She looks fresh and sexy as hell every day with very little makeup. *That's* the Dixie I want, so whatever you need to do to help her natural beauty shine through is what I want you to do." He heard something behind him and found Dixie standing in the doorway.

"I need makeup remover," Dixie said a little tentatively, and he realized she'd heard everything he'd said.

"I'll help you with that," Indi said. "I'm sorry, Mr. Stone. I'm used to working on fashion shoots where I'm asked to make the models less natural and more glamorous, and under the harsh lights, we need to go a little heavy. Don't worry. I've got this. I'll tone it all down to a more natural look. I prefer that, actually."

"Thank you. Dixie's glamorous without extra *anything*." He held Dixie's gaze as she sank down into the chair in front of the mirror. As Indi dug around in what looked like a giant toolbox, Jace gave Dixie's shoulder a squeeze and whispered, "Always trust your gut. If you feel like something is off, it probably is. There's no need for threats. I hear you, Dixie. I *always* hear you."

Jace went to talk with the guys handling the bikes, and then he checked in with Hawk and his team.

When Dixie finally emerged from the dressing room wearing the skintight black leather pants with lace trim above angled, silver-zippered pockets and a long-sleeved black lace top over a leather bralette, Jace lost his breath for the second time that day. Silver-and-diamond earrings glittered against the lush, natural waves of her hair, and her Silver-Stone boots had a silver chain and buckle around the ankle. Maddox had been right to suggest they use expensive jewelry. It added another level of elegance to the ensemble. Dixie looked like a million bucks.

She put her hand on her hip, and in pure *Dixie* fashion, she said, "You going to gawk at me all day, or are we going to get this show on the road?"

"Dixie," came out sounding as off-kilter as he felt.

Her smirk grew into a smile, and she said, "I know. Indi's a genius, isn't she?" Her eyes drifted over Jace's shoulder, and she exclaimed, "Hawk? You didn't tell me *Hawk* was the photographer!"

She rushed past Jace, snapping him from his reverie, and threw her arms around Hawk. Hawk's eyes drifted down Dixie's body as she turned in a circle, reawakening the green-eyed monster in Jace. He mentally prepared himself for another long day.

"Jace!" Dixie exclaimed. "Did you know Hawk was a Dark Knight? I've known him forever. This shoot will be *much* easier with Hawk taking the pictures. I'm already less nervous."

Jace was thrilled with her enthusiasm, but he couldn't deny that he wished he'd elicited the same excitement. "Yeah, I knew."

"Well, good for us!" Dixie looked around and said, "So, where do we start?"

Hawk took charge, ushering her across the parking lot to the area where his team had set up their equipment. Indi and the stylist, Kyra, stood off to the side as Hawk gave Dixie suggestions for poses.

Dixie listened intently, following his guidance like she modeled all the time. "Something like this? Or this?" she asked as she tried out different poses.

Hawk commended, repositioned, and guided her with a professional hand. Dixie obviously trusted him. It was a damn good thing Jace hadn't hired someone else. He couldn't imagine making Dixie deal with a stranger's hands on her, much less having to deal with it himself. The visceral thought was accompanied by a dose of *what-the-hell?* He told himself he'd be just as protective with any female friend and tried to push it away.

There was a flurry of activity as Hawk began shooting. His assistants each held a large light-modifying disc as he took pictures. Despite Dixie's initial excitement, she seemed a little uncomfortable and stiff, looking to Hawk for guidance each time she shifted positions.

"Don't worry about whether the poses are correct or about seducing the camera," Hawk suggested. "Let's just get comfortable with each other. Nothing you do will be wrong, so just go with your gut. Move how you might if there was a really hot guy standing by me."

Dixie moved stiffly through a few more poses, uncertainty written in her eyes. It was tough seeing her in such a vulnerable state. Jace wanted to help, but he didn't want to intrude, so he let the uncomfortable shoot go on for a few more minutes.

"You're doing great," Hawk coaxed. "Just relax. Act like I'm not here."

She stopped posing and said, "That's hard to do when you're staring at me through a gigantic lens and your assistants are holding up those big things. I'm sorry. I don't know why I'm all freaked out all of a sudden."

"I have an idea." Jace grabbed the bottle of whiskey and shot glass Dixie had brought with her and went to her, guiding her away from the others. He lowered his voice and said, "I know it's nerve-racking to be the center of attention. What can I do to help? Do you want to do a shot?"

"I'm afraid it'll make me lose focus," Dixie confided. "I hate that this is so hard. I'm sorry, Jace. I really wanted to do this for you, but maybe I'm not the right person."

"Where's the ballsy woman from the auction? And the Dixie from last night? The one who had me on my knees?"

"I have no frigging idea," she said defeatedly.

Jace set the bottle and glass down and pulled his wallet from his pocket, showing her the picture he'd taken from Jillian. "See this gorgeous woman? She's the face of Silver-Stone, and she's in there somewhere, Dix. All we have to do is find her."

"I was a moving target. This is totally different."

"You can do this, Dix. I know you can." He put the picture back in his wallet, catching sight of the card her mother had given him from the auction. It was the information Red would have read about Dixie as the bidding started had things not gone south. He recited the first part of it from memory, swapping her name and the word *her* for *you*. "You can whip a business into shape with your magnificent mind, shut a man down with your sassy mouth, or melt hearts with a single seductive look."

"That sounds like something my friends would say."

"It was on the card from the auction Red gave me."

"They did write it." Surprise rose in her eyes. "You *memorized* it?"

"What else was I supposed to do after dancing with you that night?" That earned an adorably shy look that was so foreign, he wanted to say more and keep it going. But that wasn't what Dixie needed, so he said, "As much as I want to tell you what *else* I've had to do to make it through these last few nights, I don't think it would help you relax."

Her eyes darkened, and she said, "I think I might need that drink after all."

He reached for the bottle. "Would it help to draw upon any of the advice my sisters or Rush gave you?"

"Yes!" She touched his hand, stopping him from opening the bottle, and said, "I don't need the drink. Rush's advice will work perfectly."

His mind rewound to last night, and he remembered Rush telling her to think about her biggest teenage crush. Jace's chest constricted, hating the idea of Dixie thinking of any other guy like that. "Great. Are you sure?"

"Yes! I know it'll work." As they headed back to the area

where they were shooting, she lowered her voice and said, "It already is!"

"*Fanfuckingtastic*," he ground out. As he stalked away, he took a swig of the whiskey, forgoing the glass.

Indi and Kyra rushed over to primp Dixie for the shoot. Ten minutes later Dixie was like a different person, posing like she was made for modeling, her eyes locked on Jace. Jace's gut burned with jealousy. Whoever she'd crushed on must have shown her a hell of a good time, because the looks she was giving him could make a dead man hard. He took another swig, but there wasn't enough whiskey in the world to get the green-eyed monster off his back.

"That's it," Hawk coaxed. "Perfect. That's hot. Lean back, good…Seduce the *camera*, Dix. We need eye contact." A few minutes later he said, "Let's take a break."

Hawk waved Jace over.

"She looks great," Jace said.

"She looks better than great. The camera loves her, but she's staring at you, Jace, and we need eye contact for the calendar."

"She'll get it. Just remind her." He glanced at Dixie, who was chatting with Indi. She met his gaze, and that feeling that had swamped him when he'd had to stop himself from taking things further returned.

"I think you're evoking the look we need," Hawk said.

He wasn't about to admit that it couldn't be him Dixie was thinking about, but some douche she must have gone out with as a teenager.

"She's just gotten comfortable in front of the camera, so why don't we make it easy for her?" Hawk suggested. "I think if you stick by my side while I work, we can get the right angle for eye contact. She'll look at you, but if you're *right* by me—as in, when I move, you move—I think it'll work. Are you willing to try?"

"Whatever you need." He never imagined the photo shoot would be uncomfortable for *him*.

Several hours, hairstyles, and sexy Leather and Lace outfits later, Jace knew he'd made a mistake agreeing to be Dixie's focal point. She wasn't seducing the camera; she was seducing *him*. Every sinful look hit with laser precision, making his body flame. It didn't help that she was dressed in the outfits he'd co-designed with the intent of being exactly what he loved, classy with an edge. The Leather and Lace line amped up her already-off-the-charts natural allure. When they took a break for lunch, she spent the entire time on the phone or with Indi and Kyra, giving him a chance to cool down. But after the break, she strutted out in the skater dress, and when she set her green eyes on him, she reignited the fire.

Dixie was blowing him away in more ways than just her ability to model and the professionalism with which she was handling the shoot. When she had tiffs with Hawk about poses, she stood her ground until they came to a compromise she was happy with. Even that was a turn-on. Watching her in action confidently wearing the clothes he helped design, straddling his bikes, brought his emotions to new heights. His hands itched to touch her. Her voice whispered seductively through his mind, bringing rise to more than just rampant desire. He couldn't stop thinking about the way her body had trembled and the needful sounds she'd made as she'd come apart against his mouth last night. How could she evoke all those sensations from several feet away, while they were surrounded by people, one of whom was barking out directions?

Late in the afternoon, when Dixie went to change clothes,

Jace got caught on a call with his assistant. When he heard Dixie's angry voice, he ended the call and found her and Hawk having a showdown. And *holy hell*, she'd done it again. She'd taken his breath away. She was wearing tight leather shorts, a silver-studded black belt, a cropped top, and a vented leather jacket that was trimmed with silver studs and black lace. The outfit was paired with Silver-Stone boots. Her hair was twisted up and secured with a leather clip, with several sexy strands framing her face.

He didn't want *any* other man seeing her in that outfit, and reality slapped him in the face. He'd made a huge mistake by asking Dixie to be the face of Silver-Stone. He'd been so blinded by wanting the only woman he truly believed worthy of representing Silver-Stone, he hadn't realized the obvious. Her brothers were right. Every asshole on the planet would be gawking at her. But there was no backing out now.

He was *screwed*.

He reminded himself she wasn't *his*. He had no right to be jealous or possessive. He forced himself to try to push those thoughts aside, but it was a futile effort. They were etched in his mind, glaring like neon lights he couldn't turn off.

"I would *never* stand like that," Dixie snapped, arms crossed, smoke billowing out her ears.

"What's the problem?" Jace asked.

"Hawk wants me to lean over the bike and stick my ass out. I'd never do that in these shorts. I *love* the clothes and I'd wear them in a heartbeat, but *come on*, Jace. Can you imagine me in *any* situation bent over a bike like that?"

Hell yes, but only for me.

Hawk turned an amused expression to Jace and said, "Keep in mind, this is for a male audience, Jace."

"Fuck the audience. Turn the bike so we can shoot it from the side," he demanded, and one of his men hurried over to move the bike. "Dixie, straddle the bike and grab the handlebars."

"You said you wanted to showcase the *clothing line*," Hawk reminded him. "We won't see her top or the shorts."

"I want to showcase the *line*, not Dixie's *ass*," Jace snapped. "Just do it."

"If I don't hold the handlebars I can put one hand on my hip while I'm sitting down and turn like this, so you can see my top." Dixie straddled the bike and put her hand on her hip, catching the leather jacket so it pulled back as she turned, revealing the cropped leather and lace top—and giving Jace another ball-busting dose of reality.

She could be wearing full-body armor and she'd melt it right off.

"That'll work," Hawk said.

Dixie smiled triumphantly, causing a twinge in Jace's chest.

After Hawk walked away, Jace said, "You can thank me later."

"Oh, I plan to," she said promisingly.

His mind went straight to the gutter.

Her gorgeous green eyes taunted him as Hawk took more pictures. His temperature spiked, and he wondered if *Whiskey fever* was a real thing after all.

He thought he was screwed by making the decision to have Dixie be the face of the company, but he'd been wrong about the reasons why. He hadn't made a mistake by asking her to do the calendar shoot. She was as authentic as they came, and she was the *only* woman he wanted representing Silver-Stone. His mistake had been letting her get under his skin.

Chapter Ten

THEY DIDN'T FINISH shooting until after seven. Dixie had a new level of respect for Jace, and for models. She'd thought Jace would put business first, but the few times she'd had issues, he'd stepped in, making sure she was comfortable above all else. He'd also demanded two unscheduled breaks when he noticed Dixie was getting a little worn out. She'd loved seeing the serious side of him as he worked with her and Hawk to get the exact looks he wanted. There was much more to Jace Stone than met the eye, and what met the eye was nothing to shake a stick at. But the biggest surprise of the day was that they'd wrapped shooting half an hour ago and her body was still humming with desire.

With one small tweak, Rush's suggestion had worked like a charm. She'd imagined herself at eighteen strutting like a temptress in front of Jace, who at twenty-seven wouldn't have touched her with a ten-foot pole, and the unstoppable power she'd felt back then came over her. It was easy to be fearless before she'd known what rejection had felt like—that had come later, when she'd realized all her strutting wasn't going to get her the man she wanted. But as she was working that teenage invincibility, she realized how silly she was being. She'd been with Jace last night, and he still wanted her today. As soon as she realized that, the teenage premise had fallen away and she'd become her womanly self, trying to seduce the man of her dreams.

She might have needed the kick in the ass of that youthful bravery, but once she'd embraced it, giving in to the seduction of Jace Stone was the easiest thing she'd ever done.

Modeling on the other hand, not so much.

It had been as fun as it had been grueling to hold certain poses with her head at just the right angle or arching her back for long periods and changing her clothes a million times. She'd used muscles she didn't even know she had, and she was sure she'd be sore tomorrow. But it was worth it. Hawk had been supportive and easy to work with, and seducing Jace had been a thrilling bonus. Plus, he'd said she could keep the clothes. His taste was incredible. She felt sexy and just tough enough in every outfit without undermining her femininity. But the outfit she had on now was her favorite. The thin black miniskirt wasn't tight, which made her feel even sexier than the snug clothing had. Kyra had paired the skirt with a clingy sleeveless lace top, open from her neck to her navel. It fastened with a button behind the lace-choker neckline. Jace had been captivated by her from the second she'd walked out wearing it. She couldn't stop fantasizing about him kissing the exposed skin down the center of her body and pushing the skirt up as he had last night to take his fill.

Her whole body shuddered.

Had the camera caught *everything*? Had Hawk seen how much she wanted Jace? Would she look as turned on in the pictures as she felt? That would be embarrassing. Jace, Hawk, and everyone else who had helped out with the shoot had been overwhelmingly supportive and complimentary, telling her how great she was doing during the shoot and showering her with accolades when they finished for the day. But what else could they say? *Hey, you look like you're going to spontaneously combust. If you want to drag Jace in the back and fuck his brains out, feel free. We can wait.*

Thankfully, they were all packing up and leaving when she went to change.

She paced the dressing room, trying to regain control of her lust-laden body. If she didn't find a way to calm her overzealous hormones fast, she'd have to take things into her own hands or she'd never make it through the night.

A knock at the door startled her from her thoughts.

"Come in." She turned as the door opened and Jace stepped in, looking scrumptious in the white T-shirt and faded jeans she'd been dying to rip off of him all day.

"Everyone else took off. You were amazing out there." His eyes slid down her body, and he made an appreciative sound. "I hope you plan on wearing that outfit tonight. I want to take you out to dinner and celebrate."

Just being close to him brought an adrenaline rush. Maybe she did need to take things into her own hands, but it didn't have to be a solo effort. Feeling bold, she walked past him and closed the door. As she turned the lock, she said, "Dinner sounds great, but maybe I'd like an appetizer first."

His arms circled her waist from behind and kissed her shoulder.

"*Jace*," she whispered.

Reaching behind her, she pushed her fingers through his thick hair, and he bit down, sending rivers of lust coursing

163

through her. She turned in his arms, and he captured her mouth with his, holding her so tight she felt exactly how much heat he was packing in those jeans. His hot hands moved roughly over her back, down her hips and thighs. She grabbed his ass and his hips thrust forward. She stumbled back against the door, and he reached for her skirt.

She grabbed his hands and tore her mouth away. "I said *I* wanted an appetizer." She released his hands and cupped his crotch. Heat exploded inside her at the feel of him, but it was the lethal darkness in his eyes that made her panties damp.

He grabbed her wrist and said, "Dix, be sure. You know I can't promise you anything beyond our time together here."

"I can't decide if you suck at listening or if you're trying to be chivalrous."

"I listen to every word you say, but I also hear the ones you *don't*."

Her heart raced at that confession, and the honesty in his eyes tore at her heart. But she'd already decided that if New York was all they'd have, she was going to take a big bite out of that apple and savor it forever. She squeezed his crotch and said, "Then you know we're on the same page."

"Dix," he ground out in a pained voice. "You're getting good at telling stories."

"Wait until you see what else I'm good at."

She grabbed his hips, turning them both so *his* back was to the door. She unbuttoned his jeans and yanked them down his hips. Her knees weakened at the sight of his formidable erection outlined by tight black briefs. He grabbed her face between both hands, taking her in another heart-pounding kiss. She swore he had the most powerful tongue she'd ever encountered, the way he possessed every inch of her mouth just as deeply as his tongue had claimed her down below last night. She pushed her hand into his briefs, palming his shaft, and sweet baby Jesus, his flesh was on *fire*. He broke their kiss with a greedy groan, and she made quick work of stripping down his briefs. As she sank down to her knees, he slid his back down the door, bringing him to the perfect height for her to pleasure him.

As she lowered her mouth toward his cock, she stopped short and met his gaze. Her heart nearly stopped from embarrassment as she said, "Am I going to need to wash my mouth out with bleach after this?"

He choked out a laugh and shook his head. "I'd have to be an asshole to let you do this if I wasn't clean."

Relief swept over her.

"Dix, you don't have to do this for me. I told you I wasn't looking for you to reciprocate."

"Don't flatter yourself. This is for *me*." It wasn't a total lie. As much as she wanted to give him pleasure, she wanted to *taste* him, *feel* him in her hands, and *make* him lose his mind, just as badly as she'd wanted *his* mouth on *her* last night.

She slid her tongue around the broad head of his cock, teasing him until his jaw was clenched so tight it had to hurt. His shaft was thick and strong, like him, and it twitched greedily in her hand. She dipped lower, licking him from base to tip, getting him nice and wet. She stroked him with her hand as she took him in her mouth, earning the sexiest moan she'd ever heard. It was such an erotic sound, she knew she'd hear it echoing in her sleep. And she wanted to hear more of it! She stroked him tight and slow, loving the way his breaths came harder. When she quickened her pace, taking him all the way to the back of her throat, he buried his hands in her hair with a *hiss*. Oh, how she loved that! Even when the tip of his cock touched her throat, she could still fist the base. The man wasn't just packing heat. He was packing a *volcano*, and she wanted to make him *blow*. The quicker she moved, the harder he thrust. Her big bad alpha was letting her set the pace, and as much as she appreciated that, she craved his *power*. She cupped his balls and squeezed.

He ground out, "*Fuuck...*"

She sucked harder, stroked him faster, and when she felt him swell in her hand, his thighs flexing, she slowed her efforts, drawing out his pleasure—and her own. She'd never gotten off on blow jobs, but everything was different with Jace. She *wanted* to pleasure him so thoroughly, he'd feel her mouth on him long after their time together was over. She wanted him to remember how she felt every time he looked at that calendar and see her when he closed his eyes at night.

"Christ, Dixie, you're killing me," he said through gritted teeth.

The rawness of his voice sent her body into a frenzy. She squeezed her legs together, trying to stave off her own neediness as she worked him faster, squeezed him tighter. His entire body went rigid, his hands tightened in her hair, and she amped up her efforts even more. His hips thrust shockingly hard as he found his release, and her name fell rough and appreciatively from his lips. She continued stroking and sucking, taking everything he had to give, even as he slumped back against the door, his body jerking with aftershocks.

When he finally stilled, panting, his fingers still tangled in her hair, he said, "Come here, kitten," in a craggy, sated voice as he drew her up to her feet. He pressed his lips to hers, and one arm circled her waist, holding her tight against him, as his other hand found her cheek. His thumb brushed over her lips.

"What'd I tell you about calling me *kitten?*" she said softly, her head spinning by how close she felt to him.

"I don't remember. My brain isn't functioning right now."

He touched his forehead to hers in such an intimate embrace, her stupid heart clung hopefully to it. She was there for two more nights. Why not be hopeful? Heck, why not throw caution to the wind and be demanding, too? Hadn't Jace made it clear that this time they had together was her only chance to be with him? She wasn't about to go home regretting not asking for what she wanted.

"Next time don't hold back," she said brazenly.

He lifted his face, gazing deeply into her eyes. She knew he was wondering if she was really asking what he thought she was.

"I won't break, and I know you respect me, so let go next time."

He looked at her like she was asking the impossible. "Dixie…"

She didn't want to hear his excuses. "Do you know *why* I've crushed on you for so long?"

"You've crushed on me?" he asked coyly.

"Shut up. I'll deny it if you ever bring it up again." She liked how her response softened his features. It made the truth come easily. "You're all *man*, Jace, and despite what people say, real men are *not* a dime a dozen. So let me feel all of you, and don't hold back next time."

His forehead touched hers again and he closed his eyes. She closed hers, too, needing a minute to come to grips with what she'd just confessed.

"You wreck me, Dix," he said just above a whisper.

If only he knew how badly he wrecked her, too. But she'd revealed enough secrets for one night, so she said, "Well, I hope you can still walk, because you promised me dinner."

DIXIE MUST HAVE sucked so hard she'd scrambled Jace's brain *and* his emotions. He'd been acting weird all evening, walking with his hand possessively on her back and staring at her for long periods without saying a word. She thought those things might be signs that he was feeling more of what she was feeling, like her crush had just been the tip of the iceberg. But during dinner, interspersed with those long stares were periods when he wouldn't look at her at all. Their conversations were clipped and awkward, and as she watched him pay for the meal, she wondered what had changed.

She smiled at the young waiter, who had been sweetly stealing glances at her since they'd arrived. In fact, she'd noticed several men looking at her. She felt special wearing the gorgeous Leather and Lace outfit, and those appreciative looks made her feel beautiful, too. But Jace hadn't missed those ogling men either. He'd shut down nearly every one of them with harsh glares. She wondered how he could pull off being possessive *and* standoffish at the same time, and she was more than confused by it.

"Come back and see us again," the waiter said, stealing another glance at Dixie before walking away.

"Let's get out of here," Jace said sharply as he pushed to his feet. His hand landed on her back like she was *his* as he guided her toward the doors.

"Why are you acting so weird?" she asked as they stepped through the doors and onto the sidewalk.

"It's been a long day. I just have a lot on my mind."

Dixie stopped walking and crossed her arms. "Bullshit. I thought we had a great day. You were happy with the shoot, and I loved doing it. You sure *seemed* to enjoy my *appetizer*, and you just treated me to a delicious dinner at a nice restaurant. So why are you acting like someone pissed on your motorcycle?"

"I told you. I've got shit on my mind."

She sighed and started walking down the sidewalk at a quicker pace. The sights and sounds of the city were vibrant and loud, but the tension rolling off Jace as he fell into step beside her nearly drowned them out.

"Where are you going?" he asked curtly.

"It's New York City. There must be a bar on every corner. I need a drink."

He took her by the arm and turned her around, walking in the opposite direction. "NightCaps—my buddy's bar—is this way."

"Perfect."

He held on to her arm the whole way to NightCaps, which thankfully was busy enough to be a great distraction from whatever was yanking Jace's chain.

Dixie headed straight for the bar, weaving around men wearing dress shirts and ties and women wearing fancy blouses with professional skirts and dresses, so different from the clientele at Whiskey Bro's. She leaned on the bar, and the bartender turned from where he was mixing drinks. "Hey, handsome. Can I get a bottle of your best tequila and two shot glasses?"

The bartender cocked a grin and said, "You bet."

"Make it a bottle of tequila and a bottle of your best whiskey," Jace said as he came to her side. That big hand of his pressed against her back again.

"Jace! Hey, man, good to see you." The bartender walked over and shook Jace's hand, eyeing Dixie. "I guess this is your beautiful lady?"

"I'm Dixie, and I'm nobody's lady," she said with a smirk.

Jace's jaw muscles bunched again. "Dixie, this is my buddy Dylan Bad. Dixie's the new face of Silver-Stone."

Dylan winked at Dixie and said, "Nice to meet you. It looks like all those months this guy spent looking for the right model finally paid off. Congratulations."

"I'm not a model, but thank you," she said.

"Let me get you those drinks. Nice ink, by the way." Dylan motioned toward Dixie's arms, and then he went to fill their order.

"He seems nice," Dixie said.

"He's happily married to a wonderful woman," Jace said, his eyes skirting over the people around them.

"I don't want to *fuck* him. I was merely mentioning that you had a nice friend."

Dylan put the bottles and glasses on the bar. He reached for a salt rimmer, and Dixie said, "No salt, thanks."

"Lemons or limes?" Dylan asked.

"Limes would be stellar," Dixie said. "Thank you."

He reached under the bar and placed a bowl of sliced limes beside the bottles. "The corner table in the back was being held for my brother and his wife, but they canceled a few minutes ago. Grab it if you'd like some privacy."

"Thank you." Dixie grabbed the tequila, the bowl of limes, and a shot glass, and headed for the table, leaving Jace to trail after her with the other shot glass and the whiskey. She was determined to break through the wall he was erecting, even if it had to happen one drink at a time.

She slid into the semicircular corner booth and turned over the RESERVED sign. Jace slid in beside her, his big body crowding her.

She put space between them and said, "You have to earn the right to sit that close to me."

"I thought I did that last night." He opened the bottle of tequila and filled her glass.

She scoffed. "Does that usually work for you? Dole out a few orgasms and you get anything else you want?"

He scowled as he filled his glass with whiskey.

"No response? Well, I can see this is going to be a fun game."

"Game?" he asked.

"*Shots for secrets.* Cheers." She clinked her glass with his and they downed their shots. She bit into a slice of lime and licked her lips, enjoying the way his eyes followed her tongue.

He refilled their glasses and said, "What are the rules of this game?"

"There's only one rule. *Honesty.* We ask each other questions, and after answering, the person who asked the question takes a shot. If you don't answer, you take the shot. Pretty simple concept, even for a knotted-up guy like you. You *in*, Stone?"

He cracked the first grin of the evening since they'd left the warehouse, and it was a devious one. His eyes took a slow stroll down her chest, and when he finally made it back up to her face, she could practically hear his dirty thoughts as he said, "How can I resist learning your secrets? I'm *in*, Dixie, and I hope to be even deeper *into* you after learning those secrets."

Her traitorous body celebrated, but she managed to keep a

straight face, unwilling to make things that easy for him, and said, "Good luck with that."

"Ready?" She didn't give him a chance to answer. "I'll go first. Why are you being so weird tonight?"

His eyes narrowed, and he gritted his teeth.

"I can see this is going to be a boring game." She pushed his glass closer to him and said, "Last chance. What's up with the hot-and-cold treatment?"

He downed his shot.

"I never pegged you for a chickenshit," Dixie said, but in truth, she hadn't expected him to answer that question right out of the gate. She just couldn't hold it in any longer.

He refilled his glass. "My turn. Why'd you really agree to do the shoot? Was it to screw with your brothers or something else?"

"Both." She nodded at his glass and said, "Drink up."

"You didn't answer the question."

"The hell I didn't. If you wanted details, you shouldn't have given me options. Now, drink up, Stone. I'm getting bored."

He did the shot, and as he filled his glass, she sifted through the questions racing around in her mind, finally landing on the one that had haunted her for years. "What did you really think of me when you first saw me at the rally with Bear? And I want *details*."

This time he didn't hesitate. "I thought you were trouble. You had a gorgeous face, a killer body you flaunted like you knew how to use it. You swore like a sailor, refused to be ignored, and had no regard for Bear's warnings." He leaned closer and lowered his voice to say, "Even then I knew you had the power to bring me to my knees."

Holy shit. That was so much more than she'd hoped. She

grabbed her glass and did the shot, needing the burn to calm her racing heart. "Why did you keep your distance?"

He sat back, leisurely draping his arm over the back of the bench, and said, "I don't think that's how the game works. *One* question, *one* answer."

Damn him.

"My turn," he said as he filled her glass. "Were you a virgin when we first met?"

She felt her cheeks flame, shocked that he'd asked such a personal question. But she had nothing to hide. "Yes."

The surprise in his eyes bothered her. As he drank a shot, she was tempted to ask him an equally intimate question, but decided to catch him off guard instead and asked, "Why did you get into the motorcycle business, and how did you pull it off?"

"That's two questions."

"Okay, then just answer the first part."

"Because bikes don't break hearts." He refilled his drink and said, "I worked at a gas station in high school and learned how to work on cars, and when I went to college, I worked for Maddox's company, Silver Cycles. I worked my way up from the bottom, starting as a mechanic. Most nights I stayed long after everyone else left. Maddox has always been hands-on, like I am with our company. He'd see me hanging around when he was in town, and over the years he became my mentor. I started designing bikes in my spare time, and Maddox let me build a few of them on my own time, in his shop. He's a great guy. He didn't get into any of the legal crap or try to claim rights to whatever I designed. He said he was 'paying it forward.' Right before I graduated from college I showed him the design for the Stroke, the bike I still ride today. I told him my plans to get a loan and open my own company. We both knew the bike had the potential to be huge. He asked if I'd consider working for him. I was a cocky little shit back then, and I said no. The way he tells it, that was the moment he knew we were meant to be partners. But being the arrogant bastard that he is, he waited until I got turned down by several banks before asking if I wanted to partner with him. He later said I needed a dose of reality to kick my cockiness down a notch. Long story short, we partnered, and neither one of us has ever looked back."

"First, that's an incredible story, and second, that was way more of an answer than I deserved, so thank you." She hadn't forgotten his first comment about bikes not breaking hearts, but she didn't want to get off subject before hearing the rest of his story. "It's amazing that he let you partner when you had no money. Didn't you have to buy into the partnership? Usually that's how it works."

"You *are* business minded, aren't you?" He slid her glass across the table and said, "Maddox is one of a kind. He's also a smart businessman. Silver Cycles had been trying to break through the glass ceiling, so to speak, but they kept falling short. He knew my designs would pay off. He advanced me the money to buy into the partnership, and I paid it off when the Stroke line rolled out."

"You're a true rags-to-riches story," she said with awe, and downed her drink.

He filled her glass and said, "It's never been about the money. It's about doing what I love. If Maddox hadn't believed in my designs, I'd have found a way to make it happen. It just might have taken me several years to do it. Now, back to *your* secrets. Have you always been tough as nails? Wait. I have a different question. What factors in your life besides your family made you so tough?"

"You're a quick study." She'd known he would be. "I was always verbally tough. It was either that or defer to my brothers. But Bullet's the one who made me capable of defending myself. Before he went into the military he taught me to fight, and it was a good thing he did." She ran her finger around the rim of her glass as memories trickled in. "I know you want to know what factors other than family made me tough, but honestly, it all comes back to them. When I was young, I could be as much of a big mouth as I wanted, because nobody fucked with the Whiskeys. But when my dad suffered his stroke, with Bullet and Bones away, and just me, Bear, and my mom handling *everything*, I felt a little lost and angry, and there were times when everything was just overwhelming. Or maybe it was most of the time. I don't know. Anyway, I've gotten into one fistfight in my life, and it was during that time. I had a lot of male friends because of the Dark Knights, but not many girlfriends. Most girls didn't know what to make of me because I wasn't like them, going to dances and worrying about hair and makeup. I was busting my butt to try to earn scholarships for college, working my ass off at the bar and at home to help my mom and Bear, and I didn't have patience for any of the normal crap teenage girls cared about. One day in the cafeteria this snotty girl was mouthing off about me. She'd just moved into town and she had no idea who I really was. She knew my family owned a bar, but that was about it. Most of the girls I went to school with respected what my family did for the community enough to keep comments to themselves if they didn't understand me or thought I was a slut. Or they'd write it on the bathroom walls." She paused as old hurt moved through her.

"Dix, that's awful. Why didn't you shut that shit down?"

"Because I had enough on my plate, and I didn't really care what they said."

"Bullshit. You had to care. That shit hurts, even when it shouldn't." He picked up his own glass and said, "I'd have scrubbed those walls clean for you, and then I'd have dealt with the bitches who did it. Here's to you, Dix."

He downed his drink and she felt herself falling harder for him, the same way she had last night and when they'd been together in the dressing room. She knew she shouldn't allow those feelings to take root, and she tried hard to shove them away as she finished telling her story.

"Anyway, the girl was talking crap about how I thought I was tough and that I'd end up working at the bar forever. I've always been proud of my family and of the bar. I lost it, walked right up to her, and with one punch I laid her out flat on her back."

"That's what I'm talking about!" Jace said loudly, making her laugh.

"It felt *good*. I remember that. But then I got suspended and my mother had to come to the school to get me. I had never felt so awful in my life. My mom had enough to worry about. We met with the principal, and I was dead silent, just waiting for my mom to let loose on me. When we got in the car, she said, 'Was all that true?' I admitted that it was and apologized, and she said, 'You defended our family, and I'm proud of that, but you know how I feel about fistfights.' I did. She *hated* them. She said she had to have a talk with Bear for teaching me to fight, and when I told her it was Bullet, she started to laugh. I thought maybe I'd made her so mad she had no other outlet than laughter. But then she said she finally understood what she'd heard Bullet say to me the day he left for the military, 'Never let a bitch knock off your Whiskey crown.'"

Jace was looking at her with a soft, curious expression.

"Did I just ramble and not answer your question?" she asked.

"No. You answered it completely. I was just picturing you in high school with the weight of the world on your shoulders." He shifted closer and then stopped himself and said, "Ask me another question so I can earn a closer seat."

She smiled at that, because she knew it took all of his restraint not to bully his way closer. "Okay, but it's not going to be an easy one."

"I like it *hard*," he said with a wicked glint in his eyes.

"Then we have that in common." She paused, letting her intended meaning sink in. The tightening of his jaw told her it had the impact she'd hoped for. "What led to your broken heart?"

His brows slanted. She covered his hand with hers, holding his gaze. "Think carefully before you take that drink," she said, her heart racing. She knew what she was about to say might backfire, but despite how she probably looked to Jace after what they'd done the last two evenings, she *didn't* sleep around. What she was about to say was important and true. "This is the only *game* I'll play, and I'd rather walk away than sleep with a stranger."

His lips curved up, eyes locked on her as he said, "I wasn't going to drink it. I had just graduated from high school and started hooking up with a woman who was twenty-seven. I was six five by the time I was seventeen. I was tough. Most people mistook me as being in my early twenties. She didn't. She had been my teacher and knew exactly how old I was."

"Oh my God, Jace! Was this your *French* teacher?"

He grinned, lifting one shoulder.

"You hound dog! So, what happened?"

He laughed. "We hooked up a *lot* for a few weeks, always at her place and always in secret. But I was full of testosterone and I was getting laid. I would have fucked her in a tree if she'd asked me to."

"I like your honesty."

He nodded, his eyes hitting his glass as he spoke. "*Just fucking* turned into more for me, and when I told her as much, she said she thought I understood that we were just having fun."

Dixie swallowed hard. *Just like us.* Pieces of Jace's mysteriousness were falling into place. "She broke your heart."

"She said she'd never *really* get involved with a guy like me." His eyes filled with pain. "That's when I learned not to get too close and not to trust *women*. That's a shitty thing to say, sitting here with you, but you wanted honesty. As fucked up as that is, it had a big impact on me. From that moment on, I focused on making myself into *something*. I worked hard at college and have remained emotionally distant from women."

"Like Bullet," she said absently.

"PTSD from the hot high school teacher?" he said with an amused expression. "Sure, I guess so. Like Bullet."

Then she wanted to be his *Finlay*. To earn his trust and show him just how much she believed in him. She scooted closer and said, "For what it's worth, I wanted you before I knew you had a dollar to your name."

"I know, Dix. There's something between us. It was there all those years ago, and it's even stronger now. But that doesn't change who I am or what I have to offer. I'm sorry if I've been a prick tonight. I'm dealing with a lot of shit in my head."

She downed another shot and said, "Another thing we have

in common."

"Have you ever had your heart broken?"

"We'll see," she said, her eyes never leaving his. "The night's still young."

"I DON'T WANT to be the man who breaks your heart."

"I'd have to give it to you first," she challenged with the sexy smirk he saw in his sleep.

Jace knew she was telling stories again, but he was too selfish to walk away. He leaned closer, catching a hitch in her breath, and said, "Lying to yourself again?"

"Maybe we both are..." She eyed his glass. "Drink up. You've used your question. Now it's my turn."

"I think we're both done playing games, Dix."

The smile curving her lips sliced through the last of his remaining tethers. His mouth came down hungrily over hers, taking without hesitation. She kissed him feverishly, their tongues battling for dominance, teeth gnashing.

God, her *mouth*...

It was heaven and hell, luscious and hot and so fucking talented he wanted to feel it on every inch of his flesh. Hell, he wanted to strip them both bare so they could explore each other's bodies until they knew every inch by heart. He leaned in, taking the kiss deeper, and knocked a glass with his elbow. He tore his mouth away and ground out, "Shit," as he slapped napkins over the spill.

He'd completely lost his mind, forgotten they were sitting in a bar. Dixie's skin was flushed, her eyes piercing through his thoughts, begging for more. He recaptured her mouth for one last taste, kissing her for so long, he caught himself getting lost in her again and reluctantly pulled away. He took out his wallet, slapped enough money on the table to pay the whole fucking staff, and climbed from the booth. His entire body throbbed as he pulled Dixie to her feet, taking her in another passionate kiss. *Fuck.* He didn't want to break away even for a second, but they had to get out of there.

"Let's go." He tucked her tight against his side, plowing through the crowd and out the front door, kissing her again the minute they were outside and breaking away only long enough to hail a cab.

He gave the driver his address, and in the next breath he lifted Dixie onto his lap, her knees straddling his hips, and ground out, "Fucking Whiskey fever."

Their mouths crashed together, their hips grinding hard and fast. He pushed his hands beneath her skirt, clutching her ass with one hand, forcing more pressure where they both needed it most. He fisted his other hand in her hair, tugging her head to the side so he could feast on her neck. She gyrated harder with every suck, moaned with every slick of his tongue. He was *this close* to fucking her when the cab pulled over in front of his building.

He quickly paid the driver, and they stumbled onto the sidewalk kissing as they made their way into the building and onto the elevator. He grabbed her hands, pinning them beside her head as the elevator doors closed. He wedged himself between her legs, ravaging her mouth. When the elevator doors opened, they stumbled into the apartment in a tangle of frantic kisses and greedy gropes. He fumbled with the zipper on the back of her skirt, got frustrated, and ripped the seam to shreds.

Dixie's eyes widened. "I loved that outfit," she said as she tugged at the button of his jeans.

"I'll give you ten more. I've been dying to do this all fucking night." He grabbed both sides of her lace shirt and shredded that, too, leaving her bare, save for her panties and boots. Ink snaked around her arms, down her ribs, and along her upper thighs. She wasn't just a beauty or a princess. She was a fucking *queen*.

In the next second, he rid her of those sexy panties, baring the manicured tuft of soft red curls he'd enjoyed last night. She boldly watched as he pulled a condom from his wallet and tore it open with his teeth. He shoved his jeans and briefs down to his knees, and she licked her lips like the sexy minx she was, reaching out to cup his balls as he sheathed himself, drawing a groan from someplace deep inside him. In one swift move, he lifted her into his arms, and her long legs wrapped around him as he entered her in one hard thrust. She cried out, her nails digging into him.

He stilled, hating himself for being too greedy. "Too much?"

"Hell no," she panted out. "*Harder.*"

He drove into her hard and fast. She grabbed his head, feasting on his mouth, unleashing the animal in him. He clutched her ass and used the wall for leverage as he pounded into her. She was so tight and so hot, he was sure the latex would melt right off. Her nails cut into his scalp and her legs squeezed tighter, sending bolts of heat spiking down his spine. He pumped faster, and her mouth left his as her body clamped down on his cock.

"Jace! Oh God, *Ja*—"

She clung to him, her sex clenching, her hips bucking wildly. He struggled to keep from coming with her, gritting his teeth. When her head fell beside his as she came down from the peak, he wasn't even close to done. He kicked off his boots and used his legs to shove off his jeans and briefs. Still buried deep inside her, he carried her to the couch and lowered them both to the cushions. Her hair fanned out around her beautiful face. Her eyes were at half-mast, her lips swollen from their kisses. Her cheeks were pink from the scratch of his beard. She smiled up at him as they found their rhythm, and his heart stumbled. He lowered his mouth to hers, kissing her rougher, more demandingly, trying to chase away the unfamiliar emotions and replace them with pure, unadulterated lust. She wound her legs around him again, allowing him to take her deeper, and when she bit down on his shoulder, her body clenching and thrusting, *holy hell…*

He found *nirvana.*

And he was in no hurry to leave.

He reached over his shoulder and tugged his T-shirt off, dropping it to the floor. Then he pulled off her boots, only to find pink socks with red hearts on them, each heart pierced by a tiny black dagger. If that wasn't the most adorably sexy thing he'd ever seen…and maybe the saddest. He hated the idea of Dixie's heart being pierced.

Then again, knowing Dixie, it was her dagger and someone else's heart.

And that was *hot.*

"Make fun of my socks and I'll castrate you," she said as he pulled them off her feet.

He couldn't resist getting a rise out of her and said, "I want to take a peek in your *lingerie* drawer, see what you're into."

"Right now I'm into *you,* so get busy."

He chuckled, loving how ballsy she was, and he wanted—

needed—more of her, to see *all* of her. He wrapped his arms around her and rolled them over, so she was straddling him, her gorgeous breasts there for the taking. He filled his palm, teasing the taut peak as her eyes swept over the ink on the right side of his chest and followed it down his ribs. When he slipped his other hand between her legs, rubbing her clit, she moaned, moving deliciously along his hard length. Her eyes closed, and she grabbed the back of the couch with one hand, arching as she rode his cock.

"That's my girl. Come for me again."

"*God*, Jace," she said breathily.

He rolled her nipple between his finger and thumb, squeezing just hard enough to feel her sex clench. She moaned as he quickened his efforts with his other hand, pumping his hips faster, until her whole body went rigid and his name sailed from her lips like a curse. She came hard, her body thrusting violently. He rose to a sitting position, taking her mouth in a passionate kiss, her sounds filling his lungs as they rode out her pleasure.

When she collapsed against him, her head on his shoulder, she panted out, "Don't move. I'm too sensitive."

"Toughen up, kitten. I'm going to make you come so hard you'll forget your own name."

He shifted her beneath him again and traveled down her body, in need of a feast. And feast he did, sending her soaring again. But before she came down from the peak, he moved up her body, capturing her pleading mouth as he drove into her, pouring all his pent-up desire into their connection. Heat and pressure spread down his limbs, through his chest, pooling and throbbing in his balls. When he felt her muscles flex and her body tremble, he gave her all he had, sending them both spiraling over the edge of ecstasy. His head spun as his climax tore through him, and he *roared* out her name, feeling like his come had erupted from his *bones*.

He cradled her beneath him, their hearts hammering, both of them breathless and shaky. They lay tangled together until they came back down to earth. Then he kissed her softly and went to take care of the condom. When he returned, his breath caught in his throat. Dixie lay naked on his couch, one arm arced over her head, one knee bent, eyes closed, a sated smile on her lips. She looked like a work of art. He wanted her in his bed, where he could hold her, safe and comfortable, all night long. He scooped her off the couch, half expecting her to bite his head off for doing so, but she remained soft in his arms as he carried her toward the stairs.

"Look at you, going all romantic on me," she said, her arms circling his neck.

He carried her upstairs. She felt so perfect and *right*, like it was exactly where she belonged. The rush of emotions freaked him out a little, so he tried to deny them and said, "You call it romantic. I call it selfish. I want you in my bed so I can take you again as soon as I recover."

He lay her in his bed and climbed in behind her, drawing her into the crook of his body. She snuggled against him. Her soft bottom pressed against his hips, making him hard again. His appetite for her was insatiable, but she was exhausted. The urge to take care of her overrode his greedy desires. She made a sweet sound as she drifted off to sleep. He listened to the rhythm of her breathing, memorizing the feel of her cradled within his arms and body, telling himself there would be no broken hearts because they were both on the same page.

A thick feeling settled in his chest, and he wondered when he'd become such a good liar.

Chapter Eleven

DIXIE AWOKE TO the sound of Jace's hushed voice. He was sitting on the edge of the bed naked, elbows on his knees, talking on the phone. His hair was tousled, revealing a mass of thick curls. Tattoos covered the top of his broad back. The intricate designs trailed down his lats, enhancing the way his body tapered into a sexy vee at his waist. She'd already had more sex in the last few days than she'd had in the last few *years*, and she was looking forward to getting enough to hold her over for several more. She got up on all fours, feeling the remnants of their wild, sexy night all over. Her inner thighs felt like she'd spent hours using an abductor machine. *Jace Stone, the fun abductor*, she mused as she crawled over to him. Her fingers and arms hurt from holding on to him so tightly. Even her jaw was achy from the intensity of their kisses. She cherished each and every one of those pains as she ran her fingers down Jace's arms and kissed the crescent-shaped marks and thin gashes her fingernails had left on the hard ridges of his shoulders and back.

She craved *seconds*. Or more accurately, fifths or sixths. She'd lost count after they'd woken in the middle of the night unable to keep their hands off each other.

Jace turned his head, eyeing her appreciatively. His forehead rested on his palm, his fingers buried in those thick curls. "That sounds great," he said into the phone.

She reached between his legs, fisting his cock. It swelled in her hand, and his jaw clenched. She began stroking him, kissing a path up the back of his neck. She loved feeling his muscles tense, knowing she was driving him crazy.

"We'll look them over and give you a call back," he said roughly, sitting up straighter and turning toward her.

She went up on her knees, brushing her breasts over his beard. He swept his arm around her and grabbed her ass. The restraint in his eyes drove *her* wild. She decided to make him just as crazy and caressed her breasts seductively. She bit her lower lip as she moved one hand between her legs, spreading her knees wide.

"Yeah," he said curtly into the phone, a warning blaring from his eyes.

She wasn't about to heed that warning when she was having fun watching him squirm. Holding his gaze, she sucked her index finger into her mouth, drawing it out slowly, and slipped it between her legs, making hushed pleasure-filled sounds. She pinched her nipple, moaning seductively, and pumped her hips. She could straddle him or drop to her knees in front of him and take him in her mouth. Both of those thoughts made her even wetter, but neither would elicit the response that teasing him was getting. Nothing was more exciting than seeing all his powerful muscles bulging with restraint and flames practically shooting from his eyes.

She dragged her finger, wet with her arousal, over his lips.

He grabbed her wrist, speaking through gritted teeth as he said, "Hawk, I gotta go. I'll get back to you by ten."

He ended the call, dropped the phone on the nightstand, and *growled* as he tackled her to the bed. She laughed, squirming beneath him as he straddled her torso. His eyes were dark as night as he fisted his cock.

She was wrong.

The sight of his big hand wrapped around that magical beast was hotter than anything she'd *ever* seen.

"You want to play, *kitten*?" he asked as he stroked his shaft.

She lifted her hips, excitement beating inside her like a base drum. "I want to watch *you* play."

His eyes narrowed. "Why would I do that when a much sweeter option is lying beneath me, wet and ready?"

"Because I want to see you do it." She could hardly believe she was asking him to touch himself, but there was no time for holding back. She knew the score. Once she stepped on the plane tomorrow morning, that was it. They were done. She'd given herself permission to ask for *everything*—and she was damn well going to get it.

"Sorry, kitten," he said as he climbed off her.

Had she turned him *off*? Disappointment crashed over her.

"There's only one way that's happening." He lifted her hand from the mattress and guided it between her legs as he shifted on the mattress and lowered himself onto his side, facing her with his head by her legs and his cock right in front of her mouth. "I stroke, you suck. I eat, you tease."

His mouth was on her sex even before her *yes* had fully left her lips. *Holy mother of all things delicious.* He stroked his cock as he fucked her mouth, and she teased herself between her legs as he pleasured her with his other hand and his talented tongue. She was swept away by the intensity of every sensation, sucking and licking as his cock pushed in and out of her mouth, rocking her hips as his tongue swept over her fingers and into her sex. It was almost too much to bear. Heat and lust consumed her, pounding and mounting inside her until she cried out around his cock as she came. When her orgasm started to ease, he amped up his efforts, sending her up to the peak again. As if *that* were too much for *him* to bear, he drew his hips back, fucking his fist with only the head of his cock in her mouth, quickly finding his own powerful release.

They lay on their backs for a long time, head to feet, trying to recover. Jace pressed a tender kiss to the top of her foot, her ankle, shin, and knee. She felt a tug in her chest as he worked his way up her hip and ribs. These tender kisses were so different from the way he took and demanded. She had a feeling she was getting a glimpse of a secret side of him he didn't let many people see. Did he let *anyone*? Or was she special? She was good at lying to herself, but not that good. He kissed her shoulder, her neck, and then sank his teeth into her earlobe, just hard enough to make her body flood with heat.

She must be crazy, giving herself so freely to the only man she'd ever really wanted when she knew it was only temporary. At this rate she was going to break her own heart.

He gathered her in his arms, turning her toward him, and pressed his lips to hers.

"You surprised me, kitten."

She'd secretly become fond of the endearment that had previously grated on her nerves, which was weird because she *hated* endearments. That was enough of a red flag for her to dig her heels in and try to stop herself from falling any harder. She knew she had to pull out the tough-girl guns and said, "I'm nobody's *pussy*."

His brows slanted. "Jesus, Dix. Give me some credit. I don't talk like that, and I didn't mean it like that. I would never disrespect you in that way."

Her heart squeezed, and she felt a little guilty, but she had to get her head on straighter. "I know. Sorry. I guess it's my turn to have stuff going on in my head." He still had that serious, upset look on his face, so she tried to change the subject. "What did Hawk say? Do we have a lot of reshoots today?"

"No, actually. Just the opposite. He doesn't think we need to reshoot any of the pictures. He's sending a contact sheet for us to look at so we can make that decision."

"Are you kidding? Wow, that's good, right?"

"It's awesome. I told you you'd be perfect for the shoot. We'll look over the pictures, and if they're good, then you're done. You nailed it."

Her heart sank. *You're done.* Suddenly feeling vulnerable, she sat up, pulling the sheet over her nakedness, and reached for her phone. "I guess I should see about changing my flight."

He covered her hand with his, lowering the phone to her lap, and said, "Slow down there, kit—*tiger*. We still need to check out the pictures."

She had to smile at *tiger*, but her amusement faded with the realization that she might be leaving to go home today instead of tomorrow.

He brushed his fingers over her hand and said, "I was thinking that if we don't have to reshoot any of the pictures, I could show you around the city, take you for a ride on one of the Legacy bikes."

"I'm not sure that's such a good idea," she said tentatively, trying to protect herself from falling any harder for him.

He kissed her shoulder, and in a softer tone, he said, "Selfishly, I think it's an excellent idea. But even if it were a bad idea, when has that ever scared you out of doing something?"

She loved the way he *got* her. He embraced her snark and toughness, challenged her at times when most men would back down. She wasn't ready to give that up just yet.

"What do you say, Dix? Nobody's expecting you back until tomorrow. It's not like you're taking advantage of anyone." He leaned closer and said, "But if you play your cards right, I'll let you take advantage of me." He traced the lines of her tattoo on her forearm. "I was also thinking about how much I'd like to get my ink in you."

"Is that a weird *octopus* metaphor?"

"*Ink*, Dixie. You know I'm a tattooist, right?"

She'd forgotten. "I think I remember hearing that at some point. Do you tattoo all the women you sleep with? Brand them with *Jace was here*?"

He ran his hand down her thigh and said, "I don't *sleep* with women. I *fuck*, *hook up*, or whatever you want to call it, but I don't *sleep* with them." He pushed from the bed and pulled her to her feet, holding her against him. "Forget I said anything. I'm hitting the shower. Want to *come*?" He arched a brow when he said *come*.

How could she deny an offer like that? "*Always*. I'll be right there."

He walked into the bathroom, and she grabbed her phone to check messages from last night. She'd missed messages from Jayla, a few from Crystal and Izzy, and one from Bullet.

She opened and read Bullet's message first. *Did you kick ass today?* She typed, *I think so. It was fun. Everything okay there?*

She read Jayla's text next. *I LOVED the pics Jace sent during the shoot! You are a natural!* She liked all of Jace's sisters and had texted with them yesterday before the shoot. She sent her a quick response, thumbing out, *Thank you! Rush's advice was perfect. It really helped!*

Crystal and Izzy had sent almost identical messages. Each of them had sent one wishing her luck and another asking how it had gone. As she responded to Crystal, telling her it went great and she'd loved it, another text from Izzy popped up. *Never heard from you yesterday. Hope it went well. If you're okay, send me a*—she inserted a thumbs-up emoji. *If you need me to send your brothers to kick Jace's ass, send me a*—she inserted a thumbs-down emoji.

Dixie responded with an eggplant emoji and a smiley face with heart eyes. She texted, *Can you still pick me up at the airport? I might need a stiff drink.*

She heard the water running just as her phone vibrated with Izzy's response. *Of course! I need details.*

Dixie sent a quick thank-you to Izzy; then she headed into the bathroom. Jace opened the glass shower door, and steam billowed out. *Lord*, he looked good dripping wet. He treated her to a rare, genuine smile that was neither seductive nor coy. It was just *Jace*, and it was the most wonderful smile of all.

He reached for her and said, "Come here, beautiful. Let me thank you properly for saying you'll stay…"

This man, naked and in the mood to *give*, was a deadly combination. He'd been right to think he had the power to ruin her for all other men, but oh what a glorious ruining it would be.

191

AFTER WALKING DOWN to one of Jace's favorite cafés for breakfast, they returned to his apartment to go over the contact sheets Hawk emailed to Jace. They were in his home office, viewing images on two computers with large monitors. There were sketch pads with drawings of random designs and motorcycles on the desk, the end table, and even the sofa. But she didn't have time to look through them. Hawk had taken *hundreds* of shots, as if he hadn't stopped to take a breath during the entire shoot. He'd even taken several pictures of Jace throughout the day, talking on the phone or with the guys handling the bikes, leaning against the building, or gazing at something in the distance with a faraway expression. Those were the pictures that fascinated her most. Her favorite was a picture of him leaning against a brick wall. One booted foot was on the ground, his other knee was bent, the sole of his boot resting on the brick. His head was tipped back, eyes closed, a bottle of water pressed to his lips. Dixie had been so busy every second yesterday, she hadn't had time to slow down and admire him. Boy was he worth admiring. He looked like a badass model who should have a calendar all his own.

Jace sat back in his chair with an incredulous smile, shaking his head. "Well, Dix, if you ever had any doubt that you were born to be the face of Silver-Stone, here's the proof."

She glanced at the images on the other screen. She couldn't believe she was looking at herself. The woman in the pictures was gorgeous, so unlike the way she saw herself. The gritty background of the warehouse enhanced the radiance of the sleek and shiny motorcycles. But it was the clothes that Jace had helped design that added an unexpected level of elegance to the pictures. She was proud that she hadn't let him down, but even more than that, she was grateful to have been part of such an important project.

"I don't think we need to reshoot any of these. You're gorgeous in every one of them. What do you think?"

"*Me?*" She couldn't believe he was asking. "All I know is that I want copies of the pictures of *you*, in my own calendar."

He laughed, and it was the best sound ever. He didn't laugh often, and she'd miss it when she went back home.

"It's your company, Jace. That's your decision. I'm just proud to be part of your project. I still can't believe that's *me* in those pictures. Your bikes and clothes sure do make me look good."

"I think it's the other way around, Dix."

"I doubt that. But I'm really glad you talked me into doing the calendar. I'm sorry I didn't realize how amazing it would be when you first mentioned it. I was thinking pinup girl, and you really were envisioning a work of art. I loved doing the shoot and working with you and Hawk. This was an experience I'll never forget." Butterflies took flight in her stomach at that last little reveal, which had as much to do with their private time together as the shoot.

She was looking forward to spending another whole day and an incredible night in the arms of the man who was more generous, family oriented, and *delicious* than she could ever have imagined. So why did that chance feel like a double-edged sword?

He covered her hand with his and squeezed. "I can't believe I almost settled for Sahara. That would have been a big mistake. I should have come to you in the first place."

His eyes lingered on hers, looking deeper than just a friendly glance. She wondered if he meant he wished *they'd* gotten together sooner, not just for the shoot.

As if he'd read her thoughts and they'd scared him away, he shifted his eyes back to the screen and let go of her hand.

"Honestly, I don't know how we'll choose from all these pictures," he said casually. "You're gorgeous in every one of them. Next week's merchandising meeting should be interesting. That's when we're choosing the pictures for the calendars and other merchandising. Why don't I reach out to Hawk and my assistant and let them know we don't need to reshoot? Then we can go out for a celebratory ride."

A motorcycle ride was exactly what she needed to break free from the whirlwind of thoughts and emotions inside her.

IF ANYTHING COULD get Jace out of a fog, it was the wind on his face and the open road, and after drooling over pictures of Dixie all morning, he needed it. The only problem was that the cause of that fog had been molded to his back for the past hour, and *man*, riding had never felt so good. But that fog still remained, and as he pulled into his parents' driveway, he ground out a curse, having no idea why he'd driven straight there. Thank God his parents were at work.

He climbed off the bike and took off his helmet, drinking in Dixie, still straddling the motorcycle in a tight black tank top, her faded jeans tucked into her leather boots. Damn she looked good, like she belonged on the back of his bike. His mind slowed her motions as she took off her helmet and shook her head, her red mane tumbling down her back. He offered her his hand, but she gave him an amused look and climbed off herself, gazing up at his childhood home, a modest three-bedroom

Colonial.

"Whose house is this?"

"This is my parents' house, but they're not home." Thinking quick, he said, "They asked me to take a look at their kitchen sink. It's on the fritz, and I figured since we were out anyway…"

"Cool," she said as they went to the side entrance. "Did you grow up here?"

He unlocked the door and waved her in. "Yeah. I used to play football out back with my buddies."

"Mm. It smells like freshly baked bread."

"My mom has always made bread. It's kind of her *thing*. When we were little, she'd pack it in our school lunches. She always said homemade bread would remind us that we were loved. As if we could ever forget." He opened the bread box on the counter and said, "Make yourself at home. Want a slice?"

"No, thanks. But that's really sweet that she baked for you guys."

She followed him into the living room, her eyes moving over the couches and coffee table to the Stone Wall of Shame, where his mother had every embarrassing picture ever taken on display. She hurried over to it, pointing to a picture of Jace at fifteen. His hair was long and bushy, and he was dressed in black jeans and a black t-shirt with a black-and-gray flannel shirt overtop and black army boots, the laces hanging open.

"Was it always your dream to be the lead singer of Pearl Jam?" she teased.

He laughed and hooked his arm around her neck, tugging her against him. "I went through a grunge phase. Give me a break. It was the nineties."

"I see, and when you were little you wanted to be Elton

John?" She pointed to a picture of him at seven, wearing a flashy light blue suit and big round sunglasses.

"You're a brat," he said in her ear, and kissed her cheek. "My mom made that suit, and I was very proud of it. My friends and I were in a talent show at school."

"What was your talent? Being extra cute?"

He smiled. "Magic."

She turned and wound her arms around his neck. "You have lots of secret talents, don't you, Mr. Stone?"

The adoring look in her eyes made his insides go soft. Dixie had a way of turning off her edge and going sweet on him, as she was now, as if standing in his childhood home looking at pictures was the most natural thing in the world. She made him want things he had never wanted before, like sharing pieces of himself he'd never even thought about sharing before.

"You tell me," he said, his arms circling her waist.

He touched his lips to hers, but one tender kiss wasn't enough, and he kissed her again, slow and deep, feeling her melt against him. He continued kissing her, telling himself the warmth inside him was just lust. But when their lips finally parted, he was swamped with the emotions he'd been trying to outrun.

"I have a feeling I don't want to know most of your secrets." She slipped from his arms and pointed to a picture of him with his sisters. He stood tall and lanky with his arms around all three of them. "How bad were you when your sisters were teenagers? Did you scare off the guys they dated?"

"Sometimes, if they were dirtbags. But mostly I just watched out for them, stood back until they needed me."

"As a sister, I'll tell you that sometimes we won't tell our brothers when we need them the most. I went out with a guy once who tried something that I wasn't into. I got out of the situation, and I should have told Bear, since he was the only one home then. But I never did because I was too embarrassed."

"Lucky for the guy. I'm sure Bear would have maimed him. Unfortunately, I know all about those situations. Jennifer missed dinner with me one night a couple years ago. She said she was sick, but I heard something in her voice that told me otherwise. She sounded *broken*. I went to see her, and she had a bruise on her arm from a guy she went out with. I told you I don't lie, but I just realized that I have lied to her. I promised I wouldn't do anything about it. The guy was a teacher at another school and she didn't want any drama. But I found him, beat the hell out of him, and made him leave town."

"Leave *town*? Isn't that a little extreme?"

Jace shook his head. "I gave him a choice. Turn himself into the police or get the fuck out of town so I didn't have to worry about him trying to get back at Jen. He left town three weeks later, and I contacted a cop buddy of mine in the area where he moved and warned him about what'd happened. He found the guy and told him he'd be watching him. He said if he saw or heard anything he didn't like, he'd put his ass in jail."

"Why didn't you just have him arrested?"

"Because he would have gotten out too fast. I wanted him to feel like he was always being watched. Honestly, I wanted to scare the piss out of him so he'd think twice about making another wrong move."

"You could have gone to jail for beating him up," she pointed out.

"After I took care of him." He winked.

"Okay, *Knuckles*, tell me about this guy right here. Is this your dad?"

She pointed to a picture of Jace at twelve years old standing next to his first mini bike with his father, smiling like a fool and holding a helmet under his arm.

"Yes. That's my old man. He's an electrician and a really great guy. The best thing about my dad is that he'd rather give you a challenge than tell you no, and he always keeps his word. When I was ten, I asked him if I could get a mini bike. He didn't want me to ride one. He's very conservative, and I was a rambunctious kid with a wild streak. I'm sure he saw trouble ahead, but instead of putting his foot down, he said I could get one when I was twelve *if* I could pay for it myself. Never in a million years did he think I'd make that happen, but I was a resourceful little bugger. I went door to door to all of my friends' parents' houses offering to do anything for money. I washed and cleaned out cars for a buck fifty, walked to the corner market and brought back groceries, fed animals when people were away, walked dogs, shoveled snow in the winter. I saved up a hundred and twenty bucks for a ratty old bike. But my old man was so proud of me for having the wherewithal to pull it off, he helped me put a new engine in it, and then he paid a guy he knew from work, his friend Morty, to teach me to ride."

"Your dad sounds like a great father. It's no wonder you turned out like you did."

"My old man's a better man than me."

"Why would you say that?"

He shrugged. "Because he is as selfless as they come. He's been with my mother since they were teenagers. He raised five kids, put up with all our bullshit, and I can't remember ever once hearing him badmouth anyone. There's no comparison between a guy who's given his life to make others happy and a guy who lives only for himself."

"You say you live for yourself, but I've seen enough evidence to know that's not true. Don't think I wasn't listening when your sisters mentioned the scholarships and mentorship programs you put together. A guy who only lives for himself doesn't do those things." She took his hand and said, "Show me your room, *Knuckles*. But don't get any ideas, because there will be no dirty business going on under your parents' roof."

He chuckled as they headed downstairs. "There are only three bedrooms upstairs. My dad and I built a room in the basement, and Jared and I shared it."

"That must have cramped your style with the ladies."

He looked at her out of the corner of his eyes as he opened the basement door. "I never brought women here. It would have been too disrespectful to my parents."

"So, tell me the truth—was your French teacher your first?" she teased. "Did you age yourself *up* so you didn't seem like a ballsy kid but really you were sixteen or something?"

"My sixteen-year-old self *wishes*. No. My first time was when I was seventeen, with a girl I met over the summer. She was twenty and just passing through town with her friends."

"I think it's adorable that badass Stone didn't get any until he was almost out of high school."

He stopped at the bottom of the stairs and said, "It wasn't adorable. It was a *choice*. How old were you your first time?"

"Twenty-one," she said without hesitation. "It was right before college graduation with a guy I'd known for three years. We were study partners. He was a total math geek, complete with high waters and thick glasses, and I just adored him. Not in a sexy way, but as a friend. His name was Ritchie Meyers. I didn't want to come back to Peaceful Harbor without having experienced being with a man, so I asked him if he wanted to sleep with me."

"Are you being serious right now? I saw how you looked, and *acted*, at eighteen. You must have had guys crawling all over you."

"Sure I did, but that's never been a turn-on to me. I told you I prefer *real* men, and real men don't chase every tail they see. They only chase the one that means something."

Holy shit. That explained a lot, including just how much respect Dixie had for herself. "But *you* propositioned *him?*"

"I did. He was a gentleman and I trust him."

"Are you still in touch with the lucky bastard?"

"From time to time. He's married and lives in New Hampshire."

"Well, Dix, you're even more impressive than I thought you were. Thanks for sharing that with me."

He walked through the recreation area and pushed open his old bedroom door, revealing what was now his mother's sewing room.

"Aw," she said with a disappointed expression. "I was looking forward to seeing posters of half-naked women, bikes, and pinup calendars."

He laughed. "You're about a decade too late. My mother took those down as soon as Jared moved out." He motioned toward the left side of the room and said, "That was Jared's side. He's several years younger than me, so I was a teenager when he was still just a boy. He used to drive me crazy asking all sorts of questions about everything I did. He'd steal my cell phone and send goofy pictures to my contacts. He was a real pain in the ass, but man, I'd have killed for him."

"Seems like you still would."

"You know it." He pulled her into his arms and kissed her.

She asked to see the yard, and they went outside. It was a beautiful day, and after much urging on her part, they walked down to the auto shop around the corner to see where he'd had his first real job.

When they finally climbed onto the bike to head back to the city, she said, "You didn't look at the sink."

Damn. "I'll do it when I see them tomorrow night for dinner."

She cocked her head, studying his face, and said, "You'd never leave a broken sink. Why did you really take me here?"

He felt a smile tugging at his lips and climbed on the bike in front of her as he said, "I honestly have no idea. I blame it on Whiskey fever."

Chapter Twelve

"I FEEL LIKE I'm in a video game or something," Dixie said in a hushed and hurried voice, clinging to Jace's arm as they walked around Times Square. The clouds had rolled in and their sunny day had turned gray, but that hadn't slowed her down or stolen the delight from her eyes. "All these people are staring at their phones. How do they walk so fast without bumping into anyone? I swear New Yorkers must have invisible sensory antennae, because I'd bump into everyone if I did that."

Jace chuckled. After their impromptu jaunt to his parents' house, which still had him a little boggled, they'd dropped off his bike at his place and set out on foot to explore the city. He thought he knew everything there was to know about the Big Apple, but seeing it through Dixie's eyes was like looking at a whole different world. They'd grabbed slices of pizza for a late lunch, and she'd insisted on eating outside as she people watched. She noticed things he'd never given a second thought, just as she was now. And she picked up scents like a blood-hound. To Jace, the city smelled like garbage and occasionally like roasted peanuts. But Dixie followed her nose to the Portuguese bakery, where they shared the most delicious honey cake he'd ever eaten, and she stopped to smell the flowers at a floral shop he must have walked past hundreds of times and had never really thought about. He wondered if she'd been that happy when she'd received the roses he'd sent.

She looked up at him and said, "Please tell me you're not usually like all these people."

"I could, but it would be a lie."

"Oh my God, *really*? The guy who found the most beautiful spot in all of Peaceful Harbor takes the incredible sights and sounds of *this* city for granted? That's a shame."

"That's life, Dix. Don't you ever get so busy back home that you don't take time to see the sights of the harbor?"

She shook her head. "Nope. Every time I walk outside I can smell ocean breezes, or if I'm across town, I'm admiring the mountains. I love it all, and I wake up happy to be there. I mean, the city is really cool, but I would never want to live here. If I did, though, I'd want to experience it each day. Otherwise how boring would life be? I'd feel like a robot going from cabs to buildings, moving through life without really living."

"Says the woman who doesn't want to go into any of the shops. Not that I'm complaining, but I thought all women liked to shop."

"The only thing I want to shop for are gifts for my babies, but if you need something, we can shop."

"Your *babies*? Do you have a double life I don't know about?"

"I mean my nieces and nephews. Can you imagine their sad little faces if they knew Auntie Dixie went all the way to New York and didn't bring them anything? I'm not into breaking hearts. We need to find a few toys."

They stopped at the corner to wait for the light to change,

and while Dixie was checking out people and skyscrapers, Jace's eyes were riveted to her. He had the same love for experiencing the world, but not when he was in the city. When he was in any of the big cities where he worked, he was usually hunkered down and focused on business. Dixie made him want to reevaluate that part of himself. Why did he overlook the very things he loved about life when he was in those places? It wasn't like he couldn't focus on work while still taking time to enjoy the areas. She was right about Peaceful Harbor, though. He'd found that spot, and he'd returned there every time he was in town. It called out to him, but what that meant, he wasn't sure.

She pointed across the street and said, "There's a souvenir shop."

"That's crap. We should go to FAO Schwarz and get them something really special," he suggested.

"Oh, *fancy*. Okay, Mr. Moneybags." The light changed, and the crowd pushed forward. Dixie held on tight and said, "You lead. I'll follow."

"It's about a ten-minute walk. Are you up for it? We can take a cab if you want."

"Are you kidding? And miss out on all this?" She waved one hand. "Let's walk."

They headed for Rockefeller Center, and from the moment they entered FAO Schwarz, Dixie's eyes were wide with fascination. She dragged Jace over to the big dance-on piano with neon lights around the keys, above which was a mirror image on the ceiling.

They waited in line, and when it was Dixie's turn, she stepped onto the keys and reached for his hand. "Come on. Do it with me."

"Go for it. I'll watch," he said, enjoying seeing her so carefree.

She crossed her arms, jutted out her sexy hip, and tapped her foot on one of the keys in a monotonous rhythm. "Unless you want to torture all these people with this sound, you'd better join me."

Just as Jace was about to relent, an adorable little boy with a shock of black hair bounced on his toes and said, "I'll play with you!"

"I would love that, if your mama says it's okay." Dixie smiled warmly at the woman holding his hand.

"Me too!" another little boy yelled.

"Can I play, too?" a little girl with pigtails asked her father.

Dixie waved them all up to the keyboard and proceeded to dance across the keys with the giggling children in tow. Jace took pictures as she hopped and danced, earning unforgettable smiles from the children and their parents.

When she finally came off the keyboard, the kids hugged her, the parents thanked her, and Jace fell a little harder for the enchanting redhead who was changing his world one minute at a time.

More than an hour later they walked out with gifts for all of Dixie's *babies*, which he found out didn't just extend to Bones and Sarah's three children, but also to Truman and Gemma's little boy and girl and Jed and Josie's son. She was particular about the gifts being just right for each child, and it was fascinating to watch her choose. She bought a pink stuffed unicorn for Bones and Sarah's new baby, Maggie Rose, because she said Maggie Rose was unique in that Sarah was pregnant with her when she and Bones first met. She bought a yellow cab for Bradley, who loved cars, and a street cleaner for Hail, who was into *work trucks*. She said she was going to tell them all about the city and knew they'd want to play Big Apple afterward. She bought an adorable stuffed giraffe for Lila, who was a year and a half, because *as the middle child, she needs to stand out.* For Kennedy she bought a make-your-own fairy garden because she loved all things fairy and princess related, and for Lincoln she got a tiny drum with a trumpet and a tambourine inside, because he loved banging on things.

"You're going to need a suitcase just for these gifts," he said, carrying her shopping bags as they left the store.

"But can you imagine their happy little faces?"

As they walked to Rockefeller Center, he looked up at the darkening clouds, hoping the rain would hold off a little while longer, and said, "You're a thoughtful auntie, Dix."

"Thanks. From what I saw the other night, you're a pretty fab uncle, too. Have you ever thought about having kids?"

"Never…" He debated the rest of his answer, having hardly admitted the truth to himself, but one look at Dixie and it came out unbidden. "Until Thane was born."

"*Interesting.* Are you saying that Mr. No Roots has the baby itch?"

"*No,*" he said with a shake of his head. Baby itch? Was there such a thing? "I'm not ready for kids, and I'm not ready to give up my freedom, but that sweet boy makes me feel something I've never felt before. Seeing him with Jay and Rush gave me perspective and made me realize if I don't have a family one day, I might miss out on something pretty incredible."

They came to the area that served as an ice rink in the winter but was now filled with diners eating under umbrellas, but Dixie was looking at *him*, not the view.

"What?" he asked.

She looked away and said, "Nothing."

He leaned over the railing, the pit of his stomach sinking. He couldn't even bring himself to think about Dixie in the arms of another man, much less having children with them. "I bet you'll be a great mom, Dix."

"Thanks."

He tried to quell that unfamiliar ache in his gut and changed the subject. "This is the ice skating rink in the winter. Do you skate?"

"I've never tried." She moved closer and nudged him with her shoulder. "What about you? I can't imagine you on skates. Then again, I never imagined you in a bright blue suit, either."

He hooked his arm around her neck, making her laugh. "I used to be great at it. You'll have to come out this winter and I'll teach you." He led her toward the Channel Gardens, which was what he'd really wanted to show her.

The Channel Gardens were built in a narrow promenade between two large buildings. They were one of the city's greatest secrets, with six granite pools and fountains, each with a large fountainhead sculpture, surrounded by beautiful flowers and leafy plants. Just as he'd hoped, Dixie's face brightened when she saw them, and it lit *him* up inside.

"What is *this*, right here in the middle of the city?" She hurried over, touching the plants with her fingertips.

"The Channel Gardens. I thought you'd like them."

"It looks like you *haven't* had your nose in your phone every time you were here after all." She leaned into him. "These are gorgeous." She pointed to one of the sculptures. "Is that a sea nymph?"

He nodded. "The sculptures are nereids and tritons. Two hundred years ago this was the site of the first botanical garden in the state." He pointed to the buildings and said, "That's the

British Empire Building and the La Maison Francaise. The promenade we're walking along represents the English Channel that separates the two countries for which the buildings were named."

Dixie looked up at him with a curious expression. "How do you know all of that? Oh wait, I almost forgot that you liked history. I didn't realize how much until I saw your bookshelves this morning. They're loaded with history books."

"I told you I liked history."

"But you didn't say you were a history *buff*." A raindrop fell on the apple of her cheek. Another hit her eyelashes. She closed her eyes and tipped her face up toward the sky. Dixie opened her eyes when it started raining harder, turned her palms up, and twirled as rain pelted her. Her arms glistened, her shirt quickly became drenched, and her hair stuck to her shoulders.

All around them people rushed for shelter, and there was Dixie, the badass biker who could bring a man to his knees with one cutting remark, twirling and laughing.

She was utterly and completely mesmerizing.

Clutching the bags in one hand, Jace drew her into his arms, and when their eyes connected, the truth spilled out. "You are too damn hard to resist."

He lowered his mouth to hers, and in that moment he didn't feel the sheeting rain slicking his skin or hear the traffic noises that had never before seemed to halt. There was only Dixie's softness pressed against him, her warm, eager kisses, and the sweet pleasure-filled sounds luring him deeper in to her.

Jace didn't know how long they stood in the promenade making out, but when thunder rumbled and lightning split the sky, they both startled. He kept her close as they ran for the street, and he hailed a cab. They climbed into the cab, soaked to the bone, laughing and kissing on the ride to his place, and continued in the elevator. They stumbled into his apartment in fits of laughter. He couldn't remember the last time he'd had so much fun. As they tugged off their boots, he realized this was the last time he'd come home with Dixie. Hell if that didn't gnaw away at him. He liked his solitude, *thrived* on it.

And yet here he stood, unable to imagine coming home without her tomorrow after he dropped her off at the airport.

THEY CHANGED OUT of their wet clothes, and Dixie towel-dried her hair, feeling lighter and happier than she had in a long time. They had Thai food delivered and ate while sitting on the couch, serenaded by the driving rain against the windows. The dark evening sky stole what light had lingered when they'd arrived, leaving a romantic glow throughout the loft. It felt strangely natural to be sitting on Jace's couch in her cutoffs and T-shirt, sharing food from each other's plates and talking about silly things.

"Favorite food?" she asked, her eyes trailing down his jeans to his bare feet. Even his feet were sexy.

He waggled his brows and said, "Do you even have to ask? It's *you*, Dix." He snagged a noodle from her plate. "If you could go anywhere in the world, where would you go?"

"I used to think it would be cool to go far away, like Greece or Paris. Someplace exotic and special." But after the last couple days, the thought of going anyplace special without him just felt lonely.

"And now?"

"I went on a road trip alone last fall, and besides the ride, which of course was great, what I enjoyed most was seeing my cousins and meeting friends. I don't think being a solo world traveler is in the cards for me. You travel a lot and seem to like it. Where do you go from here, after I leave?"

He set his plate on the coffee table and took a drink of his whiskey. "I'm meeting with Maddox in Boston Thursday, and then I head to LA to prepare for the launch. Back to business as usual. How about you? You're going to the Cape next week for Justin's art show?"

"Yes. I'm going to the opening on Wednesday, and I'll come back Sunday for *my business as usual*."

"Are you staying with your cousin?"

She set her plate down and turned to face him. "No. I didn't want to cramp Justin's style. One of the girls who runs the book club works at Bayside Resort, which is right on the water in Wellfleet. I rented a cottage there."

"Not too shabby."

"It should be fun. Thanks for letting me stay here with you. I bet you'll be glad to have your place to yourself again," she said a little tentatively.

He put his arm across the back of the couch, brushing his fingers along her arm. "I'm not looking forward to it, Dix. It's been nice having you here."

"I've had a great time." She was itching to know more about his life, and she knew this might be her only chance. "Can I ask you a personal question? You don't have to answer."

"Go for it."

"I'm just curious what your life is really like. I know you own the company with Maddox and you design bikes, and it seems like you're always going places to open offices or shops, but I don't really know what you *do*."

He finished his drink and set the glass on the table. "I guess you could say that I oversee the creative aspects and expansion of our business, while Maddox's forte is the business itself. We have directors of operations and managers who oversee our operations and report back to us. Maddox and I work together to review operations on a monthly basis, but he oversees the business end on a day-to-day basis, while I focus on scouting new locations, working with our engineers and designers to come up with future concepts, that sort of thing. I work primarily out of LA, but once we close the deal for the Boston headquarters, that'll be my home base. I've got an assistant who keeps my days in order, and she's got underlings who report to her."

"And when you travel, do you have girlfriends in different areas? Do you have buddies everywhere you go, like you do in Maryland?"

"Girlfriends?" He shook his head with a cocky smile. "No ties, Dix. You know that about me. I'm not an asshole, but I'm sure as hell nobody's Prince Charming, either. If I meet a woman I'm interested in, we might hook up, but that's the extent of it. And despite what you might think, I'm not a guy on the prowl, getting together with women left and right. That's not my priority. I put all of my focus into growing the business and have been doing that forever. Sex has never been anything more than a way to kill some stress."

She swallowed that bitter pill and said, "You really don't answer to anyone."

He shook his head. "I haven't in so long, I don't think I'd know how without fucking it up."

That stung, but she'd known that about him, hadn't she?

He'd been nothing but honest, and she couldn't blame him for her hopeful heart.

"How about you, Dix? I can't believe you're not hooking up with guys behind your brothers' backs."

"Isn't that what I've spent the last forty-eight hours doing?"

He laughed. "You've got me there."

"I try to meet guys through friends," she said honestly. "But I haven't found anyone worth hooking up with for so long, it's embarrassing. And now that you've ruined me for all men…" She said it lightly, just to hear that laugh again, and she was rewarded in kind.

"Damn, you are good for my ego." He leaned closer and slipped his hand to the nape of her neck, bringing their faces so close she could smell the whiskey on his breath. He looked into her eyes and said, "You're good for my soul, too. I'll never forget a minute of our time together."

Her heart skipped. She wanted to remember every second of it, too. "Do you still want to tattoo me?"

"Almost as badly as I want to kiss you."

That made her feel good all over. "Do you tattoo lots of women?"

"Never. That would be like bringing a woman to my apartment. It's not something I do."

"I'm here," she reminded him.

"I know. I'm still trying to figure out how you managed that."

She smiled. "You *invited* me."

"That's what I meant. How'd you get so deep into my head before I even kissed you that I forgot my own rules?"

"That's what I want to remember on my way home tomorrow, so shut up and kiss me, Stone. If I like it, I'll let you tattoo me."

"No pressure or anything," he said as he lowered his mouth to hers.

His rough hand gripped the back of her neck as he moved over her, his broad chest pressing against her. He made love to her mouth as thoroughly as he made love to her body. His tongue swept deep and invasive, his mouth ground against hers, and he made the most appreciative, *erotic* sounds. Her skin flamed from scalp to toes. When their lips finally parted, she was light-headed.

His cheek touched hers and he whispered, "Shall I get my tattoo supplies?"

"Uh-huh," she said absently.

He kissed her again, and she drank in every delicious second of it. When he disappeared into his office, she tried to pull herself together, sitting up straighter and looking around the loft. She heard him opening drawers in his office and realized she didn't want to rush the blissful feeling away. She closed her eyes and let her head rest on the back of the couch, enjoying the racing of her heart, the swoony, dizzying feeling, and the lingering taste of him in her mouth.

She felt his body heat before his hands touched the couch on either side of her shoulders and his lips pressed against hers. These were the moments dreams were made of, and she was so glad she got to have them with Jace.

"You must really trust me," he said, gazing down at her from behind the couch.

Her head was still resting against the back of the couch. "Don't get carried away. I trust you enough to give me a tattoo where I can see it. I don't want to end up with your name tattooed above my ass."

He cocked a brow as he rose and said, "Now, there's an idea."

She scowled.

"It's an honor to put my mark on you, Dix. You tell me where, and I promise not to brand you with my name."

She realized that if the situation were different, she'd proudly let him brand her with his name. "Where are you thinking?"

"Someplace you'll see it, so you'll think of me."

"You're like moss, Jace. You've invaded every inch of me. I'm pretty sure I'll think of you even without a tattoo." She held out her left arm and turned it over. "The inside of my wrist?"

He lifted her wrist to his lips and pressed a kiss there. "Perfect. Let me grab a table for my supplies and get set up."

He turned on music, set up a light, a table, and a chair beside the couch, and prepared his tools. When he was ready, he carefully cleansed the inside of her wrist. "Nervous?"

"No." She wasn't nervous at all, but she was curious. "What are you going to draw or write?"

"You'll see," he said as he grabbed his tattoo gun. "Is a little color okay?"

"Of course. Don't you need to draw it first?"

"Freehand, baby. It's the only way." His eyes flicked up to hers. "Ready?"

"Yes. Is it going to be something you designed?"

His eyes narrowed. "Do you think I'd draw someone else's design on you?"

"Not really, but I wondered. How long have you been thinking about doing this, that you're ready to go so fast?"

The side of his mouth lifted, and he said, "You don't want to know."

Oh yes she did! But she wouldn't push, because believing

he'd been thinking about giving her a tattoo for a long time felt fantastic, and clarification might bring disappointment.

She watched him work. He had a gentle touch, and his whole face changed as he worked. There was an intensity to his eyes that was different from the type of tension she was used to seeing on him—caused by restraint or desire.

"How'd you get into doing this?" she asked.

He wiped excess ink from her wrist, his eyes meeting hers for a second, then focused on the tattoo again. "When I was in college I used to draw custom tats for money, and I realized I could make more doing them. I did that for a while, but then I realized I didn't like tattooing the crap college kids wanted done, so I went back to drawing and reserved tattooing for my buddies, whose tats were meaningful."

"Did you do any of your own tattoos?"

"If I can reach it, chances are, I did it," he said as he dragged the tattoo gun across her skin.

Jace didn't say much as he worked, and Dixie was just fine with that. She liked watching him concentrating, feeling his hands on her, knowing he was marking her with something he designed. An hour bled into two as he added colors, working patiently. Dixie was curious about the design, but she was even more interested in the man holding the tattoo gun. He'd said meaningful things as casually as he had said line-defining comments, leaving just enough gray area for her to play with in both directions.

She tried not to look at the ink on her wrist, focusing on *him* instead. She felt as though she were an outsider watching a private moment, made even more special because he was doing something he loved for *her*.

A long while later he wiped her wrist, studying the design,

and said, "Almost done."

He touched up a few spots, and when he finally set his tools down for the last time, he rolled his shoulders back and stretched his neck to either side. He reached for a cloth and dampened it with rubbing alcohol.

As he wiped her wrist clean, she said, "I think I owe you a back and neck massage."

"Your hands on my body sounds great to me, but don't ever feel like you owe me anything, Dix. Like I said, it's an honor to put my mark on you." He met her gaze and said, "Do you want to see it?"

Her pulse quickened with anticipation as she moved her wrist into view. She'd never seen anything so intricate and delicate and yet strong. In the center he'd drawn a heart-shaped diamond shaded with touches of white, pink, gray, and purple. The colors were so faint they were almost invisible, but their effects were remarkable, defining the intricate facets and angles of the diamond. A black dagger pierced through the heart-shaped diamond, and a mildly thick, leatherlike band draped out from either side of the diamond to the edges of her wrist. Scalloped, intricately drawn lace hung from the band on either side of the diamond, and from that lace hung a few thin threads with tiny gray-and-white diamonds at the ends.

"*Jace*, this is beautiful. It's a work of art."

Relief swept over his face. "Then it's fitting," he said modestly as he rose to his feet and stretched. He leaned in to kiss her and whispered, "Because so are you." He took her hand in his and said, "When we were coming up with the clothing line, you'd been my muse for so long, the name came to me quickly. You're as strong as leather and as delicate as lace. But I spent long nights trying to come up with a logo for the line. What started as an idea for a logo turned into what I would tattoo on you if I was ever given the chance. In the end, I let our marketing team design the logo and kept this for you."

She was stunned speechless.

He covered the tattoo with a piece of gauze and said, "In case it bleeds. We'll take that off in a little bit. What can I get you? Do you need a drink?"

Thunder roared outside, and lightning lit up the room. All the emotions she'd been trying not to pick apart crashed over her. She pushed to her feet, feeling breathless and overwhelmed, and said, "I don't know what I need right now, but I know what I want."

She reached for him, but he was already there, his hot mouth claiming hers as he lifted her into his arms and strode across the room. He guided her legs around his waist as he carried her up the steps, slowing only long enough to grip the railing with one hand and intensify their kisses. Blood pounded in her ears as he stepped onto the landing and carried her into the bedroom, taking them both down to the mattress.

JACE WAS GOING to lose his mind, or maybe he already had. As he stripped them both naked, he tried to reel in his runaway emotions. He'd been in such a trance while tattooing Dixie, when he'd seen the elation and desire written all over her face, he'd nearly lost it. Now, as they kissed, their bodies grinding together, he needed a deeper connection, and he needed it *now*. He reached for a condom.

"No," she said, urgent and breathless.

His heart sank. Did she not want him as desperately as he wanted her? *Okay*, he told himself. He would just hold her, kiss her, and that would have to be enough.

"I want to feel *you*, Jace. Only you. I'm on the pill. It's okay."

She reached up and touched his cheek so tenderly, he felt himself free-falling into her. He laced their hands together, careful not to touch her wrist. He knew they were embarking on something even more powerful than they'd already experienced, and that terrified him as much as it thrilled him. The head of his shaft nestled against her wetness. He wanted to kiss her as he claimed her, run his hands over every inch of her skin, through her hair, feel her heart beating in the crooks of her elbows and knees. He wanted to experience every part of her, but he couldn't take his eyes off her, couldn't move his hands from their interwoven connection.

He pushed into her slowly, savoring the feel of her opening up to him, embracing his hard heat. There were so many emotions swimming in her eyes, he was afraid he'd drown. When he was buried to the hilt, rivers of warmth flowed through him, so different from the urgency of the other times they'd come together. He knew it had little to do with the thin sheath that had separated them and everything to do with how deeply she'd gotten to him.

"Hold me," she pleaded, tucking her head against his neck. "Let me just feel you."

He cradled her beneath him, her soft body molding to his, her breath warming his skin. Remaining still was killing him, but at the same time, it was exactly what he needed. To be immersed in Dixie.

When she whispered, "Take me slowly," it brought an onslaught of more unfamiliar emotions. His throat thickened, and he had the overwhelming need to make this time everything they could ever want.

He had no idea what was happening to him or how to stop it. For the first time in his entire life, he felt his world spinning out of control. He should take her hard, chase those confusing emotions away. But he couldn't bring himself to do it, because what she'd asked him to do was exactly what he wanted. He'd always known Dixie had the power to slay him. It was the reason he'd stayed away for so long. He knew how to move on from most anything, to put his head down and focus on work. But as they found a slow, sensual, *perfect* rhythm, he knew there was no going back.

He'd joked about ruining her for all other men, but he'd had it all wrong. Dixie Whiskey had cast a spell on him, and he had no idea how, or if, he'd ever recover.

Chapter Thirteen

WEDNESDAY MORNING PASSED as slowly as molasses as Dixie prepared to leave—and faster than a raging river when they finally made it to the airport. Jace set Dixie's luggage on the floor outside the security checkpoint, his gut twisting into knots. Dixie held her chin high, a stiff smile on her lips. She'd been putting on a brave face all morning, and she was so fucking good at it, it killed him.

"I guess this is it," she said lightly.

"You can't get rid of me that easily. You've signed on for appearances over the next few months, remember?"

She nodded, blinking several times, her eyes suddenly glassy. He knew she'd never let those tears fall. They were surrounded by droves of travelers, but it felt like they were the only two people on earth as he pulled her into his arms for what would be their last embrace as lovers. He couldn't remember ever missing anyone before they'd even left, but he didn't want to let her go. He closed his eyes, breathing her in, wishing things could be different and knowing they couldn't. She was going back to her stable family life in Peaceful Harbor, and he was resuming a life filled with travel and focused on work. There was no doubt in his mind about how much she enjoyed her work and her family, but he couldn't shake the feeling that she worked so many hours to avoid the loneliness she'd never admit existed. He knew all about using work as a vehicle to outrun emotions, but he'd never realized loneliness was one of them until the last few days. Maybe Jayla was right and they *were* what she'd called kindred spirits in her last text—the one where she told Jace he was being an idiot for not dating Dixie—but that didn't change the fact that he wasn't the put-down-roots man Dixie needed.

He drew back and gazed into her sorrowful eyes, his chest constricting painfully. "This isn't just *it*, Dix. This was *everything*." *Everything* wasn't a strong enough word to describe what their time together had meant or been like, but it was the best he could do at the moment.

Her lips curved up in a sweet smile. "Thanks for *everything*," she said as she reached for her bags.

He got a glimpse of her new tattoo, sparking all of the overwhelming emotions he'd nearly died from last night. In an effort to stop his throat from closing and to ease the pain in her eyes, he tried to find safer ground and said, "I'll send you proofs of the pictures we choose for the calendar."

"Right. Okay."

"And I'll hit you up next time I'm in Peaceful Harbor."

"Okay," she said softly, walking backward toward security.

She turned away, but he was rooted in place, the urge to tell her not to leave swamping him. He gritted his teeth and curled his hands into fists as she made her way through security and disappeared down the corridor without so much as a backward glance.

He left the airport in a haze, wondering if it was possible she'd taken all of the oxygen in the air with her.

By the time he got home, his muscles were so tight his whole body ached. As he walked into the loft he'd hardly noticed for years, silence echoed in his ears. He felt like Dixie had been there with him for a month, not just a few days. Her perfume lingered in the air, and as he ascended the stairs, her laughter rang in his ears. He gripped the railing, reminding himself this was for the best. He was pushing forty, and he'd never been tied down, never had a woman relying on him to be there, to listen, to pick her up when she was down or celebrate her successes. His lifestyle wasn't conducive to being *that* guy. His absence would only hurt Dixie, and that hurt would turn to resentment—and that would kill him.

He stood at the entrance to the bedroom where she'd slept that first night. Dixie had stripped the bed and folded the blankets, like she'd been a fucking guest. He went to his bedroom and picked up the pillow on the side where she'd slept. He pressed it to his nose, inhaling her intoxicating scent. Even though he'd made sure they were both on the same page, guilt at having given in to his desires ate away at him. What the hell had he done? He tore off the pillowcases and stripped the sheets from the bed in a fit of anger, throwing them into the corner.

His eyes caught on a gift bag on the dresser that hadn't been there earlier. There was a greeting card envelope beside it with his name written on it in Dixie's loopy handwriting. With his heart in his throat, he opened the card. There was a picture of a kitten on the front, and inside, *THANK YOU* was printed in fancy gold letters above Dixie's note, which read:

Jace, wipe that smile off your face. You still can't call me kitten.

She'd drawn a smiley face after "kitten."

Thank you for giving me an experience I'll never forget, and for allowing me to be part of the launch for your Leather and Lace line. I know it will be a huge success, and I'm proud to be the face of Silver-Stone. I'll cherish the memories and always be grateful for the time we shared. Now I no longer have to wonder about my biggest crush. You are so much more incredible than I could have ever imagined. Good luck with the Boston deal.

XOX, Dix

PS: The gift bag is for Thane. I couldn't buy gifts for my babies without getting him a little something, too. I loved your wonderful family. It's obvious how much they adore you. Please thank them for welcoming me so warmly.

His heart felt like it might implode. She'd seen Thane for only a few hours, and she already thought of him as one of her *babies*? Even when she wasn't there, she still burrowed beneath his skin. He read the note again to see if he'd missed anything—the admission of missing him, not wanting it to be over—but there was nothing. He was suffering this misery alone. He needed to get out of there, away from Dixie's ghost trailing at his heels. Keys in hand, he flew down the stairs. He was an idiot. He never should have opened that door, because he had no fucking idea how to close it.

DIXIE SPENT THE whole flight reliving last night, which felt like the most wonderful dream, and then replaying their goodbye. No matter how many times she tried to change what

Jace had said—*This isn't just it, Dix. This was everything*—she couldn't change the tone of his voice or his meaning. It was clear to her that he was drawing the line in the sand one last time, reminding her of their agreement that what they'd had was everything they would ever get. She decided right there and then, as tears vied for release and her heart split down the middle, she *wouldn't* cry or pine over what might have been. She wouldn't show any weaknesses at all, because she'd gotten exactly what she'd agreed to. She had never blamed others for her mistakes, and she wasn't about to blame Jace for giving her what she wanted. Or at least what she'd told him she wanted— whatever she could get, no strings attached—even if she'd thought—*hoped*—that if things were as great as she had expected them to be, he wouldn't want to let her go afterward.

That'll teach her to think like a stupid girl.

She never had before, and she had no idea why she'd allowed herself to do so now.

As she headed for the airport exit, she gave herself a mental pat on the back for making it through the flight home without bursting into tears or killing anyone. Now all she had to do was make it through the next three days. What did her girlfriends say about dieting? *Day one was hell, day two was practice, but day three made it a habit.* After that it was just part of their lives. Surely that could also be applied to forgetting a man.

She pushed through the doors and saw Izzy standing by her car in the drop-off area.

Izzy waved with a big-ass smile as she ran toward Dixie and grabbed one of her bags. "I have been *dying* to talk to you," she said as they hurried to her car. "I want to hear about *everything!*"

Forget three days.

Dixie needed to get through the ride home.

They tossed her bags in the trunk, and as soon as they were in their seats, Izzy said, "You look *different*."

That didn't surprise her. She *felt* different, too. Like she'd gone on a year-long vacation and fallen in love, and now that she was home she realized she'd been in a time warp. Nothing felt quite like it had before.

As Izzy drove away from the airport, she said, "I'm going to assume that looking different is a good thing. But I really can't tell until you say something, Dixie. Are you okay, or did Jace fuck your voice right out of you?"

Dixie cringed inside. The way Izzy said it made it sound like what they had was crass and meaningless, when in reality it had felt real and right, unbelievably big, loud, intense, and beautiful, even if only temporary. She shouldn't cringe or hold anything back, considering she and Izzy always talked like that.

But she did.

And it wasn't just Izzy's remark that had Dixie holding back. She felt protective of her time with Jace in a way she never had about anything before. What they'd shared felt private and special, and the details of it were wonderful secrets they'd carry to their graves. She'd thought Jace might text at some point, but her phone had been quiet as a church mouse—and she'd checked the volume twice.

She looked down at her new tattoo, filling up with as much happiness as sadness. *Three days*, she reminded herself. She knew today would be the worst of it, or at least she hoped so.

"I'm just exhausted," Dixie lied. "The whole thing was incredible. The shoot, spending time with Jace, seeing the city." She told her all about the photo shoot. "I swear, Iz, I didn't recognize myself in the pictures."

"I can't wait to see them."

"Thanks. They're so good. And the clothes? Oh my gosh, Jilly and Jace make an incredible design team. The outfits were chic and edgy, and they really classed up the shots. And the Legacy bikes are freaking phenomenal. It's amazing how different it felt sitting on a bike built for a woman." It struck her that she hadn't told Jace how much she'd loved the bikes. She thought about calling or texting, but she quickly nixed that idea. Hearing his voice would only make the next three days that much harder.

Day one is hell. Deal with it.

"Well, Jace *did* design them," Izzy said, distracting her from her thoughts. "I'm sure that man did plenty of hands-on research to make sure the bikes have just the right curves to fit a woman's body."

Dixie glowered at her.

"What? It's not like you're giving me *anything* to go on here," Izzy said. "Did things go bad since we texted?"

"No. I really did have a great time with Jace and everything else, but now it's over and I have to go back to work tomorrow. There's not much else to tell."

"There's *always* more to tell. He looks like he'd be an animal in bed, all *take this* and *give me* that. Please don't tell me it's all an act."

"Let's just say he was everything I thought he'd be and much more." She looked out the window as they drove toward the harbor. Izzy must have taken the hint, because she turned up the music and didn't push for more details.

When they pulled into Dixie's neighborhood, Izzy said, "I made brownies last night. Do you want to come over after you unpack?"

"As much as I love brownies, I think I need to crawl into my bed and sleep or I'll never make it into work tomorrow."

Izzy parked in front of Dixie's house and they got out to get the luggage from the trunk. Izzy looked curiously at her and said, "Are you sure you're just tired?"

"Yeah, of course."

"You'd tell me if Jace did something wrong, right?"

She loved Izzy so much. She knew her friend would do anything for her, just as she'd do anything for Izzy. But this was a private battle Dixie had to conquer on her own.

"Yes. He didn't. He was a perfect gentleman."

Izzy wrinkled her nose. "Is *that* what's wrong? Was he really a disappointment and you don't want to admit it?"

Dixie laughed softly. "Jace Stone is as far from a disappointment as a man can get. He's forthright and honest, and trust me, he's as talented in the bedroom as he is a designer. I'm just tired, and you know how it is after a really intense hookup. You need time to process. I just want to revel in it a little longer, go to sleep, dream about it…"

"Okay, *that* I understand." Izzy hugged her and said, "But if you need drinks and brownies, I'm your girl."

"I know. Thanks, Iz."

Dixie went inside and dropped her bags by the door. She'd loved her cozy three-bedroom home from the moment she'd seen it, even though it had been in awful shape after years of renters. The previous owners had stopped paying the mortgage, and she'd gotten a steal on it from the bank. Her brothers and several of the Dark Knights had helped her fix it up, repairing the wide front porch that wrapped around the left side of the house, refinishing the wood floors, and replacing nearly all of the drywall, windows, and plumbing. She'd saved every penny she'd earned to buy it, and she was proud to have purchased it on her own. But the usual comfort of coming home was missing. She felt like the walls were closing in around her.

She grabbed a water bottle from the fridge and a bag of chips from the pantry and shoved them in her leather backpack, along with her phone and wallet. She snagged her keys and helmet on her way out the door. Just the sight of her motorcycle brought a modicum of relief. As she put on her helmet and straddled the bike, memories of riding on the back of Jace's bike assaulted her, bringing waves of emotions she didn't want to deal with. She refused to give in to them as she drove away from her house.

The vibrations of the engine, the wind on her skin, and the call of the open road brought more hope of the relief she sought. She cruised out of her neighborhood and sped down the main drag, passing the auto shop and the bar, and cranked her speed as she drove over the bridge and out of the town limits. She drove aimlessly until the knots in her chest loosened and the sun dipped from its high afternoon perch in the sky, but Jace remained front and center in her thoughts. She finally gave up trying to outrun him and turned back toward home. As if her bike had a mind of its own, she found herself driving the narrow winding mountain roads she'd frequented when she was younger. When she came to her favorite trail, she followed it to her secret spot. Or what had been her secret spot before she'd realized Jace had discovered it.

She parked and pulled off her helmet as she strode through the woods, feeling Jace's presence all around her. She reached for the branches separating her from the clearing and felt a hopeful flutter in her chest, thinking Jace might actually be there.

She burst through the bushes, her heart beating frantically, but the clearing was empty. What was happening to her? She'd never been this person before, hanging on to her sanity by a thread because of a man. She shrugged off her backpack and dug around for her phone. Maybe that hopeful flutter was caused by a missed text or phone call from him. She snagged her phone, but she had no messages or missed calls. Disappointment turned that hopeful flutter into a dull ache. She wondered what Jace was doing right now. Had he delivered the gift she'd left for Thane? Had he gone to work? Or out for a ride? A drink? She shoved her phone into her backpack and plunked herself down on a boulder with a heavy sigh, pulling her knees up to her chest and wrapping her arms around them.

This is how it happens. How strong women become sad and pathetic.

She let go of her legs, astonished that she was talking about herself.

This was not who she was, and she was not going to let it consume her.

She was a Whiskey: strong and capable. There was nothing she couldn't do if she put her mind to it. She'd *chosen* to sleep with Jace knowing she was in it for only a few days and nothing more. Now she just had to *choose* to turn off her feelings for him. She dumped her backpack on the rock and tore open the chips, stuffing a handful in her mouth as she tried to come up with a plan. She was usually the one talking others down from the ledge, but her go-to advice sounded pat, not to mention unattainable—*Just stop thinking of him. The best way to get over a man is to get under another.* It wasn't like she had an on/off switch, and she definitely didn't want to sleep with another man.

How could she have ever given that advice to her girlfriends?

There *had* to be another way.

Jace had said he'd turned to work when that teacher had broken his heart. That seemed like a reasonable plan. She could take extra shifts at the bar to fill the hours, fall into bed at night too exhausted to move. Next week she'd leave for the Cape, and then she'd be distracted by Justin and her cousins. She convinced herself she could do this. By the time she came back from the Cape, the pain would lessen, and Jace would be a wonderful and *distant* memory.

I've got this.

Pleased with her plan, she grabbed another handful of chips. *Work, work, work.* She loved work. It really was the perfect way to get her mind off Jace. Her mind off *him.* It would be easier if she started distancing herself from him in every way, and not thinking about his name was a start. She gazed out at the setting sun as she finished the bag of chips. Then she lay down on her back, thinking about how smart she was to have come up with a plan so quickly. Maybe she should go into work early, too. That way she'd definitely be exhausted by the time she got home at night.

Her phone rang and she bolted upright. *Jace!* Her foolish heart nearly leapt out of her chest as she fumbled for her phone. *Bones* flashed on the screen with his phone number, and a crushing sensation started in her chest and spread to her limbs.

She pressed her hand over her heart, trying to keep her tears from falling as she answered the phone. "Hi, Bones."

"Hey, Dix. How was your trip?"

"Great," she choked out. "A lot of fun."

"You sound funny. You okay?"

No. She wiped away a tear slipping down her cheek and

said, "Mm-hm."

"I'm glad to hear it. Listen, I know you just got back into town, but I was wondering if you might be willing to babysit tomorrow night. I want to take Sarah someplace special, just the two of us."

"Sure," she said softly. Was it too much to ask to fall in love with a man who would want to be with her as much as she wanted to be with him? More tears spilled from her eyes. "What time?"

"Great, thanks. How about six?"

"I'll be there. I have gifts for the kids, so that's perfect." Memories of shopping with Jace slammed into her. She saw him picking up stuffed animals and wiggling them with the smile she'd never seen until they'd gotten close, and laughing when she put on a plastic tiara. She remembered the way he'd looked at her when she was dancing with the children on the big piano keys, driving the pain and longing even deeper.

As Bones relayed a cute story about Bradley, she thought of the gardens Jace had taken her to see and the way he'd gazed into her eyes as the raindrops had fallen. She'd never forget how they'd climbed into the cab soaking wet, laughing and kissing, or the way his face had morphed to a mask of concentration while he tattooed her wrist.

Tears flooded her eyes, and she interrupted Bones. "Sorry. I have to go. I'll see you tomorrow." She ended the call and dropped her phone to wipe her eyes. *Stopitstopitstopit.* She looked up at the sky, willing her tears to abate, but she saw Jace's face in every cloud. She closed her eyes, trying desperately to shift her thoughts, but his voice invaded her mind. *I'll hit you up next time I'm in Peaceful Harbor.*

She closed her eyes tighter, but it only turned up the volume.

You can't get rid of me that easily. You've signed on for appearances over the next few months, remember?

How had he gone back to business so easily? Swiping at the unstoppable tears, she thought about asking Bones if he needed a babysitter *right now* because she sure as hell needed a distraction.

This isn't just it, Dix. This was everything.

The pain in her chest brought a sorrowful groan. Forget babysitting. Maybe she'd just climb into bed and never get out.

Chapter Fourteen

DIXIE SAT BEHIND her desk Thursday afternoon staring at the text Jace had sent last night, picking it apart for the millionth time.

Hope you got home safe.

How was she supposed to interpret *that?* He was obviously thinking about her, or at least worrying about her welfare. It wasn't like he'd asked a question, which meant he didn't expect a reply. Or want one. She must have typed out dozens of responses from a curt *I did* to a friendly text asking how his dinner with his parents went, and finally, to a needy-sounding message asking if he missed her as much as she missed him. In the end she hadn't replied at all. At least she'd found out he'd delivered the gift to Thane. Jayla had texted to thank her for it and said she hoped they could get together next time Dixie was in New York. If the tables were turned and Dixie were Jace, she would have texted him to say she'd dropped off the gift and that they'd loved it. She also would have thanked him for thinking of her nephew. *And then I would tell you how much I miss you, how I used to love my life but now everything feels off, like something is missing. And it's all my fault because I thought I could handle a few days with you and move on with memories I would cherish. But I can't.*

Being a girl blows…

A knock on her open door drew her attention, but the doorway was empty. Jed and Truman were working until seven. She assumed she must have heard one of them banging around, but then a hand appeared from behind the wall, waving a white rag.

Quincy peered around the doorframe and said, "Is it safe to come in? Tru said you've been snappy and even got into it with a customer."

Dixie rolled her eyes. "He was a jerk arguing about labor costs."

"I remember a certain someone schooling me about proper customer service etiquette before I applied for a job at the bookstore," he said as he walked into her office. "If I recall correctly, you told me never to argue with customers no matter how right I was."

"Yeah, well, the guy caught me on a bad day." She shoved her phone in her pocket and began shutting down her computer. She had to babysit in half an hour. She'd reworked the waitressing schedule for the bar and was working Friday and Saturday nights. She planned to work late and close up the shop Saturday evening and then go straight to the bar. She'd spend a few hours doing the books and inventory at the bar Sunday, and then she would go on a long motorcycle ride. Her time was pretty well sewn up, at least through the weekend. She was on day two of trying to get Jace out of her head. So far day two was no easier than day one. She'd gone from brokenhearted to brokenhearted and angry at herself for not being able to turn off her feelings. And the worst part was that she didn't think she ever would.

Quincy tapped his finger on her desk and said, "Did you have a good trip?"

"Yes. It was amazing, and I really appreciate you handling things while I was gone."

"No worries. I left a few notes that you'll see Sunday when you do the books for the bar."

"Great. Any trouble?"

"No. The bookstore just started using a new inventory system, and I thought you might want to check out the company that makes the software. They have a program for restaurants. You'll see. I left all the details."

"Thanks. I wanted to ask you about helping me out a little more." She gathered her papers and said, "Jace reminded me that I have obligations to Silver-Stone to do some in-person appearances for marketing purposes. I don't have a schedule yet, although according to the contract I should have it by July first. The launch is in early fall, and it's going to be a lot of time at first, six events during a twelve-week period when they launch the Legacy and Leather and Lace lines and then six appearances each year for three years. If scheduling works out, would you consider handling things for me during those times? If not, no worries. I can have my mom or Bear do it."

"I could use the money, so count me in. If you get the schedule in July, I should have time to work it out with my schedule at the bookstore."

She pushed to her feet and grabbed her bag. "That's great. Bear will have his hands full with their baby by then, and Mom just cut herself loose from working at the bar. I really didn't want to lean on her."

"Dix, I'll do whatever I can to help you out. This is an exciting new adventure for you. You're going to be famous in the biker world. You know that, right?" He pushed a hand into the front pocket of his jeans and said, "Then I'll say I knew you when…"

She laughed as they walked out of her office. "I don't think calendar chicks get famous, but thanks. Where are you headed now? Did you get things worked out for your date with Roni yet?"

"Not yet, but I've got that pretty little fish on the line. I've got to grab something from my apartment, and then I'm going down to Penny's to help her out at the ice cream shop."

Truman walked up behind Quincy and put his hand on his shoulder. "That means my baby brother is going to eat ice cream and flirt."

Quincy winked. "Damn right, bro."

"I thought that ship already sailed for you two," Dixie said curiously.

"You never know when it might come back into port." Quincy waggled his brows and headed for the door that led to his apartment above the shop.

Had everyone's personal life gone topsy-turvy?

"Your brother cracks me up sometimes," Dixie said.

"Yeah, he's a great guy. Hey, are you sure you don't want to swing by and give Kennedy and Linc the presents you bought them?" Truman asked. "Gemma will be home with them by six."

"She probably has a date," Jed said as he walked around the truck he was working on, wiping his hands on a rag.

"Hardly." The only man she wanted wasn't the dating type. "I'm babysitting for Bones tonight. Can you take pictures of the kids opening the gifts and send them to me?"

"Sure," they both said.

"Thanks. I can't wait to see them. I'll see you guys in the morning."

She headed outside and climbed into her Jeep, wishing she had been able to ride her bike to work, but she'd had too many presents to carry. As she drove away, her mind traveled back to Jace. She wondered how his meeting had gone about the space in Boston and what he was doing tonight. For the millionth time, his voice whispered through her mind. *I don't answer to anyone, and I can't give you forever. Hell, I can't give you next week.*

She admired many things about him, but his honesty was definitely at the top of that list, even though it was also the cause of her pain. She gripped the steering wheel tighter, willing the hurt not to dig its claws in any deeper. She had only herself to blame, and that made it even harder to accept.

She made her way to Bones and Sarah's house on a bluff overlooking the harbor.

A cool breeze swept over Dixie's skin as she stepped from the car and grabbed the gifts from the passenger seat. She gazed out at the water as she walked up to the front door, promising herself she would *not* think of Jace tonight. She wouldn't hope to hear from him or pick apart his message from last night. Tonight she was *Auntie Dixie*, and Auntie Dixie would never slight her babies for a man.

With her rules firmly in place, she knocked on the door.

"Come in!"

She heard little feet running by the door. Picturing Bradley racing by in his bare feet brought a smile to her face as she pushed the door open.

"Surprise!" rang out from the living room.

Startled, she jumped as her parents, siblings, and their significant others came at her with open arms. But her favorite sandy-haired four-year-old, Bradley, beat them to it, throwing his arms around her legs, beaming up at her.

"Happy calendar!" Bradley jumped up and down and said, "Are those presents for *me*?"

"*Manners*, kiddo." Bones swept Bradley off his feet, holding him under his arm like a football as he leaned in and kissed Dixie's cheek. "Congratulations, Dix." He set Bradley on his feet.

"What is all this?" she asked.

Bradley grabbed her hand, pulling her into the living room, which was decorated with streamers and balloons. "Look at the sign we made!" He pointed above the mantel, to a sign that read CONGRATULATIONS, DIXIE! It was decorated with adorable stick figures and scribbles.

"We're celebrating *you*," Crystal said as she took the gifts from Dixie and set them on the coffee table.

Bradley tugged on Dixie's hand and said, "Lila scribbled. I drew our family and Tinkerbell. Do you see Tink? Do you?" Tinkerbell was Bullet's Rottweiler. Bradley had drawn the dog with four uneven legs and an enormous head with pointy ears.

"Yes!" Dixie said. "Everything you drew looks amazing."

"It's *amazing*!" Bradley hollered, running to Sarah's side.

Sarah was holding Maggie Rose. "So is your auntie," she said, touching Bradley's head and smiling at Dixie.

Lila was perched in one of Bullet's arms, looking adorable in a pink dress with white polka dots, tugging at his beard as he hauled Dixie against him with his free hand, hugging her so hard she couldn't breathe. "We're all proud of you, Dix."

"*Dissie! Dissie!*" Lila chanted, her grabby hands catching

Dixie's hair.

Emotions clogged Dixie's throat as Bullet handed Lila to her. Lila wrapped her arms around Dixie's neck.

"Finlay and Sarah cooked," Crystal said. The table was set with platters overflowing with food and a vase of fresh flowers.

"We made all your favorites," Finlay said.

"Everything looks incredible. I can't believe you did all this for me. It's just a calendar," Dixie said, although she knew how big a deal it was that Jace had chosen *her* to be the face of Silver-Stone. But she still had a hard time grasping that part.

"Believe it, baby girl," her mother said, her gaze warmer than the summer sun.

Her father limped to her side, his beard twitching with his smile. "It's not really about the calendar. You have given so much of your life to our family. We're celebrating *you*, sweetheart. It's as simple as that."

As he embraced her, Dixie's eyes filled with tears. *This doesn't feel simple at all.*

THE EVENING WAS full of love, laughter, and plenty of eye rolls. Lila hadn't let go of her giraffe since she'd unwrapped it. They were sitting around the dinner table enjoying the feast the girls had prepared, the giraffe perched beside Lila in the high chair, covered with food. Maggie Rose was asleep in Bones's arms, and Bradley was having a blast pushing his new truck along the edge of the table to Bear, who would then push it back. Dixie had just finished telling them all about the photo shoot, and she was fielding their questions.

"A clothing stylist and a hair and makeup person? It sounds glamorous," Sarah said.

"Our sister the *model*," Bear chimed in.

"Hardly," Dixie said. "It was nerve-racking, at least at first. But then I remembered some advice Jace's sister had given me when we had dinner with them, and that made it easier."

Finlay, Crystal, and Sarah exchanged excited glances.

"You had dinner with Jace's family?" Finlay asked.

"You guys must have had a really special date," Sarah added.

"Sounds like he won *more than* a date in that auction," Crystal said snarkily.

All three of Dixie's brothers glowered at Crystal.

Good thing Dixie wasn't spilling her guts to anyone in the room. "Would you all stop. His sisters live in the city. We had dinner with them. It was no big deal. He has an adorable nephew, by the way. Thane is four months old, and oh my gosh, he is a cutie."

Her mother looked at her with a curious expression. "That must have been a nice visit."

"It was. His sisters and brother-in-law are really nice." She wondered if Jayla had said anything more to Jace about her, and if so, how Jace had responded. She didn't want to go down that rabbit hole, so she said, "Anyway, Rush, Jace's brother-in-law, suggested I mentally go back to being a teenager while they did the photo shoot, because teenagers feel so invincible."

"I don't know about you, but I'm still invincible," Bullet said.

Bear chuckled. "You and me both."

Bones shook his head and said, "And it worked?"

"Like a charm." As she said it, she remembered how it had worked so well to take away her nervousness, but she'd ended up too hot and bothered to think straight.

And then she remembered what happened next.

Her cheeks burned, and she downed her glass of water in three big gulps. But the image of Jace's eyes locked on her as she loved him with her hands and mouth didn't abate, and her pulse quickened.

"You okay, sweetheart?" her mother asked.

"Yeah. Just thirsty." She refilled her glass from the pitcher and drank more water, scrambling for another subject. "I got to keep all the clothes from the shoot. Wait until you see them. They're gorgeous." She hoped they wouldn't ask to see them. She hadn't been able to bring herself to unpack them yet. She was afraid the sight of them would only bring more heartache.

"When do we get to see the calendar?" her mother asked.

"I'm not sure. Jace said they're meeting next week to decide which pictures to use."

The conversation moved from the shoot to her thoughts on the city, which led to Bones and Sarah talking about where they wanted to go on their honeymoon.

"Maybe you should pick a wedding date first," Finlay suggested. "That usually comes before the honeymoon."

Bullet put his arm around Finlay and pulled her closer. "Our honeymoon started the day you accepted my proposal, and it's never going to end."

Bear made kissing sounds as Bullet kissed Finlay. Bradley mimicked Bear, and Lila got in on the game, giggling as she smacked her lips together, spraying food all over her tray.

"Just wait until your baby is born," Bones said to Bear as he wiped Lila's cheeks.

Bear rubbed Crystal's belly and said, "I welcome it. I want our baby to be just as fun as I am, and as well endowed."

"*Bear*," their mother scolded him with a smile tugging at her lips.

"Someone's got to take over the title for the next generation," Bear said, sparking a round of hilarious comments from the adults. Their laughter brought more giggles from the kids.

Finlay laughed so hard, when she finally caught her breath, she said, "I love this family so much."

"'Course you do, Lollipop." Bullet kissed her temple.

Dixie sat back, taking it all in. Sarah was cutting up food for Bradley, who shoveled it into his mouth as quickly as she could cut. Bones cuddled Maggie Rose against his chest as he put more pasta on Lila's plate.

"How about Giraffe? Does he need some, too?" Bones asked, earning a giggle from Lila, who immediately tried to shove pasta into the stuffed animal's mouth.

Crystal and Bear were holding hands, volleying parenting comments with Bullet, who was still holding on to Finlay like he'd never let her go. Red and Biggs talked in hushed voices, their foreheads close. The image of everything Dixie wanted was right before her eyes. She'd been on the same page with Jace when she was with him, and she didn't regret a second of what they'd done. But as she looked around the table, she decided she was done selling herself short. She wanted to be with a man who wanted to be on *this* page with her. Someone who wanted to be there for all the crazy, unexpected things that happened in families and in life, a partner she could rely on, who thought about her the way her brothers thought about their wives: constantly and lovingly. She didn't even care that Jace had to travel often and couldn't commit to being physically present on a daily basis *if* he loved her the way she loved him.

But he didn't.

A dull ache sprouted deep in her chest, spreading like a thorny bush. She grabbed the edges of her chair to keep from crumbling into herself as she tried to accept reality. Jace Stone wasn't ever going to be the man she needed, no matter how much she wanted him to be.

Chapter Fifteen

THE SUN HUNG low over the horizon as Jace pulled into the parking lot of Whiskey Automotive Saturday evening, remembering the last time he'd been there. He hadn't expected that night to lead to something more, and he sure as hell hadn't expected something more to lead to sleepless nights and *Dixie Whiskey* burning through his veins. But she was *everywhere*. When he closed his eyes, he saw her beautiful face gazing up at him as they made love. When he was working, he felt her hands on his body, heard her voice challenging and seducing him. And every damn time he'd walked into his loft, he'd felt her presence. He missed her so much his chest hurt day and night, and there was no turning it off. He'd tried to drink her away the first night she'd left, but it had only reminded him of their evening at NightCaps. He'd never experienced anything like this before, and he didn't understand why it was happening or how to handle it. He'd finally given up trying, and like an addict seeking his next hit, he'd come to Peaceful Harbor.

He climbed off his bike, grabbed the gift he'd brought her from the saddlebag, and headed inside. The bell above the door chimed. Dixie was sitting behind the front desk, her gorgeous hair curtaining her face, her bare shoulders begging to be kissed. Just the sight of her sent heat and relief flooding through him, easing his misery.

"We're clos—" She looked up and dropped her pen. "*Jace.*"

"Hi, Dix. I came back to take care of a few things and make arrangements for my bike. Thought I'd stop by."

She rose to her feet, gorgeous in a pair of cutoffs and a tight tank top. "Oh," she said a little shakily. As if she caught that small vulnerability, she cleared her throat and said, "Payment for the shoot just hit my account. You said it would be five times what I earn here, and it's *way* more than that."

"You're worth every penny."

She shifted her eyes to the box in his hand as she came around the desk.

His heart thundered as she met his gaze. He'd thought he'd imagined the way her green eyes drew him in like an unstoppable force, but he found himself stepping closer. He handed her the box and said, "This is for you. What do you say we grab some dinner, get a drink?"

She looked at the box, her brows knitting. "Thank you." She set the box on the desk and said, "I can't see you tonight. I'm working at the bar."

Damn. "I can swing by your place after you're off."

She shook her head, averting her eyes again. "I don't think that's a good idea."

Ice cut through his chest. He really *was* alone in his anguish. He'd known she'd handled her leaving better than he had, but he'd thought she'd at least missed him. "Why not?"

She pressed her lips together, and he reached for her hand. She didn't pull it away, but he could see her struggling with something.

"Dix, talk to me. I have to be in LA tomorrow. I don't have time to try to guess what's going on."

"It's too hard, Jace. I can't do it. We had New York, and we agreed that was all we'd have."

She was *done*? He didn't believe it. He stepped closer, the familiar thrum of desire coursing through him, and he saw it mirrored in her eyes as he said, "It doesn't have to be all we had. We've got tonight." He ran his hands up her arms and said, "Be with me after work."

He gathered her in his arms and brushed his lips over hers. Her breathing hitched, and she grabbed his sides, pressing her fingers into him. "I can't get you out of my head, Dix. That damn Whiskey fever's got me all worked up."

The longing in her eyes brought his mouth to hers. She pressed her whole body into his, and in the next breath both of them were pawing and groping as they feasted on each other's mouths. All of the anguish and confusion fell away. *This* was what he needed, and it wasn't nearly enough.

Dixie moaned, and he tightened his grip on her hair, but she tore her mouth away, panting as she pushed out of his arms.

"No." She shook her head, walking backward until she bumped into the desk. "I can't do this, Jace. I can't be your booty call."

Now he was shaking his head, trying to still his whirling thoughts. "*Booty call?* I thought we were on the same page."

"We were," she said, touching her lips, as if they were still tingling. She folded her arms, then unfolded them, only to fold them again.

"You said you didn't need promises of more," he said a little too sharply, but he didn't fucking get it. They were good together. She sure as hell wouldn't kiss him like that if they weren't.

"I *didn't*," she snapped, her eyes pleading with him, but not for what he wanted. "I never thought I was the type of girl who would pine over a man, checking my phone and wondering where we stand. But it turns out I *am* that girl, and I hate it. It's too hard. I didn't expect to care about you or think about you so much afterward. I can't …"

"What are you saying?" He already knew the answer, but he didn't want to believe it.

She held his gaze, as still as steel, hurt simmering just below the surface. "I'm saying things changed. It turns out I do want promises. I want the frigging fantasy. I want a man who wants forever with me—kids and family dinners, the whole shebang. I'm on day *three*." Her voice escalated. "Do you know what that means? It means I'm over the worst of it. I need to move on and protect my heart, and I can't do that if I fall into your arms tonight."

The truth hit him like a punch to his gut.

He'd known she was fooling herself in New York, but she'd done such a good job of it, he'd taken a page from her playbook and fooled himself, too. *But that note…Fuck.* That note had been just another attempt to fool herself. He wasn't alone in his misery after all, but knowing he'd hurt her only drove his torment deeper.

"We're good together, Dix. Hell, we're phenomenal together, but you're asking for promises I can't give."

"I'm not asking you for anything." She lifted her chin defiantly. "I'm just explaining, and if you care about me at all, you'll let it go at this."

"Dix…" He stepped closer.

She put her hands up and shook her head, tears welling in

her eyes. "Please don't. I'll still live up to my commitments for Silver-Stone, but we can't happen."

Right that second, he didn't give a damn about the company. "You're fucking killing me," he said angrily. Her eyes implored him to hear her, and damn it, he did, loud and clear. He'd never wanted to hurt her, and he'd fucked that up.

Battling the crushing feeling in his chest and his own self-loathing, he reluctantly headed for the door. But he stopped short, needing one last look at her, and drove the dagger deeper into his heart as he said, "You're a hell of a woman, Dixie Whiskey, and you deserve everything you're hoping for and more."

DIXIE HELD HER breath as Jace stormed out the door. She heard his bike roar to life and speed out of the parking lot. The air rushed from her lungs, tears sprang from her eyes, and her legs gave out. She grabbed the edge of the desk as sobs burst free. She'd thought Wednesday had been the worst of it, but as the pain drove her to her knees, the sound of Jace's engine faded in the distance, and this time she knew she'd never be the same again.

Chapter Sixteen

SUNDAY MORNING THE numbers in the ledger blurred together. Dixie closed her eyes, refusing to give in to the heartache she'd suffered all night. It was a futile effort, and she wiped the frigging tears from her cheeks. God, she hated this! When she'd finally made it to the bar last night, she was almost an hour late, her eyes red and puffy, and she'd moved through her shift like an automaton. Izzy, Tracey, and Diesel wouldn't stop asking what was wrong, and she'd lost it, hollering at them right there in front of all the customers. *I'm having a shit day, okay? Leave it alone or I swear you'll regret it.* She'd cried herself to sleep like a pathetic child. She'd thought coming into the bar to do the books would snap her out of it. But here she sat, stuck on replay. At least the bar was closed and she could wallow in her misery alone.

She knew she'd done the right thing by sending Jace away, but why did it feel like the worst decision of her life? She pushed away from the table where she was working and went around the bar to pour herself a drink. She hadn't bothered to turn on the lights, hoping to hide from herself, but as she grabbed a bottle of tequila, she accidentally caught sight of herself in the mirror behind the bar. Her hair was piled on top of her head like a rat's nest, her bloodshot eyes looked like she was already drunk, and her nose looked like she'd stolen it from Rudolph.

Disgusted with herself, she put the bottle down and went back to the table to stare at the blurry pages of the ledger.

She must have fallen asleep, because she startled awake to the feel of a hand on her arm and found her mother sitting beside her with a concerned expression. "Mom? Sorry, I must have dozed off. What time is it?"

"Just after three."

Holy cow, she'd been asleep for *hours*. She sat up, and her mother's eyes trailed from her head down to the fuzzy slippers on her feet.

Dixie tucked her feet under her chair and folded her arms around her middle. When she'd finally gone home last night, she'd opened the gift Jace had given her. Inside she'd found copies of the pictures she'd asked for, the pictures that Hawk had taken of him at the photo shoot, and a beautiful black lace top and black skirt from the Leather and Lace line like the ones he'd torn off her in the heat of passion. In her grief last night, she'd put them on, and couldn't bear the thought of taking them off this morning.

Her mother scooted her chair closer and put her palm on Dixie's forehead. "Hm. No fever."

Jace's voice slammed through Dixie's mind. *That damn Whiskey fever's got me all worked up.* She lowered her eyes, trying to hide her emotions.

"I hear you were hell on wheels last night." Her mother put her finger under Dixie's chin, lifting and studying her face. "You look like you had a rough night, sweet girl. Diesel followed you home last night and slept outside your house. Did you know that? He was worried you were hiding something and that whoever had caused you to be upset might come back."

Dixie shook her head.

The Dark Knights took care of their own, and as the daughter of the president of the club, she'd always be one of their own. Maybe it should piss her off that Diesel had done that after she'd made such a scene about being able to take care of herself, but it didn't. It brought fresh tears to her eyes, because a teeny-tiny part of her had wished Jace would come roaring back to profess his love for her.

A knot lodged in her throat.

"Do you want to tell me why you look like you got all dressed up for a hot date, ended up being passed around a pool hall, hitched a ride to Vegas, got ditched at the altar, and woke up at the bottom of a barrel of tequila?" Her mother reached up to tuck a few loose strands of hair behind Dixie's ear, and her brows slanted. "Is that a *scrunchie* in your hair? Oh, *baby girl,* talk to me."

Dixie opened her mouth to speak, but her thoughts were jagged and painful, spilling out in an incomprehensible wail. She surrendered to the pain, collapsing into her mother's waiting arms.

"It's okay, baby." Her mother stroked her hair. "Let it all out, every last tear."

Dixie sat on the edge of her chair, weeping and clinging to her mother like a lifeline. She cried until she had no more tears to cry, until all that was left were the painful sores of a broken heart.

When she finally pried herself from her mother's arms, she felt like a husk of a person, empty and soulless. Her mother put a handful of napkins in her palm, curling her fingers around Dixie's, her eyes moving to the new tattoo on her wrist. It was crusted with scabs.

Her mother's brows knitted, and she said, "*Jace.*"

It wasn't a question or an accusation, but a confirmation Dixie knew she didn't need to acknowledge. Her mother's face crumbled in hurt, and she pressed her lips together, her chest rising as she nodded in understanding.

"Just tell me one thing," her mother said softly. "Should I let the boys go after him?"

Dixie was wrong. She hadn't cried all her tears, because more filled her eyes as she shook her head. "It's not his fault. He did everything right," she said through her tears, unable to stop the truth from pouring out. "He was honest from the start about what it would be if we got together. He warned me, and he tried not to do *anything*. Mom, he really tried. I pushed it, and I thought I could handle it. I thought I could just hook up with him and be done with it, but…" Her voice was lost to her sobs.

"Oh, my sweet darlin'." He mother embraced her again. "You can't have a taste of love and turn it off like a faucet. Don't you know that's why Bullet lost his mind when Jace claimed you at the auction?"

"What?" she choked out.

"Baby, Bear told us all those years ago how you lost your heart to Jace in the space of a heartbeat. Bear said Jace had looked at you in a way that made him want to tear his head off, but you know Bear. Even as a boy he could read emotions better than any of us, and he knew Jace was chaining himself down to keep from going after you. You were just a young thing, and he was a full-grown man making big strides with his life. He was too smart to get tangled up in a situation like that."

Dixie pulled back, shocked at what she was hearing. "Bear saw that?"

"He did. You're a Whiskey, baby, and when Whiskeys set their mind to something, we don't let anything stand in our way and we don't hide our feelings. Your brothers *all* know that. They knew it was just a matter of time until you and Jace gave in to what you felt. We thought things would come to a head long before now, even before Bear started working for Silver-Stone. But Jace was strong. He kept his distance until the night of the auction, when he *claimed* you. Trust me, Bullet knew *exactly* what was going to happen. We all did."

"I didn't!" Dixie snapped. "Couldn't you have warned me? Or stopped me?"

Her mother laughed softly, shaking her head. "I raised four ornery children to be even stronger adults. That was one hornet's nest I wasn't about to step into, although Bullet did his best to stop you. But our girl Finlay saw something more between you and Jace and yanked Bullet's leash until he backed off."

"Maybe she should have let him go," Dixie said, wiping her eyes.

"You don't believe that."

Dixie shook her head, trying to dry her remaining tears. She told her mother about Jace showing up last night. "I thought I was protecting my heart by sending him away, but it just broke it even more. Am I *wrong* for wanting what you and Dad and everyone else has? I thought he might come back, but last night I realized he wouldn't. He's not the kind of guy who chases women, and I don't want a man who doesn't want me."

"Oh, baby. There's a big difference between not wanting a

woman and respecting her wishes. You sent him away, and he listened."

"It doesn't matter," she seethed. "He can't be what I want, and I don't want to be any man's sometimes lover."

"Like I said, I raised a strong woman. I think it's time you got away from everything. You haven't had a real vacation in years. Why don't you see if Daphne can give you the cottage a few days early and head up to the Cape? I'll fill in for you this week and get Babs to watch the babies for me." Daphne Zablonski was one of the founders of the book club Dixie was in, and she handled the reservations for Bayside Resort, where Dixie had rented a cottage for her trip to attend the opening of Justin's show at the gallery.

"But I'll miss the opening of Josie's gingerbread shop on Tuesday, and she's worked so hard. She's doing a ribbon cutting. I hate to let Josie down."

Her mother took her hand and said, "Just for once can you please put yourself first? Josie loves you, and she knows you support her. Gemma is writing a story about the opening of Ginger All the Days for the community newspaper. I'll make sure we take lots of pictures, and you can read the article. I didn't want to wave this in front of you, but not only is being here going to make you crazy, but if your brothers get wind of your situation, Jace might very well end up with two broken legs."

Dixie gasped. "They *can't* know. It's not Jace's fault. This is *all* on me. It was *my* choice to be with him and *my* choice to end things."

"Which is exactly why I'm suggesting that you get out of here until you can pull yourself together. Get rid of that Cyndi Lauper hair and those broken-heart slippers. You can get back to work Monday. Hopefully by then you'll be able to do that gorgeous outfit justice. Why does it look like you *slept* in it?"

Dixie lowered her eyes.

"Oh, Dixie. You are even worse off than I thought." Her mother sat and said, "That's it. Mama Red's taking control. Don't try to fight me on it. I'll do the books. I'll handle the shop and waitressing. I want you to go home, call Daphne to extend your reservation, and if she can't accommodate you, then call Violet, that friend of yours at Summer House, or stay with Justin or Madigan." Justin had three brothers—Blaine, Zander, and Zeke. Madigan was their only sister. Their mother, Dixie's aunt Reba, was Biggs's sister. "And I want you to take off that outfit before you start downing ice cream like alcohol and get stains on it. Take a hit of Benadryl or a shot of whiskey, and get some sleep. Tomorrow morning, you climb your pretty little ass into your Jeep and get the hell out of Peaceful Harbor. I don't want you to stop at the shop or say one word to your brothers. Do you hear me? You're lucky Diesel called me. If he'd called Bullet or your father, things would be going down very differently. Take your time going to the Cape. Stop in Mystic and walk around the seaport to clear your head. The fresh air will do you good."

Dixie sighed. "My heart feels like it's been ridden hard, wrung out, and tossed on the pavement."

"And then run over a few times, if I remember the feelings correctly," her mother said.

"How would you know? You've been with Dad forever."

"Because you don't get to forever without first walking through fire. You think your brothers met their significant others and everything was peachy? Heck no, Dixie. Theirs are not my stories to tell, but trust me, all of us have gone through our own private hell, and we each came out stronger on the other side. *Fate's* not to be fucked with. That bitch blows into your life at full speed, rides right up to you so you can smell her power, and then she lets you know who's in charge by leaving you to wonder if you'll ever feel whole again."

"If this is fate's hand at play, I'm going to hunt that wicked bitch down and you'll have to visit me in prison," Dixie said solemnly.

"Better ask Tru for some pointers first." Her mother chuckled and leaned in for a hug, squeezing Dixie tight. "I love you, baby." She rose to her feet and helped Dixie up, too.

"Thanks for rescuing me from myself."

"You didn't need rescuing, sweetheart. You've never been in love before. You just needed someone to part the trees so you could see beyond them and remember that you're a strong, smart woman and it's going to take an even stronger man to give you everything you need."

"I thought Jace was that man," she said, feeling raw.

Her mother picked up Dixie's keys from the table and put them in her hand, covering it with her own as she said, "Don't give up on him just yet. You're a force to be reckoned with. My guess is that you've knocked that big, burly man off-kilter and he's trying to figure out which way is up." As they walked toward the door, she said, "And if not, then he's a fucking idiot and he's lost out on the best thing he's ever had a shot at."

Chapter Seventeen

ALL THE OPEN road in the world wasn't enough to clear the image of Dixie Whiskey with tears in her eyes from Jace's head. It didn't help that she'd been *literally* everywhere he was since returning to LA Sunday night, when he received an envelope from Hawk containing dozens of prints from the photo shoot. Now it was Tuesday, and he was meeting with Maddox and their marketing team, as he had all day yesterday. They were choosing the final images for the calendar and the other marketing materials for the launch of the Legacy and Leather and Lace lines. They were down to eighteen possible pictures for the calendar, each of which were blown up to poster size and displayed on easels along one side of the conference room. Ten more poster-sized images were displayed on the other side of the room for the promotional packages. And at the front of the room was a projection screen that they were using to revisit pictures they'd already decided against, just in case they'd missed something.

Jace tried to focus on the discussions taking place. Work had once been the place where he could put his head down and drown out the rest of the world. Now even that was shot to hell.

Everywhere he looked, Dixie's face smiled back at him, but in his mind all he saw were the tears she'd shed, the hurt she'd tried to mask when she'd sent him packing. He'd thought about drowning those images with alcohol, but he couldn't bring himself to drink more than one shot. The only Whiskey he wanted had overpowered his ability to concentrate on anything other than her, which made these meetings even more of a nightmare. He was stuck listening to a room full of men and women pick at the woman who had touched him so deeply, she felt like she was *part* of him.

"Her legs look a little too skinny in number fifteen," one of the women from marketing said.

Too skinny, my ass. They're perfect.

"She looks older in number three," Maddox said. "And she looks younger in number eight than in all the others, so both of those stay, catering to different demographics."

A marketing assistant moved those two pictures off to the side.

"This is splitting hairs," one of the guys said. "But we are down to that, aren't we? Does anyone else think her breasts look a little *too* perfect in number four? That could be a turnoff for women buyers."

"Definitely splitting hairs," one of the women chimed in. "I'd give my left arm to have that problem."

The group laughed.

Jace scowled. He imagined most women would give their left arm to look like Dixie.

"I like the look in her eyes in twelve better than fifteen," another guy said.

The guy next to him nudged him with his elbow and said, "That's because you're imagining the pictures above your bed."

Jace gritted his teeth for the dozenth time that day.

Maddox glanced at Jace from the other end of the conference room. He was wearing the black leather jacket he almost never took off, his elbows resting on the table. One hand covered his other in front of his chin. He wore thick silver-and-gold rings on two of his fingers and several leather, beaded, and silver bracelets on his wrist. The edge of a tattoo snaked out from under the sleeve of his jacket. His face was weathered, his thick silver hair and beard flecked with black, and his eyes held the hard look of a man who had not only been *around* the block, but he'd worn a path so deep, he *owned* it.

Maddox had been looking at Jace for the past two days like he was trying to puzzle him out. Jace shifted uncomfortably in his seat. Maddox knew him better than any man ever had. Could he read the fucked-up chaos wreaking havoc in Jace's head?

"We should use number sixteen for the life-size cardboard cutouts in the retailer outlets," another woman said. In that picture, Dixie was standing in front of the bike, one arm across her stomach, the elbow of her other arm leaning on it. Her tattoos added vibrant color to her flawless skin. Her hand rested by her shoulder in an alluringly feminine pose. Her chin was angled down, and she was looking at the camera with a taunting challenge in her eyes *and* on her lips. Her hair fell over the shoulders of her Leather and Lace bralette, which was paired with leather pants with silver zippers and lace accents and a pair of high-heeled leather boots.

"Good call. She looks tough but approachable," Maddox agreed.

"She does have that *come on, baby, try me* look in her eyes," one of the guys said.

Jace didn't like the way he said it. He must have looked annoyed, because the guy mouthed, *Sorry.*

"I'm ordering one of those for my place," another guy said. He leaned forward with a teasing expression and said, "I know we can't mix business and pleasure, but can't you make an exception just this once?"

Not in this lifetime. Jace was *sick* of hearing comments and innuendos about Dixie, and he was also growing irritated with the concerned looks Maddox was giving him. He narrowed his eyes and pointed at the guy. "You. *Out. Now,*" he said in a deathly serious voice, leaving no room for negotiation.

The guy stilled like a deer in the headlights, as did everyone else in the room. The offender's eyes darted right, then left, his lips twitching as if he were expecting it to be a joke, waiting for the others to laugh. "Sorry, Jace. I meant no disrespect. It was a joke."

"The fact that you need to explain should tell you how off base you were." Jace looked at the door, dismissing him.

After the guy left the room, an underlying hum of tension remained. The staff fidgeted uncomfortably, and Maddox arched a brow, as if he were trying to work out why Jace had suddenly reacted to what had been going on all day. Or maybe he was amused, in which case Jace would give him shit later.

"What's next?" Jace asked firmly.

"I've got something," Leni Steele said. She was sharp as a tack and had been spot-on when she'd recommended Hawk. "I just received an email from Shea. Jillian Braden is slotted to attend Fashion Week, and they pulled some strings and got the Leather and Lace line in!"

There was an uproar of cheers.

Jace held up his hand, and the cheers quieted. He looked at

Maddox and said, "When did fashion shows become part of the launch?"

"I spoke to Shea over the weekend while you were traveling," Maddox explained. "It wasn't part of the original launch plan, but she thinks it'll take our clothing line mainstream."

"That's great, but Dixie didn't sign up to do fashion shows." And he couldn't picture anyone else representing the line.

"Oh, that's not a problem," Leni reassured them. "Shea has a dozen models ready to do the show, and if we give her approval, she thinks she can use this to get the line into two other prominent fashion shows."

"That could be huge," one of the other women said.

"I don't care how huge it could be," Jace said firmly. "We signed Dixie Whiskey as the face of Silver-Stone, and that means something."

"With all due respect," Leni said, "I don't even think it's possible for one model to do a show of this caliber."

"Not to mention that she's *not* a model," Maddox reminded him.

"Turning this down would be like cutting your legs off at the knees," Leni urged. "It's impossible to get in on Fashion Week this late in the game. They almost never—"

"I know how big a deal this is," Jace interrupted. "That doesn't change the fact that I don't like the idea of it."

"Jace." Maddox leveled him with a stare and said, "Be reasonable."

How could he be reasonable when his mind was fucked beyond repair? He pushed to his feet and paced by the windows. "Clear the room," he demanded. "I need a minute with Maddox."

As the others gathered their things and filed out of the

room, Jace tried to get his head on straight—an impossible task.

Maddox closed the door and crossed his arms, watching Jace pace like a caged tiger. "You've been acting blue-balled and bitchy since we met in Boston last week. I'd tell you to take the day off, but we're signing the Boston deal at five. I think you'd better tell me what's going on with you."

He looked at the man who had been there for him since he was a cocky kid, his brilliant mentor who had turned into a loyal friend and trusted business partner. For the first time in their dealings, Jace was at a loss for words. He sank down to a chair and said, "We gotta talk. I'm so fucked…"

Chapter Eighteen

WEDNESDAY MORNING DIXIE sat on an Adirondack chair behind the cottage she'd rented, gazing out at Cape Cod Bay with a book in her lap and several hours to kill before Justin's show at the gallery. She planned on spending it in that exact spot, with the sun warming her cheeks, the bay lapping at the shore, and the sounds of families on the beach floating up the dune with the afternoon breeze. Her mother had been right. Coming to the Cape early had given her the space she needed to try to begin clearing her head, even if it hadn't touched the hurt in her heart. She'd decided not to stop in Mystic and had driven the whole ten-plus hours straight to the Cape. She'd settled into the adorable one-bedroom cottage Monday evening, and then she'd wallowed in self-pity for the rest of the night. But yesterday morning had greeted her with a nudge in the right direction when she was walking along the edge of the dunes and Daphne's almost two-year-old daughter, Hadley, had toddled over for a visit.

Daphne and her daughter lived above the offices of the resort. They had been on their way to have breakfast with their friends who owned Summer House Inn, the property next door, when Hadley had spotted Dixie and detoured in her direction. Hadley had clung to her with a serious scowl on her adorable face. Apparently the precious little girl didn't smile very often. Daphne had invited Dixie to join them for breakfast with their friends, and she introduced Dixie to more of the women she knew from their online and video book club chats. She also met a few of the women's significant others, and it was obvious how happy those couples were. Dixie had hoped to find that kind of happiness with Jace, and she'd felt herself slipping back into a dark abyss. It was then, while sitting with her new friends, with sweet little serious-faced Hadley on her lap, that Hadley had surprised her with a smile. Dixie's heart had melted, driving home how much she wanted a family of her own. She'd realized that life was too short to wallow in heartache and had vowed once again to try to find a way to come to grips with the fact that she and Jace were *done* and move on.

It would be one thing if Jace had lied to her or had led her on and then broken her heart, but he hadn't done either of those things. Even if she was never able to love another man, she couldn't allow herself to be miserable over her *own* stupid mistakes forever. She'd forced her own hand yesterday and given herself a push in the right direction. Instead of shutting out the world, she'd called her aunt Reba, her father's sister, to say she'd arrived in town early and would like to hang out. Reba was very much like Dixie's own mother: strong, loving, and unwilling to put up with bullshit. As the wife of a Dark Knight, she couldn't be anything less. Her aunt had said, "Say no more, sweet pea. Get your butt over here." It turned out that her mother's bragging about the auction and Dixie's appointment as the face of Silver-Stone had traveled quickly through her family. It had been as exciting as it was difficult to relive those events with her cousins and friends, but she'd spent the rest of the day surrounded by family, and it had been the perfect remedy for her aching heart.

Until she returned to her cottage and the silence had pressed in on her.

She'd spent the evening looking at the pictures she'd brought with her. One picture of Jace—her favorite of the ones Hawk had taken, in which Jace was leaning against the wall talking on his phone—and a picture of her family and friends. First, she'd admired the picture of Jace until she'd missed him so much her chest hurt. Then, to soothe the ache, she'd looked at the picture of her family and friends that was taken at the hospital the night Maggie Rose was born. That picture never failed to make her happy. She knew how messed up it was that she'd brought Jace's picture with her, but she *wasn't* trying to *forget* him. She was only trying to come to grips with going back to being friends and not lovers. The truth was, she hoped she'd never forget a single second of their time together.

That endless cycle of stabbing a dagger in her heart and then soothing the wound, only to stab herself again, had gone on until she'd fallen asleep hugging the pillow as if it were Jace.

The whole night had pretty much sucked, which was why she was trying a different tactic this morning—getting lost in the romance novel her book club was reading. It was actually working, at least part of the time. She'd get drawn into the story, which was a great distraction, but then she'd come to a sexy scene and immediately replace the hero and heroine with Jace and herself. That got her hot and bothered, which led to reality, and then, inevitably, to sadness.

A gust of salty air swept up the dune. Dixie tucked a wayward lock of hair behind her ear and picked up the book, diving into her next distraction.

SPENDING THE DAY reading in the sun had helped ease the tension that had been Dixie's constant companion for the past several days. As she sipped her champagne at Justin's art show later in the evening, she was glad for the reprieve, even if she knew she'd be sucked right back to sadness when she returned to the cottage. She'd been at the gallery for hours, and it was still standing room only. The Dark Knights had turned out in droves, as had local residents and tourists. Justin's sculptures were a huge success, and it was wonderful to see him honored by so many people. Justin was incredibly talented, although his artwork had always tugged at Dixie's heart. Every piece looked a little bit *tortured*, like the one Dixie stood before now, depicting a naked, armless woman lying on her back on top of what appeared to be waves. Her head was tilted back, eyes closed, her delicate features beautifully crafted. Thick straps of stone wound around her torso and legs like a flat python squeezing its prey. She looked at another piece a few feet away, an enormous sculpture of a woman's face emerging from chipped and textured stone. Her lips and nose were smooth, polished, and well defined, but the area from the apple of her right cheek to the bridge of her nose appeared to have been broken off, as though the woman had been battered and that part of her face had crumbled to pieces. His other sculptures were equally interesting and powerful.

Dixie set her empty glass on a tray and glanced across the room at Justin surrounded by a flock of pretty women. All of the Wicked brothers were big and brawny, even Justin. Though he had been adopted, he looked like he was made from the same strong stock. Like most of the Dark Knights, they were tough, mouthy, and fearless.

Justin glanced over, and that fiendish grin he was known for slid across his handsome face. He lifted his chin, excused himself from his harem, and headed for Dixie. Justin didn't walk; he *swaggered*. He was broad shouldered, sported plenty of tattoos, and depending on his mood, he was either cocky and playful or he had a chip on his shoulder the size of Antarctica, which went well with his ice-blue eyes. His dark hair always looked like he'd just made out with someone, and his beard was short and neat.

He sidled up to her and said, "Hey, Dix. Which piece is your favorite?"

"I think that one." She pointed to the woman tangled up like prey and said, "But you know I love all of them. Which is your favorite?"

His gaze moved to Chloe Mallery, the regal-looking blonde holding a champagne flute across the room. Chloe had started the book club with Daphne. Dixie knew her through their chats, and she'd met her in person at breakfast yesterday. Chloe was funny, sharp, and *definitely* the type of woman who would call Justin on his shit, which made sense since she'd told the girls in the book club that she would never date a *bad boy*. She was *also* there with a date, whom she'd met on a dating app.

"Does *she* know that?" Dixie asked.

Chloe looked over before Justin answered, and the distance between them practically caught fire before her cheeks pinked up and she turned away.

"You tell me," Justin said arrogantly.

Dixie laughed. "How well do you know her?"

"Well enough to know she'd be hot in bed." Justin finished his champagne.

Dixie rolled her eyes. "Then you know she won't date a biker."

"This pretty-boy Ken-doll shit is just a phase. She'll get tired of hanging out with guys with training wheels soon enough. When she's ready for a real man, I'll be there to welcome her to the club."

"Good luck with that," Dixie said, as Zander, one of Justin's younger brothers, joined them.

"Hey, Zan," Justin said, bumping fists with his brother.

"Great show," Zander said, his eyes dancing with mischief as he nodded toward the door where their brother Zeke was talking with two pretty brunettes. "Zeke and I are heading out. We'll catch you at the Hog later, okay?" Their aunt and uncle owned a restaurant/bar called the Salty Hog, and they were throwing a big celebration in Justin's honor after the show.

Justin's face grew serious. "Definitely. Who are the babes?"

"Tourists." Zander waggled his brows. He was the playboy of the family, and he had a knack for finding trouble.

Justin frowned and said, "You treat them well, you hear me?"

"That's the only way I fly, bro."

"Dix, excuse me for a minute." He grabbed Zander's shirt-sleeve and dragged him away.

Dixie chuckled at the pot calling the kettle black. She spotted Madigan coming her way and waved. Madigan was in her early twenties, the youngest of Justin's siblings. With wavy mahogany hair and eyes the color of a spring sky, she was as sweet and slight as her brothers were tough and brawny.

"What did my brother do now?" Madigan asked, watching Justin lecturing Zander.

"Zander's just being Zander."

"I see nothing's changed while I was away." Madigan was a puppeteer and a greeting card designer. She'd returned to the Cape a few weeks ago after being away for several months touring the country for her puppeteer business. "Did you meet Justin's friend Gavin before he left? That man is *tasty*, isn't he?"

Dixie had seen the tall, handsome, clean-cut man with wily green eyes who had caught the attention of every woman within a twenty-foot radius. "He was hot, but too squeaky clean for me."

"I forgot, you like your boys rough."

"*Men*, Mads," Dixie corrected her as two of Madigan's brawny and bearded cousins, Tank and Baz Wicked, strolled through the door, drawing the eyes of just about every female in the room.

Tank was the eldest of Madigan's three Wicked cousins, and at six four, he was also the biggest. He had dark hair, a body full of tattoos, and several piercings. As usual, he was wearing his leather vest sporting the Dark Knights patches. He had a couple of inches on Baz, a handsome veterinarian who ran an animal rescue with their youngest brother, Dwayne. Though they weren't related to Dixie by blood—their father and Madigan's father were brothers—they were all one big family through the Dark Knights.

Baz greeted a woman by the door with a hug as Tank made his way to Justin. Baz had longish dirty-blond hair and puppy-dog eyes. Women around town called him *prime husband material*. Baz, however, had other plans for himself.

"I'm glad Tank made it," Dixie said. "How's he doing?"

Tank hadn't been around yesterday when she was visiting with her cousins and Tank's family, and she was worried about him. Their younger sister, Ashley, had committed suicide several years ago. While it had taken everyone a long time to move past Ashley's death, Dixie knew some of the Wickeds still hadn't fully dealt with their grief, Tank included.

"He's still trying to save the world," Madigan said solemnly. Shortly after his sister had passed away, Tank had joined the fire department, making it his life mission to rescue everyone.

"I guess that's a good thing."

"We can only hope. Who knows for sure, though, right? You know Tank. He's not big on sharing his feelings," she said as Tank cut through the crowd, heading toward them.

Dixie was glad to see a smile lifting his lips as he joined them, though the bottomless pain in his eyes remained.

"Well, aren't you a sight for sore eyes, *chili pepper*," Tank said as he draped an arm over Dixie's shoulder, hugging her. He smelled like leather and fresh air, and he had called Dixie *chili pepper* forever. When they were young he'd called her *Red* and Dixie's mother had been quick to nip that in the bud.

"I could say the same about you," Dixie said.

Tank kept his arm around her neck and said, "I've got a chair with your name on it in my shop. You going to let me tattoo you while you're here?" In addition to volunteering as a firefighter, Tank owned a tattoo parlor.

"We'll see. I just got inked a few days ago." She showed them her new tattoo.

"Oh! That's beautiful," Madigan said.

Tank whistled, studying the tattoo. "Nice line work. Who did it?"

"A friend," she said, trying to ignore the quickening of her pulse.

"I hear you're a supermodel now." Tank leaned closer and said, "And that your brothers just about had coronaries the other night at the auction."

"It was interesting, that's for sure," Dixie said lightly.

"I've got to give it to Jace Stone. He's got *big ones*," Tank said. "I guess he really wanted you for that calendar."

A knot tightened in Dixie's chest.

"I've known Jace from Bikes on the Beach since I was yay high." Madigan put her hand out about two feet from the floor. "That man is better than crunchy peanut butter."

Tank scowled. "And he's old enough to be your *father*."

"I don't want to *date* him. I'm just saying he's hot. Anyway, Dix, I'm *so* proud of you!" Madigan said. "You're brave standing up to your brothers and your father like that. Your mom told my mother that she's never been prouder of you. I could *never* do anything like that."

Tank arched a thick dark brow and said, "You'd have to stick around long enough for them to give you a hard time first, Mads."

"Aw, Tanky, did my big ol' cousin miss me while I was gone?" Madigan put her arms around him, hugging him tight.

"You caught me," Tank said.

Madigan flashed a cheesy smile.

Tank chuckled. "I'm going to get a drink. Can I get you anything?"

"No thanks," Dixie and Madigan said in unison.

As Tank walked away, Madigan peered around Dixie and said, "So, Dix, exactly how many dates does forty grand get a guy?"

"*One*. Why?"

"Because someone's looking at you like he's here to collect his due." Madigan pointed toward the door.

Dixie spun around, losing her balance at the sight of Jace striding determinedly through the gallery, his eyes locked on her. She grabbed hold of Madigan's arm to steady herself, wondering what the hell he was doing there and why he looked angry.

JACE CUT THROUGH the crowd toward Dixie, who was stunning in a sexy black miniskirt, a dressy white tank top, and the leather boots she never seemed to be without. She appeared oblivious to the other guys in the gallery who were checking her out, but Jace wasn't. The tension in his gut was gnawing away at him. Her mouth twitched, as if she wasn't sure if she should bare her teeth or smile.

"Hi, Jace," Madigan said excitedly, leaning in for a hug. "I didn't know you were in town."

"Neither did I," Dixie said. "What are you doing here?"

"Taking care of business," Jace said as evenly as he could when every muscle in his body was corded tight.

Dixie put her hand on her hip, lifting her chin as she said, "Of course. Why else would you be here?"

"*Geez*, Dix." Madigan looked disapprovingly at her. "The way Jace made a beeline for you, I was sure he was here to collect a second date for all that money he plunked down at the auction."

"I've already paid that debt," Dixie said coldly.

Jace gritted his teeth and quickly schooled his expression.

"You may have paid your debt, but we still have unfinished business to discuss." He took hold of Dixie's arm, feeling her go rigid, and said, "If you'll excuse us for a minute, Madigan."

He led Dixie toward the door as she snapped at him in hushed, angry whispers. "What are you doing? I thought you were supposed to be in LA. Answer me, Jace. *Jace?*"

She was so mad, and though he hadn't known what to expect, he hadn't expected *that* reaction. Had he made a mistake by coming there? After flying across the country from LA to New York, picking up his bike, and driving straight to the Cape, he was exhausted and didn't trust himself not to snap right back at her, so he bit his tongue as he pushed through the door.

"*Jace!*" she seethed as he led her outside and around the side of the building, where they could be alone. She yanked her arm free, breathing hard, anger and confusion staring back at him. "*What* is going on? You can't just drag me away from Justin's show like you own me."

He felt like he was cracking open, and at the same time, anger brewed in retaliation to that pain. Despite the war raging inside him, he stepped closer, craving the connection that had driven him there.

"You're so *angry*," he said gruffly. "And here I am, Dix, after too many torturous days and fucking hellish nights, *finally* standing with the woman who has infiltrated my every thought, feeling like I can breathe for the first time since you left New York."

Her expression softened, and she looked like she might say something, but nothing came out.

"Tell me I didn't make a mistake putting my business obligations on hold to be with you this week." He touched her hand, his heart hammering against his ribs, and said, "Fuck, Dix. Say *something*."

She blinked several times and said, "I...I still don't know what you're doing here. You know where I stand."

"I do. I told you that I hear everything you say, but I also hear the things you don't. I heard everything you said in Peaceful Harbor, and as much as it killed me to do it, I did what you asked and I left. But damn it, Dixie, it was the things you didn't say that had me pushing off days of meetings, flying across the country to be here with you. I know you're missing me as much as I'm missing you."

He gathered her in his arms, relief consuming him when she didn't freeze up. "I know you need promises, and you know I'm a man of my word. I haven't answered to anyone in so long, I can't stand here and promise you something I'm not sure I can give. But you are the *only* thing I can think about. What you're doing, who you're with, wondering if you're thinking about me. The pain I saw in your eyes when I came to see you gutted me. I don't ever want to see that look again, and damn it, Dix, you're all I see when I close my eyes. When I get on my bike, I *feel* your arms around me. And if that doesn't tell you just how much you've messed with my head, then this will. When I walked into my place in LA, where you've *never* stepped foot, I felt your absence like a missing limb."

"Jace," she said in a shaky whisper.

Her lower lip trembled, but he had to get the rest out. "I can't promise you next week or forever, but I'm here *now*. If you're still into me, which I think you are because what we have is too fucking powerful to dissipate, then I'm yours for the rest of the week. It's a *start*, Dixie, and it's the best I can do right now. Lord knows it's the biggest step I've ever taken with a woman. What I *can* promise you is that I have no interest in being with anyone else and that I will do everything within my power not to hurt you again. The choice is yours. I've been up all night, and I'm sure I'm not saying this as eloquently as you deserve, but I hope I've said it clear enough—"

"It's *enough*," she said with tears in her eyes, pressing her lips to his.

Like a starving man to a meal, he greedily took more. She was the balm to his anguish, the very oxygen he needed to breathe. When she melted against him, returning his kisses with all of the passion and intensity he remembered, the tangled and broken pieces of himself started falling back into place. He slowed their kisses, savoring their closeness and thanking the heavens above that she was giving him another chance.

Chapter Nineteen

FOR THE FIRST time in her life, Dixie felt *giddy*. She knew how big a step it was for Jace to put his work on hold even for a few days, but to have come after her? To give even the promise of a *start*? He was giving them a *real* chance. She remembered what he'd said about not trusting a woman, and that made what he'd done, and all the things he'd said, that much sweeter. The longer they kissed, the more he filled up the empty spaces he'd left behind.

He touched his forehead to hers and whispered, "God, I've missed you."

"I can't believe you put everything off to be with me."

"Believe it, Dix. I couldn't stay away for another day. I know I'm not perfect, but I'm trying the best I can." He took her hand in his and said, "Can we get out of here? Go some-place to be alone?"

Her mind screamed *yes*, but there was one obligation she couldn't get out of. "I want to more than anything, but Justin's cousins are throwing him a big celebration at the Salty Hog and I promised I would go."

"Then the Salty Hog it is." He kissed her softly and said,

"It's going to be hell keeping my hands to myself."

A thrill skated through her. "That makes two of us."

"The past week has felt like a month. I wasn't sure how you'd react to me showing up like this, but I had to come."

"You kind of blew me away." *Kind of* was the understatement of a lifetime. The man who didn't chase or make empty promises had not only come after her, but he'd promised her a start. *A start!* Would she ever be able to think about those two words again without getting giddy?

"I'm crazy about you, Dixie. Thank you for giving us a chance."

Her heart soared. "Where are you staying?" she asked, hoping he'd stay with her.

"I didn't get that far. I figured if things went badly, I'd crash at Jared's place in Truro."

"I'm staying at a cute cottage in Wellfleet, and the bed is *way* too big for me," she said with feigned innocence. "I guess I can make do if you want to stay at your brother's place."

His hands slid down her back and he pressed her tight against his hard body. "Like hell you will."

BY THE TIME they pried themselves apart, everyone was leaving the gallery and heading to the bar. They made a quick stop at Dixie's cottage to drop off her Jeep and Jace's bag—enjoying dozens of steamy kisses—then they went to join the others for the celebration.

The Salty Hog was a two-story restaurant and bar in Harwich Port overlooking the harbor. There was the restaurant on the main floor and a bar on the upper level. Tank's parents had owned it for as long as Dixie could remember. She had fond memories of sipping sodas on the back deck with her cousins and other Dark Knight families when they were young. The older kids kept an eye on the younger ones while the parents danced and carried on upstairs, where there were pool tables, darts, and almost always a live band. Unlike Whiskey Bro's, which catered primarily to bikers, the Salty Hog was a favorite haunt for locals and tourists from all walks of life. Though tonight, for the celebration in Justin's honor, motorcycles outnumbered other vehicles in the parking lot.

Jace kept his hand on Dixie's lower back as they made their way upstairs, his dark eyes taking everything in. Her giddiness had calmed to a constant vibration, though she was trying to tamp down her expectations. She'd never realized how easy it was to get swept away when a man made such a meaningful gesture. *Everything* was different between them. *She* felt different, less like she had to stand her ground and protect her heart. Not only had he *heard* every word she'd said, but he'd acted on them, making her feel more than special, like he would protect her heart now, too.

That was an incredible feeling. She was proud to be with him as they stepped into the crowded bar.

"Dixie! Jace!" Madigan waved from where she stood by a table, surrounded by her four brothers and three Wicked cousins.

Jace's arm circled Dixie's waist, holding her closer as they made their way over to the table. Justin, Madigan, and Tank were watching them curiously.

"Jace, my man. Thanks for showing up," Justin said as he filled two shot glasses. Justin handed Dixie and Jace drinks and waggled his finger between them. "This is *new*. Did I miss something in the last hour?"

All the men around the table chuckled.

"I knew it!" Madigan exclaimed with wide-eyed delight. "I could tell by the way you were looking at Dixie that there was something between you two."

Tank eyed Jace over the rim of his glass and said, "Collecting on that forty-grand auction win, Stone?"

"Absolutely *not*," Jace said gruffly, holding Dixie tighter.

"Hey." Dixie pointed at the amused Wicked clan. "Cut the crap. This is *my* life, and I did not just take a frigging stand at the auction to be heckled by you nitwits. If I hear *one word* out of any of you about this now, or from my family back home, I will hunt you down and make you regret it. Not a word, *got it?*"

All the men held their hands up in surrender, except Tank. His eyes remained trained on Jace and Dixie, softening only when Dixie gave him a reassuring look.

Dwayne whistled. "Back up, boys. Dixie's in the house."

"We know better than to get in your way," Baz said with a wink.

"Give me enough to drink and I won't even remember this tomorrow," Zander said, and then he guzzled his drink.

"You heard the woman." Justin cocked a grin. "What happens at the Hog stays at the Hog!"

There was a round of cheers and commotion as the men filled their glasses for another shot.

"I was about to shut them down," Jace said to Dixie. "But that was *hot*."

"I had to nip it in the bud. You give these guys an inch and they'll take a mile." She clinked her glass with his and they drank their shot.

Justin lifted a bottle to refill their glasses.

"No more for me." Jace set his glass on the table. "I'm transporting precious cargo tonight."

Dixie swooned and caught a dreamy sigh from Madigan.

"You're a good man," Justin said. "Dix? You in?"

"No, thanks." She didn't drink when she was riding, *and* she wanted to be sober to enjoy every second of her night with Jace.

"To Justin!" Justin's older brother, Blaine, shouted, and another cheer rang out.

"I'm not drinking either," Madigan said. "You guys are so cute together. How long have you been going out?"

"Jace!" An exotic-looking brunette wearing a flouncy floral dress pushed through the crowd, squealed, and launched herself into Jace's arms.

Dixie's chest constricted as Jace lifted the hot little number right off her feet. *Do you have a woman in every town? Because I did not sign up for this shit.* She fought the urge to pry the woman from *her* man.

When the effervescent chick's high heels touched the ground, she smiled at Madigan, and Jace reached for Dixie, bringing her possessively to his side. "Marly, this is my girl, Dixie."

"Your *girl?*" Marly's face lit up. She turned to Madigan and said, "Mads? Is it true? Please tell me it's true!"

Madigan laughed. "I can confirm that Jace and Dixie are an item, although they don't want to talk about it."

"*Girl...*" Marly grabbed Dixie's and Madigan's arms and said, "We need to talk."

As Marly dragged them away from Jace, Dixie looked over her shoulder at him. He held his palms up with an apologetic expression.

"Don't look to him for help," Marly said. "I've known that man for eight years and not *once* has he brought a girl around. So you've got some explaining to do, chickadee."

"I could say the same for *you*." Dixie pulled her arm free and planted her hand on her hip. She didn't even *try* to hold back. "Are you an old flame? Because I won't put up with that cheery, hugging shit if you've slept with my man."

"Forget the explanation. *Wow.* I get it," Marly said with a knowing smile.

"Right?" Madigan said as they gathered around a high-top table. "They're a perfect match. But we're *not* talking about that."

"Got it, and to answer your question, Dixie, no, I'm not an old flame of Jace's." Marly's expression turned serious. "The first time I met Jace was at Bikes on the Beach, almost two years after my older brother Paul was killed."

Dixie's stomach pitched. "Oh, Marly. I'm so sorry."

"Thank you," she said kindly. "He was taking a joyride on his buddy's motorcycle, and he wasn't wearing a helmet. He was thrown from the bike and died instantly. He shouldn't have been on the bike. He'd never ridden a motorcycle before, but twenty-year-olds don't always think things through." She sighed, hurt passing over her face. "I was eighteen when Paul died, and it pretty much destroyed me. I wanted to do something to try to keep other families from going through the same heartache, so I started the Head Safe motorcycle safety program."

"You started that program?" Dixie had heard about it. "That's a required course as part of the Department of Motor Vehicles licensing requirements in the town where I live."

"It was a huge deal when it went national," Madigan said. "We're all very proud of Marly."

"I'm just glad I was able to get people to see the seriousness of riding without a helmet." Marly glanced at Jace, who was talking with a few of the Dark Knights, and said, "I met Jace right after I started the program. I was a naive twenty-year-old, totally out of my element at Bikes on the Beach, standing by a card table trying to pass out flyers. I was much shyer then and had never been around people like this." She waved to the crowd of bikers, many of whom were bearded, tattooed, and wearing their leathers. "Nobody paid me any attention, but Jace walked up and asked for a flyer, and I swear my heart nearly stopped. He looked so much like Paul. He was older, but the similarities were striking, and I lost it. Bawled my eyes out, blubbered like a fool to the one person who actually spoke to me. Jace didn't even know me, but he wrapped me in his arms and held me as I cried. I was so embarrassed, but he kept saying, 'Whatever it is, it'll be okay.'"

A lump lodged in Dixie's throat.

"I need to go get a pitcher of soda, or I'm going to cry." Madigan headed for the bar.

"I love her," Marly said.

"She's sweet, and so are you, Marly. I'm sorry I jumped the gun before. I've known Jace a long time, but our relationship is new, and I got jealous. But I'm really not a jealous bitch."

Marly laughed. "It's okay. Jace is a special guy and definitely worth getting jealous over. When I finally stopped crying that day and explained myself to him, he sat down and we talked for, like, two hours straight. And then he spent the rest of that day, and the next, handing out pamphlets for the program with me. I had no idea he was a bigwig in the biking community. I thought he was just a nice guy. He said he had sisters and hoped that if they were in the same situation, someone would be there for them. It wasn't until the last day of the event, when he showed up with an outline of a business strategy and marketing plan for Head Safe and walked me through them that I realized this kind gentleman knew a heck of a lot about business and bikes. I finally asked what he did for a living. He said he was with Silver-Stone, but he said it so nonchalantly, he could have been low on the totem pole. He connected me with Alexander Gallow, the director of marketing at Silver-Stone's LA head-quarters and said he'd forward a copy of the business plan to him, along with a list of people in the industry for me to contact when I was ready. That's when I googled Jace and found out that he was one of the owners of the company, and of course I was floored. Alexander has been a godsend, but Jace was like my guardian angel. I've never met anyone like him."

Neither have I.

"Without Jace, the program never would have gotten off the ground," Marly said, bringing Dixie's mind back to her story. "He funded an initiative to take it statewide, then helped me get funding to take it nationwide. And I'm sure you know how he is. He still won't allow me to do anything in return. He says educating people is saving lives, and that's enough of a payback. To this day he calls me on the anniversary of Paul's death, and he helps me at the booth for a few hours each day during Bikes on the Beach, and he gives twenty-five percent of every helmet sold by Silver-Stone to the program."

"That's incredible," Dixie said, feeling guilty for having accused Jace of throwing money at the auction and not wanting to give his time to help others. Now she understood how little time he had to give and the ways in which he was already helping so many. She glanced across the room at him, wondering why he hadn't set her straight.

She turned her attention back to Marly and said, "You're incredible, too, Marly, for starting such a great program. I'm sure your brother is smiling down on you, proud of all you've done."

"I'd like to think so, but knowing Paul, he's the one who dropped Jace in my path. He was a really good brother. I miss him."

Madigan set three glasses on the table and said, "Are we past the crying part?"

"*Part?* That would be the *whole* story." Dixie pointed to the empty glasses and said, "Did you get a little thirsty on the way over?"

"*No,* she did *not.*" Conroy Wicked's deep voice sailed over Dixie's shoulder as he filled the glasses. His deep-set eyes glittered playfully. He was a tough biker with movie-star looks: a long, straight nose, wavy silver hair he wore long enough to brush his collar, and a warm smile that set off his dimples. The apples had not fallen far from the tree. All four of his children had inherited his killer dimples. Tank also shared their father's burly stature, Dwayne was every bit as cocky as Conroy, and Baz shared their father's ability to remain calm in any situation. Before the tragic loss of his daughter, Ashley had shared their father's zest for life.

Conroy set the pitcher on the table and said, "How're three of my favorite girls? The guys get too rowdy for you?"

"No. I was just getting to know Marly," Dixie said.

"She's quite a gal." He clapped a hand on Marly's shoulder and said, "I'm surprised you two haven't met before. She's one of my honorary daughters."

"Aren't all the girls around here your honorary daughters?" Madigan teased. "I swear, between my parents, Dixie's parents, and you and Aunt Ginger, nobody within a fifty-mile radius of our town or of Peaceful Harbor could be parentless if they tried."

Conroy flashed his pearly whites and said, "Good, then maybe you girls and my boys can remember that for the next generation."

"You know we will," Dixie said, looking around the crowded bar. "This is quite a party."

"We'll take any reason to get the gang together," Conroy said, looking around the crowded bar. "It was great visiting with you last night, Dix. You need to come out and see us more often."

"Or you could drag your butt down to Maryland." She took a sip of her soda and said, "My parents would love to see you."

Conroy glanced at the bar and said, "We'll do that. But right now I'd better go help serve drinks. You girls have fun."

When he walked away, Marly said, "Not that I'm into your uncle, Mads, but he is so *hot*."

"He does have three available sons," Madigan pointed out.

"Don't get me started…" Marly glanced around the room and sighed. "Do you ever feel like you'll be single forever?"

"I know I will, and I look *forward* to it," Madigan answered.

"I forgot about Little Miss I Don't Believe in Love," Marly teased.

"I believe in love for other people," Madigan insisted. "I like going on dates, and I like that feeling of excitement when you're just getting to know someone. But I just don't see *love* in my future."

Madigan had never been one to sleep around or play head

games with guys. She was in her early twenties and always seemed happy doing her own thing.

"Well, I hope that's not true, because I think love is beautiful. Dixie, how did you and Jace meet?" Marly asked.

"It was a day I'll never forget." Dixie remembered the thrill of trying to get Jace to notice her. "I was at a bike rally with my brother Bear, and he kept talking about this motorcycle designer he wanted to meet named Jace. I literally stopped dead in my tracks when I saw him." She told them the whole embarrassing story, which led to Marly and Madigan exchanging their embarrassing stories.

The conversation turned to other topics, like family and hobbies, and Dixie told them about the book club. She gave them the link to join, and then she and Marly exchanged phone numbers so they could keep in touch after Dixie returned to Peaceful Harbor. When they circled back to talking about relationships and the girls discussed their opposing viewpoints, Dixie's thoughts returned to Jace. She reveled in all the wonderful things he'd said to her earlier when he'd poured his heart out like he couldn't hold anything back. She didn't want to hold back either.

She picked up her glass and said, "I'm going to leave you two to discuss the merits of love while I go do a little hands-on research."

JACE WATCHED DIXIE making her way across the room. She stood out among the crowd like a diamond among gemstones. Though he knew she'd refute it if he said it aloud, she moved with as much strength and confidence as she did grace. She stopped to chat with Justin's mother, her eyes darting to him, that secret smile he adored curving her lips. She was so different from the women he knew. Most women dreamed of being showered in diamonds and furs. He knew Dixie didn't dream of those things. She longed to be wrapped in his arms at night and to wake up in them in the mornings. She dreamed of him joining her in the world in which she was happiest, surrounded by her family and a sense of security.

She hugged Justin's mother, and then she set her catlike eyes on him. He had no doubt that he'd started falling for her years ago. His attraction at first had been physical, but it had taken only a matter of minutes before he'd realized all that she was and that attraction had burned stronger than anything he'd ever known. He'd compared all women—*grown* women—to the tough, confident eighteen-year-old she had been. Over the years he'd noticed how loyal and loving a sister and daughter she was. He'd watched her from afar as she'd grown into a sharp businesswoman, wiser and even more beautiful with each passing year. She was the most intriguing woman he'd ever known, and he'd fought the urge to get close to her, to get to know her, building impenetrable walls around himself in order to keep his distance, to protect her from his unwillingness to be the man she needed. Their time in New York had tipped the scales. He wanted to give her everything she'd ever dreamed of. But he was a man of his word, and he would never in a million years let Dixie settle for empty promises.

His heart beat faster as Dixie set her glass on the table and lowered herself to his lap, claiming him in front of her family and friends. He thought she might chat with her cousins and friends, but her eyes were still on him, making him feel like a fucking king. As his arms circled her, the approving looks coming from around the table also felt pretty damn good.

"Why did you sell yourself short?" she asked so sweetly he didn't recognize her tone.

"What do you mean?"

"When you first asked me to be in the calendar, I gave you a hard time about not taking part in the auction. I said some harsh things about you giving money so you didn't have to donate your time. But Marly just told me how you two met and everything you've done for her, and your sisters mentioned scholarships, internships, and mentoring programs that you set up at Silver-Stone."

"Dix, those are just things I wanted to do. I didn't do them so I could get a pat on the back. Marly needed a guiding hand, and college kids need a leg up. It's hard to find a place in our world. I was lucky that Maddox gave me a shot and believed in me when I was just a college kid trying to make something of myself. It's no big deal."

"It's a very big deal." She pressed her lips to his in a tender kiss, and then she whispered, "What do you say we get out of here so I can apologize properly?"

She didn't have to ask twice.

They said their goodbyes, congratulated Justin on his show, and promised to catch up the next time they were in town.

On their ride back to the cottage, with Dixie's warm body pressed against his back, her hands playing over his stomach, he was consumed with *missing* her. Every day without her had felt like an eternity. She was with him now, and *still* he longed to be closer. He thought about the first time she'd ridden on the back of his bike and how proud he'd been, how right she'd felt. He hadn't admitted it to himself at the time, but he *had* been staking his claim.

He cruised down the long driveway of Bayside Resort and followed the gravel road to the cottage. A gust of salty air swept up the dunes as they made their way inside. They didn't turn on the lights or say a word as they took off their boots and socks by the door. Dixie took his hand, leading him into the bedroom. Moonlight spilled through the windows as he pressed his lips to her shoulder, trailing kisses along her warm skin. He lifted her shirt off and then kissed her softly as he unhooked the front clasp of her bra and slipped it off, too. He dipped lower, tasting her neck and bathing her breasts in kisses and slow slicks of his tongue. Dixie breathed harder, pulling at his shirt. He tugged it over his head, and as he reached for her, she put her palm on his chest, her eyes riveted to the new tattoo over his heart.

She traced the design that matched the one he'd tattooed on her wrist. Her eyes flicked up, her silent question hanging between them. He covered her hand with his, holding it over his heart while trying to come up with the words to explain himself, but the closest he could come was "I felt too far away from you."

Her eyes dampened, and he gathered her in his arms. He held her for a long moment, their emotions filling the silence. Then he cradled her face in his hands and covered her mouth with his, pouring all of himself into their kisses. When he knelt to help her step out of her skirt and panties, he had the overwhelming urge to *worship* her, to show her just how special she was to him.

He ran his hands up her legs, kissing along her knee, thigh, and hip. He slowed to kiss her belly and felt her watching him as she threaded her fingers into his hair. He continued caressing, kissing, *treasuring* her. He stepped back to strip off his jeans and briefs and she brazenly drank in every inch of him. He hadn't been kidding when he'd told her that their time in New York had been *everything*. She had changed who he was and opened his eyes to who he wanted to be.

He pulled the covers down to the foot of the bed, in no hurry to rush their time away. She lay on the sheet, and he came down over her and cradled her in his arms, filled with a sense of coming *home*. He wanted to savor their closeness and gazed deeply into her eyes. Moonlight reflected in them, heightening the greens, bringing out the golds, drawing him even deeper under her spell. *My Dixie.* He didn't think it was possible to feel so much, so *close*, to another person. *God*, when had *she* become his *everything?*

"Dixie..." he whispered with a sense of awe as their bodies came together slowly, *perfectly*. The intensity of their connection pulled a long, surrendering sigh from both of them, bringing rise to another all-consuming sensation.

For the first time ever, Jace felt *complete*.

They lay in each other's arms, their bodies joined so deeply, they felt like one being. Neither one of them moved, their hearts beating to their own private revelry.

"I never knew it could be like this," Dixie said softly.

Jace brushed his lips over her cheek, breathing her in as he whispered, "I always knew it would."

Chapter Twenty

JACE WAS IN no hurry to open his eyes, much less move from where he lay with his head on Dixie's stomach, his arms around her. He'd wanted this—*her*—for so long, he didn't want to rush it away. But now that his brain was firing, his dreams came rushing back with such clarity, they felt real. He'd dreamed of a life that wasn't his, one in which Dixie was walking along a beach with a baby in her arms and he was watching from afar. He'd seen flashes of her and the baby with her family, but he couldn't get to them. They were on the other side of a treacherously deep and craggy, uncrossable ravine. He'd seen himself riding his motorcycle, desperately trying to find a road that led to her. But road after road brought him to the edge of the cliff, close enough to hear her voice and see her holding that baby, separated by the jagged abyss.

His heart raced, and he opened his eyes, hoping to forget those dreams. Dixie's beautiful face came into focus, easing his panic.

She ran her fingers through her hair, smiling sweetly, and said, "Thank God you're up. You've been holding me so tight it was hard to breathe, and I have to pee."

"Sorry, babe." He kissed the pink marks his beard had left on her skin, then leaned up to kiss her lips. "You should have woken me up."

"You were so tired last night, I didn't have the heart to. And you were holding me like you were afraid I'd run off."

"Can you blame me?" he asked as she stepped from the bed, enjoying the playful look she gave him almost as much as the view of her gorgeous naked body as she headed into the bathroom.

He sat up against the headboard and stretched, surprised to see one of the pictures of him that Hawk had taken on the nightstand. He loved knowing she'd brought it with her. Beside it was a framed picture of Dixie and her family—and the people the Whiskeys treated as family, Truman, Gemma, Josie, Jed, and all their children. They were *all* wearing pajamas, even Biggs and Red. The men wore flannel pajama pants with their boots. Bullet also had on his leather vest. He probably slept in the damn thing. The women wore various sleeping outfits, but his eyes were drawn to Dixie, wearing a short black nightshirt and her favorite knee-high black leather boots. He loved those boots. She was facing away from the camera, and I DARE YOU TO BRING OUT MY DARK SIDE was printed on the back of her nightshirt. She was holding Truman and Gemma's son, Lincoln, kissing his little cheek.

You and your babies...

She came out of the bathroom, hair brushed, a bright smile on her beautiful face, and his heart did a double take. He held up the picture and said, "Please tell me how you convinced a roomful of bikers to wear pajamas."

"That was taken in the hospital the night Maggie Rose was born." She climbed onto the bed beside him and said, "Sarah went into labor when we were celebrating Hail's birthday with a pajama party. He and Josie had a tradition of spending his birthday in their pajamas. I didn't have to convince anyone. We all love Hail and Josie. We'd do anything for them. Anyway, the night of Hail's birthday, when Sarah went into labor, we all went to the hospital to wait for the baby to come."

"You're telling me these guys went out in *public* dressed like that?" He laughed.

"Yup. I'm sure you've heard about Halloween when Kennedy asked the guys to dress up like cheerleaders because she wanted to be a football player. I'll have to show you *those* pictures sometime." She bumped him with her shoulder motioning to the picture, and said, "That was a really big night. Besides Hail's birthday and Maggie Rose being born, Jed proposed to Josie in the waiting room of the hospital in front of everyone. He was just so overcome with love, he blurted it out."

"In a hospital waiting room, wearing *pajamas*?"

"I know it doesn't sound romantic, but it *was*. There's something beautiful about a man who's so in love he can't hold back, and everyone was there to witness it. I think it was especially cool that Hail got to see it. I don't think he'll ever forget *that* birthday." She snagged the frame from his hands and set it on the nightstand. "You're just jealous that nobody threw you a pajama party."

"Oh, is that what I am?" He tickled her ribs, and she laughed, rolling away from him. He grabbed her hands, pressing them down to the mattress as he shifted over her. "The only thing I'm jealous of is that I wasn't there to take you up on that *dare* you were parading around."

"I had lots of offers," she said tauntingly.

His gut twisted. "I bet you did. I see you brought the picture of me with you, too. Guess you missed me as much as I missed you."

"That is why I brought it, but I actually came to the Cape early to try to *move on* from you." She paused and then said, "I thought I was just your booty call."

He released her hands, remembering the pain in her eyes that had driven him to come to the Cape, and his heart sank. "Christ, Dix. *Seriously?*"

"When you said New York had been everything, I thought you meant it was all we would ever have."

"How could you think that?" His voice escalated with his frustration. "I meant that our time together was everything *to me*, as in enough to fuck up my head so badly that I couldn't think of anything but you. Why do you think I came to Peaceful Harbor to see you?"

"I assumed to fuck me," she said as casually as if she'd said he was there to buy her an ice cream.

"You don't mince words, do you?"

"No, and you *like* that about me."

"Hell yes I do." He loved how vehemently she stood up for herself, but didn't she know how deeply she'd sunk her claws into him? "Dix, you have no idea what you've done to me. I sent one of my employees out of a meeting because he wanted to go out with you, and he was *lucky* I didn't fire him. Yes, I wanted to fuck you when I went to see you—good and hard, too. But *my God*, woman, I also wanted to be with you. Don't you get that by now?"

Her eyes narrowed. "You need lessons in communication, *Stone*."

His head dropped between his shoulders in defeat, and she laughed softly.

He met her amused gaze and said, "I ought to keep you in bed all day and *communicate* six ways to Sunday just how much you mean to me."

She ran her fingers through his hair again and said, "I am so glad you're a man of your word." A wicked grin spread across her face as she dragged her finger along the seam of his lips and said, "Because I'm holding you to that."

DIXIE HADN'T HAD to hold Jace to anything. Neither one of them had wanted to be anywhere other than in each other's arms yesterday. They spent the entire day loving on each other, dozing off, and lazing around the cottage. They read steamy passages aloud from the book Dixie was reading for her book club and then acted the scenes out, christening the surface of nearly every piece of furniture in the cottage. They laughed, talked, and spent long, silent stretches of time doing nothing more than being together. They had dinner delivered and ate it on the patio as they watched the sun set over Cape Cod Bay. It was the most wonderful day Dixie could have ever imagined. She was in a dangerous position, falling deeper in love with Jace with every passing moment. When they'd made love Wednesday night, she'd had to fight with everything she had to keep *I love you* from rushing out, reminding herself that this was only a *start*, even if it felt like so much more.

Friday morning greeted them with the promise of a warm, sunny day. They showered together, which had become one of Dixie's favorite things when they were in New York. It wasn't just that they took things slower in the shower or that the water made their intimacy even more erotic. What she loved most was the way Jace relaxed and the sounds he made when he first got into the shower. It was always the same: He tipped his head back and closed his eyes as water rained down on him. His shoulders relaxed, and the stress that so often showed in the tightness of his jaw and arms dissipated. A good ten or fifteen seconds would pass before he'd let out a deep, relaxing sigh. That sound was music to her ears. She liked knowing that the man who was busy traveling and working, and didn't seem to have set schedules or continuity, had at least a few moments of letting everything go.

Those few moments at the beginning of his showers seemed like the nonsexual equivalent of the blissful aftermath of their lovemaking, when it was just the two of them without any pretense or expectations.

She pulled on her skinny jeans, catching Jace watching her in the mirror. She turned with her hand on her hip, wearing her jeans and bra. He was shirtless and barefoot, the button of his jeans open, and her eyes were drawn to his matching tattoo, proudly inked over his heart. She'd nearly cried when she'd seen it the first time. It meant more to her than if he'd given her a diamond ring.

Jace waggled his brows.

"Don't give me that look." She snagged the black lace-up tank from the Leather and Lace line and slipped it over her head. "We are *leaving* this room today." Yesterday, in one of their quiet periods, Dixie had searched for historical sights on the Cape, and she'd found a few she thought Jace might like to see.

"What if I don't want to share you with the outside world yet?" he asked, stalking toward her.

Her heart soared, but yesterday Jace had confessed that he couldn't remember the last time he'd taken a vacation, and not to take it personally if he became edgy with too much down-time. She wasn't a vacationer, either, hence the forced time off by her mother. She knew neither one of them would get edgy if they stayed in the cottage the whole time they were together. They were too into each other for boredom to set in, and they laughed as much as they loved, which confirmed what she already knew. They were a perfect match, whether they were in or out of the bedroom. But Jace had gone to such great lengths to show her how much she meant to him, she wanted to do something for him in return.

"You need sustenance if you're going to keep up with me, *old man.*"

He hauled her against him, his dark eyes boring into her. "*Old* man? That's funny, I don't remember hearing any complaints in the shower this morning."

"Mm…That was *nice.*" She kissed the tattoo over his heart, "The truth is, I want to experience everything with you, including being a tourist, since neither of us has really done that. I made a list of some historical sights I thought you might want to see."

"You're just full of surprises, aren't you?" His gaze softened. "I want that, too, Dix. But I'll also always want *this.*" He grabbed her ass.

His eyes smoldered as his lips covered hers, his beard burning and tickling at once. He buried one hand in her hair, sending lust ricocheting through her. Shouldn't she be used to his kisses by now? They were so consuming, when he kissed her it was like nothing else mattered or even *existed.* He eased his efforts to a series of feathery kisses, leaving her breathless for more.

He smacked her butt and said, "Now I'm ready."

"*Me too*," she said, full of innuendo. "You're a *cruel* man."

He laughed and hugged her again. "Just reminding you of what's waiting when we get back here."

THEY HEADED OUT on Jace's motorcycle, stopping at the Blue Willow Bakery for breakfast, which they ate at a picnic table outside the general store two doors down. Dixie didn't want to ruin the surprise of the places she'd mapped out, so instead of telling him where they were going, she gave him directions without naming the final destinations. They drove into Eastham, a neighboring town, and stopped at the Eastham Windmill, which was set in the middle of a grassy area along the main drag.

He shaded his eyes, looking up at the enormous structure. The slatted blades were much larger than they appeared from the road. The cedar siding had aged to gray, and the trim and front door were painted maroon. The windmill looked stately and important.

Jace reached for her hand and said, "I've actually never been in a windmill. Have you?"

She shook her head. "When I come to the Cape, it's all about hanging out with my family."

"Good, then it's a first for both of us. You're about to see me in full-on history-geek mode."

"If you didn't drive a motorcycle, I might have to trade you in for a tougher model."

He shook his head. "I don't believe that for a second. I know the Ritchie Meyers story, remember?" He gave her a chaste kiss, and they walked inside.

It smelled like old wood, which made sense since practically the entire structure was made of it.

"Good morning," a thin, older gentleman with white hair and a thick gray beard greeted them. "I'm Jim. Welcome to the Eastham Windmill."

Jace shook his hand. "Hi. I'm Jace, and this is Dixie. We're both new to windmills. Would you mind telling us about the history of this one?"

"Have you got some time on your hands, or do you want the condensed version?" Jim asked.

"We have all the time in the world," Jace answered.

Jim rubbed his hands together with a glimmer of excitement in his eyes and said, "This is my lucky day. This is believed to be the oldest windmill on the Cape, dating back to about 1680, when it was built in Plymouth. It's also the last working gristmill…"

He told them about how the windmill was moved from Plymouth to Truro, and later to different locations in Eastham, before finally landing where it now resided. He showed them the millstones and explained the process of grinding corn. Jace had dozens of questions about the structure, the moves, the process of making flour and cornmeal. The two men talked about how things had changed over the years. When they went up a narrow wooden staircase to the second level, Jim's history lesson continued.

It was interesting to watch Jace learning rather than being the man in charge, and it was even more interesting to hear him befriend the elderly gentleman, asking about how long Jim had lived there. Dixie could tell Jace wasn't just being kind. He was actually interested in this man's background, and the longer they spoke, the more interested Jace became, asking about his family and his personal thoughts on how the Cape had changed over the years.

More than an hour later, when they were getting ready to go to their next destination, Jace insisted they take a selfie with Jim in front of the windmill.

"Since you're history buffs, be sure to stop by Fort Hill—check out the buildings and walk the trail." Jim gave them directions, along with a short history of that property.

"Thanks. We'll do that." Jace shook his hand and said they'd be back the next time they were in the area. Dixie's hopeful heart clung to his use of *they*.

Since Dixie had a number of places she'd already scouted, they decided to visit Fort Hill tomorrow and headed to the Salt Pond Visitor Center. They explored the museum and bookstore and watched a movie about the changing landscape on the Cape. Dixie didn't realize how much she would enjoy learning about the history of the area, but Jace's excitement was contagious. He held her hand, kissing her often and pulling her close as they looked around. They wanted to take a walk around the marsh and trails, but they had other places to see before the day got away from them.

Their next stop was the Museum of Natural History, where they learned about the environment and wildlife around the Cape. Jace made friends there as well. While he was listening and learning, Dixie was admiring *him*. His endless curiosity made him even more intriguing, revealing another side of him that he kept well hidden.

At the suggestion of a woman who worked at the museum,

they drove into Brewster, another small town, and had lunch sitting outside at a café, sharing kisses as they ate their meals. They visited the Brewster General Store, a quaint little shop Dixie had seen online, and then headed to the Bird Watcher's General Store, which the waitress at the café had recommended.

When they climbed back on his bike, Jace lifted Dixie's hand from his stomach and kissed her palm before putting on his helmet. It was those little touches, along with the way he'd been looking at her throughout the day, that told her he was falling just as hard for her as she was for him.

It was late when they finished seeing all the places on Dixie's list and returned to the Salt Pond Visitor Center to take the romantic walk they'd missed out on earlier. The sun set as they walked along the marsh, casting beautiful ribbons of pinks and purples over the horizon. Jace kept Dixie close, kissing her temple or her cheek, as they talked. She wished they could have a month worth of days like these, but what she really wanted was a lifetime of them.

Jace kept her close as they made their way up the final trail. "Thank you for planning such a great day. Nobody has ever done anything like this for me before." He stopped walking and gazed into her eyes. "You're changing me, Dix."

"Is that good or bad?"

Her pulse quickened as she waited for him to respond. He looked back the way they'd come, then up at the sky and out at the marsh.

Please don't say bad.

When he finally looked at her, he exhaled that relaxed sound he made in the shower. Then he kissed her lips, tucked her against his side, and continued walking to the trailhead.

"Jace...?"

He grinned and said, "I'm still deciding."

"You're an ass," she said teasingly.

"What was that?" he asked as they crossed the dark and almost empty parking lot. "You want me to spank your ass?"

She laughed and socked him in the arm, making him laugh, too.

He tugged her against him and said, "You don't have to hit me. I'll happily spank your ass."

She wasn't about to let him get away with not answering her. "You're skating on thin ice, Stone."

"Why? You might *like* it," he taunted.

She felt her cheeks flame and glared at him. "I like a lot of things, but that doesn't mean I want you to *talk* about them."

"I see," he said, his mouth a breath away from hers. "I'm allowed to *take* or *spank* as long as I don't talk about it."

"And I'm allowed to *withhold* until you answer my question."

He kissed her hard, then handed her a helmet and said, "I already answered. I'll happily spank—"

"Stone!"

He laughed and leaned down as if to kiss her and whispered, "It's *good*, Dix. Very, very good." Then, louder, he said, "Now, get that sexy little ass on my bike, because we never had our auction date, and I've got plans."

"Care to clue me in?" she said casually, though she was already excited to see what he had in store.

"Nope." He straddled the bike. "Climb on or get left behind, babe."

She climbed on and put her arms around him. He moved her hands between his legs, pressing them over his formidable package, and then he started the engine. As they drove out of the parking lot, the vibrations of the bike and the feel of *Jace* worked their magic.

When he turned off the main drag and into the road that led to the Wellfleet Drive-In Theatre, happiness bubbled up inside her. She couldn't believe Jace remembered what she'd said at dinner with his family.

He paid at the ticket booth, then cruised into the crowded lot, where rows of cars were parked beside poles with speakers on them. He stopped the bike and told her to close her eyes and hold on tight, which she did, even though she was dying to peek.

It was unsettling having her eyes closed on a moving bike, but Jace drove slowly. When he finally stopped the bike and cut the engine, he told her not to open her eyes yet as he helped her to her feet and removed her helmet.

"Okay," he said. "Open your eyes."

She was facing the back of the parking lot, not the movie screen. Jace looked a little nervous, which was something she'd never seen on him before. What could possibly make badass Jace Stone nervous?

"If this isn't cool," he said with a serious expression, "I have a backup plan. Reservations at a fancy restaurant with dancing and all that jazz."

She was touched that he worried she might need to be wined and dined. Didn't he know that time with him was all she really wanted? She didn't care what they were doing. "Being here with you is the perfect date."

He turned her by the shoulders, and "Oh my God," fell from her lips. She couldn't believe what she was seeing. A blanket was spread out in front of the motorcycle, several battery-operated candles flickered in the moonlight around the edges, and a bouquet of red roses lay across one of two large pillows. In front of the pillows were place settings for two, and beyond that were silver-covered dishes, a bottle of wine, and two wineglasses. Not once in her entire life had anyone done anything so romantic for her.

Her eyes dampened as she turned to thank him, but the words lodged in her throat, so she wrapped her arms around him and kissed him. Whistles and cheers rang out around them, and they both smiled into the kiss.

"Thank you," she finally said. "This is beyond perfect. How did you get it all set up? We've been out all day."

"I have a few friends who were happy to help."

Dixie spent the evening in a bit of a daze. They enjoyed a feast of seafood, rice, and vegetables as they watched a romantic comedy. After dinner, she sat between Jace's legs, nestled in his arms, her back to his chest. He must have kissed her shoulder and neck a thousand times as they sat under the stars, surrounded by hundreds of strangers. Dixie soaked in each and every one of those sweet touches, wishing she could spend forever just like this—no dinner or movie necessary.

Chapter Twenty-One

JACE WOKE SATURDAY morning in the same position in which he and Dixie had fallen asleep, with her cradled within the curve of his body as he spooned her. He buried his nose in her hair, inhaling her intoxicating scent. He'd thought she'd gotten to him after their trip to New York, but she'd become a part of him now. He was even addicted to her smell. They were leaving tomorrow morning, and he couldn't imagine spending a single night apart, much less days, weeks, months...

He was so screwed, but there was no honor in empty promises, so he forced those thoughts down deep and focused on making the most of today. He kissed her shoulder, then opened his mouth, sucking gently, earning a sleepy, alluring moan. His cock twitched against her ass. He couldn't get enough of her. Dixie reached behind her with one hand, her fingers playing over his face. He turned into her touch as she stroked his cheek.

One more day...

He rolled her onto her back, and that sexy smile did him in. He covered her mouth with his, kissing her rougher than he intended, but she arched beneath him, wrapping her legs around the back of his thighs. Her kisses made him lose his mind, but those long, lean legs? *Fuck...*He needed them wrapped around his *head*. He tore his mouth away, but before he could move down her body, she grabbed his hair, guiding his mouth to her breast. He teased and grazed the peak with his teeth and tongue.

She bowed off the mattress, moaning as she pleaded, "*Harder—*"

He did her one better. He shifted to the side as he sucked harder and pushed two fingers into her slick heat. She whimpered and moaned, rocking her hips, fisting her hands in his hair so tight it stung. He teased her clit with his thumb as he moved to her other breast, giving it the same attention. Her inner muscles clenched, pulling his fingers deeper into her. He curled them up, stroking over the spot that made her inhale sharp gasps.

"*Don'tstopdon'tstop,*" she pleaded.

He quickened his efforts, and she grabbed the sheets in fisted hands, her hips rocking furiously as she rode his fingers. The sexy sounds she made were like a mating call, luring him in. He kissed his way down her body, still using his fingers to keep her at the edge, and sucked her clit into his mouth, expertly giving her what she needed. She cried out long and loud, her hips bucking wildly, her sex pulsing around his fingers like a vise.

When she collapsed to the mattress, he sealed his mouth over her sweet, hot sex, and she wrapped her long, luxurious legs around his head. *Man*, that made him even harder. He feasted on her, using his teeth and tongue, rough and deep, then slower, licking her sensitive, swollen flesh, drawing out her pleasure. She grabbed his hair, spreading her thighs wider. He knew what she wanted, for him to fuck her with his tongue, suck her clit, make her come fast and hard. But he loved feeling her *need*, her *greed*, too much to hurry. He licked slowly up and down along her silken flesh, until she was panting and writhing.

"Jace, it's too much. *Please*—"

He couldn't deny her another second and gave her everything she craved, sending her soaring. She cried out loudly, and he stayed with her, holding her at the peak of ecstasy as she bucked against his mouth. When she sank limply to the mattress, he moved swiftly up her body, capturing her mouth with his, still drenched with the taste of her arousal. She sucked his tongue, clawed at his back. She was an *animal*, his every dream come true, and he wasn't nearly done.

He tore his mouth away. "I need your mouth on me, baby. I need you to suck me hard, take me to the edge before I fuck you."

She scooted down the bed, guided his cock into her mouth, and *holy fucking hell*, she sucked and stroked, teasing the tip, squeezing his balls, doing all the things she knew drove him out of his mind. He was on all fours above her, watching as she loved his shaft. Seeing her feast on him was as erotic as feeling her hot, wet mouth on his cock. He grabbed the base of his shaft, squeezing hard, staving off his orgasm so he could enjoy her mouth longer.

He gritted his teeth until he was on the brink of exploding, and then he pulled out, greedily demanding, "On your hands and knees, baby. I want to take you from behind."

She was quick to comply, her gorgeous ass in the air. Her hair curtained one eye as she looked at him over her shoulder, watching as he aligned their bodies. She was so wet, she drenched the head of his cock, making it impossible for him to hold back. He drove into her in one hard thrust.

"Oh, *yesss*," she hissed.

He held her hips as he pounded into her, her muscles clamped down so tight, she nearly drew the come right out of him. But he held back, wanting to enjoy every second of her. She lowered her shoulders to the mattress, reaching beneath them, and tickled his balls.

"Fuck, Dix. Don't make me come yet. I'm not done with you."

He wrapped his arm around her waist, rising onto his knees and bringing her up with him. He cupped one of her breasts, using his other hand to pleasure her down below as he drove his cock deeper, faster. She dug her fingernails into his arms.

"Harder," she panted out. "There, there, *there!*"

Her nails drew blood as her climax tore through her. Jace withdrew when she was mid-orgasm, and she cried out.

"I need to see your face," he said through gritted teeth, fighting his own release as he helped her onto her back.

She reached for him and he plunged into her. Her eyes widened as she cried out, "*Ohmygod...*"

Her arms and legs wrapped around him so tight, she lifted off the mattress. His thrusts drove her back to the sheets, and he put his arms around her, his cock drilling into her. She came hard and loud, her inner muscles squeezing tight. The pleasure was so intense, he lost all control. Moans tore from his lungs as they rode the waves of their passion higher, until they both cried out, clinging to one another as they descended from their peaks, falling spent and sated to the mattress.

Jace remained buried inside her, cradling her beneath him, wanting to hold on to every last second of their magnificence. He rolled them onto their sides, their bodies still tangled together.

"I think I'm dying," she whispered.

"That's funny, because I finally feel like I'm living." He brushed her hair from her cheek and kissed her there. Then he kissed her lips and the tip of her nose. "Does that mean you don't want to go on that hike today?"

She groaned.

They lay together for so long, they drifted back to sleep. When they awoke, more than an hour had passed. Dixie nestled into him like she wanted to crawl beneath his skin. She was adorable, and *too* warm and alluring. If he didn't get the hell out of that bed, more of his emotions would come tumbling out, and she'd be left hoping for more than he could promise.

He kissed her cheek and forced himself to get out of bed. "Come on, babe. It's our last day. If you don't get your babies presents, you'll be bummed when you go home empty-handed."

She rolled onto her stomach and put the pillow over her head with another pouty groan.

He rubbed his hand softly over her ass and said, "You sure that's the view you want to give me?"

She threw the pillow at him. He lunged for her and she scrambled to her knees. He lifted her up and tossed her over his shoulder, giving her ass a loud *smack*.

"*Ack!*" She laugh-squealed as he carried her toward the bathroom. "Jace!"

"You liked it, didn't you?"

She went silent, her answer blaring in his ears as he lowered her to her feet and then turned on the shower.

She wrapped her arms around his waist and looked over her shoulder in the mirror, her brows knitting. "You made my cheek pink."

"Sorry, babe, but at least I know every time you feel it you'll think of me." He rubbed his hand gently over her offended cheek.

She rested her cheek on his chest and said, "I always think of you."

He tipped her chin up, and as the bathroom filled with steam, the three words he'd been fighting climbed up his throat. He pressed his lips to hers, then stepped into the shower, pulling her in with him. He held her under the water and tipped his face up to the warm spray, willing himself to swallow those words. When he was sure they were stuffed down too deep to escape, he sighed with relief, and maybe a little regret.

FOR THE FIRST time in Dixie's life, the thought of going home filled her with dread. She and Jace had enjoyed another romantic, fun day. They headed up to the artsy community of Provincetown to shop for souvenirs for the kids and spent the entire day enjoying the street performers and shops, but mostly enjoying each other. Then they went for a motorcycle ride down to Harwich and had dinner at Common Grounds, the coffee shop where her cousins held their annual anti-suicide rally. It was open mic night, and people sang, read poetry, and told stories. Now it was Saturday evening, and they were walking along the beach in front of the cottage, bundled up in sweatshirts to ward off the chilly bay breeze. Jace's arm was draped over Dixie's shoulder, and she'd never been happier—or more sorrowful. She wasn't sad, like she'd been after their trip to New York. This was different. She was already mourning the end of their time together. She tried to ignore it and focus on their conversations. They'd talked about everything from the weather to their favorite movies—his was *Road House*, hers was *Pretty Woman*—avoiding anything that might lead to the elephant at their backs.

"Your favorite movie is about a *hooker?*" Jace asked.

"Yes! Vivian is badass. She did what she had to to make her way through life, and she didn't need a man to take care of her."

"She fell in love with a billionaire," he reminded her.

"No. She fell in love with a *man*. She left his money on the bed and *walked away* from him when they fought, standing her ground and demanding respect. That movie could have made her out as a woman who needed rescuing, but it didn't. She knew what she wanted in life and she held out for it. I loved that she didn't let anyone drag her down. She just pulled herself up by her bootstraps, made a plan, and moved forward."

"Sounds like a certain someone I know," he said with a grin. "I never saw the movie."

"Well, that needs to go to the top of your bucket list, because you're missing out."

"Have you seen *Road House?*"

"I have three older brothers. What do you think? It's one of Bear's favorite movies."

He kissed her temple and said, "Then maybe you can use your womanly wiles to convince me to watch *Pretty Woman* sometime."

"I guess that's the least I can do, considering you put your life on hold to come see me this week." She snuggled closer, wanting to know where they would go from there, but at the same time, she didn't want to sound needy. This was their *start*, and it was a beautiful, glorious start. But Dixie's *start* had begun the first time she'd seen him. Her feelings had grown over the years, one interaction at a time, and then New York had kicked them into hyperspeed. Sadness moved through her, remembering the heartache of leaving, the anguish of hoping to hear from him, and the worst feeling of her life, the evening she'd sent him away. The sounds of the bay lapping at the shore and Jace's warm body pressed against her side calmed the anxiety that accompanied those thoughts.

She refused to be that needy woman again. This was obviously *Jace's* start, and she needed to respect that. Instead of asking for more of a label, or firm future plans, she said, "Where do you go from here? Back to LA?"

"Among other places. On top of the launch, I've got a lot of travel coming up over the next several weeks: Oregon, Mexico, Ohio, and Pennsylvania. But first I have to catch up on all the things I put off to come here. I was so sidetracked with thoughts of you when I was in LA, I was a danger to the business." The tease in his voice brought her eyes to his, and he said, "I told you I almost fired a guy who didn't deserve it. But now I feel ready to jump in again with both feet. Thankfully, we finalized the pictures for the calendar before I left, which of course are stunning. I'm excited about getting back in the game."

He leaned down for a kiss, and her heart was stuck fluttering like a bird that couldn't catch wind. He was excited to get back to business, but was he excited to see her again, too? *Soon maybe?*

"There are going to be life-size cardboard cutouts of you in all of our retail stores," he said with a grin.

She couldn't even imagine that. "I'll be sure never to go into your stores again."

He laughed. "Well, you're going to have to. We'll be traveling together to the in-person events."

That made her all sorts of happy. "I know. I'm proud to be representing your company, but it'll be embarrassing to see cutouts of myself."

"Nah. You'll get used to it. Did I tell you that they want to have the Leather and Lace line represented at Fashion Week?" he asked.

"Seriously? That's fantastic! I'm not surprised. It's such a gorgeous line."

"I'm not sold on the idea. You're the face of the Leather and Lace line. I just can't picture a bunch of random models taking your place. I think I might nix the idea."

She stopped walking, floored by what he'd said. She didn't have to ask for a label, because in his own way he was telling her how important she was to him. But her elation was chased by the magnitude of what he was considering giving up.

"Jace, you can't give up that big of an opportunity. Fashion Week is *huge*, and not just for your company. Think of Jillian. She's your business partner. That's *her* chance to present the new line, too. You can't pass that up for something as ridiculous as wanting *me* to do it. I'm not even a model. I mean, hearing you say you can't imagine anyone else representing the line means a lot to me, but it's a really bad idea to pass up this opportunity."

"You sound like Maddox. I don't know, Dix."

As they walked down the beach, she said, "I could never even pull off walking a runway at an event that big."

"Bullshit."

"You have no idea how stressful it is. Jace, you have a history of making *great* business decisions, but this would be downright stupid. Hopefully Maddox won't let you make that mistake."

He stepped in front of her and put his hands on her hips. "Then tell me you'll do it."

"No way. I'd be so nervous, I'd probably fall on my ass."

"You did Jillian's show."

"It was a million times *smaller*, and my friends who weren't models were also walking the runway. It was totally different."

His brows knitted, and a second later his eyes brightened. "Then we'll use other models for the show and *you* can walk out at the end with me, Maddox, and Jillian as the face of the line."

Her heart tumbled at his vehemence.

"Tell me you'll do it, Dix," he said. "It's one walk down the runway, and you'll be on my arm so you don't have to worry about falling."

"Does it mean that much to you?" She tried to tamp down her excitement and expectations, telling herself this was all for Silver-Stone. But the look in his eyes made it feel so much bigger.

"This means *everything* to me," he said. "Please, Dix?"

Everything. She'd misinterpreted that once. She wasn't going to make that mistake again. "Okay. I'll do it."

"Yes!" He wrapped her in his arms, kissing her hard as he spun her around.

The move was so unlike him, she gave in to her giddiness, giggling like a fool as he set her on her feet.

"This week has changed me, Dix. Now I understand why people take vacations. I'm revitalized and ready to plow through this launch. But enough about work." He took her hand, and they headed up the beach toward the path that cut through the dunes to their cottage. "We only have a few hours until we have to say goodbye, and I want to spend them holding you naked in my arms."

That sounded just perfect to her.

Chapter Twenty-Two

DIXIE STOOD AT the top of the dunes Sunday morning, a cool breeze kissing her skin as she gazed out at the water. She'd come to the Cape grasping for a way to move forward without Jace. And here she was getting ready to leave with a full, hopeful heart, telling herself to stop wishing they could stay there forever, because this was a hell of a start and they had so much more to look forward to.

She heard movement and turned to find Jace walking toward her with a handful of wildflowers, roots dangling from a few of the long stems.

He shrugged innocently and said, "I didn't think the flower shop would be open this early, and you like flowers so much…"

God, she loved him, and she was nowhere near ready to say goodbye.

"Do you think your friends would believe a rabbit ate them?"

She laughed and shook her head. "You're crazy."

"I'm definitely crazy about you." He put his arms around her and said, "Thank you for giving us a chance."

"I'm still kind of floored that you put your life on hold for me. I really underestimated you. This time together has meant the world to me."

"To me, too."

He embraced her, and she closed her eyes. They stood at the top of the dunes, swaying in each other's arms, each lost in their own thoughts. When they'd said goodbye in New York, she'd wanted to cry. This goodbye was different. She felt confident about their relationship, not worried that this was all they'd ever have. She knew when she drove away she'd have a new companion, *Sorrow*, and that Sorrow would take up residence in the passenger's seat for the long drive home. She also expected Sorrow's pal *Longing* to hunker down in the back seat. But on this trip there was a third companion. *Love.* They may not have given it a voice, but now she knew that love didn't always need one. It was as real and present between them as the ocean was deep.

Jace gazed down at her and a smile lifted his lips. "I probably didn't tell you this enough, though I think it all the time. You are so beautiful. Truly beautiful, Dix."

She pressed her forehead to his chest, and he kissed the top of her head, then rested his cheek there.

"We've had a great time, haven't we?" he said.

"Yes."

"You know this isn't the end, right?"

She looked up at him and said, "I know."

He pressed a kiss to the space between her eyebrows. "Then why do you have those worry lines on your forehead?"

"If I can get Daphne to believe the flowers were eaten by a rabbit, would you believe I'm just stressed over the ten-plus hours' drive home?"

He chuckled. "Probably not, but it was worth a try." His

face turned serious and he said, "You don't want empty promises, Dix."

"I'm not asking for them." But she saw something in his eyes. Half promises? The desire to make promises? She didn't know. It could be wishful thinking.

"I realize that, but you have to know that this time together has been fantastic. We both needed it, and now we have to go back to reality. I have to catch up on all the work I've put off to be here, and you have your life to carry on with, gifts to give to your babies."

Her throat thickened, but she refused to fall apart. "I'm just going to miss you, that's all."

"And I'm going to miss you, too." He kissed her forehead and said, "You know it's not like we're going our separate ways and then that's it, right? You're on my mind every second of the day, Dix. That's not going to change."

JACE LOOKED OUT at the water to try to regain control of the emotions thundering through him. He'd thought he would draw out their goodbye as long as possible, stay with her until the very last second. But the idea of her driving away again drove spikes into his chest. He thought back to their very first kiss, his first taste of her, and wondered how he'd ever believed he'd be able to be close to Dixie and then leave it all behind. He had no idea how he'd fought what he'd felt for her for so many years without losing his mind. He should go down in *The Guinness Book of World Records* as the strongest man on earth for that alone.

Who was he kidding? He was the stupidest man on earth to have waited so long.

She took his hand and said, "I should get going. I have a really long drive."

He nodded, unable to wrangle in his thoughts enough to trust his voice. He wasn't the only one who had changed. Dixie wasn't saying goodbye with tears in her eyes. He saw trust this time. He recognized that look because for the first time since he was a teenager, he trusted a woman. He trusted Dixie enough to have handed her his heart in the biggest way he was able.

"Would you mind if I went to Bikes on the Beach with you next time?" she asked as they walked around the cottage. "I would really like to help Marly at her table."

He remembered how she'd looked like she wanted to kill Marly when Marly had hugged him. It didn't surprise him that the two of them had gotten along so well. They were both bighearted, doing all they could for others. What did surprise him was how much it meant to him that she would go to an event she had already said she wouldn't enjoy, just to see a new friend and help her with her cause.

"I'd like that," he said, wanting so much more.

They stopped by her Jeep, which was already packed, and he gathered her in his arms again. "I wish I had gotten you something while we were here. A piece of jewelry or something to commemorate our time together."

She looked at him with a dreamy expression and said, "You did. You gave us both something. You gave us a *start*."

"*God, Dix*," he said in one long breath, hugging her tight against him. "Goodbyes fucking suck."

She mumbled her agreement, and then she rested her chin on his chest and said, "Then let's not say goodbye."

"Okay," he said just above a whisper.

"Just kiss me, Stone."

He lowered his lips to hers, trying to silence the sadness in her eyes—and in his heart. His life seemed to be built on futile efforts lately, and this was no different. When their lips parted, her eyes dampened, and he hugged her again. He cradled her face in his hands and brushed her tears away. "Tell me not to make empty promises, Dix, because right now I'd say just about anything to see you smile."

Her lips curved up and she said, "Empty promises are for assholes."

He laughed and then he kissed her again and helped her into her Jeep. As she started it up, he said, "Have a safe trip. I'll let you know when I'm back in Peaceful Harbor, but I'm sure we'll talk before then."

He watched Dixie drive away, the sense of loss overwhelming. He'd been burying himself in work for so long, hiding from decades-old heartbreak for fear of being hurt again, that he'd almost forgotten how hurt had the power to strengthen a person's resolve. He could continue hiding forever, losing himself in projects and designs, stockpiling wealth and professional achievements. Was that really *hiding*? Or was it self-preservation? Or maybe a glowing example of determination?

He thought about that long after Dixie's Jeep faded from sight. Somewhere between his lack of promises and the opening of his heart, he'd discovered the man he was always meant to be. But he'd been wrong about so many things lately. Could he keep from adding another item to the list?

Maybe this wasn't a *start* after all, but an end to what could become his biggest mistake yet.

Chapter Twenty-Three

DIXIE CLOSED THE accounting software program for Whiskey Bro's Monday evening, speaking into her cell phone to her mother. "Thanks again for handling things while I was away. You were right. I really needed a break."

"Anytime. I heard you had a visitor at the Cape."

"*Ugh.* I told Justin and the guys if they opened their mouths they'd regret it!"

"Calm down," her mother said firmly. "I didn't hear it from any of the guys. You know the girls' club always has your back. Aunt Reba and Ginger put the kibosh on gossip where the men are concerned, but they had to call and gush about how happy they are for you. Heck, darlin', I'd worry if they didn't." The girls' club was what her mother had always called the wives of the Dark Knights, who could lock down secrets better than Fort Knox.

"Well, maybe they shouldn't rave too much," Dixie grumbled. It had been a day and a half since she and Jace had said goodbye, and she hadn't heard a peep from him.

"Uh-oh. Talk to me."

Dixie sighed. "I don't want to talk about it." It was too

embarrassing. She had been sure that Jace felt the same immense love for her as she felt for him, but if he had, wouldn't he have reached out? Wouldn't he have missed her like she missed him? *Achingly* so?

"Ginger said you and Jace looked inseparable. Conroy even made a comment to her about how nice it was to see a man looking at you like you were his entire world."

Dixie closed her eyes, seeing exactly that look in Jace's eyes in her mind. "He did look at me like that, but…" She bit back the rest of the truth. She'd been so upset earlier today she'd thought she was going to break down in tears—and she hated herself for feeling that way. It had been only a day and a half, not a *week*. She knew how busy he was, but she also knew that nobody was too busy to send a two-second text. One line was all she needed. *I miss you*, or even the lame text he'd sent after she left New York. *Hope you got home okay* would be better than radio silence.

"Listen, Dix. You of all people know that sometimes men need to be knocked upside the head before they get things right."

Dixie pushed to her feet and paced the office, unwilling to rationalize for him. "Maybe so, but if a man loves me, he shouldn't need to be knocked in the head."

"Oh, baby," her mother said softly. "Jace said he *loves* you? That's such a special moment. I want to hear all about it."

So do I…

A burning sensation seared through Dixie's chest, bringing a rush of sadness.

"There's nothing to tell. He never said he loved me." She rubbed at the center of her chest. But he'd said so many other wonderful things, and he'd gotten a matching tattoo. Those things mattered, but she couldn't go down this path with her mother. No matter what anyone said to her, it wouldn't take away the sting of his not reaching out. "Mom, church starts in half an hour and the bar is packed. I've got to get back out there and serve."

Church was what they called the meetings of the Dark Knights, which took place Monday nights in the clubhouse behind the bar. Dixie's father and brothers were already there, but some members hung around the bar until just before the meetings began.

"You can't drop a bomb like that and leave me hanging," her mother complained.

Dixie rolled her eyes, breathing deeply. It wasn't her mother's fault she was upset. "He *acted* like he loved me. I felt it. It was *real*, not just hopeful thinking. But now I haven't heard from him. Maybe you're right and he just needs to be smacked in the head, but that's not the type of love *I* want. So, can we please drop it? I really appreciate you taking over for me while I was gone, and please tell Aunt Reba and Ginger that I appreciate what they've done to keep things under wraps." She also appreciated Jace taking so much time off to be with her, even if it hurt to be put on the back burner. "But I have to go before Tracey gets overwhelmed."

After they ended the call, Dixie went into the crowded bar. Monday nights were always the most trying, and tonight she wasn't in the mood to deal with any shit.

"Hey, Dix. I brought some cookies Josie made for you," Jed called from over by the pool tables, where he was hanging out with Crow, Court, and a handful of other Dark Knights.

She walked over and said, "I'm sorry I wasn't able to make it to her grand opening. Izzy said it was amazing and that practically the whole town turned out to celebrate."

"No big deal. Red told us you'd gone out of town. Finlay hung up a copy of the article Gemma wrote behind the bar." Jed motioned toward the bar and said, "But you might want to grab those cookies. Diesel's been eyeing them all night."

"Will do. Please thank Josie for me." A tray of cookies and a quart of ice cream *might* take the edge off, but a bottle of liquor would do it quicker. Unfortunately, as she wound through the crowd, stopping to pick up empty bottles and take orders on the way, she knew neither of those were options at the moment.

"Hey, hot stuff?" a shaggy-haired, clean-shaven guy she didn't recognize called out to her as she walked by.

She feigned what she hoped was a tip-worthy smile as she sized him up. He and the other two men he was sitting with wore dress shirts and slacks, and she wondered how they'd ended up in a biker bar. "What can I get you boys?"

He looked at his buddies and lifted his chin, as if he were saying, *Watch this.* "We're *men*, for starters."

Real men don't need declarations was on the tip of her tongue, but she withheld that cutting remark and said, "What'll it be?"

"A round of Jack and Cokes." He raked his eyes down her body, making her wish she'd worn jeans instead of the leather shorts from the Leather and Lace line. "Nice shorts. They'd look great on my *bedroom floor.*"

If it were any other night, she would probably have laughed and said *You wish*, but her simmering anger hit the boiling point. She grabbed him by the collar, lifted him to his feet, and got right in his face, seething, "Bet your teeth would look great on the floor of this bar"—she was vaguely aware of silence descending around her and the Dark Knights closing in on them—"because that's what's going to happen if you make another crack like that." She lifted her eyes to Diesel, who stepped beside the table, looming as she pushed the guy back down to his seat and released his shirt. "I've got this, Diesel."

None of her guardians retreated, which pissed her off even more.

"I said, I've fucking got this," she snapped.

"Okay, show's over," Izzy said, pushing through the crowd. She took Dixie by the arm and dragged her into the office, closing the door behind them. "What the hell? Are you trying to start a rumble? Diesel damn near jumped over the bar."

Dixie was breathing hard, pacing the floor, too mad to speak. Izzy had cornered her earlier when she'd been lost in her own thoughts and Dixie had told her about not hearing from Jace.

"Oh, Dixie. You still haven't heard from him?" Izzy asked in a softer, more empathetic tone.

Dixie shook her head.

"Have you considered calling him?"

"What do you think I've been thinking about since last night?" Her thumb had hovered over his name in her contacts so often, her thumb muscles hurt, and she'd typed dozens of texts, only to delete every single one.

"I don't know. Maybe you're just thinking about all the great sex you're missing," Izzy teased.

Dixie rolled her eyes. "This is ridiculous. I'm not this person, Iz. You *know* that."

"What I know is that you must really love him to be like this after only a day."

"A day and a *half*, and don't say it. I *know* how ridiculous it is, and I hate myself for feeling like this. How did he turn me into the kind of woman I can't stand?" She leaned back against the desk.

"He slayed your heart one orgasm at a time. Now you're in withdrawal, made worse because his silence has left you wondering if all those amazing things he said were real or fake." Izzy leaned on the desk beside her. "This is why I don't date on a serious level. I hate wondering where I stand. It's much easier to lay down ground rules and stick to them."

"We kind of did. He didn't make any promises about calling or even seeing me. Not even when we said goodbye. He said he'd let me know when he was in Peaceful Harbor and he was sure we'd talk before then."

"And...?"

Too anxious to sit still, Dixie pushed from the desk and paced. "And then he kissed the life out of me, and I drove away in a state of fucking bliss."

Izzy sighed. "The man really must have a magical mouth."

"Every part of his body is magical."

"Then you have only two choices. You can sit back and wait, or you can call him and tell him exactly why you're upset."

"I'm not going to call him. I'm not chasing *any* man."

"Then you'd better get this shit under control, Dix, because you had every Dark Knight out there ready to tear that yuppie apart. What did that guy say to you, anyway?"

"That my shorts would look good on his bedroom floor."

They both laughed.

"Lame," Izzy said. "But those shorts are freaking hot."

"Jace and Jilly designed them. Come on. I'll try to keep my big mouth under control," Dixie said as she pulled open the door.

Diesel was standing there, hands on his hips, blocking the

doorway. "I got rid of those guys."

"You didn't have to do that," Dixie snapped, trying to push past him, but it was like trying to move a house. "Can I walk past, please?"

Diesel crossed his arms over his massive chest and said, "You've been uppity all night. Need me to take care of something?"

"No. What I need is to make it through tonight without killing anyone." Dixie squeezed past him with Izzy on her heels. "You know what's wrong with the male gender?"

"They're either thinking with their dicks or they're not thinking at all?" Izzy offered.

She didn't buy that Jace had only been thinking with his dick, and she sure as hell didn't buy that the man who'd built an empire wasn't thinking at all. The problem was, she didn't have an answer that made sense. She was kind of hoping Izzy had one, so she came up with the best she could. "No. That they don't come with an instruction manual."

Chapter Twenty-Four

"ARE YOU ONE hundred percent certain you want to do this?" Maddox asked as Jace signed the contract for the office and manufacturing space for their new East Coast headquarters Tuesday afternoon.

Jace turned the pages looking for the next place he had to sign. "Hell yes. It's for the best. I've already held the deal up for a week."

"You sure you're not making a mistake with Dixie?" Maddox asked.

Jace lifted his eyes, meeting Maddox's concerned gaze. "We've been over this. She needs a guy who is willing to put down roots."

Maddox scoffed and shook his head. "I don't get it. She's known you forever. How can she even think…?"

"Mad, I haven't slept in days. If you value your life and our friendship, you won't push me today."

"It's your life, but don't you think you should at least call her? Talk this shit out before committing to something as major as this? I can hold off the deal for another week, just in case."

"Hell no. I know where she stands." Jace signed the last

page and shoved the papers across the conference table. "She had my undivided attention for several days, and as unbelievably incredible as it was, it cost us enough time. What I need to do is *focus*, take care of business, and get all the shit done that I've put off for the past week, so we can move forward with the new headquarters and the launch of the Legacy and Leather and Lace lines. We're on the cusp of life-changing transitions. We can't afford to let anything slip through the cracks."

Jace's cell phone rang, and Shea's name flashed on the screen. He held up a finger to Maddox as he answered the call. "Hi, Shea."

"Hi. I'd like to go over the schedules for the in-person events. Do you have a minute?"

He checked his watch. "I have a conference call in less than ten minutes. I reviewed the schedules yesterday and saw no issues with them. But you need to reach out to Dixie and make sure to keep her in the loop in case she has any scheduling conflicts."

"Will do. Also, while I have you on the line, I spoke to Jilly and we're on for Fashion Week. Maddox told me you were dead set against the idea last week. I'm really glad you changed your mind."

"You know my stipulation about Dixie walking with me, Mad, and Jilly."

"I'm already on it. Jilly has agreed to it, and she knows you want Dixie in the sleeveless lace top with the slit in the middle and the choker collar, black miniskirt, and knee-high black leather boots. You must really love that outfit."

He loved *Dixie* in that outfit, which was why he'd chosen it as the cover of the calendar. "I do, and I want Indi to do Dixie's hair and makeup. She did a great job last time."

"Jilly has her own team—"

"I want *Indi*," he said firmly. "Please make it happen."

Maddox tapped his watch, reminding him of their conference call with Drew Ryder, the architect handling the design of their new Boston retail space.

"Okay, Indi it is," she said.

"Great. I need to go. Is there anything else?"

"No, we're good. Thanks. I'll report back after I confirm with Dixie."

They ended the call and Maddox pushed to his feet and said, "Let's take the call in my office. Leni has a meeting and needs the conference room."

Jace stood up, and Maddox offered his hand.

"What's this for?" Jace asked as he shook it.

Maddox cracked a rare smile. "You've been a little out there, a little lost, for the past year or so. It's good to have you back on board with your head on straight."

"Thanks, man. I needed that time with Dixie to figure things out and get my priorities in line."

"I guess so." As they left the conference room, Maddox said, "Some people are meant for putting down roots, and some of us are meant to ride alone and follow the open road wherever it may lead."

Jace clapped a hand on Maddox's back and said, "To each his own and all that crap. Time to get busy creating our next best store."

DIXIE SET THE empty miniature bottle of bourbon on the

table next to the other two bottles she'd already drank and shoveled another spoonful of ice cream into her mouth. It was Thursday evening, four and a half days since she'd said goodbye to Jace. Four and a half days since she'd held his hand, kissed his lips, or heard his voice.

Except in her dreams, where he was front and center every night.

After four and a half torturous days of radio silence, Dixie had cruised right past sadness to flat-out *pissed*. Well, that wasn't *exactly* true. She *was* angry as a cat in a river, but she was also painstakingly heartbroken. How hard was it to make one phone call or send one text? She felt like she'd stepped into *heartbreak quicksand*, and no matter how much she tried, she couldn't find her way out. She'd spent this week refusing to believe that what she and Jace had was anything less than *true* love, and in the next breath she was calling herself a fucking idiot. She was a weepy mess at home and a grouchy bitch at work. But she'd kept the reasons a secret from her brothers, because the idea of them blaming Jace made her even more upset. Bear had called Izzy earlier today asking her to find out what was wrong, which was why Izzy had stormed into the auto shop, pretending like she had no idea why Dixie was upset, and demanded an ice-cream intervention.

Now here they sat in Luscious Licks, Penny Wilson's ice cream parlor, trying to snuff out thoughts of Jace with rich, sugary goodness and bourbon. Penny made the best homemade ice cream in all of Peaceful Harbor and was known for her array of sundaes and specials suitable for any occasion, like the Go Away Gloomy Day and No-Good Pile of Poop sundaes and the Celebrating My Awesomeness special.

Dixie picked up an empty bottle and wiggled it in the air.

"Another bourbon please, Pen."

"Okay, but if anyone asks, you brought your own booze. This is way over the legal limit of liquor toppings." Penny climbed out of her seat in the booth across from Dixie. She was a Zooey Deschanel lookalike with bright blue eyes and walnut-brown hair and looked nothing like her blond older sister, Finlay.

"Done!" Dixie promised, shoving another spoonful of her Broken Heart Special into her mouth. The thick slab of pecan brownie smothered in several scoops of cookie-dough-chunk ice cream and topped with crushed cherries and bourbon definitely hit the spot.

At least for the next ten minutes, which was about how long it would take her to finish it.

The door to the shop opened, and Quincy strolled in as Penny reached into her *hard knocks* cabinet, where she kept miniature bottles of liquor for the sundaes that required a little *more* than sugar.

"Don't do it, Pen! You don't need a hard-knocks bottle! I'm here for you," Quincy teased with a cocky grin.

"Give it up, Quincy," Dixie said matter-of-factly. "Trust me, you don't want to get all tangled up in a woman. Love sucks." She stuffed more ice cream into her mouth.

Quincy gave her a perplexed look, eyeing her enormous sundae.

Dixie hunched over the bowl and said, "Touch my sundae and die, Gritt."

He chuckled. "I heard you've been in a mood since you came back from the Cape. What the heck happened up there? Aren't vacations supposed to leave you totally chilled out?"

"Leave it alone, Quin," Penny warned as she set the bottle

of bourbon down on the table beside the three empties.

Dixie snagged the miniature bottle and tipped it up to her lips, emptying it in one gulp.

Quincy's eyes widened. "Damn, Dix. Is whatever's going on the reason you're wearing the shirt Bullet has broken up fights over when you *know* he's working tonight?"

She looked down at her black halter top with THERE AIN'T NOTHIN' A LITTLE WHISKEY CAN'T FIX written across the front. All of the words were written in white-block letters except Whiskey, which was written in red script. The halter and skinny jeans hadn't been her first choice of outfits that morning. She'd dressed in the same outfit she'd worn home from the photo shoot, the one Jace had shredded and then later replaced. She'd felt so close to Jace the night after the photo shoot, she'd wanted to revel in those feelings and not let hurt destroy them. But every time she looked in the mirror, she missed him even more, so she'd changed into jeans and the halter top. The top made her feel *strong*. Bullet's hatred of the top made it an even better choice—she'd be forced to fight instead of weep.

"That shirt is classic *Dixie*," Izzy said.

"Agreed," Quincy said as he slid into the booth beside Izzy. "Dix, you said 'love sucks,' so I'm assuming this has to do with a guy? I'm going to tell you what I tell the people in NA when they're facing tough situations."

"Please don't," Dixie said flatly.

Izzy and Penny shook their heads, warnings flaring in their eyes.

"We're handling it," Izzy assured him.

"'Handling it,'" Quincy repeated, looking unconvinced. "Who's the dude?"

"There's no *dude*." Dixie dug her spoon into the thick

brownie, chopping off a hunk and shoveling it into her mouth.

Quincy arched a brow. "So this is about a *chick*? Wow, that's not something I expected. Things just got even more interesting."

Dixie pointed her spoon at him and said, "You need to stop talking before I stab you with this."

"You've always been there for me, Dix. I just want to help," Quincy insisted.

The sincerity in his voice brought a sliver of guilt. "Thanks, but I'm good, or I will be. If you really want to help, you'll keep your mouth shut around anyone outside of this store. You never saw me stuffing my face. Got it?"

"Sure. Whatever you need." He leaned across the table and lowered his voice. "But you know I'm happy to catch a flight to the Cape and teach some asshole a lesson."

Dixie gritted her teeth. Jace was *not* an asshole. She loved him, and damn it, she was sure he loved her too. But on the off chance that she'd lost her ability to read people and he turned out to be a bastard who had played her like a fucking fiddle, he still hadn't promised her a damn thing. This was on *her*, not him.

"Quincy," Penny said sharply, pulling him to his feet. "Why don't we catch up another time?" She ushered him toward the door. "I'm sorry. It looks like I'm closing early."

Dixie felt horrible for sending him away. It wasn't Quincy's fault she'd spent the last several days trying to put her shattered heart back together while also dodging so many questions and comments from the guys at the auto shop and Diesel and Bullet at the bar that she was ready to rip someone's head off.

"No, he doesn't have to go." Dixie pushed to her feet, feeling a little light-headed. Had she forgotten to eat lunch *again*?

She grabbed her backpack and said, "It's fine. I have to get to work at the bar anyway."

"Want me to take your shift?" Izzy asked, snagging Dixie's keys from the table.

"Nope. If I go home I'll just…" *Cry or punch my pillow.* "I need to go to work." She held her hand out for her keys.

"Oh, no, bourbon girl." Izzy took her arm and said, "I know you can hold your liquor, but in fifteen or twenty minutes you'll have a nice buzz going. There's no way I'm letting you drive."

"*Fine,* whatever." Dixie leaned over the table, shoveling more brownie and ice cream into her mouth. After she scarfed that down, she said, "Thank you, Penny. I owe you a *real* bottle of bourbon. And, Quincy, remember, you open your mouth about any of this and I'll have to kill you."

"Got it. Call me if you want a guy's perspective on this *non-guy*-related situation." He hugged her and lowered his voice to say, "Whoever has upset you is making a huge mistake. I'm sorry you're going through whatever this is."

Tears burned Dixie's eyes, and she turned away before he could see them and said, "Let's go, Iz." She pushed through the door and filled her lungs with the warm evening air. Her stomach burned, her heart ached, and the buzz from the bourbon was already taking effect, but instead of dulling her tangled emotions, it magnified them.

"You're gonna cry, aren't you?" Izzy asked as they headed for her car.

"Not if I can help it."

Dixie climbed into the car and rolled down the window, thankful that Izzy knew her well enough not to try to talk about what *was* or *wasn't* going on with Jace. She cranked the radio, giving Dixie a chance to try to pull herself together on the way to the bar. The ice cream and liquor hadn't helped. She felt a little woozy, but maybe that was because her heart was so confused it wasn't functioning properly and her brain wasn't getting enough blood.

Or maybe she was just buzzed and missing Jace.

Izzy pulled into the parking lot at Whiskey Bro's and threw the car into park. She turned to Dixie, looking concerned, and said, "Are you sure you don't want me to take your shift?"

"I'm sure, thank you. I'm just...I don't get it, Iz. Maybe you're right and I should reach out to him, but I can't bring myself to do it. Every time I try to, I get upset. I mean, think about it. Let's say I call and he answers the phone. Then what? I'll sound like a child asking why he *hasn't* called. I'm not that person, and he knows it. And the weirdest thing about all of this is that no part of me thinks he doesn't love me. If you could have seen the way he looked at me, felt what I felt when he held my hand, kissed me, or..."

"I *know* you feel that way," Izzy said. "Do you think something could have happened to him? Maybe he got into an accident?"

Dixie shook her head. "His sister Mia texted me the other night with a picture of a pair of Leather and Lace heels Jace had sent to her. If something had happened to him, she would have mentioned it."

"Did you ask if she'd spoken with him?"

"No. I'm not that person either." She grabbed her backpack and said, "I always thought I knew who I was, but I was wrong. *Now* I know the truth."

Izzy handed Dixie her keys and said, "Are you going to clue me in on what that is?"

"Sure. I'm a badass Whiskey chick." Dixie stuffed her keys into her backpack, trying to convince herself that what she'd said was all there was to it. The part she wanted to share with Izzy, but couldn't for fear of being overcome with sadness, was that Whiskeys were only human after all. Whiskey strength *wasn't* unbreakable, and the family she adored *wasn't* everything she needed.

"That's not *new*, Dix. Not for me, or you," Izzy said.

Dixie opened the car door and put one foot on the pavement, prepared to flee.

Izzy grabbed her arm and said, "Spill."

"*Fine*, but we are not talking about it. After I tell you, you are going to put this car in drive and get the hell out of here."

"Okay. Promise." Izzy made a cross over her heart.

Dixie knew she could trust Izzy. She just wasn't sure she could trust herself not to blubber like a fool. "When Whiskeys give their hearts away, I'm not sure we ever get them back."

Chapter Twenty-Five

DIXIE HEADED STRAIGHT into the bar without a backward glance, hoping to quell the lump in her throat. She was instantly sucked into the comfort of the familiar bar. The scents of leather, liquor, and testosterone, the din of the crowd, the sounds of balls sinking into the pockets of pool tables and darts hitting their mark wrapped around her like a warm scarf on a cold winter night. Bullet and Jed were manning the bar. Tracey was waitressing, chatting with a group of men as she took their orders.

Dixie headed straight for the office, feeling the weight of Bullet's eyes tracking her every step. She should have worn something different. The idea of fighting with Bullet suddenly made her feel even worse.

"Hey, Dix," Tex Sharpe said as she passed the table where he sat with two of the Bando brothers, who were also Dark Knights.

"Our local celebrity," Vaughn Bando, a brawny contractor, said.

She didn't dare slow down to greet them while she felt so unlike herself. She stepped into the office and closed the door behind her, exhaling a breath she hadn't realized she'd been holding. How the hell was she going to make it through this shift? Maybe she should just get it over with and call Jace. She tossed her backpack on the desk and dug out her phone. She saw she had a text from Shea and plunked down in the chair behind the desk as she read it.

I emailed the schedule for your appearances. Can you take a look when you get a chance and try to get back to me by the end of the day tomorrow?

Jace's voice whispered through Dixie's mind. *We'll be traveling together to the in-person events.* She'd been so happy when he'd said it, but now she realized he could have only meant that they'd be at the events together. He wasn't exactly the most accurate communicator.

Ugh. She hated ambiguity. And yet she'd allowed it throughout these last couple of weeks. *Because I love him.* Tears welled in her eyes. She'd told her mother she didn't want to make excuses for him, but at the same time she wanted to make a million of them, because the alternative was excruciating. Her eyes caught on that tattoo on her wrist, and tears streamed down her cheeks. She closed her eyes against them, but they just kept coming. Why was this so hard? She dropped her phone on the desk, crossed her arms over the desk, and lowered her forehead to them, giving in to her heartbreak. Tears slid down her nose, her cheeks, wetting the desk.

The door opened, and Dixie jerked her head up as Bullet blew in and said, "Are you—"

She wiped her arm over her eyes, spinning the chair around so he couldn't see her face. She heard the door close and choked out, "I'll be right out for my shift."

"Like *hell* you will." Bullet strode around the desk, staring down at her, angry and worried. "What's wrong?"

"Nothing." She sniffled and spun the chair the other way.

Bullet grabbed the back of her chair and whipped it around. "Bullshit. Bear said you've been crying on and off at work, and last night you told me you hurt your fucking knee. You think I'm buying that shit?"

She pushed to her feet, her heart pounding. "I don't care what you're *buying*. So what if I'm crying? Big deal! People cry, Bullet, even *Whiskeys*." She pushed past him.

He grabbed her arm, stopping her in her tracks. "Dix, talk to me," he said less angrily. "Do I need to call Justin and find out for myself what the hell went on up there?"

"No! *God!*" She yanked her arm free. "Don't you get it? This is *my* life to break or fix or do whatever I please. I'm not crying because of anyone but myself! I got together with someone at the Cape and made more of it than I should have. That's all this is. That's on *me*, Bullet, and you don't know the guy anyway, so back off."

He gritted his teeth and seethed, "You want me to just sit back and watch you like this?"

"*No*. I want you to go back out there, do your job, and let me do mine. I can take care of myself." She crossed the room and threw the door open.

Bullet stormed past her, hands fisted, teeth gritted, and said, "I'm going to fucking tear Stone's head off."

"Bullet!" she hollered.

Bullet turned just as the door to the bar opened and Jace walked in, sending Dixie's heart into her throat. Jace looked exhausted and gorgeous. He smiled when he saw her. She wanted to *run* to him, but she was too hurt, too angry, and too fucking confused to do anything more than spew venom.

"What are *you* doing here?" she fumed, striding toward him. "You can't spend days acting like you love me, making love *to* me, and then leave me hanging!"

Jace's face morphed to a mask of confusion. "Dix, I had to—"

"*Stone!*" Bullet growled, nostrils flared, eyes cold and dark.

As Jace turned, Bullet's fist slammed into his jaw. Jace stumbled back, and all the men in the bar sprang to their feet. Before Dixie could blink, Jace plowed forward, grabbed Bullet by the collar, and threw him against the wall.

Jace crushed him against the wall, hand fisted in Bullet's shirt as he growled, "That was your one *free* shot."

"You hit him?" Dixie hollered at Bullet. "If anyone gets to hit Jace, it's *me!*"

She cocked her arm, and Jace's other hand shot out, grabbing the front of her shirt, keeping her *and* Bullet at arm's length. The door to the bar burst opened, and Biggs and Red rushed in.

Jace's eyes flared angrily as he snarled, "I can't fucking believe I want to marry into this crazy-ass family."

Dixie wobbled on her feet, the room tilting around her. *Marry into?* She tried to make sense of what he'd said, but days of anguish had her heart racing, her head spinning, and his words just fueled her rage.

Jace glowered at Bullet and said, "I'm going to let go. If you hit me, I *will* fuck you up."

"Bullet!" Biggs hollered as he and Red pushed through the crowd. "*Stand down.*"

Bullet's cold, dark eyes remained trained on Jace.

"*Now,*" Biggs commanded.

Jace lowered his hands and turned toward Dixie, just as she

cocked another punch and let it fly, hitting him square in the jaw.

"*Fuck*," Jace shouted, rubbing his jaw.

"Oh *Lord*," Red said.

"What the hell, Dixie?" Jace's eyes drilled into her.

"What the hell *yourself?* It's been days since I've heard from you! You think I'm just sitting around waiting for you to march in here and play with my heart? I *cried* for you, and I don't fucking cry! You didn't call. You didn't text—you just *forgot* me!"

"*Forgot* you?" Jace looked up at the ceiling and grabbed the sides of his head, emitting a tortured groan. He lowered his chin, stalking toward her with eyes as serious as they were loving. "Jesus, Dixie. You're *not* doing this to me again. I left last time, and I'm not leaving you again, so *stop* giving me shit long enough to hear me out. I couldn't forget you if I wanted to. I have been running all over creation so that I could do *this!*" He pulled papers from his back pocket and pressed them into her hand. "I didn't call because I knew if I heard your voice— the voice that is *constantly* in my head, driving me out of my fucking mind—I'd tell you what I was up to, and damn it, *Dixie*, I told you I wouldn't make empty promises. I wasn't about to show up to your parents' house *empty-handed* to ask your father for his blessing to marry the toughest, brightest, most *stubborn* and beautiful woman in all of Peaceful Harbor."

In a state of shock, she looked at her parents. Her father nodded in confirmation. Her mother's hand covered her mouth, but a smile shone in her eyes.

"*Fuck*, Dix," Jace said in a pained voice. "I'm doing this all *wrong.*"

He dug something out of the front pocket of his jeans and

sank down to one knee. He lifted his hand, looking up at her with the most honest expression and so much love in his eyes, Dixie's knees weakened. In his hand he held a gorgeous ring with a stunning round black diamond surrounded by smaller white diamonds.

"I have never answered to anyone since the day I moved out of my parents' house," Jace said emphatically. "I have never wanted to put down roots, or start a family, or live my life for someone else, until now. Until *you*, Dixie. You captured my heart as a beautiful, confident young woman of eighteen, and not a day has passed that you weren't on my mind. I messed up by not calling, but that doesn't mean I'm not head over heels in love with you. It means I'm *not perfect*, and I may never be. But for you I want to try. I'm sorry I didn't call, but in the last four days I've been to Boston, LA, New York, and now here, taking late-night flights, rearranging my life so I could spend the rest of it with you."

Her heart leapt into her throat and tears streamed down her cheeks as her heart healed one loving word at a time.

"In your hand is proof of sale for two properties. The first is for your favorite spot and mine, the property in the woods where we went the first time you rode on the back of my bike. You were right that day, Dixie. I knew exactly what it meant to have you ride with me. I want to make a life with you, Dix, to build a house and fill it with kids. The second proof of sale is for Silver-Stone's new Peaceful Harbor manufacturing plant and headquarters, which is my home office from this day forward."

He rose to his feet, gazing deeply into her eyes, and said, "Dixie Lee Whiskey, I am so in love with you, it hurts. I can't eat, can't sleep, and I know it's Whiskey fever, but I don't want a remedy. I want to put down roots and have them tangle with yours until they're inseparable, here with all the people you love, so you never miss being Auntie Dixie."

Dixie couldn't breathe. Tears blurred her eyes as he took her hand in his, his own eyes dampening as he said, "If you can see past my faults, if you're willing to try to teach an old man new tricks, then say you'll marry me, Dixie. Be my wife. Let me learn how to be the man you deserve. I promise to text you three times a day if you want me to. I'll always be faithful, and above all else, I promise to never, *ever* call you *kitten* again."

A choked laugh escaped her lips.

He brushed her tears from her cheeks and said, "I love you, Dixie. I love your green eyes and fiery hair, your beautiful, generous heart, and your fierce spirit and determination to get everything in this life you deserve and not accept anything less. Will you be my wife, my *queen*, and let me give you the world?"

"I don't want the world," she said through choked sobs. "All I've ever wanted was *you*."

"You've had me since day one, baby, and if I have my way, you'll have me forevermore."

"If you ever leave me hanging for days again, you'll regret it," she said, only half teasing.

A rumble of laughter rose around them. She'd forgotten they weren't alone.

"As well I should," he said with a smile. He held her hand, the ring perched in front of her finger, and said, "Say yes, Dix. Please say yes."

She choked out, "Yes, Jace. I'll marry you!"

"On both sides of the band of this ring are diamonds in the shape of infinity signs," he said as he put the ring on her finger. "I designed it so you would always know that what we have is forever. You own my heart, Dix. *Don't* tread lightly."

She laughed and launched herself into his arms, crushing her lips to his. As cheers and applause rang out around them, Jace kissed her like he'd been waiting his whole life to do it. And when their lips parted, he said, *"God I love you,"* and pressed his glorious lips to hers again, like he'd never let her go.

JACE WAS ON cloud nine as he and Dixie were swept into her parents' open arms and then passed around the room, congratulated, and patted on the back. He kept one eye on his beautiful bride-to-be with her tear-streaked face and mile-wide smile. The proposal hadn't gone quite as he'd pictured it, but Dixie had said yes, and that was all that mattered. By the time he came face-to-face with Bullet, Jace's head was still in the clouds—and his future brother-in-law looked like he still wanted to kill him. It had been forever since Jace had taken a punch, much less *two*, but even the pain in his jaw couldn't dampen his elation.

He went for humor, hoping to make peace with levity. "That was a cheap shot."

Bullet's lips tipped up in a smirk, and he said, "Welcome to the family." He offered his hand, and when Jace shook it, Bullet pulled him into a manly embrace. "We cool?"

"Yeah, we're cool," Jace said, stepping back and looking for Dixie again. Red had put the word out that Jace was proposing right after he'd left their house, and news had traveled fast. The rest of Dixie's family had already arrived and congratulated them, and more friends were still filing through the door. He spotted Dixie standing by the bar with Crystal, Bear, and Bones. Dixie was holding Lila, her little fist wrapped around a lock of

Dixie's hair. Dixie looked in his direction, and their eyes connected with the sizzling heat he'd come to expect. But his heart beat to a new rhythm, stronger and louder than ever before.

"Are you really moving here?" Bullet asked, drawing his attention back to their conversation.

"Moving here, working here. Maddox and I reevaluated my responsibilities and I delegated some of my oversight to our directors. I'll still have to travel, but not nearly as often. I'm going to try to work it out so Dixie and I can travel together whenever possible." He stole another glance at Dixie and said, "There's nothing I won't do for your sister."

"Except *call*," Bullet said with a teasing lilt to his voice.

"I know I fucked up. But in all fairness, I had a lot of shit to rearrange. I don't know if she told you or not, but I surprised her at the Cape. I made the decision before going to the Cape, but I couldn't tell Dixie until I knew all my ducks were in a row. I was negotiating deals on the properties and changing not only my entire life, but redirecting the company and all our plans for the second headquarters. I still can't believe I pulled it off so fast. I was running around like a chicken with my head cut off, taking night flights from Boston to LA, then LA to New York to pick up her ring, and then I drove here from New York. I know I screwed up by not calling or texting, but I'm learning, Bullet. I'm changing, and with Dixie's help, I'll get there."

"Good, but I'm still holding it over your head." Bullet clapped him on his back and said, "I'm just giving you shit. Sorry for the punch, but I saw her tears and…"

"I get it. If she were my sister, I'd have taken you *down*."

"You would have *tried*," Bullet said. "Listen, if Dixie's happy, I'm happy."

"I've been chasing goals my whole life, man." Jace glanced at Dixie and said, "From now on, her happiness is at the top of my list."

Red yelled, "A round of drinks, on the house!"

Cheers rang out, and as Bullet went to find Finlay, Jace made his way to Dixie, who was now talking with Red, Bear, and Crystal and rubbing noses with Lila. He could hardly believe he no longer had to fight his attraction to the woman who had stolen his heart when she was just a girl, spreading her wings and learning to fly.

Jace put a hand on Dixie's back and leaned in for a kiss. "How's my beautiful *fiancée*?"

"So *happy*. *Fiancée*—I like the sound of that," she said softly.

"Me too." He tickled Lila's chin and said, "And how's this little princess?"

Lila reached two grabby hands toward Jace, flashing a toothy grin. Her wispy blond hair was pulled back in a pretty pink headband that matched her jumper. Dixie transferred Lila into his arms.

"Someone's got a fan," Sarah said as she and Bones joined them. Bones had his arm around Sarah, and neither of them were holding their baby.

"Where's my littlest granddaughter?" Red asked.

"Finlay has her." Bones answered. "Jace, I heard about the fight. Was Bullet giving you a hard time just now?"

"Nah, we're cool."

"When the Whiskeys give you a hard time, it means you're part of the family," Crystal assured him. "It's when they *stop* that you have to worry."

They all laughed.

Red said, "She's right. As you found out, Bullet would give his life to save Dixie if he thought she was in trouble. But seeing our girl smile? All you'll get from him for that is a lifetime of harassment, and that's a *good* thing." She patted Lila's back and said, "And we *all* love a man who's not afraid of babies."

"Jace is a baby *hog*," Dixie exclaimed. "You should have seen him with his nephew, Thane."

Not only wasn't he afraid of kids, but he hoped to have a family with Dixie when she was ready. But that was a discussion for another day.

Crystal rubbed her burgeoning belly and said, "If you two are thinking of having babies right away, you should know that we have dibs on Nana Red's babysitting services at least once a week after Cubby's born."

"Unless this is going to be a shotgun wedding, I don't think Jace and Dixie are the ones you need to worry about." Red lowered her voice and said, "You didn't hear this from me, but you might want to start negotiating with Finlay and Bullet."

"What?" Crystal's eyes widened.

Red put her finger over her lips and then walked away.

"Oh, I won't tell a soul," Crystal said before cutting a path through the crowd toward Finlay.

"I guess I wasn't the only one keeping secrets," Dixie said. "I hope I'm going to be an auntie again!" She went up on her toes, watching Crystal and Finlay hug.

"Looks like Bullet might have put a bun in her oven. Good for him," Bear said. "Speaking of Bullet, I hear he knocked you back a step or two, Jace."

"Yeah, he caught me off guard. That was *fun*." Jace rubbed his jaw. "I turned, and he clocked me. And then I turned the other way, and your sister busted my jaw. Bad timing, I guess."

Bear nudged him and said, "They say bikers and lovers have two things in common. Good balance and superb timing. Sorry, bro, but that doesn't fare well for you on the road *or* in the bedroom, since you don't seem to possess either."

"Bear!" Dixie smacked his arm and yelled, "Jace is a *god* in the bedroom!"

The din of the crowd silenced, and all eyes turned toward them. Jace straightened his shoulders. Yeah, he'd *own* that proclamation.

"Oh, *shit*," Dixie said under her breath, stepping behind him.

Biggs tapped his glass with a knife, thankfully calling attention away from them and up to the stage, where he and Red stood arm in arm.

"Papapapa!" Lila babbled, reaching toward the stage.

"She wants my dad," Dixie said.

"Papapapapa!" Lila rocked and wiggled, trying to squirm free.

"Son," Biggs said through the microphone, "why don't you bring that little darlin' *and* my daughter up here and join us."

With Jace's arm around Dixie and sweet Lila in his arms, they made their way up to the stage. He handed Lila over to Biggs, and she wrapped her little arms around Biggs's neck, hugging him tight.

Jace pulled Dixie closer and said, "I look forward to the day our children will do that."

She looked at him like he'd promised her the world. He intended to honor that promise.

"This is a big night for all of us," Biggs said in a slow drawl. "When our little girl was born, I swear she came out looking for a country to rule."

"That's our Dixie!" someone hollered from within the crowd.

"You've got that right." Biggs looked lovingly at Dixie and said, "I could not be prouder of you, darlin'. You will always be my little girl and the light of my life."

Dixie teared up.

"I knew it would take a strong man to win your heart, and to be honest, I wasn't sure there was a man on earth I'd feel good about giving my blessing to." He shifted his gaze to Jace and said, "Then Jace Stone showed up at my door, nervous as a rat in a snake's den and about as in love as any man I'd ever seen. I mean look at him, all swoony-eyed over my precious girl."

Another rumble of laughter rolled through the crowd.

"Damn right," Jace said, and he kissed Dixie's temple.

He'd been a wreck when he'd shown up to ask Biggs for Dixie's hand in marriage, and Biggs had made him sweat it out. He'd listened to Jace's every word without giving away a hint of what he was thinking. Jace had not only professed his love for Dixie, but he'd explained how he'd restructured his work responsibilities and finalized their decision to open the manufacturing plant and headquarters in Peaceful Harbor instead of Boston, though they were still opening a second retail store in Boston. He'd also told Biggs about the property he'd purchased for their home in Peaceful Harbor. Biggs had only asked him one question. He'd wanted to know what had taken Jace so long to finally pursue Dixie. The answer had come easily. *I had a lot of growing up to do and achievements to conquer before I could even think about being the man Dixie deserved. I am that man now, Biggs, and with your blessing, I'll make you proud to have me as your son-in-law by proving it to her each and every day.* Biggs had welcomed him to the family with a warm heart and open arms.

"Y'all know there's nothing that I respect more than honesty," Biggs said to the crowd. "Jace looked me dead in the eyes and told me that he wasn't perfect. In fact, he said he was pretty damn sure he'd mess up more than a time or two, and then he vowed to always be faithful, to protect my darlin' daughter until his dying days, and to try to give us a grandson who would protect her after he was gone. *That*, my friends, is a good man."

"Grandbabies!" Red cheered, causing more ruckus from the crowd.

Biggs laughed. "She's going to hold you to that, Jace."

"I am, too!" Dixie said, hugging him.

"I am proud to welcome Jace into our family and, my Dark Knights brothers, you should be, too." Biggs raised his glass and said, "To Jace and Dixie!"

"To Jace and Dixie!" the crowd toasted.

Jace and Dixie kissed, causing more cheers.

"I can't believe you went to see my parents, or that you were *nervous*," Dixie said softly. "I can't even picture you being nervous."

"If your father hadn't given me his blessing, I would have had to wait to propose until I proved to him that I was worthy of you, because I'd never put you in the position of having to choose between me and your family. *That's* why I was nervous."

"Oh, *Jace*." She wrapped her arms around his neck and kissed him.

"I think I'd better get my toast in before these two lovebirds get too carried away," Red said as Dixie and Jace ended their lip-lock. "You all know my daughter well enough to realize that she was never like other little girls who played with dolls and dreamed of big white weddings. Dixie asked her father for a motorcycle for her fourth birthday, and when she got a Big Wheel instead, she stormed out to the garage and said she was going to build her own."

"That's my girl," Jace said.

"Growing up with three older brothers wasn't easy. Dixie had to be tough and smart." Red looked adoringly at Dixie and said, "My beautiful little girl, who was special *because* she was different, never wanted to be seen as *different*. And there was nothing she wouldn't do to prove that she was just as tough and capable as the boys."

"Like the time she taped on a penis!" Bullet hollered, causing uproarious laughter.

"*Ohmygod!*" Dixie buried her face in Jace's chest.

"I want to hear this one," Jace said, and Dixie scowled.

Red looked at Dixie and said, "May I?"

Dixie put her palm up and said, "Why not? They know almost everything else about me."

"See that?" Red said. "My daughter isn't afraid of *anything*, and she never has been. When Dixie realized her brothers could pee standing up, she drew herself a penis, taped it on, and headed outside to prove she could do anything they could do."

Everyone laughed.

"That's my beautiful, badass queen!" Jace said, hugging Dixie and eliciting more cheers.

"It got a little messy, but she proved her point. That was the day I knew my baby girl would get everything she wanted in life, and it was *also* the day I realized that she'd never want the things that came easily." Red sighed and said, "Love is not always easy."

"No kidding," Dixie, Jace, and several people in the crowd

said in unison, causing more chuckles.

"I'm glad we're all in agreement. Some of you got an eyeful tonight, with flying fists and raised voices, and you probably wondered what the heck was going on. What you witnessed was love worth fighting for, more than a decade in the making. Let's lift our glasses and hear it for our baby girl and our soon-to-be son-in-law. May they have loads of love and happiness and *many* grandbabies for me and Biggs!"

As cheers and applause rose from the crowd, Jace swept Dixie into his arms, dipped her like a dancer, and kissed her so long, Red cleared her throat and said, "I guess the honeymoon starts now."

He and Dixie laughed as their lips finally parted, and she said, "I'm so glad you bid on me at the auction."

"Baby, when I saw you on that stage, beautiful and badass, I didn't stand a chance. It was either bid on you or carry you over my shoulder like a caveman and take you back to my lair, because I wasn't going to let any other man get his hands on you."

Her eyes darkened. "I like the sound of you going all caveman on me."

"Want to go back to your place and I'll put on my loincloth?" He nipped at her lower lip.

"Can I call you Thor?"

"As long as you're mine, you can call me anything you want."

Epilogue

DIXIE TURNED OFF the hair dryer, listening to Jace's deep voice coming from the other room as she put on her makeup. It was Sunday afternoon. She'd worked in the morning and had brought breakfast home with her, but Jace had had other ideas. They'd ended up back in bed, where he'd enjoyed his breakfast of choice—*her*.

She started to put a dab of concealer on the love bite he'd left on her neck and then decided against it. She stood back, taking a last look at herself in the mirror. *Yup*, she still had the goofy smile she'd been wearing since Jace had proposed three months ago. When they'd left the bar that night, she'd told him he didn't need to change his entire life for her. Plenty of couples had to travel and take care of business, and she was so proud of him and all he'd achieved. She wanted to support his efforts, not hinder them. But he'd said, *I want to come home to you, Dix, not a hotel room. I want to be there for walks on the beach with our babies, for our steamy showers and endless lovemaking. I want to be the cool dad who shows up at our kids' school plays and sports games. And don't forget, Mia's life plan for us includes lots of trips to New York City so our kids' three aunties can spoil them rotten.*

How could she argue with any of that?

Jace had moved in right away, and a few weeks later they'd broken ground on their new property. They were excited to see the progress on their new house after they got back from their bike ride later. She followed his voice out of the bathroom, smiling at the sight of their neatly made bed. Jace's penchant for neatness was just one of the things that had surprised her after he'd moved in. He also helped with chores around the house and ran errands without her even asking. There were definite benefits to Jace having been a bachelor for so long. He'd also proven once again that he was a man of his word by keeping his promise and volunteering at the women's shelter. When they'd had dinner with Jace's family to deliver their happy news, Dixie had thanked his parents for raising such a remarkable man. It had been easy to see how he'd become so wonderful. His parents, Jacob and Janice, were good natured, even keeled, and openly adored *all* of their children.

As great as their life together was, they'd run into a few kinks here and there since they'd begun living together. Jace had gotten better about communicating, and although Dixie loved every second of living with him, she'd had to get used to a burly man taking up space in her small home. But the biggest issue they'd encountered was that Jace didn't like guys hitting on her at work. Although news of their engagement had spread quickly, there were still customers who didn't know Dixie or Jace. Jace had wanted to hang out at the bar and shut down any advances, but Dixie hadn't taken a stand with her family only to be babysat by her fiancé. It had taken a week or two for them to figure things out, but in the end Jace had relented, allowing Dixie to handle any issues that arose. If the rock on her finger wasn't enough of a deterrent to flirtatious men, Dixie let the offenders know in no uncertain terms that she was *not*, and would never be, on the market.

The only man she wanted was standing shirtless and barefoot in their kitchen talking on his cell phone, looking scrumptious. His thick dark hair was still wet from their shower, the curls she loved so much not yet tamed.

He shifted the phone away from his mouth and said, "Hey, babe, can you grab my wallet from the table?"

She grabbed his wallet from the dining room table, and it slipped from her fingers, bounced off a chair, and fell to the floor. His credit cards fell out, along with the picture he'd taken from Jilly and the card her mother had given him from the auction. She gathered it all and brought it to him.

"Thanks." He read the credit card number into the phone and said, "Perfect. The card should read *much love, Dixie and Jace*." When he ended the call, he set his phone on the counter and put his arms around Dixie, pressing his lips to hers.

"What was that about?"

"Bear and Crystal have their hands full with their new baby, so I asked Finlay to cater their dinners for the next two weeks."

Dixie's heart warmed at his thoughtfulness. "That's the sweetest gift. Thank you."

They'd visited with Bear, Crystal, and baby Axel last night. Bear and Crystal couldn't be happier or prouder. Axel was the cutest little guy, named after their uncle, who had owned Whiskey Automotive and taught Bear everything he knew about mechanics before they'd lost him to cancer. Jace had lived up to his baby-hogging reputation, cuddling the sweet boy for most of the evening.

"Apparently it wasn't an original gift idea," Jace said. "When I called, Finlay said she'd planned on bringing lunches over this week. She also fought me on paying for the dinners, but with their baby on the way, I wasn't going to let her do that." Finlay had announced her pregnancy the week after Jace proposed. She was due in early January, and everyone was thrilled for them.

"You just earned bonus *naughty* points."

He made a guttural, appreciative sound and kissed her. "Can I collect right now?"

"No," she said, pushing from his hands, although she hoped he never stopped craving her as much as he did now. She leaned against the counter and said, "I wasn't snooping, but I saw the auction card and picture of me in your wallet. I didn't know you still had them in there."

His lips curved up and he said, "My stuff is your stuff, and I've got nothing to hide. You can snoop all you want."

"I wasn't *snooping*. I dropped your wallet and they fell out. Why do you still carry them?"

"Because I like having you with me at all times."

"We're always together," she said, but hearing her uber-alpha man say something so mushy made her feel good all over.

"Not while we're at work," he reminded her, showing more of his soft underbelly.

Although Jace had delegated away most of his travel, he still had to go away for meetings for a day here or there. They'd traveled together to Mexico for his meetings there and had spent five wonderful, romantic days and four love-filled nights enjoying each other. They'd also decided to tie the knot while they were there. After tearful and joyous calls with both of their parents, they'd gotten their blessings. Dixie and Jace exchanged their vows on a warm summer evening beneath a starry sky, and when they'd come home, her parents had thrown them a huge party. Jace's family, Maddox, and several of Jace's friends had attended. Mia had been bummed because she'd been secretly planning their wedding since their engagement, and Jax and Jillian were also not thrilled to have missed out on the chance to design Dixie's wedding gown and bridesmaid dresses. But their family and friends had all understood that Jace and Dixie were so in love, they hadn't wanted to wait.

Dixie glanced at Jace's wedding ring, and goose bumps rose on her arms. It was such a magical feeling to be married to the man she loved with her heart and soul. She'd never forget the day he proposed, the way his whole face had lit up when she'd said yes, or the look in his eyes when they'd gotten married and he'd said, "I do." She'd also never forget the tears she'd cried at their family's celebration when the Dark Knights had formed a circle with their motorcycles around her and Jace and each of her brothers had delivered touching speeches. Bones had said he hoped his daughters would grow to be as strong as Dixie and went on to tell tales of when they were young. He wished them all the happiness in the world and *lots* of babies in their future, adding that his children needed more cousins. Bullet had said that Dixie was her own woman and that he understood that she needed to blaze her own path, but he was glad she had Jace by her side. And Bear had paid tribute to Jace for having proved that when love hit, nothing could stand in its way—not even his ornery sister's own bullheadedness.

It was the perfect way to celebrate the start of their new life together.

"Hey, beautiful? Where'd you go?" Jace asked, putting his arms around her. "You had a faraway look in your eyes."

"Just revisiting a few really great moments."

He touched his forehead to hers and said, "Like that new

thing I did with my tongue when I ate *breakfast?*"

Her stomach flipped, and heat trickled down her spine with *that* memory. "Among other things." She pushed him playfully and said, "Go get your shirt or we'll never get out of here with you talking like that."

His eyes flamed.

God, she loved him!

She pointed toward the bedroom.

"I'm going," he said reluctantly. On his way out of the kitchen, he said, "Now I'll think about *that* all day long, so you'd better be ready to be devoured tonight."

A thrill skittered through her. She'd be thinking about it, too, and she doubted they'd make it through the day.

AFTER A LONG afternoon ride with his beautiful wife plastered to his back, one of their favorite pastimes, Jace drove down the new gravel driveway toward their property. He had a surprise for Dixie, and he'd timed it perfectly. The sun was starting to set as their two-story home came into view. Happiness swelled inside him. He'd never imagined that putting down roots could bring such a sense of peace, and being with Dixie, sharing the smallest of things, making joint decisions as their lives came together, and just being there for each other made life so much sweeter. Jace had begun integrating into the close-knit community, meeting local business owners, spreading the word about the internships and mentoring programs they'd bring in once Silver-Stone's manufacturing plant was up and running. He was also working to put scholarships into place for the local high school, and he'd even signed up to make a Silver-Stone float for the Halloween parade. He just hoped Kennedy didn't ask them all to be ballet dancers or something equally feminine this year, because she and the rest of Dixie's *babies* had Uncle Jace wrapped around their little fingers.

The exterior of the house was finished, and the glass windows surrounding the crow's nest reflected the setting sun as beautifully as they'd hoped they would. They'd worked with Jillian's brother Beau, a custom-home builder and renovations expert, to design a gorgeous four-bedroom home with an open floor plan, a spacious home office, a large deck, and a glassed-in sunroom. Since he and Dixie loved the open road, they wanted to bring as much natural sunlight into their home as possible. They were also building a multicar garage and a workshop for Jace to tinker in.

"This is so exciting!" Dixie said as he grabbed the bag of food they'd bought at Jazzy Joe's on the way over. "Everything is happening so fast. I'm glad the house will be done before we start traveling for the launch. I can't wait to see you honored for all your hard work."

The launch of the Legacy and Leather and Lace lines was about a month away. The calendars had turned out even better than Jace had hoped, and Dixie would be signing them at the launch events. Their families were all planning to attend the launch party in New York City, and Jace was excited to introduce his new *wife* to his world in a bigger way. He and Maddox were scheduled to do several television interviews, and though Dixie didn't know it, he was going to reveal that she had been his muse for the Leather and Lace lines. He'd spent years holding back his feelings for her, and now that he could shout it from the rooftops, he planned on doing just that.

Dixie looked around the yard and said, "It's hard to believe this is where it all started for us."

As Jace unlocked the door to the house, he thought of the surprise waiting for her inside. "You think *this* is where it started? Baby, it all started the minute you stood before me at that rally years ago and said, 'I'm Dixie Whiskey, and don't you forget it.' You cast your spell on me. I was a goner from that moment on."

"It's a good thing I have a big mouth."

"For *many* reasons," he said wickedly, and followed her inside.

The walls were framed, but there was no drywall up yet, making it possible to see the entirety of the first floor and right out the French doors in the back. But Jace had set up a movie screen and projector that ran off a laptop. He'd spread out a blanket, pillows, and battery-operated candles, just as he had the night at the drive-in. This time there were rose petals spread out around the blanket and flowers in vases. By the way Dixie's eyes were lighting up, he knew he'd chosen the perfect surprise.

"What is all *this*?" she asked excitedly as she went to investigate.

"I promised you I'd watch *Pretty Woman*, and I figured what better time than now?"

"We're watching *Pretty Woman*?" She looked down at the blanket and candles as he set the bag of food down. "Our *first* movie night!"

He wrapped her in his arms and said, "I told you I'd never let you down again." He kissed her and said, "Why don't you get comfortable and I'll start the movie."

"You're amazing," she said as she set out the food.

They ate while they watched the movie, and Jace couldn't

imagine a better way to spend an evening. She laughed, teared up, and even snapped at Richard Gere when she thought he was being stupid. And after they ate, she cuddled with Jace on the blanket and pillows.

After the movie, she lay on her stomach beside him, running her finger over the tattoo on her wrist, and said, "Now do you see why it's my favorite movie? Vivian is a badass."

"You're even more badass than she is."

"I don't know about that, but I do have a cooler tattoo than she does."

He kissed the tattoo and said, "Have you figured out why that tattoo is special yet?"

"What do you mean? You already told me about how you designed it."

"Did I?" He rolled onto his back and said, "Or did I leave out one important part?"

"Do tell, Mr. Stone." She draped her arm over his stomach and put her head on his chest.

He ran his fingers through her hair and said, "I'll give you a hint. A diamond is a precious stone."

She looked down at him, her brow furrowed.

He lifted her wrist and kissed it again. "Think about it, *Mrs. Stone*."

"Oh my God! You marked me!"

He laughed, and she rose and straddled him, pinning his hands beside his head, grinning down at him. "You *were* branding me!"

He couldn't do more than grin.

"What if we hadn't ended up together?"

"Then my life would suck, wouldn't it? But that wasn't going to happen."

"It could have," she insisted.

"No way, baby." He swept her beneath him and said, "Unforgettable Dixie, do you remember what I said to you when you told me not to forget your name?"

She bit her lower lip, her eyes glittering with love. "You said you'd never forget because my name was etched in stone."

"That's right. Stone with a capital S."

"*Jace...*" she said, a little breathless and awestruck.

"I told you, babe. I hear *everything* you say." He kissed her deeply, and when she went soft and boneless beneath him, he said, "And I also hear everything you don't." He moved down her body, rolled her shirt up, and kissed her stomach. She closed her eyes, arching beneath him as he dragged his tongue around her belly button. "Like right now," he said softly. "I hear you asking me to make love to you right here on the floor where we'll raise our babies."

She opened her eyes, looking happy and beautiful as she reached for him.

He gazed into her eyes and said, "I hear something else. Do you hear it?"

She tilted her head and said, "That depends. Did you hear how much I love you?"

"I always hear that, my love." He kissed her tenderly and cradled her in his arms, whispering, "Close your eyes and listen. Maybe you can hear it, too."

She closed her eyes, and he dipped his head beside hers and said, "You once said that better men than me had tried to tame this Whiskey."

"They weren't better," she said anxiously.

"I know, babe." He kissed her and said, "They weren't good enough for you, because they didn't see what I've always known. You're perfect just the way you are, wild and mouthy and so fucking brilliant, you tamed *me* and I never even saw it coming."

Ready for More Whiskeys? How about the Wickeds?

If this is your first Whiskey book, each of Dixie's siblings' books are available for your binge-reading pleasure! Below you will find information on those titles, as well as details on the next book in the Whiskey series, **THE GRITTY TRUTH** (featuring Quincy Gritt), and **A LITTLE BIT WICKED** (featuring Justin Wicked), the first book in **The Wickeds: Dark Knights at Bayside** series. Don't worry, The Whiskeys series is *not* ending! The rest of our Whiskey-world friends will also be getting their own love stories, and you'll soon meet many more Whiskey relatives. But when I met the Wickeds, I knew they needed a world of their own. I cannot wait for you to get to know them.

THE GRITTY TRUTH

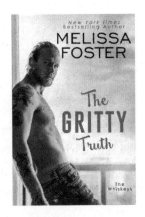

Quincy Gritt has fought his demons. He's confessed to his crimes and conquered his addictions. But when his past comes back to haunt him, can he learn to live with the gritty truth, or will he spiral back into the darkness? Come along for his sexy, emotional ride and fall in love all over again.

Get ready to fall hard for the Wickeds!

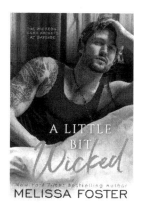

What do a cocky artist/biker and a businesswoman who has sworn off dating bad boys have in common? According to Chloe Mallery, not much. But Justin Wicked has had his eye on her for a long time, and he is sure the inescapable heat between them runs far deeper than just physical attraction. Could their difficult pasts be drawing them together, or will Justin's protective nature be too much for Chloe's independent heart to accept? Find out and fall hard for the Wickeds in A LITTLE BIT WICKED, a Dark Knights novel.

The following Whiskey books are waiting for you at all book retailers:

Tru Blue (Truman and Gemma)

Truly, Madly, Whiskey (Bear and Crystal)

Driving Whiskey Wild (Bullet and Finlay)

Wicked Whiskey Love (Bones and Sarah)

Mad About Moon (Jed and Josie)

Taming My Whiskey (Dixie and Jace)

And don't miss out on *River of Love*, the book that first introduces readers to the Whiskey family. *River of Love* features Sam Braden, from The Bradens at Peaceful Harbor series.

Remember to download your Whiskey/Wicked family tree here:

Whiskey/Wicked Family Tree

melissafoster.com/Wicked-Whiskey-Family-Tree

Love Melissa's Writing?

Discover more of the magic behind *New York Times* bestselling and award-winning author Melissa Foster. **The Whiskeys are just one of the many family series in the Love in Bloom big-family romance collection** featuring fiercely loyal heroes, sassy, sexy heroines, and stories that go above and beyond your expectations! See the collection here: www.MelissaFoster.com/love-bloom-series

Free first-in-series ebooks, downloadable series checklists, reading orders, and more can be found on Melissa's Reader Goodies page.
www.melissafoster.com/libfree
www.melissafoster.com/RG

More Books By Melissa Foster

LOVE IN BLOOM SERIES

SNOW SISTERS
Sisters in Love
Sisters in Bloom
Sisters in White

THE BRADENS at Weston
Lovers at Heart, Reimagined
Destined for Love
Friendship on Fire
Sea of Love
Bursting with Love
Hearts at Play

THE BRADENS at Trusty
Taken by Love
Fated for Love
Romancing My Love
Flirting with Love
Dreaming of Love
Crashing into Love

THE BRADENS at Peaceful Harbor
Healed by Love
Surrender My Love
River of Love
Crushing on Love
Whisper of Love
Thrill of Love

THE BRADENS & MONTGOMERYS at Pleasant Hill – Oak Falls

Embracing Her Heart
Anything For Love
Trails of Love
Wild, Crazy Hearts
Making You Mine
Searching For Love

THE BRADEN NOVELLAS

Promise My Love
Our New Love
Daring Her Love
Story of Love
Love at Last
A Very Braden Christmas

THE REMINGTONS

Game of Love
Stroke of Love
Flames of Love
Slope of Love
Read, Write, Love
Touched by Love

SEASIDE SUMMERS

Seaside Dreams
Seaside Hearts
Seaside Sunsets
Seaside Secrets
Seaside Nights
Seaside Embrace
Seaside Lovers
Seaside Whispers
Seaside Serenade

WILD BOYS AFTER DARK (Billionaires After Dark)
Logan
Heath
Jackson
Cooper

BAD BOYS AFTER DARK (Billionaires After Dark)
Mick
Dylan
Carson
Brett

<u>HARBORSIDE NIGHTS SERIES</u>
Includes characters from the Love in Bloom series
Catching Cassidy
Discovering Delilah
Tempting Tristan

More Books by Melissa
Chasing Amanda (mystery/suspense)
Come Back to Me (mystery/suspense)
Have No Shame (historical fiction/romance)
Love, Lies & Mystery (3-book bundle)
Megan's Way (literary fiction)
Traces of Kara (psychological thriller)
Where Petals Fall (suspense)

Acknowledgments

I hope you enjoyed Dixie and Jace's story as much as I loved writing it. I'm looking forward to writing love stories for Quincy, Penny, Diesel, Izzy, and the rest of our friends in the Whiskey world! Don't worry, that series is not ending. You'll soon meet many more Whiskey relatives. I hope you will also fall in love with the Wickeds. When I met them, I knew they needed a world of their own. I cannot wait for you to get to know them.

If this is your first introduction to my work, please note that every Melissa Foster book can be read as a stand-alone novel, and characters appear in other family series, so you never miss out on an engagement, wedding, or birth. You can find information about the Love in Bloom series and my books here: www.melissafoster.com/melissas-books

I offer several free first-in-series ebooks. You can find them here: www.MelissaFoster.com/LIBFree

I chat with fans often in my fan club on Facebook. If you haven't joined my fan club yet, please do!
www.facebook.com/groups/MelissaFosterFans

Follow my author page on Facebook for fun giveaways and updates of what's going on in our fictional boyfriends' worlds.

www.Facebook.com/MelissaFosterAuthor

If you prefer sweet romance, with no explicit scenes or graphic language, please try the Sweet with Heat series written under my pen name, Addison Cole. You'll find the same great love stories with toned-down heat levels.

Thank you to my awesome editorial team, Kristen Weber and Penina Lopez, and my meticulous proofreaders, Elaini Caruso, Juliette Hill, Marlene Engel, Lynn Mullan, and Justinn Harrison. And last but never least, a huge thank-you to my family for their patience, support, and inspiration.

Meet Melissa

Melissa Foster is a *New York Times* and *USA Today* bestselling and award-winning author. Her books have been recommended by *USA Today's* book blog, *Hagerstown* magazine, *The Patriot*, and several other print venues. Melissa has painted and donated several murals to the Hospital for Sick Children in Washington, DC.

Visit Melissa on her website or chat with her on social media. Melissa enjoys discussing her books with book clubs and reader groups and welcomes an invitation to your event. Melissa's books are available through most online retailers in paperback and digital formats.

Melissa also writes sweet romance under the pen name Addison Cole.

www.MelissaFoster.com
Free Reader Goodies:
www.MelissaFoster.com/Reader-Goodies